Shadows

by

Brenda Huber

Shadows

Cover Art by *Rae Monet*

The Wild Rose Press
PO Box 706
Adams Basin, NY 14410-0706
Visit us at www.thewildrosepress.com

Publishing History
First Black Rose Edition, 2010
Print ISBN 1-60154-771-4

Published in the United States of America

"Why are you saying these things?"

She fought to pull her hands from his, struggled to put space between them. "What are you trying to do here? Werewolves, Cam? I may be a little off my game tonight, but I'm not crazy. Why are you doing this?"

"JJ...just please, please let me explain. When I'm done...just give me a chance to explain." And then, because he'd fought the truth for too long and realized he only had one chance to do this right—one chance to truly claim his mate—he gathered her resistant form into his arms and pressed her close. His breath skimmed her lips as his eyes bore into hers. "I love you, JJ. I need you to remember that, when you see... I need you to remember that I love you more than anything."

His kiss was explosive, fast and hard. His lips demanded a response, would accept nothing less than honest emotion from her. Her response was immediate. She wound her arms around his neck and surrendered with a small whimper. Satisfied, filled with dread, he pulled back and set her away from him before pushing to his feet.

He kept his eyes on her as he slowly worked the buttons of his uniform loose. His gear, boots, and pants followed. Once he'd stripped down to the skin, he offered her one last resigned smile. She was so beautiful—with her big, shining blue eyes, and her damp, golden hair falling all around her shoulders, curled up there in on his sofa, wearing his shirt—that his heart ached. "I love you, Jillian."

Then he closed his eyes, centered his focus, and gathered inside him all the power the Great Spirit had bestowed upon his ancestor so very long ago.

Even a man who is pure of heart
And says his prayers by night
May become a wolf
When the wolfsbane blooms
And the Autumn Moon is bright.

~Old Gypsy Poem

Dedication

This one is for my sisters-in-law, Holly and Brooke...
It's not where you go, but who's beside you
that counts.

And for Theresa, Tammy, and Treva... Wonderful
additions to our extended family.

Acknowledgements

As always, deepest thanks to my editor,
Joelle Walker,
for unfaltering encouragement and priceless insight.
You are truly a godsend!

Special appreciation to Rae Monet
and her magical talent for providing me
with insightful cover art for my stories.

Prologue

He perched at the edge of a cold, dented folding chair, resting his elbows on one end of the long table, his thumb clicking his pen in rapid-fire succession as the mayor called the council meeting to order. What a bunch of sanctimonious, hypocritical bastards they were. Every last one of them. His condemning gaze skimmed over the small group, lingering on particularly deceitful faces sprinkled here and there throughout the gathering. He stifled a disparaging snort, covered it beneath the guise of a cough. This assembly held enough skeletons to open up its own bone yard. Among these corrupt, ignoble men and women, he was a veritable saint. But then, saint was such a strong word.

No, perhaps not a saint.

But, surely, an Apostle...

Across the table reclined humble Mayor Hughes...the pompous windbag. What would the good people of Sutter Hollow think if they knew about the mayor's predilection for Texas Hold'em? What would they say about his sticky fingers dipping into public funds with startling regularity to keep the wolves from clawing at his door?

His gaze wandered to the man at his left. From beneath lowered lashes, he eyed the saintly humanitarian Councilman Andrews. Passing a hand over his mouth, he hid the disgusted sneer. Andrews certainly had a convincing song and dance, pandering to the local ladies-aides, offering substantial donations to the clinic, all in the name of awareness and prevention of domestic violence.

Were those do-gooder church socialites really so gullible? Or were his donations so generous they were willing to look the other way...pretend his meek little wife simply had an unnatural attachment to sunglasses indoors, and long sleeves on hot summer days?

He shifted in his seat, realigned the yellow notepad in front of him, clicking his pen. Their monotonous voices droned in his ears. He gritted his teeth against the urge to leap from his chair and shout of their misdeeds.

Voting for new playground equipment in Juniper Park began. The nays had it. Next, the council voted on repaving some of the more troublesome roads in town. Again, the nays carried the vote. Finally, they voted on improving council chambers with new flooring—white carpet, of all things—and new furnishings. The ayes had it.

Of course.

As long as the council got its white carpet, who cared if the town's roads had potholes large enough to lose a whole fleet of VW Bugs? As long as the council got new, cushy chairs to pamper their fat, spoiled asses once a month, who cared if the community's children played on dangerous equipment? As long as money lined the council members' pockets, who cared if the town's residents barely scraped by, pinching pennies and recycling pop cans to pay this month's utility bill?

This gathering was—as was the town itself—peppered with sinners. Infected with the unrepentant. It was a sad state of affairs, to be sure. The Devil had knocked on Sutter Hollow's door, and its population had blithely flung the door wide open, inviting him in for dinner.

He forced a brittle smile to his lips as the meeting adjourned. Pushing to his feet, he shuffled through the door along with the rest of the crowd.

Fortunately, the meeting had been short tonight. He needed fresh air, could barely tolerate another moment with such a duplicitous bunch. He stepped clear of the outer door as he buttoned his coat, tugged at the collar, and watched a fellow councilman and councilwoman bump shoulders. The sly couple floated down the sidewalk, exchanging a warm, albeit fleeting caress and a covert, intimate smile before hurrying off in opposite directions to separate spouses and families.

Sinners, one and all. His mother's harsh voice, reproving and unyielding, echoed in his head. *Lust and gluttony. Greed and sloth. Wrath and envy. Pride... Beware, lest the Devil sink his claws into you and drag you from the path of righteousness.*

The chafe needed separating from the wheat, or God's hand would smite them all as surely as it had brought down the walls of Jericho. It was time. The town must be shown the error of its ways before it was too late. Sin was insidious.

God's children must be protected.

He strolled down the sidewalk as streetlights began blinking on overhead. Maggie's was slowing down for the evening. He veered inside and slid into a booth, shrugging off his jacket. A glass of ice water slid beneath his nose before he'd even managed to pull his attention from the laminated menu/placemat.

"Hey there, handsome," Lori purred. Her bold gaze swept over him, leaving him cold and angry.

And wanting.

Damn her.

Lecherous sin surrounded him. It was infectious.

Cocking a hip, she shot him a wink, snapped her gum. "What can I getcha tonight, sugar?"

Rubbing his damp palms down the thighs of his slacks, he forced the sinful lump of desire from his throat. His guts twisted in revulsion. It was wrong to want her. The Devil was at work here, offering him carnal sin from every wicked smile and lush curve this woman so blatantly offered. Her bright, painted eyes laughed at him. Her glossy red lips beckoned him to partake of eternal damnation, as surely as Eve had offered Adam the cursed fruit of his downfall.

God has handed me over to the godless, and cast me into the hands of the wicked.

She was the Devil's tool. His lure.

Well, he refused the bait. *He* was God's hand to smite the sinners.

Let my anguish plead the cause of a man at grips with God, just as a man might defend his fellow.

Lori had ignored the warnings. She hadn't changed her ways. She was unrepentant. She'd soon pay for her sins. Forgiveness would be between her and God now. Relaxing against the vinyl-covered booth, he smiled up at her, much more at ease. Yes. It was up to God to have mercy on her soul...and Lori's judgment was at hand.

Nonetheless, my hands are free of violence, and my prayers are pure.

He smiled up at her. "I'll just have the usual, Lori."

Chapter 1

Evil tracked JJ through the house, ruthless and methodical. Panic stole her voice, cut her scream off before it could become more than a feeble gurgle in the back of her throat. Terror, cold and vicious, squeezed her heart in its unrelenting, icy fist. His breath grated in the darkness nearby...too close. His sinister, husky chuckle echoed in the stillness, sending shivers crawling up her spine and gooseflesh slithering down her arms. Death stalked her, nipping at her heels. Nowhere to run. Nowhere to hide.

No place he wouldn't find her.

Her sister's dying cries filled her head, coursing grief and adrenaline through her veins.

Run, JJ. Run...

The flashing, gas pump-shaped indicator next to the speedometer drew her gaze to the dash, and she exhaled on a harsh expletive. Her eyes burned, as if someone had plucked out her eyeballs, rolled them in superheated sand, and shoved them back into her skull. Still jittery from the nightmare, too much caffeine, and not enough sleep, JJ drilled her fingers against her temple, desperate to ease the throb taking up permanent residence there. Six a.m. glared in luminescent green from her silent radio display, the numbers cold and unsympathetic.

How could she be running on fumes already? She'd begun this impulsive flight with a full tank, already stopped to refill twice, grabbing a large mug of not-so-great convenient store coffee and a carton of individually wrapped brownies both times. She'd put mile after mile behind her, but the memories refused to fade. The brownies had left behind the vicious crash that inevitably followed a sugar buzz, and the thick, stale coffee was nothing more than a sorry reminder irritating her stomach.

And the gas was gone.

Holy crap, she'd done it again. How far had she driven this time? The answer came at her with a sharp pang of self-disgust. The answer was simple...too far. She pressed the brake, angling her car for the off-ramp. At this point in her recovery—what a sad, sorry lie that optimistic euphemism was—even one, singular mile was too far. There'd been a trigger. Something innocuous most likely. Something she may never be able to recall. Then the dreams had come. She'd panicked.

And she'd run.

She'd driven all night, hour after hour. How then was it she couldn't outdrive the nightmare? What she wouldn't give to be able to put distance between her and the things haunting her sleep the way she'd put mile after mile, city after city behind her.

Her psychiatrist had urged her to take the next step in recovery, move beyond her grief. That was the normal, sensible thing to do...but something always held her back. Sooner or later, she always found herself in the same position. Fighting for every breath. Tunnel vision focused solely on escape, everything else blurred around the edges by the dark shadows of fear. Her hastily packed bags tossed in the back of her Grand Cherokee. Her white-knuckled fists clutching the steering wheel in a death grip. Her booted foot crushing the accelerator to the floor before the cold sweat of terror had a fighting chance to dry.

Anxiety attacks, her shrink had called them. The term was far too tame as far as JJ was concerned. This was something far worse than anxiety. It had to be. This was cold and clawing and blood curdling. And this...this *thing* crippling her wouldn't bother itself with a mere attack. No, it went for all-out, no-holds-barred, brutal assaults.

JJ flinched as a blur of honey-gold rocketed from the ditch. The massive animal dodged the beam of her headlights, disappearing down the opposite embankment. Damn dogs. Damn *big* dogs. Didn't they have leash laws around here? Swearing softly, she ground a palm against one eye and caved to the urge to yawn.

Almost a year had passed since the night of unanticipated violence and vicious betrayal. Three hundred and thirty-eight days since the night the man she'd loved as a brother snapped, shattering her life. She knew she couldn't go on this way, running every time the memories caught up with her. Sarah wouldn't have wanted this for her little sister. JJ knew it.

Somewhere deep, *deep* inside, JJ understood.

It didn't help.

The shrink she'd visited on a regular basis for almost four months after her sister's brutal murder had spent many, *many* billable hours encouraging her to acknowledge that her sister had been an adult, responsible for her own actions.

Her sister—the responsible adult—had chosen to remain in an abusive marriage. Still, the knowledge—and all the therapy in the world— couldn't alleviate the debilitating guilt gnawing at JJ. She should have been able to do more. Do something.

Anything at all.

And when the darkness closed in on her, and her sister's lifeless eyes haunted nightmares stained with blood, nothing could stifle the urge to run. Guilt and self-doubt were her constant companions. Things could have been so different if JJ had been more effective in convincing Sarah to leave him—leave him and stay gone, but she'd failed Sarah.

She should have been prepared when Jerry Dewitt had finally snapped.

Pushing free from the tangled web of guilt and stifling memories of sobbed pleas, JJ traversed the shadow-filled blacktop, following the road signs to the nearest city, Sutter Hollow.

She squinted at a large green rectangle with shiny white lettering. Her voice echoed inside the car, the sole sound aside from the hum of the engine and the roll of tires in over three hundred miles. "Population eight hundred fifty-five," JJ murmured. "Can you consider a city a *city* with less than a thousand people?"

"No," she debated aloud a moment later, quirking her lips. "Less than a thousand should make it a town."

Then, after another moment of consideration, she snickered, "Town, ha! A village...*maybe*."

JJ cast a wary glance at overgrown ditches on either side of the road, half expecting cornfields to pop up and spooky little kids with funky eyes and possessed smiles to peep at her from between the rows. Giving a mirthless, nervous chuckle, she shook her head. "Cornfields belong in Minnesota and Iowa, JJ, not Maine, and possessed children are the stuff of movies. Pull it together."

But her mind had already begun wandering down exhausted, disconcerting pathways as the age-old argument of who was the bigger monster, Freddie or Jason, began to fill her thoughts. *Did a cornfield full of possessed children trump an abusive, murderous brother-in-law?* She didn't debate long. She'd take a cornfield full of those creepy little freaks any day of the week and twice on Sundays. Her monster won...hands down.

Her monster was real.

She had the scars to prove it.

She rubbed at the knot at the base of her neck with trembling fingers. She wasn't even going to touch the whole *Children of the Corn* thing, but she'd bet her last commission Dr. Greene would've had a field day analyzing that one. She blinked, squinting at the dashboard as endless miles of driving caught up with her. Maybe Sutter Hollow had a nice, padded psych ward. She could check in for a day or two, just until the shakes were gone. Kinda like those big-name celebrities did with rehab. She could hear it now. *Paging Dr. Greene...*

Groaning aloud, rolling the kinks from her neck and shoulders, JJ eased up on the accelerator.

The drowsy little New England town snuggled at the edge of a serene lake, bordered on two sides by dense, rolling woods. Thin tendrils of mountain mists streaked down from the ridge behind the town, curling possessive fingers around pristine buildings, blanketing the quiet structures and empty streets with memories of another, simpler time. A time when horse and wagon traversed dirt pathways. A time when the plaintive hoot of an owl punctuated the steady hum of grasshoppers, and cheerful birds greeted the dawn. A time long before chaotic rattle of automobile and irritating chime of cell phone stirred the air.

Now cold metal beasts sat motionless on impersonal, aging asphalt at haphazard intervals, but the overall impression was much the same. Peaceful. Hypnotic.

Drawing a deep, cleansing breath, she squared her shoulders and readjusted her grip on the steering wheel. A small sigh of relief escaped her lips as her vehicle coasted into the small Terry Redlin-esque community on the last wisps of fuel. Some of the tension eased from her shoulders as she scanned the streets for some sign of a gas station. Quaint little houses, with their picket fences and perfectly manicured yards, surrounded her on all sides. Cozy. Soothing. She glanced in the rearview mirror, blinked in surprise as her own smile flashed back at her.

Exhausted and wan, but a smile nonetheless.

JJ spotted the antiquated filling station and heaved a sigh of relief. A landmine of potholes rattled her teeth as she eased her vehicle from the county blacktop onto a crumbling paved lot. The lights were just beginning to blink on, a good thing since there wasn't a cardtrol pump in sight. She eased her Jeep alongside pumps that must have accommodated the gas rationing of World War II. Palming her keys, she scoured the shadows and slid from behind the wheel. As soon as her feet hit the time-ravaged concrete she yawned and stretched, groaning as her stiff muscles screeched protest over the abuse of confined inactivity. Stifling another yawn, JJ fumbled with the gas cap.

A gruff voice—small-town congeniality wrapped in sandpaper—called out from a few feet behind her, "Mornin' there, missy."

Her heart slammed into her throat, blocking the first jagged edges of a scream. She whirled around, pressing against the car, balling her hands into defensive fists at her sides.

The man, whose faded work shirt identified him as Joe, greeted her with a harmless gap-toothed smile. Forcing herself to relax, she straightened, easing away from the vehicle. He had to be somewhere on the far side of sixty if he was a day...the very far side, indeed. His hairline had long since yielded to time, and his aging, sun-weathered skin had, in all likelihood, sent the local Avon Lady screaming in terror. Despite the arthritic slump of his back, he moved with a youthful spring in his step.

"I can do that for ya." He buffed his bulbous nose with a faded red rag. "Full service here at Joe's."

At her confused blink, he shoved the rag into his back pocket and slung a knobby thumb over his left shoulder toward the smudged window displaying an old-fashioned, hand-painted sign. A defunct Coke machine—the kind that dispensed glass bottled soda for a dime—slumbered beside the sign. She half expected a man in a sheriff's uniform and a little boy would come strolling by any minute now, whistling as they swung fishing poles from their shoulders.

Joe twisted the gas cap off with practiced, one-handed efficiency while reaching for the gas pump with the other. Not knowing what else to do, JJ thanked him and climbed back inside her car. She snatched up her purse, intent of digging for her cash. A shadow fell across her windshield, and she jerked, dropping her purse.

JJ bit down hard on a gasp. Her gaze snapped to the windshield as Joe slapped a sloppy squeegee against grimy glass. He set to scrubbing petrified bugs loose with a symphony of wet squeaks. Holy crap. Why didn't he just shoot her and have it over with? It'd be much more humane than spooking her to death by slow degrees. Her breath leaked out on a long, slow hiss, and, once again, she told herself to get a grip. There was no reason to be this damned jumpy. He was a harmless old man.

Her hands shook as she picked her purse up from where it had fallen on the seat beside her, and she scooted from her car once more. One glance through the plate-glass storefront, however, convinced her she'd be lucky to find so much as a stale candy bar in there.

"Ah, excuse me…Joe, is it? Is there a convenience store nearby? Somewhere I can get something to eat?" Her stomach rumbled, loud and clear, punctuating her words. Lord, what she wouldn't give for an IHOP right about now.

Joe gave a lazy nod, extending another toothless grin. "Maggie's just opened, oh, 'bout half past five. Take a left two blocks down 'at-a-way." He tossed this thumb west by southwest, apparently his own personalized version of GPS. "Can't miss it. She'll fix you up," he added with a game wink.

"Thank you." JJ shifted from one foot to the other, then gave herself a stern mental shake and dug in her purse while she waited for Joe to finish topping off her tank. He clanked the ancient machine off, and she thrust two twenties at him, one crisp and new, the other ragged and worn.

"I'll get yer change." His easy, toothless smile was fast becoming very endearing.

"No, that's all right." She returned the smile, charmed. "Consider it a tip for the directions." And the smile, she silently added.

"Thank you kindly, missy. You tell 'em down at Maggie's yer a friend of Joe's."

Nodding, she murmured, "I'll do that."

Back behind the wheel, steadier now, JJ guided the Jeep out of the lot. She glanced in her rear view mirror, smiling as Joe settled into a faded rocker beside the smudged glass door, buffing his nose again. A giggle burbled up the back of her throat as he set the rocker in motion, slow and easy, waiting on the sunrise.

Following Joe's "'at-a-way" directions, she found Maggie's Place. The diner proved to be another step back in time, a throwback to the fifties. She wouldn't have been at all surprised to find bubble-blowing teenyboppers in poodle skirts and saddle shoes pushing through the doorway. Or, perhaps, a slicked up man in a white tee and leather bomber jacket to come strolling out and shoot her a thumbs up and a wink.

Instead, as she pulled into an open parking

space feeling as if she'd fallen into some endless loop of *Nick at Night*, a tall man wearing a postal uniform stepped out into the first rays of dawn. His hair was the deepest shade of sable she'd ever seen, trimmed with meticulous care. His chest was broad, his shoulders wide. A linebacker if ever she'd seen one. Fascinated, she watched while he angled his smooth skinned, square-jawed face to the east. His smile was a pleasure to behold as confident rays of pink and gold streaked across the morning sky, illuminating his features.

When was the last time she'd done that...taken time to stop and enjoy a sunrise? Had she ever?

Stirring herself, she palmed her keys and anchored her purse over her shoulder. Glancing first to the right, then the left, she checked her mirrors and slid from her car, locking the door as she stood. As was her habit, she tested the handle to double check the lock had engaged before she made her way to the door of the diner. As unobtrusively as a stranger in a small town can, she slipped inside the establishment and eased onto a chair at a table near the door, back to the wall, eyes darting over the place in a quick sweep, drinking in the details in one fast, greedy gulp.

Old-fashioned, leather-covered booths lined the far wall, their centerpieces a hodge-podge of condiment bottles and small ceramic containers brimming with tiny, multicolored packets. A horseshoe-shaped counter rested along the back wall, around which several customers perched, nursing their morning cup of java, exchanging the latest gossip in sleepy, muted voices.

Somewhere in the rear of the building, perhaps from the kitchen, a radio announcer predicted sunny skies and unseasonably warm temperatures for the rest of the week. As the announcer's voice disappeared, the soft, sorrowful strains of Patsy

Cline's *"I Fall to Pieces"* filled the air. A perky little redhead sailed from customer to customer with coffee pot in hand—as graceful as a ballerina, as efficient as a four-star general—topping cups off as she went.

She shot JJ a curious nod of acknowledgement and a bob of her head to indicate she'd be right along. A husky, disembodied female voice snapped above the radio, "Order up."

JJ twisted in her seat to face the long service window at the north end of the room, flinching as a head popped into the long opening behind the counter. A slim pair of work-roughened hands clunked two plates overflowing with steak, hash browns, toast, and eggs on the narrow counter, then snatched a trio of tickets from the tarnished silver clip.

JJ blinked, and the hands and head disappeared back inside the kitchen. The waitress scooped up the plates without breaking stride, delivering them to random customers with a teasing smile. She looped around to pick up a glass of ice water and drew a slim green pad from the abbreviated apron tied around her waist as she made her way to JJ's table.

Sliding the water onto the table, the waitress smiled, pen poised over paper. Her bright blue eyes noted every detail from the top of JJ's head right down to the tips of her scuffed black boots. "What can I get 'cha, sweetie?"

JJ glanced down at the laminated menu/placemat. The tantalizing scents of sizzling bacon and fresh cinnamon rolls hung heavy in the air, and her mouth watered. She'd considered asking for a cinnamon roll and a large coffee to go, but after eyeing that loaded plate in the service window, she hadn't entertained the notion for long. If the scents were anything to judge by, the coffee alone would be several steps above what she'd existed on for the last several hundred miles. Oddly compelled to linger, she ordered a full breakfast—the blue-plate special—and a bottomless cup of coffee. The waitress jotted down her order before leaving her with another sunny smile. JJ settled back in her chair to soak up some local flavor.

She couldn't put her thumb on it, but ever since she'd arrived in town, she'd had this niggling feeling this was where she was supposed to be. Not necessarily Maggie's, per se, but Sutter Hollow in general. It was restful here. She was...calm.

Definitely odd.

She dusted off another smile when the waitress returned with a cup and the pot of coffee that seemed a natural extension of her arm. The motion felt rusty, but the curl of her lips seemed to be having the desired effect.

"Name's Brandi, by the way," the redhead chirped with a reciprocal smile. The coffee pot remained perfectly balanced. "What brings you to town, if you don't mind my asking?"

"Just passing through," JJ hedged, but another smile tugged at her lips. "I guess I'm a friend of Joe's."

Fond warmth seeped into Brandi's expression. "Well, now. In that case, coffee's on the house."

The last of the tension in JJ's shoulders melted away. "Thank you."

Brandi nodded, bustling off to see to the latest patron who'd joined the growing crowd at the counter. He was younger than everyone else there, perhaps in his early thirties, but the older crowd welcomed him into their fold with gracious ease. He was a tall one, with tousled, wheat-colored hair and a fair amount of powerful muscle packed onto his lean frame. His jeans were snug, as was his plain white T-shirt. Both bore a fine, white powdery residue, and both left little to a girl's imagination.

15

Her mouth watered, and this time her overactive salivary glands had absolutely nothing to do with the celestial aromas of cinnamon and Folgers.

Dried splatters of bright yellow paint speckled his oh-so-flattering jeans. A carpenter or handyman, JJ guessed. It was a game she sometimes liked to play, guessing someone's profession by the way he or she dressed. More often than not, her speculative dart didn't fall far from the proverbial target. As if her perusal had summoned his attention, his intense regard swung in her direction, and she forgot her game.

She forgot to breath.

Never before had she seen eyes of such clear and brilliant emerald. His stare was frank, assessing and appreciative. His gaze lingered on her for several long moments. Then he turned away, taking the secrets of her soul with him.

Unsettled, JJ counted out four sugar and three creamer packets, pouring them into her cup with trembling fingers. Her attention roamed over the small diner as she stirred, vigilant now to avoid the newcomer, though she could literally *feel* his bold stare return to her time and again. A strange tingling caressed her skin with every brush of his gem-like eyes.

Reminding herself to breathe, forcing herself to remain composed, she leaned back in her seat and lifted the cup to her lips, sipping cautiously at the steaming, creamy liquid. She briefly closed her eyes and stifled a groan of ecstasy. The coffee was heaven. Her gaze wandered to the large window at the front of the diner, and she surveyed the storefronts across the street. From where she sat, the tidy faces of a small grocery store, a pharmacy, and sheriff's department were visible. Inviting and neat as a pin. She'd noticed some kind of doctor's office and a hardware store on either side of the diner when she'd come in. For being such a small community, the town seemed self-sufficient, thriving.

In record time, a heaping plate landed in front of her with a slight clunk, accompanied by another of Brandi's sunny smiles. JJ dug in, savoring the food like only a woman who'd existed on stale coffee and prepackaged brownies for the last several days could. Not even the curious stares of the diner's patrons bothered her one wit. *His* stare didn't even bother her.

Well, not too much.

Okay, maybe a little, but not in the usual, object-of-strangers-stare way. No, his stare sparked funny little tugs deep in her belly...and the uncomfortable urge to giggle like a schoolgirl.

Another oddity.

Brandi stopped by to top off her cup, bringing her a large Styrofoam cup with a lid, at JJ's request, along with her ticket. JJ rummaged through her purse, pulling out another rumpled ten, more than enough for the cost of the meal as well as a very generous tip. She couldn't help sneaking a peek toward the horseshoe counter. He sat with both elbows braced on the counter on either side of his empty plate, nursing a cup of coffee.

His unnerving stare followed every move she made.

Giddy pressure fluttered, tingling in the pit of her stomach as their eyes connected. Heat filled her cheeks, and, for one startling moment, she couldn't look away. At last, shaking herself free of the snare of his eyes, she slung her purse over her shoulder and strolled from the diner. The heavy burden of her nightmare had been, albeit temporarily, plucked from her shoulders...even as she felt the weight of those probing, enigmatic green eyes on the back of

17

her neck.

She smiled into the morning sunshine, much as she'd seen the postal worker do earlier, and savored the warmth on her skin. She was content. Content was enough for her, more than she could ask for really, even if it wasn't likely to last more than a few weeks at best.

The memory of those green eyes left a pleasant, lingering hum in her bloodstream.

She wasn't sure why, but rather than taking the most direct route back to the interstate, she wended her way up and down the waking streets of Sutter Hollow. Every time she came across one of the town's residents, they waved, smiling warm greetings. The generosity of those greetings thawed her heart, and she returned the waves with a grin. She hadn't the foggiest clue who any of them were, but wave she did.

Then, having made up her mind she'd dawdled long enough, JJ rounded the last corner on the far side of town, and she saw it. A stately, if rundown Victorian slumbering at the end of a long drive, tucked back into an intimate pocket in the woods. A quick glance at the street sign and the house number tugged a chuckle from her. 123 Shady Lane. Could any address be more trouble-free? More perfect?

Antiquated gables and noble turrets offered a glimpse of quiet dignity. She couldn't tear her eyes away. Sagging shutters, accented with peeling trim, drew her down the drive. The front porch sagged on one end. The warped steps should have had caution tape strung from one newel post to the other. The grounds were beyond overgrown. A drooping trellis in the side yard marked what she supposed was to have been a flower garden; the wooden frame listed to the side, staggering beneath the weight of triumphant weeds.

JJ huddled in her idling vehicle, gazing through the now spotless windshield, struck by an odd feeling of kinship. The dilapidated structure reflected her soul. Both needed attention and a caring touch.

Both were in sad need of a major overhaul.

Her eyes snagged on the for sale sign. She considered. She calculated.

With narrowed eyes, she squared her shoulders. Her hands choked the steering wheel. If she ever wanted to move beyond the past, she needed to set down roots. Dr. Greene had suggested something along those lines, at least. So had her friends...the ones her erratic, insane behavior hadn't driven away altogether. The smile spreading across her face grew wide, intrigued with the possibilities. Determination set her jaw. A solid reflection of the old JJ peeped back at her from the rear view mirror.

What better place could there be than this soothing, little community to make a new life for herself? What better place than this rocky New England soil, and this once dignified house to set down roots?

JJ nodded to herself, more certain of this decision than she'd been of anything else since the day her sister had died. She needed this house. And it needed her. It was safe here. She was safe.

Jerry couldn't hurt her, or anyone else, ever again.

Chapter 2

In less time than she'd imagined possible, JJ stood on the sagging front stoop of the old Victorian, keys in hand and a silly grin plastered on her face. According to the real estate agent, the furniture and appliances inside went with the place, as did anything else she found. The woman who'd lived there had passed on a number of years back. Her grandchildren had already picked the place over before putting it on the market and forgotten it.

That was fine with her. She'd pick and choose at her own convenience, keeping what she liked and discarding the rest. She could buy whatever else she needed. Thanks to a large corporation's decision to acquisition several of her pieces, money wasn't a problem...and wouldn't be for quite some time.

If one wanted to get technical, she already owned a house back in Minneapolis, and all the furniture and trappings that went with it. It had been Sarah's home...and her prison. The site of Sarah's murder. But that was another life. A life she had no intention of returning to...ever again. She hadn't been able to bring herself to step foot inside the house since that night. Couldn't imagine surrounding herself with any of the memories. Nor could she bring herself to sell it. She wouldn't touch the life insurance. It was tainted money, stained with the blood of her sister's death.

As Sarah's sole beneficiary, she'd inherited it all.

She didn't want any of it.

Steadying herself with another deep breath, she forced her focus back to matters at hand. Using the name and address on the sign, she'd located the real estate agent responsible for the property.

From the comfort of his office, the agent gave her the specifics about the Victorian on Shady Lane. He even offered to take her on a walk through. She declined the tour, assuring the man she'd take it as it stood. The agent stared at her as if she'd lost her mind, but he accepted her check all the same. Even she had to acknowledge the precariousness of her sanity was a distinct possibility, but she bought the place nonetheless, sight unseen, and so far she had no regrets.

So far so good.

She didn't waste any time returning to the house. Now, standing here, in the bright light of day, she could already imagine herself, a strong cup of steaming herbal tea in hand, reclining in an old wicker rocker just like Joe's, enjoying the sunset from her own front porch. Maybe she'd get a cat, or a dog. Or both. She'd always loved animals but never had a pet of her own—never had the time for one.

She'd never *made* the time. Well, that would all change. This was a new start for her, a second chance to do things right. Something she both wanted and needed with a desperation bordering on obsessive.

JJ glanced over the front porch one more time with a delighted sigh. This was all hers, every warped board and paint chip, every weathered turret and aging gable. Well, hers as soon as the final paperwork went through. Until then, for all intents and purposes, she was renting the space. The legalities didn't matter to her. She was here, and she was determined to make a go of it this time. Nothing would stand in her way. Not the nightmares. Not the anxiety attacks.

Not *her.*

A solid, warm sense of belonging filled her as

she ground the old key inside the rusted lock. The mechanism grated, scraped, resisted for a moment, and yielded with a reluctant clack. Every crumbling scratch thrilled her to the very marrow of her bones.

Welcome home, JJ.

Home. Something she'd not *allowed* herself to have in the many long months following her sister's death. Shaking her head, she thrust those unsettling thoughts aside, determined to leave them in the past. Where they belonged. Setting her shoulder against the door, she shifted her weight. The screeching hinges gave at last. Drawing a deep lungful of musty air, she stepped over the threshold into a long hallway running the length of the house.

A staircase with an intricate, carved banister climbed up one wall. Doublewide pocket doors opened to her immediate left and a wide-open archway yawned to her right, giving her a glimpse of the rooms beyond. Aged, faded wallpaper curled at the edges in every room. The floor stretching throughout the house looked to be hardwood, mahogany perhaps, though it was difficult to tell beneath the thick layer of dust and grime.

Odd shapes huddled beneath dust cloth in the parlor on her right, ghosts biding their time, waiting to rise up and frighten the unsuspecting intruder. Overhead, a small, tarnished chandelier offered the promise of illumination beneath its thick coating of dusty cobwebs.

In the room to her left, centered along the middle of the north wall, slumbered an over-large, decorative fireplace. The mantle and grate were bare but for a coat of grime, waiting for knick-knacks and dust catchers and a pile of wood to warm the room. The very idea of wanting dust catchers, while so much dust already surrounded her, brought a surge of laughter to her lips. But want them she did. Shaking her head, she wandered toward the back of the house, past a large, empty dining room. Stopping in the next doorway, she stared in awe.

The kitchen was enormous, easily occupying a majority of the rear of the house. It was her idea of heaven, with endless miles of countertop and acres of space. The appliances were hopelessly outdated. The linoleum was worn and dull. The paint on the walls and cabinets had faded with time, chips and gouges speckled the washed out colors from years of wear.

The room, as a whole, looked as if it, too, had fallen into a nineteen-fifty's time warp. Charmed silly, she stepped inside the room and tumbled deeper in love with the place. It reminded her of her grandmother's farmhouse, and she could almost smell the pot roast and fresh bread baking. A quick survey of the cupboards revealed a lifetime clutter of mismatched pots and pans, dishes and glasses. To her complete delight, a dented enamel teakettle rested on the rear burner of an ancient gas stove, just waiting for the chance to whistle one more time.

Pleased with what she'd found so far, she finished her tour through the rest of the house, including the second floor where she discovered three spacious bedrooms and another door leading up to a finished attic. A quick swipe of the windows with the tail of her shirt convinced her this room would be the perfect spot for her studio. She'd put her easel here, near the wide, east-facing windows. The morning light would be exceptional. She pivoted toward the far wall.

That space, just there, would serve as storage for her canvases, and the long folding table across the way would work well enough for framing. She could set up another work surface close to the easel for her paints. Though the thought of hauling all the necessary supplies and equipment up two flights of stairs was daunting, everything about the attic called to her, promising endless days of losing herself in the pleasures and depths of colors.

Rubbing her palms on the hips of her faded jeans, she thumped her way down one flight of stairs, then the other. JJ made short work of hauling her bags in from the trunk and switched the rusty lock back into place behind her before heading back to Main Street.

In short order, she'd made arrangements for the delivery of a long list of groceries and cleaning supplies for her new home. The store's owner, a robust older woman who reminded JJ portentously of Harriet Olson from *Little House on the Prairie*, took down the order herself and promised personal delivery by five o'clock. She'd visited the Post Office and opened a box, though she didn't expect to receive much more than junk mail and bills. Even that was a welcome foray into normalcy, a symbolic statement of permanency giving her tremors of both fear and excitement.

The postmaster, the very same man she'd seen coming out of Maggie's that morning, was exceptionally helpful, if a trite obvious. He'd introduced himself as James Henner. With dark good looks, a charismatic smile, and an athletic build, he looked as if he'd be more at home on a football field than manning a postal counter. As he spoke to her, he twisted just right—a practiced motion if ever she'd seen one—flexing an arm while he reached for something behind the counter. The bulge of muscle commanded the eye. The sly grin he shot her brought a flush of heat to her cheeks.

Were stares like that legal? Probably not without a special permit in most states.

She amended her mental picture, dropping him square into a triple-x rated movie. Mortified at her shocking line of thought, she offered him a wan smile and edged a little closer to the exit. Her skin tingled again...but this was no pleasant sensation like those startling green eyes at the diner had provoked. This man's leer was a little too knowing for her piece of mind.

Seemingly oblivious of her uncomfortable retreat, he kept right on talking, pointing her in the right direction should she need any assistance with competent lawn maintenance, electrical work, or plumbing. Jim—he'd insisted she call him—was all too happy to recommend a general all around handyman by the name of Cam something-or-other. By that point, all the names he'd thrown at her had begun to blend into an unwieldy mess, and so she just smiled and nodded, relegating the name to the back of her mind along with all the others.

Then, Jim leaned an elbow on the counter, offered her a loaded wink, and let her know he was on the town council, and, should she have any concerns, she was more than welcome to bring them straight to him. Day *or* night, he insisted with emphatic resolve, *anytime.*

Of course, the way he emphasized the last word made her wonder what other services he was offering besides his stint as the local yellow pages director and gossip coordinator. By then the walls had begun to close in on her. Jim was just a little too obvious in his interest, his smile grew more unsettling by the second. She'd back-pedaled out the door with all due haste, vigilant to hide her alarm behind an impersonal smile.

Shaking her head over the encounter, half cringing at what this next visit might reveal about the town she'd just become a citizen of, JJ shouldered the door of Connor's Hardware open and stepped inside to the light accompaniment of bells. The interior was cheerful and well organized, each aisle clearly marked with bold lettering for ease of use.

Brenda Huber

"I'll be with ya in just a minute," called a muffled voice from somewhere in the back.

"No hurry," JJ replied, letting out a tiny sigh of relief. At least, by the female tones of the voice greeting her, she wouldn't have to fend off another Jim in here. She wandered forward and began scanning shelves.

"What can I help you with?" A tall, slim brunette swaggered down the main aisle a moment later, a tool belt strapped around her narrow hips, wiping her hands on a small blue shop towel. Her smile was warm, her gentle brown eyes curious.

"Ah, hmm... I don't really know just yet." JJ stepped up to the cleaning section and hefted a mop, considered a pail. "I guess I should have made a list or something before heading this way."

"Well, whatever you need, either we got it, or we can get it." The brunette stepped closer, offering JJ a clean hand. "Name's Virginia Connor, by the way, folks mostly just call me Ginny. I own the place."

"It's a pleasure to meet you, Ginny." JJ returned the smile, shaking the offered hand. "I'm JJ. I'm buying the old Victorian out on Shady Lane."

"The old Caruthers's Place," Ginny remarked, nodding. She lifted a fine brow and adjusted the hammer hanging from her belt as she eased a hip against the counter, crossing her arms over her plaid-covered chest. "Must have been real fast, or that purchase would have been the first thing to hit Maggie's this morn—hold on a minute..." Ginny tilted her head and narrowed a discerning stare at JJ's face and ponytail. Her eyes dipped to JJ's worn hiking boots. "You were *in* Maggie's this mornin', weren't ya?"

JJ blinked and frowned, wracking her brain. She hadn't seen Ginny there, had she? No, surely not. Even if names didn't stick too well, she was very good with faces, and a blind man could have picked this beauty out of a crowd.

"Word gets round fast in a small town, especially when someone new pops up at Maggie's at the crack of dawn. Best get used to it if you're plannin' on stickin' round, 'cuz that ain't ever gonna change." Ginny's laughing brown eyes fluttered over her once again, and she clucked her tongue. "You must have a helluva good metabolism. You look like a good stiff wind could blow you away, but I heard it on good authority you polished off one of Maggie's blue-plate specials without batting an eyelash." A dimple flirted in Ginny's cheek. "You earned a healthy amount of admiration with that feat, by the way. Folks yammered about you well on to three hours after you left."

"Oh, well...I, ah..." Heat swam up her neck to flood her cheeks. Holy crap, she hadn't blushed this much in one day in her entire life.

"Oh, now, I've gone and embarrassed you. Don't pay me any mind. I have a tendency to open my mouth a little too wide sometimes." Ginny didn't look the least little bit ashamed, and JJ couldn't help but like her. In a way, her candid ramblings reminded JJ a lot of Sarah.

JJ's lips twitched at the bittersweet reminder as she set the mop and a pail on the counter and reached back for the broom. "That's all right. Like you said...I better get used to it." She added some basic gardening supplies to the pile and then counted out her cash as Ginny rang up her bill. "Is there someplace nearby that sells art supplies?"

"Hmm," Ginny murmured, tapping a neatly trimmed, unpolished nail against her lips. Her brow creased as she gave the matter some thought. "You might find what you're looking for over at Paper Cutouts. It's a hodge-podge craft store a block down. If June doesn't have what you're wantin', she could order it, I'm sure." Ginny handed JJ her change and added, "I heard the Caruthers's Place came fully furnished, but the old lady's been gone longer than I can remember. If you decide you're in need of new furniture or appliances, Shoemakers over on Park Street has a decent selection. Just go in with the attitude you're only looking, keep your nose up in the air a bit, and George will climb all over himself to cut you a good deal. If he doesn't have it in the store—"

"He can get it," JJ cut in. Grinning now, she nodded and thanked a smiling Ginny. In short order, she stowed her purchases in the back of her Jeep and set out for Shady Lane with a blossoming sense of purpose.

Before long, every window in the house stood wide open. Dust shrouds cowered on the laundry room floor. Armed with a case of Pledge, a gallon of Windex, and a stack of old rags she found on a shelf in the back of the walk-in pantry, JJ set to whipping her house into shape, one room at a time. On the kitchen table rested an ever-growing list of things to do and repairs needing attention, as well as a second list of items for her next trip to the hardware store. Sometime around half past four, the doorbell rang. The slurred, discordant notes caught her by surprise, and the ladder rocked beneath her.

Lemon-scented dust rag in hand, JJ grasped the rickety wood, and glanced down at her dingy T-shirt, damp with patches of sweat, and her grungy jeans. Wisps of hair had escaped her ponytail to straggle around her neck in sticky strands. Decades of grime clung to her skin, making her itch and long for a shower...which reminded her, the bathroom was next on her cleaning list. Climbing down, she swiped her forearm across her brow and moved from the parlor into the hallway to answer the door.

It was "Harriet" from the mercantile.

"Hello," JJ greeted her, stepping back into the

hallway. The door groaned as it swung wider, and JJ mentally added a can of WD-40 to her list for Ginny. "Thank you for delivering my order. I'm sorry. I don't think I caught your name earlier."

"Johnson, my dear...Betty Johnson," the woman crooned as she motioned to a wiry teenager standing near the car. Stepping into the entry, she offered JJ a smile, even as her neck craned to the side and her attention skimmed past JJ's shoulder toward the parlor. "The delivery is our pleasure, Miss Frost. It's a service we offer all our patrons. I can't tell you how pleased we are to have someone moving in here. This was such a grand old home, and it's fallen into such a sad state of disrepair."

"Yes, well—" JJ stopped as a mountain of grocery bags attached to a pair of long, skinny legs staggered through the doorway. She motioned down the hall, directing, "The kitchen's back there."

The grocery bag mountain offered a muffled thanks before tottering away.

Turning to her companion, she stifled a smile as the older woman snapped a guilty gaze back to JJ. "I really do appreciate the delivery service. As you can see, there's a lot to be done."

Oh, yes, the woman's eyes were all but bugging out of her head as she craned her neck once more to drink in every nuance of the den. JJ stepped back to allow the boy another run to the car. With a shy, red-faced smile, he bobbed his baseball-cap-covered curly hair in her direction and scurried on.

"I'd invite you farther in, but, as you can see, the place isn't up to visitors just yet." She herded the storekeeper back out onto the porch, careful to avoid the loose boards while the delivery boy made a third and final trip.

On his way back, he paused, ducking his head. His voice cracked and shifted with the changes of puberty, and his freckles disappeared in a rush of self-conscious color. "If you need help with the lawn, ma'am, I'd be happy to oblige. It's my second job. Name's Mike Becker, by the way. You can find me down at the grocery store most days."

Smiling, JJ nodded, promising, "I'll remember that. Thanks, Mike."

Beaming, cheeks flaming, Mike shuffled to the car.

The nosy Mrs. Johnson looked ever so disappointed as she turned her car around in the lane. JJ just smiled and waved.

With a determined set to her jaw and contentment curving her lips, JJ marched back inside to take on the pile of bags cluttering her kitchen floor. Her muscles ached with every step she took, and her hands burned from the industrial strength cleaner and disinfectant cocktail she'd used to scour the kitchen with earlier. She was filthier than she'd ever been in her entire life, and she hadn't been this happy in over a year.

Chapter 3

Cam took the scene in with one wide, sweeping glance. He swore beneath his breath. Stepping up to the long ribbon of yellow tape fluttering in the gentle breeze, he cleared his throat and forced unruffled professionalism into to his voice. "What do we got here, Red?"

Green around the gills, the deputy glanced up from where he knelt on one khaki-covered knee on the damp forest floor. A camera dangled from shock-numbed fingers, all but forgotten. He visibly forced a swallow, his youthful face lined with grim dismay.

"Sorry to call you in on your day off, Sheriff, but..."

Red's voice trailed away as his glassy gaze fell to the naked woman laying face down on a pile of black video tapes, gaudy skin magazines, and dozens upon dozens of condoms, wrapped and unwrapped. Most shocking of all were the huge letters scrawled across her back in gruesome crimson, like a child's twisted finger painting.

LUST.

"It's Lori Watson, Sheriff. She's dead."

"I see that," Cam murmured, setting his hands on his hips, studying the letters with a frown.

Odd. Well, not so very odd when you considered the evidence, and the woman's reputation. But odd that someone—no, not someone...her killer—odd her killer should choose to leave that particular word as his message. Why not something more obvious, more common...like whore or slut?

Cam dragged his gaze from the defiled body to

survey the surrounding woods. He drew in a long, concentrated breath through inconspicuously flared nostrils, then let out a disappointed sigh. The rain last night must have washed away whatever trace scents the killer might have left behind. His keen eyesight picked up nothing Red hadn't already marked with a large plastic number.

Right about now he was beginning to fervently wish someone else could have accepted responsibility just this once, wished someone else could shoulder the weight of this crime scene and what looked to be a damned puzzling murder investigation. Unfortunately, Sutter Hollow didn't have its own police department, falling a few people shy of a map dot, and so it fell under the Fulwick County Sheriff's jurisdiction. Convenient, considering the Sheriff and most of the deputies not only lived in Sutter Hollow, but had grown up here as well.

And so, officially, this was Cam's problem

Cam stole one more glance at the garish red scrawl on the victim's back. His gut churned. Was this another of his acute gifts rearing its head? Was he scenting trouble on the wind, or was this just plain old common sense?

Red had already cordoned off the standard perimeter with official yellow tape. He'd kept everyone else well outside the boundary lines. Despite his lack of experience—and his obvious shock—Red had done a good job of following protocol, keeping the scene secured. Besides Cam, Red had called the County ME to the scene, as well as Deputy Judy Blake who now stood with Jeff Williams, a local hunting fanatic. Like Cam, Judy was also off duty and in civilian clothes. The last two stood a little way outside the tape, the female deputy talking in reassuring, hushed tones with the pale-faced hunter while the ME hovered near the body muttering to himself.

Red stretched a finger toward the blood red, silk stocking cinched around the victim's throat. His voice wobbled. "Looks like she was strangled, sir."

"I see that, too," Cam replied in hushed tones. The muscle in his jaw flexed as he worked to ignore the scornful snort the ME coughed to cover up.

Cam bent to step beneath the tape, but stopped in his tracks as a fine wisp of white dust sifted from his hair down onto his T-shirt and paint splotched jeans. Straightening, he backed up a step. "I can't get any closer, Red. I'm covered in sheetrock dust, and I don't want to contaminate any evidence."

Red nodded, but he couldn't seem to tear his eyes away from the corpse. It wasn't every day Sutter Hollow produced a dead body, and never one displayed with such lascivious care.

"Son of a bitch," Cam swore under his breath again as his gaze fell to Lori once more.

He couldn't see her face from where he was standing, but even from this distance, the bruises covering her body were brutal. Acid churned in his stomach at the undignified sprawl in which the killer had taken such obvious care to pose her. The ME had secured bags over her hands, but he'd wager next month's pay the chances of gleaning DNA from her nails were slim to none. Her fingers were a broken, bloody mess inside the clear plastic.

Shaking his head, he called out, "Tell me you got what you need so we can at least cover her up, Jarvis."

Dr. Jarvis English, Fulwick County ME, nodded as he covered the distance to Cam, adjusting his wire-rimmed glasses, gazing at the clipboard in his hands with myopic absorption. A slight breeze whistled through the trees, stirring the budding leaves overhead, ruffling the hair at his silver streaked temples. "I believe the preliminaries are covered. The rest can wait till I get her back to the morgue."

"Can you give me anything so far?"

"Not anything conclusive...and you know me better than to ask for speculation." Jarvis stepped closer, shot a glance at Jeff—the only civilian on the scene—then offered in a lowered tone, "I can say, however, it appears as if there was cadaveric spasm involved."

Cam frowned at his friend as he sifted through the crime scene terminology lodged in long forgotten corners of his brain. He couldn't quite pin the term down. Death wasn't something he'd dealt with much in his ten years on the force...unless you counted road kill of the hoofed variety. Fulwick County was relatively small, and, for the most part, minor crimes were the rule of thumb. Run of the mill domestics, petty vandalism, under-aged drinking, the occasional B and E, and the rare meth lab were his area of expertise.

Edward Whitlock—the bane of Cam's existence—was the only regular in Cam's jail. Whenever the mood struck, which was more often than not, Ed went on a bender and busted up Pappy's, the local drinking hole. His offenses were usually nothing more than public intox with slaps on the wrist for being a nuisance. Fulwick County hadn't seen a murder in damned near fourteen years, and that one had been cut and dry. Man comes home. Man finds wife in bed with plumber. Man shoots plumber. Man shoots wife. Man shoots himself. Case closed.

The communities *other* population was very careful to maintain anonymity. Too careful for something like this. Besides, if they did hunt, they *never* hunted humans. And, rain or no rain, he would've been able to pick up one of *their* scents from five miles away.

He swerved a troubled gaze to the doctor and

blinked, momentarily taken aback in an abstract sort of way as he noticed for the first time the faint crow's feet at the corners of his friend's gray eyes. When had that happened? Jarvis was only a handful of years older than Cam. They'd worked out twice a week together down at Fitness Connection for the last eight years, ever since Jarvis had moved to town. When had Jarvis taken on such a dignified...*doctorly* air? Shit. So much for Cam's uncanny powers of observation.

"Sorry, Jarvis," he rumbled, pulling himself back to the conversation. "The term sounds familiar, but I'm drawing a blank here."

The ME turned his back on the hunter and lowered the clipboard in one hand as he explained with quiet patience, "In the final moments of death—particularly a violent or emotional death—certain groups of muscles lock tight, usually those of the hands and forearms." He lifted a hand and made a fist for demonstration, adding, "Often when the victim is clutching something." Jarvis held up a finger, then stepped away for a moment to dig through a small pile of clearly labeled, plastic bags. He returned with one and held it up for Cam's inspection. "I found this in her fist."

"Is that a rosary?" He frowned when Jarvis nodded confirmation. His gaze swerved back to the form now huddled beneath a white sheet. "Red?"

"Yeah, Sheriff?"

"Aren't the Watson's Methodist?"

"Yeah, Sheriff."

What in the hell was Lori doing with a rosary? Cam let out a long, aggravated sigh while he toed at the soggy debris near his boot. At least they wouldn't have to freeze their balls off looking for evidence out here. A few weeks back, and this search would have been downright miserable. Then his gaze skitters over the sloppy mulch around the body, and he changed his mind. Searching for any clues in this mud and decomposing debris might well be a miserable task after all. He'd have to come back later, after everyone else had cleared out, and go over the scene on his own. His senses were sharp now, but they'd be fifty times stronger after he'd shifted.

Shit. Well, there went a quiet night at home with a take-out tray from Maggie's and a cold one while he watched the game on his big screen. Hell, who was he kidding? The game might be on, but, like as not, it'd be like everything else today...pushed to the back burner by unexpected fantasies about that gorgeous blonde in Maggie's this morning.

He hadn't been able to shake her from his thoughts all day no matter how hard he'd tried. She'd been like a constant buzz in the back of his brain, an unceasing hum in his veins. What the hell was wrong with him? He'd never, *never* had this problem before...and sure as hell not off one little glance at a woman.

Scrubbing his hand down the side of his jaw, he conceded the point that he'd stolen more than one little glance. Hell, he'd been hard pressed to tear his eyes away from her for more than a handful of minutes, from the time he'd stepped inside Maggie's until the moment she'd sashayed out the door. He'd never had a woman affect him like that. He'd never *let* a woman affect him like that. Hell, it was probably just a fluke. Next time he saw her—and there definitely would be a next time now that she'd moved to town—he wouldn't pay her any more attention than he did anyone else.

Heaving a resigned sigh, he glanced down at his clothes before addressing Judy.

"Give me ten minutes to go home and shower this dust off and I'll be back to walk the scene with Red. I know Tommy's big game is tonight, so I'll hurry, then you can go on. Just sit tight for now, detain anyone who stumbles out this way. Radio in and have Emma pull Austin in if she can find him, but have her keep it low key. I don't want this to turn into a media circus. And I sure as hell don't want this getting back to Steve until I drive over to break the news."

"Aw, shit," Red muttered beneath his breath. It must not have occurred to him next of kin had yet to be notified. Steve, Lori's husband, and Red were old drinking buddies from high school. Cam stifled the urge to offer sympathy. Right now Red wasn't a friend of the deceased's family. He was a lawman with a murder scene on his hands.

Cam couldn't stand to look at Lori any longer, covered as she was or not. He couldn't afford to think of her as anything more than a faceless victim now, or he'd have a real mess on his hands. Turning to the hunter, he ordered, "Jeff, I'm gonna need you to stick around just a little longer. Judy will take your statement."

The hunter bobbled his head, a feeble motion, oblivious to the subtle nod Cam shot Judy. Jeff's reluctant, wide-eyed gaze dropped to the sheet-draped body and his Adam's apple bounced. The man was built like a brick shithouse, but right now, he looked as if the slightest puff of breath might knock him off his feet.

Cam could sympathize.

He trekked back up the hill and jumped inside the cab of his truck. The big diesel roared to life. He left the lights and the siren off as he flew down the gravel road toward home in the fading daylight. He didn't have far to go. Out of habit of years of patrol duty, his gaze flickered down the long driveway to the old Caruthers Place. He almost stomped on the brake when he caught the faint glow of lights at the rear of the house.

Recalling the pixie-like blonde—the very source of his tormenting fantasies...and his new neighbor—he stopped himself from charging up the lane to scare off any would-be vandals. He'd heard she'd moved into the place. Bought the house as it stood, without so much as stepping one of those tiny little hiking boots inside. She'd stirred up a regular hornet's nest of speculation all over town, flitting here and there, ordering supplies and whatnots right and left.

He'd also heard through the gossip mill, she was some kind of artist, though he'd tried not to pay much attention at the time. The old place she'd chosen to hang her hat was in complete shambles, and if she intended to live there, she had her work cut out for her. Then again, after his stolen glances at her in the diner, he didn't figure she'd last long. Probably just as well, given his inexplicable reaction to just the sight of her. She'd been so prim, so aloof, sitting there all alone. She'd worn those faded, frayed jeans and that worn T-shirt better than most swimsuit models sported their sexy bikinis. Lord knew her effect on his system had been infinitely much more devastating.

He gave a weary shrug and punched the accelerator again. He had enough to deal with right now without worrying about some artist with a passing fancy for rundown buildings...even if she was about the prettiest thing he'd laid eyes on in longer than he cared to remember. Chances were she wouldn't last the summer anyway. Hell, once she heard about the dead body sprawled damned near in her back yard, she'd be lucky to last the week. No, he wouldn't worry about her. And he wouldn't be wasting any more time daydreaming over her.

The sway of her hips as she'd left the diner that morning flickered through his mind.

He puffed his cheeks out and blew a long breath.

Damn. She'd had a sexy little swing going on there.

She'd seemed rather frail though, had a deer-in-the-headlights look about her. Vulnerable. He didn't usually go for the helpless type, preferring confident, self-reliant women instead. Still, something about her nagged at him. Something uncomfortable, something he couldn't quite put his thumb on...and couldn't quite shake.

Something that raised the hair on the back of his neck.

Swearing beneath his breath, he chastised himself for being nosy. Contrary to common perceptions about territorial sheriff's departments, Cam did not, in fact, believe it his God-given right to stick his nose in everybody's damned business. There were enough dirty little secrets floating around this town to contend with as it was without adding more into the soup. His own included.

There'd be hell to pay if the town council found out about his foray into insanity last summer, though now, what with Lori's murder and all, it'd be a might difficult to keep *that* particular secret under wraps. Heaven help him if they found out the rest. The Salem Witch Trials would probably have offered more leniency than Fulwick County's esteemed citizens. The chilling thought of mob lynchings and genocide sent shivers crawling down his spine.

He steered his truck down the neighboring drive, 125 Shady Lane, and slammed the truck into park, refusing to allow emotion to rise to the surface. Red wasn't the only one who needed to be a cop right now. Cam couldn't let his emotions anywhere near this investigation. Sliding the keys from the ignition, he leaped from the truck and jogged across the yard toward the front porch. Bounding up the steps, he raced inside and back to his bedroom where he dug out a change of clothes.

Cam rushed through the house—stripping as he

went—past construction materials and power tools, skidding inside the bathroom he'd just finished this afternoon. He caught his own reflection in the mirrored panels of the medicine cabinet, and his footsteps faltered. Bracing his hands on either side of the sink, he leaned closer and examined the face in the mirror. Hell, if he had that face sitting in an interrogation room, he'd have a cell waitin' and a handy place to throw away the key. He'd never seen a face wearing so much guilt. How long did he have before someone else noticed it too?

Haunted green eyes stared back at him from a face pale beneath his natural tan. His wheat-colored hair was white with the dust of his labors. That same powder caked in the tiny laugh lines at the corners of his eyes, exaggerating them, making him look far older than his age. His cheeks looked gaunt, his mouth grim.

He *felt* old. Decades and decades older than his thirty-one years. Hell, where had the time gone? It seemed just yesterday he'd had nothing more to worry about than whether or not he'd throw the winning touchdown at the state playoffs...no worries other than if he'd be able to score with Mary Jane Patterson when the game was over.

Nothing more to worry about than concealing the abnormal changes taking place inside his own adolescent body. He jerked his mind away from that bitter train of thought and centered his focus on the here and now.

Here and now, his troubles consisted of a dead body and notifying the next of kin.

Shit.

Sometimes being the one in charge of upholding the law really sucked. His right hand smoothed over the tattoo covering the entire left side of his chest, yet another symbol of his transition from naïve, careless youth to jaded, responsible adult. The griffin—with its massive wings spread, lethal talons poised to strike—surveyed his reflection with piercing, ageless eyes. A personal reminder of the burdens he so proudly bore, every bit as much as the shiny badge he wore pinned to his uniform shirt.

Just now, those burdens felt like the weight of the world upon his shoulders.

Shaking his head, he hopped into the shower before the water had sufficient time to warm up. He toweled off, dressed, and was back on the road in record time. His gaze tracked back to 123 Shady Lane as he drove by, but nothing seemed to have changed. Turning back to the road ahead—resolved to keep the beguiling woman out of his mind—he edged the truck onto a side road wrapping around and back into the woods, bracing himself for the long night ahead.

Red had already set up floodlights, warding off the encroaching darkness. Drawing a deep breath, he jumped down from the chrome runner and made his way to the crime scene. Pulling on rubber gloves, he scanned Jeff's statement, nodding his approval to Judy. She was a damned thorough officer. Cam advised Jeff to keep silent about what he'd seen before sending both Judy and Jeff on their way. After helping Jarvis load the victim's body in the back of the ME's van, he stood at the side of the road, watching as the van's taillights went around the bend and out of sight.

"Aside from the tapes, magazines, and condoms, there ain't much to go on here," Red called out as he approached. Red's voice sounded steadier now, more in control. "Dr. English said as how he figured she was probably left out here sometime last night." He stood, brushing damp, decaying leaves from the knee of his uniform. "Rained last night...hard tellin' if we'll be able to lift any prints. How the hell did he manage to dump her without leaving a single footprint?"

Cam remained silent and focused as he took a walk through the crime scene. His narrow-eyed stare followed the steady sweep of his flashlight beam. Then, with the blinding kick of a sucker-punch to the gut, Red's next words stopped Cam on a dime. "You suppose this might have something to do with last summer?"

Cam's alarmed gaze swung around to the young deputy. "What do you mean?"

Red's eyes swept over the surrounding woods, as if he expected eavesdroppers to tumble from the treetops. "You know... Lori didn't exactly live like a nun when she split with Steve last spring. She spent damned near all summer kickin' her heels up with just about any man she could lay hands on." Red's troubled gaze dropped to the toes of his boots. "Cam..."

Uneasy, Cam tilted his head, his brow creased.

A nasty taste crawled up the back of Cam's throat as Red looked up at him from beneath lowered brows and admitted, "Cam, I should have said something before now. I should have told you that I..." He paused, swore beneath his breath. "I never told anyone. I didn't figure people would approve if they heard she was steppin' out with one of Sutter Hollow's finest..."

Cam's palms began sweating inside his latex gloves. His heart thumped just a little harder. "Look, Red—"

"No," Red interrupted, holding his hand up. "Let me get this out. I know it was wrong. I must have been out of my mind. I knew about her and Austin. I knew I... I never—"

Lori and Austin?

Cam stuttered, "Austin? But I—"

"—never should have slept with her. She was a friend's wife, damn it, even if they weren't together at the time. Then they reconciled, and I couldn't say anything—"

"What?" Cam stared at Red in open-mouthed shock. Red had been with Lori too? *And* Austin? Cam knew he hadn't been the only man to tangle the sheets with her last summer, but, good Lord, how many others had there been?

"I didn't kill her, Cam. I swear I didn't." Red's grief-filled eyes pleaded with Cam for understanding.

Slinging his head back on his shoulders, staring for a moment at the dusky sky, Cam drew a long breath. Letting it out on a long slow whistle, he straightened and crossed the clearing to stand at his deputy's side. "Red—"

"Cam, I'm—"

"Will you just shut up for one damned minute?" He glared Red silent, then closed his eyes, forcing his nerves to level out. When he opened his eyes, Red stood before him with a hang-dogged expression. At any moment, Cam half expected him to thrust both wrists out to be cuffed.

"I didn't figure you killed her. And no, I didn't know you'd been with her. Or Austin either, for that matter. Hell, Red...last summer... Shit." Cam kicked at a small pile of leaves. "I was with her myself. Once. I had too much to drink and... Well, it doesn't matter. What matters is half the damned town was probably with her, but it won't do any good to start pointing fingers." Cam turned away from the raw, stunned disbelief etched on Red's face. Cam had clearly tumbled from his pedestal. "We treat this crime scene just like any other. We do our jobs, and we find her killer."

Silent and pensive, Red fell into step beside Cam as they resumed their sweep.

"When we finish up here, I want you to head back to the station. Take whatever evidence we have back to my office and lock the door. I don't want any of this stuff compromised by curious hands. I'll head over to the Watson place to talk with Steve. Write up your report. By then I should be back, and we can go through this stuff together."

That prospect, in and of itself, left a cold ball of dread swimming in the pit of his stomach. Steve Watson's moods ran the gamut from maudlin to lashing fury. His unpredictable moods had been one of the reasons for the split with Lori last summer, one among many. There was no telling how he'd take the news of his wife's murder. Heaven help them all if he found out about the men she'd been sleeping with...including a sizable portion of the Fulwick County Sheriff's Department by recent account.

Unable to stand the guilt in Red's eyes for a second longer, unable to deal with his own remorse, Cam motioned toward the east. "You sweep that way. Don't go farther than the Dutton barn, though. Holler if you find anything...otherwise meet me back at the scene. Be careful."

Nodding, Red set off as instructed. Then he stopped dead. "Shit, Cam..." The beam of his flashlight cut around to catch Cam dead in the eyes before he recalled himself and aimed the light toward the ground. "You don't think Steve would've..."

Gritting his teeth with grim resignation, Cam returned to his work, but his words hung in the air between them, heavy with dismay. "As of right now, he's at the top of the list of suspects."

Chapter 4

JJ bounced off the doorframe of the small utility room and lurched inside. As she skidded into the cold metal casing of the washing machine, tingling pain burst in her elbow, shot through her toes. The upright freezer loomed nearby, but there wasn't enough space to squeeze between it and the wall. The wicker laundry basket in the corner offered no hope of concealment, and she wasn't exactly a kid who could climb inside the dryer.

That left her three options...only three. The kitchen she'd just staggered through. Even now, his booted heels creaked over the old linoleum near the stove.

He was getting closer.

The basement door shot past her gaze, a blur without a second thought. Any idiot who'd ever watched a horror flick knew that path lead to certain, agonizing death. The squeaky floorboard near the sink gave beneath his weight. She could almost feel his frenzied breath on the back of her neck. On shaking legs, she edged toward the back stairwell leading to the second floor. If she made it upstairs, maybe she could get to the main staircase leading down to the front door, and then outside...

Creak, creak. Creak, creak. Creak, squish. *Her eyelids sagged closed, and bile slammed into the back of the throat. Bloody footprints... Hysteria gurgled ever closer, filling her mind with vivid images. He'd track bloody footprints all over Sarah's pine-scented, spotless kitchen floor.*

JJ bolted upright on the sofa, clutching the

cushion beneath her in one fist and her throat with the other. Her breath sawed in and out, her chest heaved. The darkened room spun before her blinking eyes, then righted itself. Where was she? How had she gotten here? She had to get away. She had to hide.

Run, JJ. Run...

Halfway to the door, she tripped on a pile of dingy, lemon-scented rags, banging her shin on the stepstool. The bright slash of pain brought the room into crisp focus, snapping reality into place. She must have fallen asleep on the sofa when she'd sprawled to take a break. She was safe. She didn't need to run. Not this time.

Still, it was next thing to impossible not to give in to instinct. Her hands trembled with the need to feel the cold bite of her car keys against her palm.

Drawing a shaky breath, she made her way to the kitchen. Jerking open the prehistoric refrigerator door, she thrust her arm inside, groping blindly, and yanked out a bottle of water. Fumbling the cap off, she put the bottle to her lips and guzzled. The chilled water slid along her burning throat, dislodging the hot ball of terror on its way down. When the bottle was empty, she crossed the room on quivering legs and tossed the bottle into the recycling bin beneath the sink. Turning the faucet on, she bent over the sink, using both hands to splash water onto her face, over and over, until the cold sting cleared away the last haze of panic.

Feeling infinitesimally better, JJ reached for the towel and blotted her face dry. Then something caught her eye. Whatever it was, it flashed and bobbed in the dark, out in the woods just past her back yard. She went up on tiptoe and leaned over the sink, closer to the window, straining her eyes. There it was again. And that glow farther off, it was...eerie.

Like a freakin' space ship had landed in the woods.

Oh, yeah, that was rational...*not*. Maybe instead of standing here, staring out the window, thinking about going out there to investigate, she ought to be dialing Dr. Greene. What would the good doctor have to say about aliens?

Have you been taking your medications, Jillian?

Well, that'd be a big hell no. She hadn't been able to take another minute of pharmaceutically induced tranquility, and so she'd ditched the pills two months ago, bottle and all, and she hadn't looked back once.

Chewing her bottom lip, JJ watched another, smaller light separate from the eerie glow, bobbing in a different direction. Dare she go out there? Or should she dial 911 and pray they didn't haul her off to the nearest loony bin? One of those lights was coming closer, its arc slithering back and forth over the ground in slow, methodical patterns. Damn it. Someone was out there, trespassing on *her* property.

Find your backbone, JJ, it's around here somewhere.

Jerry is dead and buried.

Literally.

She was not a victim. Not anymore.

It was, in all likelihood, nothing more than some kids out searching for a good place to get a buzz on. She rocked back on her heels and planted fists to hips. Well, not on *her* property. Narrowing her eyes, she dug through one drawer after another until she found the flashlight she'd stowed away earlier. At least she'd thought to replace the batteries this afternoon.

Glancing out the window, JJ bit down on her lower lip. The light was still there, still moving closer. It might just be kids, but she had no way of knowing that for sure. No. She'd rather be safe than sorry.

She went to the back door, stopping long enough to pull on a light jacket. With a spare moment's hesitation, she squared her shoulders, and slipped down the back steps, around the side of the house, and across the yard. Her vehicle sat, cold and dark, in the night. Safety—protection—nestled in the glove box. Careful not to rattle the keys, she opened the door and snatched the gun from its hiding place. The brush of cool metal against her skin bolstered her courage.

She was taking control of her life, wasn't she? If this was where she had to start, then so be it.

Jerry's dead. Jerry's dead. Jerry's dead.

She repeated the litany—over and over—as she tucked the gun into the back of her waistband.

It didn't help much.

****

A muffled pop in the darkness somewhere to the west brought Cam's palm to the butt of his gun in a patent move of pure instinct, though he didn't draw. Those same instincts that had him reaching for his gun—his survival instincts—also urged him to shift. Primal instinct was harder to control than trained instinct. He crouched and froze, thumbing the switch to kill the power to his flashlight.

Straining to hear the slightest noise, attuned to the very shift of the wind, he crept forward on silent feet, relying now on his keener-than-your-average-human senses. His lungs burned, but he fought to keep his breathing slow and shallow. Someone was out there, slipping in and out of the shadows. He shoved his flashlight into his back pocket, freeing up one hand while he kept the other close to his gun. Ready. With cautious steps, he eased around the thick trunk of a tree, slinking deeper into the night, peering into the shadows.

Slipping closer to becoming the predator he'd

been born.

Snap. A low, muttered curse. A shadow wavered, moving closer.

He slipped back, pressing his spine against unyielding, rough bark. Drawing a measured, quiet breath, Cam tensed, poised to spring.

****

"Damn it," JJ muttered beneath her breath as another twig snapped under her heel. She may as well have tramped out here with a full marching band for as much noise as she was making.

Holding her breath, she paused. When deafening silence met her ears, she moved forward. The lights had disappeared completely. Holy crap. Whoever'd been out here, they apparently suspected they were no longer alone. Damn it. She should have dialed 911.

JJ took another step forward and stopped. A chilly breeze stirred the loose tangles of hair against her neck, sending goose bumps scooting over her flesh and unease snaking down her spine. The night had been deceptive in the back yard. There, moonlight had taken the edge off fear. Here in the woods, the shadows were so deep, so dense she couldn't see three feet in front of her face. Tree branches came alive, snagging at her jacket and tweaking her cheek with hungry, questing fingers. They danced in the breeze, swaying and stretching into the night sky, like giant arms preparing to strike.

It was so very silent here. Deathly still. She'd expected some kind of noise, a rustle, a hoot, a symphony of crickets, or...or something. But there was nothing. And the silence hurt her ears.

JJ eased forward. Quietly. Gingerly. Shifting her weight, she put one foot after another, faster and faster. The toe of her boot caught in something solid, something that refused to budge. Her momentum carried her onward without her feet. She went sprawling, face first, with a soft whoosh of expelled breath into a thin scattering of leaves and twigs. Damn it, could she be any more clumsy tonight?

Muttering foul curses beneath her breath, she swiftly rolled over, twisted around and picked herself up. Passing the flashlight from one hand to the other, she brushed her palms over her thighs, dislodging dirt and pieces of dead leaves.

Did something move? She swung to the right. There? She wheeled to the left. No, just there? She dare not turn on her flashlight. It wouldn't be wise to give away her location on the off chance whoever was out here had less than innocent intentions. Her nostrils flared, and she sucked in a sharp breath, her wide-eyed gaze darting this way and that.

The air was pure and layered here. The tang of pine and the clean wash of approaching rain hung in the air. Beneath that, honeysuckle and some nameless, cloying-scented flower perfumed the night. And beneath that layer hovered moldering grass and fallen, decomposing vegetation. If her nerves hadn't been strung so tight, she might well have stopped where she was to drag in lungful after lungful of the heady stuff.

As it was, panic made it difficult to breathe.

A soft crackle nearby spun her on her heel. Her heart vaulted into her throat, and then hung there, thundering like a racecar, revved and ready to cut loose. She clutched the flashlight like a club, but, she refused to turn it on. She wouldn't draw any more attention to herself than she already had. A shadow shifted, and her head whipped around. She reached for her gun. Panic surged through her. It was gone. Oh God, it was gone. Where was it? Dare she drop to her knees and shuffle around in the leave trying to find it?

A soft shushing sound filtered closer. The sound

of stirring leaves.

The instinct to cut and run swelled. Yeah, 911 sounded damned good right about now. She'd worry about finding her lost gun tomorrow. In the daylight. Spinning on her heel, disoriented, she took a quick, measured step.

She smacked into a brick wall.

Or rather, the brick wall slammed into her. It flew through the night with a dark growl and the force of a freight train, knocking the breath from her lungs, slapping stars into her eyes. She hit the ground, hard, too stunned to move, with a terrifying weight planted firmly astride her. Panic, hysteria warred with angry incredulity. She'd survived Jerry only to come here—to this picturesque little community—to die?

Oh, *unfair.*

Her heart slammed against her ribs, reminding her there was life in her still. She hadn't gone down without a fight the last time. She sure as certain wasn't going to go like a meek little lamb this time around either. Gun or no gun. Curling her fingers into claws, she flailed her arms and kicked with all her might. Thrashing and wiggling, clawing for her freedom, JJ snapped her teeth at anything unwise enough to get close to her face.

The dark shadow grunted as she connected a knee with a hard thigh. Large hands grabbed and grappled. A solid, heavy chest pressed into hers, and her wrists were pinned above her head in a viselike grip. Thrusting her head forward, she snapped her teeth again. This time she caught more than air. Her teeth clamped down hard, and through the cotton, she caught her attacker's collarbone.

He jerked back leaving her with nothing but his shirt in her mouth. A deep voice barked with violent insult near her ear, "Son of a bitch!"

An angry hand fisted in her hair, yanking her

head down against the ground, and the hand pinning her wrists tightened, threatening her circulation. Threatening to crush bone. That rock solid chest crushed hers now, deliberately, restricting her very ability to breathe. A heavy leg flopped over her straining legs, and slid down, clamping one of them between hard thighs. Ragged breath rasped against her cheek. Sandpaper bristles on a hard jaw scraped her neck.

Then her assailant's ragged breathing went utterly silent, just for a sliver of a moment.

His chest expanded against her as he buried his nose in the side of her neck, just below her earlobe. Was he *smelling* her? His entire body went rigid. The low rumble began deep in his chest, vibrating its way up until it escaped him in a wary growl. His nose nuzzled her flesh a second time, and he drew another impossibly deep breath. The ominous rumble altered, shifted, slid into a definitive purr of approval, and she shivered beneath him.

No, no, no. Oh, no, please... Her mind screamed the plea, but she refused to let the words roll past her lips. She wouldn't beg. She'd never beg again...but, damn her eyes, tears began to well. No. Stop it, damn it. She couldn't show weakness. Weakness of any kind invited prolonged torture. That was a lesson she'd learned well. Her mind screamed she fight on, but her body wouldn't cooperate. Her traitorous limbs had turned to jelly.

"I'm gonna let go of your head," a disturbingly sensual, husky voice informed her. Her assailant's lips brushed her ear, velvety smooth, and a chill coursed through her. "Do *not* bite me again."

She nodded understanding. She'd agree to anything...right now. Once she was loose, they'd be in a different ballpark altogether. With obvious caution, as if he were just waiting for her to lunge again, he loosened his fingers first, then slowly dragged his palm away from her head, though he kept her wrists caged.

Mud soaked her from the back of her head to the backs of her boots. She wanted to squirm, but she didn't dare. She lay still, until a sharp beam of light lanced into her face. Snapping her eyes closed, she jerked her face away, humiliated by the trail of moisture leaking from the corners of her eyes.

"You!" It was a harsh, disbelieving accusation—that one word—and it carried a wealth of emotion behind it. Peeping an eye open, JJ eased her head back, but the face beyond the light was locked in the shadows, featureless and threatening.

"What are you doing out here?" He didn't sound any less dangerous the more he spoke.

Reckless fear shot through her, turning the edge in her voice to snapping fury. "This is *my* damned land. What the hell are *you* doing out here?"

That gave him pause, even if only for a moment. Good. Now he knew he couldn't intimidate her. She bit her lip to quell the disloyal trembling.

"I'll be the one asking the questions here," he grumbled.

"Like hell you will," JJ hissed, praying the last dregs of terror weren't as clear in her eyes as she feared they were. "Get off me."

He shifted atop her, easing his grip a bit, but by no means did he release her...or get off her. He eased the hold he had on her thighs, sliding one of his legs between hers as he eased some of his weight from her. No, her assailant seemed to be doing nothing more than getting comfortable. Damn him.

"I don't think so, honey," he murmured near her temple, his hips shifting a little more, centering, as he readjusted his grip on her wrists. "Not until I get some answers."

Despite her fear, his voice slipped over her like luxurious velvet. Sensual and enticing. She shivered, gritting her teeth, unwilling to acknowledge the involuntary movement as anything more than a reaction to the temperature, though, truth be told, he was radiating enough heat to thaw half of Alaska in the dead of winter. He didn't even have a coat on.

Why wouldn't he *move*?

"Well, that's not likely to happen, *asshole*." She squirmed beneath him, trying to wriggle her way to a little more breathing room. Instead, all she managed to do was thrust her breasts against his chest and settle his pelvis more firmly against the juncture of her thighs. She cut his sharp hiss of breath off with a snarled, "Get off me, you rotten son of a—"

"Now, now, honey," he cut in, sounding oddly pained. "Don't go saying something you'll—"

"—*bitch!*" JJ ground out between clenched teeth, jerking at her arms. "Get off me, now!"

A low, appreciative chuckle met her demand. "You know, you're awful bossy for such a little thing. Didn't your mother ever teach you that you can catch more flies with a little sugar?"

"Sugar, my ass... Get that damned light out of my eyes, I can't even see your face," she snapped, squinting against the beam.

He paused, as if weighing his options, then the beam angled away. With the loss of the glare in her eyes, she got her first good look at the man pinning her to the ground. The glittering emerald eyes that met hers knocked the wind from her sails...just as they had early that morning at the diner. Her eyes widened, and she gasped, "You!"

Her assailant was the carpenter from Maggie's...the one with the come-hither eyes and the worship-at-my-altar body. Oh, hell, wasn't that just freakin' perfect? The first time in over a year she so much as snagged a glimpse of a man who could ignite sparks of interest, and he turned out to be some demented nighttime prowler. Go figure. It must be a genetic aberration of the women in her family, this fascination for the wolf in sex-god skin.

Narrowing her eyes, she tamped down on the urge to sink her teeth into him again. He was twice her size. He still held her pinned to the ground. And she still didn't know whether he intended to hurt her, or worse. She wasn't out of the woods here, not by a long shot.

She forced level calm into her voice, a calm she was a long way from feeling. "Get off me."

Ignoring her demand, he cocked his head to the side. His eyes gleamed like jewels as they searched her face, and a groove began to form in his cheek. "What are you doing out here in the dark?"

"I asked you first," she spit back, yanking at her wrists, serene façade forgotten.

She bucked against him. She gained not an ounce of leeway.

Above her, his eyes widened, then narrowed and darkened. He shifted atop her, the edge of his lips—attractive, sensual lips—curved up.

The bastard.

He was enjoying this. Her nostrils flared and her teeth clacked together loud enough to make that sexy groove in his cheek a little deeper. Sucking in a deep breath, she willed herself to relax. No way was she pushing at him with her body again. She flat out refused to give him any more opportunity to cop a feel.

"I saw lights moving around out here." Her frigid tone threatened frostbite. "I came to investigate."

"Well, now, that's just plain stupid."

"Excuse me...*stupid*?" This from the man who seemed perfectly comfortable carrying on a conversation while lying in the mud.

"Stupid, I said." He scowled down at her now,

and his voice took on a decidedly scolding tone. "You could've been hurt. You're new around here. You have no idea the kinds of things that might be lurking around out here in the dark. Damn it, you could have been attacked."

She dropped her head back on the ground, lifted a sardonic brow. Her stare bore into his, but she uttered not a sound.

"Don't look at me like that," he snapped, sounding very much like her mother had whenever JJ'd gotten herself grounded. "Why the hell didn't you call 911?"

"You know, you're right," she agreed, sticky-sweet, smiling thinly veiled malice. "Why don't you let me up, and I'll just run along like a good little girl and do that right now?"

Answering her sarcasm with a snide snort, he pressed, "Did you see anything suspicious out here at anytime today?"

"You mean other than the glow of your spaceship? Or maybe you mean a big, arrogant prick who might jump out of the shadows, knock me into the mud, and sit his heavy ass on top of me?" By the time she'd gotten to the end of her spiel, her nose was an inch from his while she glared daggers at him. If she couldn't bloody him with her claws, she'd damned well do her best to draw a few drops with the sharp side of her tongue. "If this is your version of the welcome wagon, thanks, but I think I'll pass."

Grim admiration danced in his eyes, but the smile fell from his lips. "Look, honey, this is serious. I'm—"

"You're damned right this is serious," JJ ground out through clenched teeth, giving her wrists a vicious, useless tug again. "This is assault, and trespassing, and holding me against my will, and...and Lord knows what else you're involved in out here. Is it drugs? It's drugs, isn't it? No, do *not* tell me, I don't want to know, just get the hell off me. And stop calling me that."

The way the word "honey" kept dripping off his tongue was a little too familiar...and much too intimate...for her comfort.

Forgetting her vow not to give him any more jollies, she arched her back, planted her heels in the mud, and strained to buck him off again. He only settled farther into the vee of her thighs. She bucked, and his hips wedged tight against her. He swore beneath his breath, ferocious and feral, and the light in his eyes shifted, darkened even more. His hungry gaze slid to her lips, smoldering with an intensity that stole her ability to breathe, robbed her of all lucid thought.

For half a second, she froze, lost in the deep awareness in his gaze and the searing jolt of desire etched on his face. Would his lips be soft and persuasive, or hard and demanding? An odd pressure swelled where his pelvis rested against her—a rigid, thick, long line hard as steel—and it didn't take her more than a heartbeat to realize it wasn't the gun strapped to his hip.

Desire pooled, molten liquid, deep in her core, but panic chased the lust from her veins. His nostrils flared, and he drew a deep breath. His eyes dilated, until only the smallest sliver of emerald remained. As if of their own volition, his hips did a slow, rolling surge, grinding his all-too-evident erection hard against her. The corner of his mouth curled upward in seductive invitation, and his delectable lips began an unmistakable descent.

She gasped. Her eyes flared, and she renewed her struggles, but her efforts were no more effective than a lamb defending against a wolf. Then, without warning, the strangest expression flickered over his face. As if he'd just been caught with his hand in the cookie jar. He looked startled. Embarrassed.

Releasing her, he bound to his feet in one graceful economy of motion, bending to offer her a hand.

She wouldn't have accepted his help had she been practicing her breaststroke in quicksand with an anchor sailor-knotted to each ankle. Scrambling to her feet with much less grace than determination, she leaped back a healthy foot or two. Her entire body shivered with awareness, tense and prepared for flight. Her eyes darted from him to the general direction of the house and back. Was she fast enough?

"Look, this is easy to settle," he coaxed in a hypnotic, husky voice.

She hadn't missed the Glock at his hip, stark black against his faded jeans. Oh, yeah, let's be reasonable. That's easy to say when you're the one with the gun. Damn it, how the hell could she have dropped hers? Maybe if she hadn't, he wouldn't be so damn confident, so damned smug.

One large, calloused hand lifted, empty palm toward her. He took a step closer as his other hand slowly reached around behind his back. Terror raked icy claws through her, instantaneous and brutal. She panicked, and, for a moment, the sexy handyman in a skin tight, plain white T-shirt no longer stood before her. Jerry did. And he was covered in blood. Her sister's blood. Hers. She couldn't give him time to pull the knife out from behind his back.

She wouldn't give him the chance to run her to ground.

Launching herself at him, she brought her knee up as hard as she could between his legs. As he sagged to the ground, his hands clutching his abused privates, wheezing in shock, she doubled up a fist and swung with all her might.

She needed to improve her aim. She'd been angling for his nose, but ended up delivering not much more than a glancing blow off his cheek. Still, it was enough to surprise him, whip his face to the side. JJ didn't stop to see if he would follow. She didn't pause to search for her fallen flashlight or that cursed gun. She just ran. Ran as if the hounds of hell were snapping at her heels. Tree branches tore at her hair, ripped at her jacket, slapped at her face. Tree roots and loose stones made every step a treacherous gamble, but still she ran.

Run, JJ. Run...

****

From behind the thick trunk of an ancient oak some distance off, the killer watched it all, his night-vision binoculars trained on the woman tussling with Cam in the mud, struggling for the upper hand. At first glance, one could easily mistake her for timid, frail even. A poetic soul might have dubbed her haunted. She was a looker all the same. Feminine and fair. Delicate. The kind of woman that made a man want to toss her over his shoulder and carry her off, protect with his life.

He'd underestimated her, though. He could see that now. He cringed in male sympathy as she rammed her knee into Cam's balls. From the way the good sheriff dropped to the ground at her feet, it was safe to assume Cam had underestimated her as well.

God helps those who help themselves.

He chuckled, even as his eyes narrowed in speculation. This little beauty had gumption and spirit, more than met the eye. She was a little spitfire all right. God would surely smile on one such as her. Interesting.

Very interesting.

Miss JJ Frost, brand new owner of the derelict Victorian at 123 Shady Lane, had just earned herself a blip on the Apostle's radar.

Chapter 5

JJ's boots pounded across the yard. Blood thrummed in her ears, a raging river of adrenaline and terror, her breath ragged on her trembling lips. The cool night air seared her heaving lungs. She took the steps of the back porch two at a time, and slammed into the door with a bone-jarring crunch. Frantic, she jiggled the handle in fumbling hands, tossing a terrified glance over her shoulder. The solid panel of wood refused to budge.

Sinister shadows at the edge of the woods swayed and bowed, but no man-shaped silhouette broke free. That fact offered little solace to her erratic pulse. Wrenching her attention back to the doorknob, she broke a nail wresting with the tarnished metal. Cursing aloud, JJ pounded her palm against the peeling paint near her face in desperation, kicking at the unyielding barrier between her and safety. The door gave at last. Sobbing, she shoved her way inside, slammed the door behind her, and forced the decrepit lock into place with weak, shaking fingers.

Oh, no. Oh, no. Oh, no.

How could she have lost her gun? She wasn't about to go back outside in the dark to search for it now though. The phone...she had to call for help. Her phone was in her purse, wasn't it?

Where was her damned purse?

The parlor...on the secretaire...

Scrambling through the kitchen, she stumbled down the long hallway and tore into the parlor. Her feet tangled in the pile of dust rags again. Careening to the side, she narrowly avoided a pail of filthy water, but luck was not on her side. She crashed into an end table instead. The small antique lamp wobbled and tipped. Instinct took over. She dove, arms outstretched, to catch the delicate bit of brass and stained glass before it crashed to the floor. Just that quickly, the memories sucked her back.

She staggered past the freezer, groping in the dark for the banister. Each step of the back staircase was a landmine of sound, creaking and groaning beneath her. Somewhere near the top—was it the third or the forth step that creaked the loudest? Heaven help her she couldn't remember—she tripped, knocking her shin on the next step up, banging her already smarting elbow against the landing. She reached out, fingers splayed, clawing to regain her balance.

Torn nails dragged bloody trails across the wall beside her. Dozens of tiny cuts stung her bare feet as they slapped against polished mahogany, leaving behind weaving smears of blood. A tiny shard of glass, still embedded in her heel, sank ever deeper as she hobbled through the long, second floor hallway. JJ braced her hand against the wall as she threw a frightened glance behind her, fleeing for her very life.

Her breath sawed in and out of her burning lungs. Cold sweat dripped in her eyes and trickled down the side of her battered face, tracing an icy finger down the middle of her back. The gash on her forearm and the slash across her shoulder blade burned like a red-hot poker had dragged against her bare skin. But she didn't have the benefit of cauterization, no, her wounds inexorably dripped more of her strength away, leaving behind an unmistakable path of dark splotches leading Jerry straight to her.

She wrapped an arm around her middle, her hand fisting in the drenched material covering her

61

throbbing ribs. It hurt so much. A slow creak from the bottom step spun her around, and crimson splattered across the vintage, Victorian wallpaper she'd helped Sarah hang only a few short months ago.

Her momentum and dizzying waves of lightheadedness tipped her off kilter, and she slipped on a decorative braided rug. Arms flailing, she crashed into a small hall table, tipping the crockery vase atop it sideways before regaining her balance. Diving for the container, her heart lurched in her chest. If the vase shattered, the sound would give her away. He'd know right where to look, and he'd find her faster than she was prepared to die. Not that she wanted to die. She'd never be ready to die.

Oh, God, Sarah...

No. No, Sarah was dead. And JJ wasn't there anymore.

She wasn't in *that* house.

Frantic hands swiped across the wooden surface of the desk, propping the lamp on its side, knocking she knew not what to the floor as she fumbled for her purse. Tearing it open, JJ thrust her hand inside and stirred around in the mess until her fingers closed over the slim device. Her wide-eyed gaze skidded over the room, her ears straining for the tiniest sound. Just as she flipped the phone open, her alarmed stare collided with the window...the *open* window.

Every window in the house was wide open.

Her heart plummeted to her hiking boots. Her vision blurred, and her knees buckled. She clutched at the side of the secretaire for balance as the blood in her veins turned to sleet. Forcing down the bitter taste of fear swimming up her throat, she thrust her hand inside her purse once more and wrenched out the bottle of pepper spray. The purse fell to her feet, contents scattering in wild abandon. Her gaze flew to the stairs in the hallway.

JJ's skin crawled at the very idea, but she forced herself to ascend them. Déjà vu was a sticky poison, damned near paralyzing, and she couldn't quite shake free of it.

She had to hide. At this point, every one of the downstairs rooms held potential danger. She had nowhere to go...nowhere but up. Remembering the large chest of drawers in the second bedroom on the left, she scrabbled up the stairs, skidded inside, and dragged the door closed as quietly as possible. After pushing the old lock below the doorknob into place, she rushed to the side of the chest, pushing and shoving with every ounce of adrenaline coursing in her hypothermic veins. At last, with the chest lodged in place, JJ crouched in the dark on the far side of the bed and flipped the phone open, blindly jabbing at numbers. Her fingers were trembling with such force, though, that she punched the eight instead of the nine. Cursing, she started over.

The call took an eon to connect. She sobbed aloud when a cool female voice vibrated through the line.

"911...do you have an emergency?"

"Help me." Her hoarse croak ended on a humiliating sob. She swiped at a damp cheek, sagging against the side of the mattress. Falling apart now wouldn't help.

"Ma'am, you have to tell me what's wrong," the confident, soothing voice advised. "Are you injured?"

"Yes—no." The air was like soup—like stew— and she couldn't draw enough in to make her lungs work properly. "No, no. I'm not hurt."

"Has there been an accident?" The voice was patient, reassuring. The clacking of computer keys in the background settled JJ's nerves, somewhat. The dispatcher needed facts, information. She had to keep her head.

"No. My name is JJ Frost. I live at 123 Shady Lane in Sutter Hollow," she stammered. Good. At least if he killed her now, they'd know where to look for the body.

Shaking her head at her own morbidity, JJ pushed on, "There was a strange light in the woods behind my house." Oh yeah, *that* sounded sane. Now they were going to think she was calling to report a UFO. Instead of sending the cops, they'd be radioing the little men in white lab coats for a straightjacket. "I...I went out to look around, and a man...jumped me. He knocked me down, but I...I managed to get away."

"Are you inside your home now, ma'am?" The clacking increased in speed. "Are you alone in the house?"

"Yes, I'm inside. But all the windows are open downstairs," she rushed to explain. "I...I think I'm alone, but...I don't know for sure. He could have...climbed inside."

"Okay, ma'am. This is what I want you to do. Can you stay on the line and still make it into a closet or a room that you can hide, somewhere you can barricade yourself inside?"

"Yes," JJ mumbled, letting out a ragged breath. "I'm already in a second floor bedroom. I shoved the chest of drawers in front of the door."

"Good, that's very good. Okay. Stay on the line with me, ma'am. It's important that you stay calm," the voice cajoled. "We have a unit nearby. I'm sending an officer over right now."

The dispatcher's voice drifted away from the phone, began rattling codes and JJ's address in a level, professional tone. The scratchy response of a police radio replied in the distance, and the female voice came back to JJ. "Do you have a weapon, ma'am? It's important that you do not use it on the responding officer by accident."

"Pepper spray. I have pep—"

A crash from below, the reverberating clang of metal against the hardwood floor, cut her words off on a sharp hiss. Her startled gaze flew to the door as she edged the top half of her face up over the side of the mattress.

"Ma'am? Are you still there, ma'am?"

"Yes. I... Oh, no..." She tamped down on the fierce urge to curl up into a ball and sob. "He's inside. I think he's...inside the house. Something crashed...down there. Oh, shit... He's armed. In the woods...he had a gun."

The voice drifted away to the dispatch mike to report the latest development to the responding unit, but JJ couldn't make sense of the words. He was *inside* the house. He'd kill her and be gone before help arrived. A broken sob clogged her throat. Then a wild swirl of red and blue burst across the walls, and JJ's forehead dropped to the bed.

"Ma'am, the officer is on the scene now. Where are you?"

"Second floor bedroom...on the left," JJ responded without conscious thought. Rolling waves of relief sucked the last of her strength from her.

The voice transmitted her location to the deputy. "I'll wait with you, ma'am, while he searches the house. Stay on the line with me, can you do that?"

JJ mumbled what she hoped would pass for a positive response, her relief making coherent speech next thing to impossible. The next several minutes crawled by. A creak on the stairs lifted the fine hairs on the back of her neck. A door opened and closed nearby, and her stomach clutched. Then another and another. The scratchy radio echoed over the phone line.

"Ma'am," the dispatcher's voice broke the silence. "The officer is on the second floor with you. The house is secure, but I'll stay on the line until you have visual confirmation of the officer. It's safe to open the door now."

"Miss Frost," a deep male voice called out from the other side of the door. "I'm Deputy Austin Perry with the Fulwick County Sheriff's Department. Are you all right, ma'am?"

"Okay," she mumbled to the dispatcher, pushing to her feet. "I'm here," she croaked.

Her knees wobbled, and she steadied herself against the bed for a moment. On shaking legs, she crossed to the chest and braced her back against it, shoving for all she was worth. Wood grated on wood and the chest gave way with groaning reluctance. Unable to force any more words through her dry throat, she fumbled with the lock and opened the door.

Light flooded into the room from the hallway, and she blinked, squinting at the man standing before her. He was tall and spindly, with wisps of silver streaked through his dark hair. The badge pinned to his uniform brought a surge of tears to her eyes. She sagged against the doorjamb. Her gaze swept over the hallway before catching on the small bundle he cradled in the crook of his arm. Remembering the dispatcher, she pressed the phone to her ear. "I see him. Thank you."

Once dispatch acknowledged her words, she snapped the phone closed, only now aware that the fingers of the hand holding the pepper spray had cramped so tight she wasn't sure she could release the can.

"Ma'am, I found your noisemaker," the deputy assured her, holding his bundle of gray fluff up for her inspection. To his credit, he held the smile in his kind brown eyes locked firmly away. "I'm assuming this little critter don't belong to you?"

Straightening, JJ's mouth fell open in surprise. The fluffy gray shape shifted in his hands. A tiny nose poked out and sniffed the air. The animal in question peered at her with unmistakable curiosity through a white-ringed black mask.

"A raccoon..." A raccoon? Holy crap, she was an idiot.

"Yes, ma'am," he responded. "A young one, barely weaned, I'd guess. Musta climbed in through a window. His mama's probably lookin' all over for him. You're gonna want to get yourself some screens if you're gonna leave the windows open all the time, ma'am."

No shit, Sherlock.

JJ caught herself before she opened her mouth, or rolled her eyes, but the thought was there all the same. She stepped out into the hall, the raccoon forgotten. "There was a man, out in the woods." Her eyes flew to the officer's face, gauging his reaction. After the whole raccoon thing, he probably thought she was some delusional crackpot. "I know who it was. I've seen him in the diner. I can give you a description."

"How about we head down to the kitchen? If you don't mind my saying so, Miss Frost, you look like you could use a good stiff drink." Then he paused, his eyes rounding as if he'd made some tactical error, and he mumbled, "Ah, tea, or...or something. I can take your statement there."

Nodding, she led the way down to the kitchen. The deputy was right. She did need a drink. Tea sounded divine right about now. She'd use it as a chaser for the Cuervo. But then she remembered there wasn't any Cuervo in the house. Or Jack, or Jim, or Captain. Not unless the old lady had a stash the grandkids hadn't found.

Unfortunately, she hadn't found it either. Not that it would have done her much good. She'd tried that route once before, just after Sarah's murder. She'd learned—the hard way—she didn't have the stomach for oblivion via liquor. Every time she had more than a drink or two, she was immediately ill. JJ let out an aggrieved sigh. Tea it was...straight up.

The mud had begun drying in her hair, plastering her clothing to her skin. Muscles, already stiff and sore from her efforts with the house, began to protest in earnest. She wouldn't be the least surprised, once she stripped down later, if she had one big, long bruise from hip to shoulder.

Just as JJ lifted the teakettle, the back door rattled beneath the weight of an angry fist. She jumped, her heart screeched to a halt, and the kettle clattered to the floor. Drawing an unsteady breath, she chastised herself for her reaction. Her attacker was hardly likely to come knocking on her door. Yet her hands still shook as she retrieved the kettle.

"That's probably Red...ah, Deputy Thorpe," her companion remarked in reassuring tones. "He was investigating a...ah... Ah, he was nearby. I'm sure he's just checking in on the radio call since he was so close." Deputy Perry slipped from the kitchen to answer the summons at the back door.

JJ filled the teapot and returned it to the burner as male voices spoke in hushed tones on her back porch. A shuffle of footsteps moved toward the kitchen, and JJ glanced at the teapot with sudden uncertainty. Maybe she should be making coffee instead. Cops drank coffee, didn't they? What did a little caffeine really matter to her anyway? It wasn't as if sleep held any appeal to her. Ever again.

Shrugging, she set the full kettle on the stovetop and returned to the table on liquid legs. Lowering herself to one of the kitchen chairs, she glanced to the door as the deputy stepped back inside the room. Close on his heels was another officer in uniform. She didn't have to wonder long why he carried the name Red. His hair was close cropped, and red as a fire engine. He was young and well built, but not so tall she could miss the man behind him.

She shot from the chair, vibrating with livid indignation as the three men filed into the room. What in the hell was wrong with these deputies? They hadn't even put the bastard in cuffs yet. She was so stunned, so angry she couldn't speak.

"Thanks for taking the call tonight, Austin," her attacker addressed Deputy Perry, though his fulminous emerald eyes never left hers. "If you want to go on back to the station now, we can take it from here. Take care of the coon on your way."

She gaped in astonishment as the deputy nodded, assured her she was in good hands, and shuffled out the door with a lazy yawn, the raccoon tucked securely beneath his arm like a football. She couldn't believe her eyes. What kind of law enforcement did they have around here? Why were they allowing the criminal to run the show? Damn it, what was going on?

His cold emerald stare drilled clean through her, and she shrank back despite her resolve not to cower. His voice dipped another degree...or ten, every bit as chilling as his stare. "Have a seat, Miss Frost."

JJ remained on her feet, her chin jutting stubbornly. She shot a wide-eyed stare to the remaining deputy, jabbed a finger in the handyman's direction, and demanded, "Get him out of my house and put him in a cell where he belongs."

"Now, just hold on a minute," the young deputy coaxed, spreading his hands, palms out. "I think it'd be best if we all just sit down and talk this out."

"The hell I will," she exploded. "That man attacked me. He knocked me down and held be against my will. It's your duty to arrest him, *officer*."

The handyman rocked back on his heels, crossed his arms over his chest, and narrowed distinctly unfriendly eyes at her. The same mud covering her backside coated the entire left side of his body, both forearms, and both his knees. A smudge of blue was beginning to form high on his cheek, just beneath his left eye. She took small comfort in that. At least he'd received some punishment for his crimes, as it didn't appear the law around here intended to dole out any.

The deputy motioned her to take her seat. Hell would freeze over before she sat down to tea with this jerk. "Now, Miss Frost—"

"JJ," she corrected out of hand, all the while glaring at her assailant.

"JJ," the deputy obliged her. "There's been a mistake made here tonight. Cam—"

"You're damned right there's been a mistake made," she interjected with enough heat to steam the faded wallpaper clean off the walls. "The mistake is yours if you think for one damn minute I'm just gonna let this go because he's one of the good old boys."

She paused to draw breath, but before she could comment further, the infernally sexy handyman stalked forward, stopping mere inches from her. Had she been able to draw a deep breath, her breasts would have pushed against his chest. As it was, she had to tilt her head back—way back—in order to maintain eye contact. She scooted back a step, purely out of self-preservation, halting when the back of her knee connected with the seat of the chair. Her chin thrust up a notch. She wouldn't cower to him. She wouldn't give him the satisfaction.

The deputy didn't move a muscle, didn't even blink. Lot of help he was. Or was that the point? Was he here to help with the clean up? Two shovels dug a hole faster than one did.

Oh, Lord, what had she gotten herself into?

He towered over her, glaring down at her with glittering, entrancing eyes. The muscle in his jaw jumped with a steady beat. With studied deliberation, the man reached behind his back and drew forth a slim, black leather wallet. Flipping the leather open, his blistering eyes locked on hers, he slapped the wallet onto the table with enough force to send the small centerpiece dancing. Furious emerald pierced clear through to the back of her skull, challenging her to look away. Forcing a cautious swallow, she lowered her gaze to his hand where it rested on the table. Her eyes just about rolled out of her head when he lifted his hand away to reveal his identification badge.

Holy crap.

It was a good thing she was so close to a chair, because her knees buckled without warning.

Dropping to the seat, she closed her eyes and groaned aloud. Her shoulders sagged. Dragging air into her lungs, she turned back to face him and opened her eyes, intent on offering embarrassed apologies. He hadn't moved back even half a step, and his fly was now at eye level. Instant heat burst in her face as that moment she'd lain beneath him, enthralled by the irrefutable desire on his face—with his unmistakable erection pressed hard against her—flooded her mind.

He must have remembered too, because he took a hasty step back. Hot color rose in his cheeks as well. Then again, maybe he was remembering her parting shot before she'd left him lying in the mud, and sought to avoid more of the same.

"Miss Frost...JJ." Deputy Thorpe's voice rang hollowly in her ears as the room spun. "Allow me to introduce...Sheriff Cameron Walker."

Chapter 6

The way she dropped onto her chair gave him no small amount of satisfaction. Finally, she'd shut up long enough for him to get a word in edgewise. However, when her eyes popped open and leveled on points south of his belt—the way her face flamed with instant awareness—his uninhibited reaction to her in the woods came back to haunt him, and he backpedaled. Never before had he behaved so unprofessionally. Damn it, he'd been ready to kiss her senseless—and a whole hell of a lot more, truth be told—like some horny teenager his first time out of the starting gates.

Like a Werewolf who'd found his mate, a niggling, unwanted voice in the back of his head chimed in.

And with crime-scene tape still fluttering from the trees where a body had been found just a couple hundred yards away. Shit, what the hell had possessed him?

Even now, as angry as he was with her—as badly as his groin still throbbed from her cruel blow—he wanted her still. And not just with an ordinary, boy-meets-pretty-girl want. No, this was a pagan, snapping-at-the-leashes-of-restraint *need*. She was a stranger—prickly as the back end of a porcupine—but, Lord Almighty, was she sexy...and soft in all the right places.

She'd kneed him in the balls and walloped him a good one, damn it.

And still, he wanted the hell out of her.

Not freakin' cool, Cam. Not cool at all.

She was covered in damp forest floor and grungy as a person could be. Her attitude rubbed him raw. But the fire in her eyes provoked him, and he'd never seen anyone so drop-dead beautiful. Vivid images slammed through him like another knee to the groin. It was all too easy to picture himself scooping her up in his arms and carrying her off to the nearest shower, where he'd strip her down and...

Sweat beaded on his brow before he could cut the vision short.

Shit. Get a grip, Cam.

He shook his head and retreated to drop onto another kitchen chair, praying she hadn't noticed the significant tightening in his jeans. The full length of the table rested between them like a defensive barrier, but, as he caught her stunned gaze, that flimsy obstacle didn't seem near formidable enough. Something about her called to him on an elemental level. Primal. Feral. Damned if he knew what it was.

Damned if he didn't resent the hell out of it.

Bracing his forearms on the table's polished surface, he leaned forward, clasping his hands together. The nagging, analytical part of his brain wondered if he hadn't done that—clasping his hands like that—to keep from reaching for her, keep from dragging her across the table and onto his lap.

Cam stared at her for several long minutes, then he leaned back in his chair, sucking in a deep breath. The citrusy scent of lemon coated the sharp bite of bleach, and he remembered the flavor too well. It had filled his nostrils, along with that elusive, feminine fragrance she wore, as he'd held her pinned beneath him.

Pinned. Beneath. Him.

He'd been cradled between her warm, lithe thighs...

Shifting in his seat, he stifled a groan as the

tightness in his jeans threatened to cut off circulation to parts he'd rather die than lose.

What the hell was wrong with him? He'd never lost control of his brain like this, not to mention certain other parts of his anatomy. In fact, now that he thought about it, even this morning at the diner—with nothing more than a cursory glance passing between them—that specific part in question had taken on a mind of its own.

Right now, that particular aforementioned body part was deep in the throes of rebelling in outright glee.

Focus. She'd been tramping through the woods. In the dark. Near the scene of a crime. Near the scene of a murder. Was she involved somehow? Or had she been telling the truth? Had it been nothing more than dangerous curiosity that sent her into the woods...and into his arms?

Was her skin as soft as it looked? Her lips as kissable?

Don't go there. Focus.

"Miss Frost," he addressed her at last, careful to keep his tone and his words cold and impersonal. "We have a serious situation here."

He paused, waiting for her to insert some sarcastic comment the way she had earlier. Instead, she leaned back in her chair, perfectly still now, and starred at him, deadpanned, no glimpse of emotion showing but for the hint of warm color lingering in her cheeks.

"Start at the beginning, and tell me why you were in the woods tonight." Tell me why I can't get your delectable scent out of my head.

Focus.

For a moment, he thought she might refuse to respond, but then she spoke. Her voice was smooth, controlled. It skated down his spine, a thousand silky fingers unraveling his control. "I fell asleep on the sofa. When I woke up, I went into the kitchen for a drink. As I was standing at the sink, I noticed a strange light in the distance. Then, a smaller light broke away and started moving over the ground. It looked like it might be headed this way."

She paused, slicked the tip of her tongue over her lower lip. Every nerve in his body locked on the motion, and the tightness in his jeans grew unbearable. Then she caught that luscious lip between perfect, pearly teeth, and he nearly groaned aloud, remembering how those teeth had sunk eagerly into his flesh.

Would she be uninhibited—wild even—when he...

Focus, Cam!

She pressed back against her seat a bit, as if sensing his inner struggle to keep a leash on thoughts he had no business thinking, and muttered, "I figured it was nothing more than some kids out looking for a place to party. So I thought I'd go out..." She lifted a slim shoulder. "Scare them off. Instead," her accusatory eyes narrowed on him, "I got jumped."

As prone to flights of fantasy as his mind seemed tonight, her last words were not conducive to rational thought on his part, and so he shifted the topic to safer waters. "What time did you arrive in town this morning, Miss Frost?"

Her brow wrinkled, and she tilted her head. "What does that have to do with anything?"

"Please answer the question."

Crossing her arms over her chest, she tapped out a belligerent rhythm beneath the table with the toe of her boot. "I guess around six maybe. I stopped for gas at Joe's and then went straight to the diner."

"Have you ever been to Sutter Hollow before today?"

Her eyes narrowed. She tipped her head, and

drew the suspicious syllable out, "No."

"Why did you buy this particular house? You told Brandi you were just passing through. Isn't this an awfully impulsive decision? Purchasing a house on your first day in a town you've never before visited? A house you've never even stepped foot inside? Are you prone to impulse, Miss Frost?"

Any hint of tolerant civility in her beautiful eyes blinked out in a flash. "My reasons are none of your business. What are you getting at, Sheriff?"

He stared at her again, long and hard, unblinking. If he told her about the body in the woods behind her new home, would she pack up her Jeep and run for the hills? Would she leave town as quickly, as unexpectedly as she'd arrived?

It might be far safer for his peace of mind if she did exactly that.

His stomach plummeted, fast as the first drop from a rollercoaster, at the mere thought.

Normally he wouldn't dream of discussing an ongoing investigation with a civilian, part and parcel with standard police procedure. Maybe he was just that off his game tonight, but procedure didn't hold much weight right about now. His mind was a muddled mess, firmly under the influence of an unexpected, unwanted, physical obsession.

He could hardly be held accountable if he were less than professional at this point.

"A few hours back, a local hunter found a dead woman in your precious woods, Miss Frost." He leaned forward again, doing his best to ignore her slight gasp and the icy shock rolling through her eyes. In the periphery of his vision, Red straightened away from the counter across the room, but he remained silent, and Cam ignored him too.

"A dead woman," she breathed. The color drained from her face making the dark smudges beneath her eyes stand out in sharp relief.

"That's right, a dead woman," he confirmed, biting down on the surge of remorseful protectiveness. He couldn't offer her comfort, not any more than he could rightfully offer her his lust. "Where were you last night, Miss Frost?"

Shock faded slowly, leaving behind a horrified, glazed stare. Then, in the snap of a finger, she came to the edge of her seat. Her glaring eyes threw sparks and her tone breathed fire as she gripped the edge of the table. "Are you accusing me of something, Sheriff? Do you think I had something to do with that poor woman's death?"

"Did you, *Miss* Frost?" Cam emphasized the title, deliberately—desperately—keeping the interaction between them formal, trying in vain to fend off the unreasonable urge to sooth her ruffled feathers.

He had to keep her at arms length, had to keep himself impersonal and objective. If he couldn't do it on his own—and damned his sorry hide if that didn't seem the case—then he'd extend every effort to flat out piss her off, let her brick up as much of a wall between them as she could. Hopefully, that would be enough. Too bad the fury in her eyes only served to pour fuel on the flames of lust already roasting him alive.

Her chest heaved in and out with her obvious outrage. Her hands, locked on the edge of the table, tightened. "I was on the road, *Sheriff* Walker. I drove all night. I don't have an alibi, though you're welcome to check my credit card receipts to verify my whereabouts for whatever time that poor woman was killed.

"I don't appreciate your accusations, and I don't appreciate your attitude...just as I didn't appreciate getting tackled in the mud, though now I at least understand your warped logic at the time. At the risk of repeating myself, if this is your version of the welcome wagon, I'll pass." The frigid disdain in her voice would have given a lesser man a lethal case of hypothermia. As it was, a delicious shiver rippled just beneath his skin...a ripple of pure lust. She was sexy as hell when she was pissed off. "Now, I'd like for you to get the hell out of my house."

Cam stayed in his chair for a moment longer, wishing he could find the willpower not to react to the icy flames in her eyes. *If wishes were horses, then beggars would ride...*

Without another word, he pushed to his feet. Guilt had begun to ball in his gut, slick and greasy. He'd always made it a personal rule never to accuse anyone of anything before he had sufficient proof. Not only could you endanger an investigation, but you also burned a hell of a lot of bridges that way. He'd seen that indisputable fact proven firsthand, time and again, with his predecessor.

Old Sheriff Wilkes had ruled his county with intimidation and ignorance. Abuse of power had been the rule of thumb, not the exception. No, this high-handed interrogation didn't sit too well in Cam's gut at all. An apology formed on his lips, but, for reasons beyond his understanding, he remained silent, the words firmly locked away. Cam nodded, tipped his chin at Red, and strode toward the door. He swore to himself he wouldn't give in to the urge to steal one last glance at her.

Three steps from the door, he shot a glance over his right shoulder. That ball of guilt swimming in his guts expanded until he was in serious danger of choking on it. Drying mud matted her hair to the back of her head and the long graceful line of her neck. The same dark muck coated her entire backside, from nape to boot heel. She hadn't moved an inch since he'd walked past her, and, even now, her spine was so rigid he could have used it as a straightedge on his next remodeling project. Gritting his teeth, Cam stalked from the house, stomped down the back steps.

He didn't speak again, and, praise the Lord, neither did Red as they tramped through the woods back to the scene of Lori Watson's demise. Silence hung between them like dead weight until they finished loading the crime scene gear into the back of Red's cruiser.

Cam slammed the trunk and addressed Red at last. "Head on back to the station now, work on your report. I'll stop off at Steve's, then I'll be along shortly. Hopefully Jarvis will have something for us by then."

Red nodded, but as he opened the cruiser's door and placed one foot on the floor mat, he paused, shooting Cam a cautious look over his shoulder. "You gonna tell him? About Lori...I mean, about Lori and you...and Lori and me?"

Grinding his teeth together, struggling to meet Red's remorse riddled stare, Cam dug his hands deep in his pockets, rocking back on his heels. He rattled the change in his pocket and drew a long breath.

One long moment of mutual guilt passed between them before he heaved a disgusted sigh. "I already had my balls shoved up my throat once tonight, what the hell do you think?"

Turning away, Cam climbed into his truck. He slouched against the seat with the engine idling for a long time after Red left, staring at the spot where the woman he'd shared one night of lonely, drunken foolishness with had died a cold and brutal death. He thought then of his next stop and shuddered. Swearing, he shifted the truck into gear.

His night had gone straight to hell in a handbasket...and it was about to get a whole lot worse.

Chapter 7

The Apostle—that was how he thought of himself now, he was God's chosen messenger after all—smiled at Ginny, thanked her once again, and picked the white plastic sack up from the counter. The tinny clank of the hacksaw blade reverberated against the counter, shushed beneath the crinkle of plastic. Once outside, he pivoted to face the sunlight, savoring the gentle, golden rays as they bathed his face. God was surely smiling down on him this fine day.

He was euphoric. His first mission had gone off without a hitch. Lori had been all too willing to slip away with him. Of course, once she'd realized judgment was upon her, she'd begged. She'd pleaded for her life...but not for her soul. She hadn't beseeched God for forgiveness. She hadn't been truly penitent...not until he'd explained the error of her ways.

By then, of course, it was too late.

He'd brought along a rosary—just in case—a wise insight that, since she claimed she didn't own one. Shameful. He'd even supplied the words for her prayers, as she couldn't remember them by herself. God loved all his children, and he wanted them to have one last chance for redemption. The Apostle was proof of that. He was a sinner redeemed. After all, God had led him through his times of trial and sent him forth as His messenger, to spare the righteous, and to punish the wicked.

Vengeance shall be mine, so sayeth the Lord...

He could still see Lori, kneeling among the

rubble of her sins. He hadn't meant to lose his temper, to beat her like that. It had been her own fault, provoking him, begging, offering to do all those vile things if only he'd spare her life. It had been a slip, a miscalculation on his part. He'd be better prepared next time, wouldn't be surprised or provoked by the Devil's tricks.

The poor thing hadn't even known what to do with the rosary he'd given her. Perhaps God would forgive her ignorance. He gave a small shrug.

Her soul was in His hands now.

Smiling, he waved at Emma through the large window on the front of the sheriff's office as he shuffled by, swinging the bag at his side. Now there was a good girl. She dressed a little strangely, but she was in church every Sunday, come rain or shine...unless she had to work, of course. Then she'd always made a point of attending Mass the night before. She didn't run around, getting herself into trouble, the way some people did these days.

He rounded the corner of the building, and his footsteps faltered. The contented haze he'd been wearing since he'd fulfilled God's wishes for Lori began to slip through his fingers. He surveyed the large man stumbling from the liquor store, a case of beer tucked like precious cargo beneath his arm. Another sinner if ever there was one.

Another soul in need of guidance.

The unkempt sinner stopped to dig in his pocket, swaying on his feet. His beard was shaggy, his hair dirty and wild. His clothing was mismatched, soiled and torn. He swore with exaggerated precision as he switched the beer to the other arm. The man lurched two uneven steps forward, then stopped to dig in his back pocket, listing to the side.

Filled with renewed purpose, the Apostle stepped forward, directly into the drunkard's path.

Smiling benevolently, he reached out to steady the sinner he'd been called to save. "Hey there. It's a might early in the day for that," he said, nodding toward the case of beer, "don't you think?"

Bloodshot, glazed green eyes swung to his face, blinked. Sour sweat and stale beer pummeled waves of nausea against the back of the Apostle's throat. The drunk gave a vicious snarl and batted the hand on his shoulder away. His momentum spun him halfway around, and the beer slid from his arm. He fumbled the case, his coordination too sluggish to accomplish much more than to give it a slight spin on its way down. The carton landed flat on the ground with a sharp crack and a vicious, slurred curse.

Snatching the beer up, cradling it against his chest, the drunk snarled, "Mind your own f-fuckin' business."

Muttering to himself, the sinner staggered away, clutching the Devil's brew in a death-grip, as if he feared someone would try to wrest it from him if he let his guard down for even a moment. The Apostle stepped back, his eyes narrowed, and he exhaled a pent-up breath laced with resolve.

And so Solomon answered, 'Should he bear himself honorably, not one hair of his shall fall to the ground...but if he proves difficult, he shall die.'

****

JJ knelt in one of the flowerbeds lining her driveway, tugging at a particularly determined weed. A wailing horn blared from nearby, barely discernable over the enthusiastic roar of an archaic motor. Shielding her eyes against the bright midday sun with one hand, she glanced up, her curious gaze following the trail of dust swirling ever closer.

JJ swiped the back of her grimy wrist along the side of her forehead. A stray wisp of hair stuck to her temple. The damp curl twisted up and around to tease her lashes. She sighed and swiped again, rocking back on her heels when the truck veered off the main road, angling down her drive. A battered, red Chevy—coated with more rust than paint— barreled down the washboard gravel straight toward her.

A long, slim arm thrust out the truck's open window and set to waving with impressive enthusiasm. The truck jerked to a stop alongside the flowerbed, and the roar of the engine cut out on a sputtering cough. A bare elbow poked in JJ's direction as Ginny Connor leaned out the driver's side window, grinning with warm ease. "Are you winnin'…or are the weeds?"

JJ surveyed the tangled mess around her. "Right now, I'd say it's a draw…though the weeds might have a slight advantage."

"I got a truck load of deliveries for ya, brought along a jug a tea too. Figured you could use a break…know I sure could."

The need for fresh air and sunshine had driven JJ from the house as the first rays of dawn broke over the horizon. It'd been considerably cooler then. Sunshine and fresh air or not, as the saying went, there was no rest for the weary. The sight of the overgrown flowerbeds, more weeds than flowers, were more than she could stand, and it didn't take long before JJ found herself elbow deep in weeds and dirt. For all that it was early spring, the day was a warm one—much warmer than JJ had anticipated— and by the fourth small bed of weeds, she'd begun daydreaming about a tall glass of something cool to slake the thirst.

"You read my mind," JJ announced, pushing to her feet.

She tugged the gardening gloves from her hands, dusted the knees of her ragged jeans, and brushed a stray, withered bit of green from the threadbare Atlanta Braves T-shirt she'd dragged on earlier this morning. Bending, she retrieved the small gardening tools. She dug her knuckles against the kink in the base of her spine as she straightened.

Ginny disappeared from view for a moment as she leaned across the seat. The passenger door swung open with a loud, creaking protest, and Ginny's smiling, gamine face popped back into the window. "I know it's hardly worth the ride, but you better hop in. You look like you're 'bout ready to drop where you're standin'."

It wasn't that far to the house, but JJ rounded the hood and hoisted herself up inside the cab nonetheless, hauling the creaking door closed behind her with a grateful grin.

"When I bought this place, I'd decided to do as much of the repairs as I could by myself, but I'm about to yield on this yard. There's a lawnmower in the shed out back, but I think it's older than I am. I couldn't even get it to cough. Somebody should have taken it out and given it a decent burial long ago."

Ginny chuckled, and the engine roared to life once more. The truck didn't sound much better than the lawnmower probably would have *if* it had started. JJ didn't try to make conversation over the grumble of the motor, and her driver seemed content to navigate the short length of the lane in companionable silence. By mutual consent, the two opted for tea first, leaving the supplies for later.

Once inside the house, Ginny glanced around the kitchen as JJ stretched for a shelf inside a tall cupboard. Accepting a slim, bottle green glass, Ginny poured the dark, iced liquid from the jug, commenting with a nod toward the general vicinity of the rest of the house, "You've been busy."

"Mmm," JJ sighed as she accepted the offering, taking a long draw of sweet, iced bliss as she sank onto a chair at the table. Her eyes nearly rolled back in her head with ecstasy. When she could find her voice again, she remarked, "There's still a lot to do, but it's getting there."

JJ glanced around her, smiling with pride. Her kitchen gleamed now, spit-shined and lemon-scented. The rest of the downstairs wasn't looking half-bad either. Oh, there was a list of repairs a mile long, but she'd chased the coat of dust and grime away to her satisfaction, and some of the smaller repairs were behind her. The grounds... Well, they were another story altogether. Later this afternoon she'd give that boy, Mike, down at the grocery store a call. Then she'd be free to tackle the attic. She almost rubbed her hands together in anticipation.

"I'm sorry," she added as an afterthought. "I don't have much aside from some packaged cookies to go with the tea. I've been so focused on cleaning I haven't bothered much in the way of cooking yet."

"No problem," Ginny assured her, hefting her glass. "This is all I need."

Before long, they fell into the easy companionship of long-lost friends newly found. It was a peculiar sensation for JJ, this experience of female bonding. She hadn't allowed anyone close since Sarah, finding comfort only in her work. Even before that, she'd never been much for collecting friends as some were wont to do. A loner by nature, she'd always preferred to isolate herself with her paints and her brushes, living vicariously through the colors that poured out onto her canvases.

The initial stages of awkwardness gave way in the face of Ginny's warmth and vitality, and JJ couldn't help but welcome the familiarity. Ginny brought her up to speed on the nuances of small-town gossip, and, inevitably, the talk shifted to the victim discovered in the woods behind JJ's house her first night in town. Until now, she'd been able to push the matter from her mind, at least until the dark of night pushed back. She'd avoided going into the stores, thereby avoiding the inevitable question, and placed her orders by phone instead. All good things must come to an end though...as had her reprieve of blissful ignorance.

"Her name was Lori Watson," Ginny filled her in. "She was the night waitress down at Maggie's...good one, too. She'd have your plate on the table waitin' for you before your ass hit the seat." Ginny set her glass down with a baleful thump. She clucked her tongue against the roof of her mouth. "Pitiful, though, the way they found her. Stripped naked and laying on a pile of porn. She had pantyhose wrapped around her throat, I heard. Poor woman. No one deserves that, no matter what kind of life you've led."

Glancing up, JJ set her glass down and met Ginny's eyes, waiting with bated breath, like a bystander at a horrific crash site, unable to help, unable to look away. Her companion leaned an elbow on the table, lowering her voice to a conspiratorial tone.

"Between you and me, after her and Steve split last spring, that woman saw more action than the Bowl-a-Rama on league night. 'Course, if you believe the rumors around town, she was playin' fast and loose long before then. Shameful..." Ginny tsked, shaking her head, and took another long draw of tea.

JJ remained silent, toying with the slim gold watch on her wrist. Pondering that last bit of information, she lifted the cool glass to her lips once more, savoring the clean bite of the tea. From there, the conversation drifted to more mundane topics.

Although JJ didn't offer much more than the fact she was from Minnesota, Ginny didn't seem inclined to pry. Instead, she offered her own history.

"I originally came up from Bridgewater—a hole-in-the-wall Podunk town that makes Sutter Hollow look like Nashville." Ginny let out a hoarse chuckle and took another draw off her tea. Her eyes took on a reminiscent twinkle. "I met Todd my first year at college. He was a senior, and so damned handsome you'd swear he just stepped down off some fashion billboard for designer underwear. I was a goner the first time I laid eyes on that man." She rolled lively brown eyes, but her face softened with fond memories. "My grandmother'd passed on the year before...both my parents died when I was a youngster...and I didn't have anything to pull me back to Tennessee, so I followed Todd up here like a stray puppy."

JJ leaned forward in her seat with an interested murmur of encouragement, charmed.

"With a mind like his—to say nothing of the body—I could never figure what drew him back here...or what attracted him to the likes of me." Ginny shook her head, leaning back in her seat, her eyes a million memories away. She shook her head again, as if trying to shake a baffling question she'd asked herself a thousand times and never been able to answer. "Anyway...here we were. After an abbreviated engagement, we bought the hardware store and settled in. Life was good...better'n I'd ever hoped for."

Ginny held a finger up as she dug in her pocket. Dropping a battered keychain onto the table between them, she flipped over a small locket and held the tiny pictures up for JJ's perusal. On one side of the locket, a man's handsome visage grinned at her with wicked charm. He was, indeed, every bit as attractive as Ginny had claimed. On the opposite side of the locket, a small boy peered back at her. He was adorable, with hints of the woman sitting across the table from JJ around his eyes. The rest of him was all Todd. There was no doubt about it...he'd be a real heartbreaker when he grew into all that potential.

"That's my Todd...he's been gone going on two years next month. Big lug went and got himself shot in a hunting accident up north." Her sorrowful eyes glittered bright then, gleaming with pride, as she went on, "And that's our Tanner. He'll be seven come July."

"He's a beautiful boy." JJ handed the locket back, tilting her head as she considered Ginny in a new light. "I'm sorry about your husband."

Ginny gave a small, uncomfortable shrug.

"And you kept the hardware store going?"

"I couldn't close up shop. That store meant so much to Todd, and the town needs it. You close up one shop in a town this size, pretty soon they all start to topple." Ginny cleared her throat, offering JJ a warm smile. Her eyes held not an ounce of self-pity or regret in their clear depths. No, they were too full of pride in her son and confidence in her store. She looked entirely too young to shoulder the burdens she carried, but shoulder them she did, with a style and grace that left JJ in awe. "Besides, I have a son to support, and at twenty-nine I'm a long way from retirement...and a hell of a lot farther from having one foot in the grave. A girl's gotta have something to do."

By now, JJ was certain, she would have packed it up and crawled back to Gloria's doorstep, tail tucked firmly between her legs. Even her aloof mother's holier-than-thou attitude would seem warm and welcoming compared to facing the responsibilities Ginny did, day in and day out. Alone.

After a while, Ginny flicked a glance to the masculine watch strapped on her wrist by a wide leather band, and she pushed to her feet with a resigned groan. "I guess I best be headin' back soon. Tanner will be home from school soon, and I've still got end-of-the-month bookwork to tackle." Helping JJ clear the table, she waved the tea jar away. "You keep that."

"Oh, but—"

"Just make sure it's full the next time I come for a visit, and we'll call it even," Ginny suggested. Then, pausing in the doorway, she shot another warm smile over her shoulder. "It's nice to sneak in a little girl time once in a while. I'll give you a call the next time we all get together. You'll fit right in."

"You all?" With a curious smile, she followed Ginny from the house to the back of the truck where her supplies awaited unloading.

"A few of us get together every Tuesday night. We do something different most every week, just to break up the monotony." Ginny leaped up onto the truck bed with the grace of a ballerina. She toed a smaller box toward the tailgate and JJ's waiting arms, and then, with a slight grunt, she bent to pick up a larger box with the Paper Cutouts logo stamped in bold black lettering on the side.

"Lord A'mighty," she grunted as she set the box down and leaped to the ground, where she hefted the box once more. "I never imagined paints and such could weigh so much."

Grinning, JJ stretched over the rust-pocked truck bed and locked her fingers around the folded legs of a wooden easel. "You'd be surprised."

"Where do you want this stuff?"

Chewing on her lower lip, JJ frowned. The supplies had come in much sooner than she'd anticipated, and the attic wasn't yet ready. "My supplies can go in the den for now, I suppose." Her gaze fell to the antique bench and coat rack she'd bought from the furniture store for the front entry. "I think we'll have to put those in the shed around back, though. I don't want to ding them by accident while I'm working on something else."

The bench was heavy, and by the time they'd wrestled it around to the shed, both women were winded and laughing. JJ's merriment died on her lips, however, as soon as she reached for the lock on the shed door...or, rather the place where the lock should have been. The errant lock now rested on the ground a few feet away, the wood around the bent latch scratched and gouged.

Stepping closer to the door, JJ squinted at the damage, planting bemused fists on her hips. "I was out here last night. I put some of the old end tables and lamps in here," she murmured, more to herself than to Ginny, while her companion moved closer, a concerned frown marring her smooth brow. "The lock was fine then," JJ went on, "And no one else has been here today. I would have noticed. I was outside all day."

"Austin mentioned there's been some trouble with vandalism the last few weeks." When JJ reached for the lock, Ginny put her hand on JJ's forearm and cautioned, "You better call this in. Might not want to touch anything in the meantime."

JJ grimaced but dropped her hand to her side. The last thing she wanted to do was deal with that overbearing, obnoxious jerk that passed for a sheriff in these parts. She could already see the disapproving scowl on his gorgeous face...and the accusing questions in his brilliant, jewel-like eyes. She wouldn't put it past him to blame her for breaking into her own shed. No. She'd rather just add the shed to her list of repairs and go on with her day. It wasn't like there was anything of value out here anyway.

As if sensing her reluctance, Ginny drew a slim cell phone from her hip pocket and began punching numbers before JJ could object. "Ill just call Emma and have her send a deputy over to take a look around."

JJ relaxed a little. The soothing, silver-streaked deputy who'd responded to her 911 call last night came to mind. He wouldn't be so bad. Even that young red-haired deputy would be a better bet...a safer bet...than the sheriff. Besides, whoever broke into her shed could easily break into someone else's property, take something valuable from someone else. No, she couldn't object to having a deputy come over. She was just being ridiculous. She listened with half an ear to Ginny's side of the conversation as she wandered around the shed, looking for any other signs of disturbance.

"Someone will be over soon," Ginny informed her as she crammed the phone back into her right hip pocket. "Emma said we better not mess with the shed for now. Is there anywhere else we can store this bench and the rest of the stuff in the truck?"

JJ jerked the elastic band from her loose ponytail and scooped the wild tresses back into some semblance of order, rewinding the band. "I guess we could shove it all into a corner in the den."

The two of them wrestled the bench back across the yard and up onto the front porch. By the time they gained the top step, a huge, fresh-off-the-lot new Dodge Ram had already charged down her lane, easing alongside Ginny's decrepit truck. The Dodge's spotless, gunmetal-gray paint job and sparkling chrome put the rusted-out old Chevy at a distinct disadvantage. The light bar over the cab, the extra gear across the grill, and the large decal on the door announced her latest visitor was from the Fulwick County Sheriff's Department. The two women set the bench down on the porch and straightened. Ginny smiled affable recognition as JJ lifted a hand to shield her eyes against the glare from the front windshield.

The bottom of her stomach dropped away when the very man she'd been hoping to avoid stepped down from the cab. He shot Ginny an easy smile steeped in sin and ambled toward the house like a self-absorbed, over-confident Greek god come down from Mount Olympus with the express purpose of reducing any and every female he crossed paths with into weak-kneed puddles of greedy hormones. JJ shot a sidelong glance at her new friend. Ginny didn't appear to have any problem with malfunctioning salivary glands and gawking eyes. Perhaps JJ was the only one he'd deigned to torture.

Her traitorous gaze wandered back to the demigod. He utterly radiated the promise of sexual gratification. Once again clad in snug jeans and a fitted T-shirt, he was delicious enough to nibble from head to toe...nibble or gulp down in large, greedy mouthfuls, leaving the guilty calorie—or in this particular case, sin—counting for later. Lord help her.

With any luck, he'd be like the flu, or some other common ailment...with repeated exposure maybe she'd build up immunity. Her heart flip-flopped inside her ribcage when his cool eyes flicked over her.

Damn it. She'd settle for semi-tolerance at this point.

A much-welcomed breeze stirred the treetops, rustled through the overgrown yard, ruffling his honeyed locks. Gilded sunlight kissed his carved-granite features. Her lingering resentment over his high-handed treatment of her on her first night in town was the only thing to keep the drool locked firmly behind tightly compressed lips.

"Hey there, Ginny," Sheriff Walker crooned with effortless familiarity, adding another layer of resentment to JJ's defensive walls. His eyes chilled again, just the tiniest bit, as he swiveled her way. He dipped his chin in a miniscule nod of professional acknowledgement. "Miss Frost."

"Sheriff," she responded tonelessly. "Hey, yourself," Ginny greeted the lawman. Her palm rested sassily on a cocked hip as she tilted her head. "I thought you had the day off, handsome."

"That was the general idea," he drawled as he ascended the steps. JJ would have preferred he'd stayed down on the bottom step, or, better still, in his truck as he headed back down the lane. Up here on the porch, he towered over her, crowding her with undeniable masculine appeal. "We've been a little busier than usual. Austin and Judy are already out on calls, and Red worked last night. Had a couple B and E's. The shop room down at the school was vandalized, and somebody got inside the movie theater, left a hell of a mess there." He tipped his head toward the bench. "You takin' this in or out?"

"In," Ginny supplied helpfully.

Without warning, he stepped around JJ and tipped the bench on its end. Taking a firm grip in the middle of the seat, he lifted it with astonishing ease. The whipcord strength of his lean frame stunned her. Though the muscles in his arms and shoulders bunched and flexed, not an ounce of strain flickered over his smooth features. JJ swallowed, blinked, and sucked in a deep breath. That bench was heavy. *Really* heavy. It had taken an enormous amount of energy for her and Ginny to lug it across the yard again and up the steps, yet he'd just hefted it like a flimsy piece of dollhouse furniture.

Whaa...

Suck the drool up, JJ, before it runs down your chin.

Not bothering to stifle her appreciative smile, Ginny stepped to the door and braced it open. Cam stood still, though, and lifted a patient eyebrow at JJ. His muscles flexed and rippled, but his arrogant grin was completely relaxed. Stirring herself, she shot forward, leading the way into the den.

"You can..." JJ cleared her throat after that embarrassing croak. "You can put it down over there in the corner."

"If you don't mind my saying so, Miss Frost," he commented, striding confidently—effortlessly—into the room, "this doesn't seem like it belongs here."

"Ah, no," she murmured, surprised he'd noticed. "It'll eventually go back into the front entryway. I didn't want to worry about scuffing it or dinging it while I was working on something else. In here it should be relatively out of the way." She was babbling. What was wrong with her?

JJ leaned to the side, stretching around him to move the edges of the long drapery out of his way as he set the heavy piece of furniture down. The sheriff straightened as he pivoted toward her, but she was so close that his nose brushed her cheek.

And he froze.

His eyes glittered bright, wild and confused, as they peered into hers. His nostrils flared and he leaned closer, close enough for his breath to stir the loosened tendrils of hair at her temple, once...twice. He was smelling her again, drawing her scent in just as he had that night in the woods when he'd pinned her beneath him. He drew her scent in as if he were savoring it...as if it were the last thing he'd ever do on this planet. JJ was too stunned to move away. It was like finding herself in the roll of prey, trapped in the crosshairs of a hunter's dangerous weapon, knowing she needed to flee, but instinctively sensing that so much as a flinch would trigger the inevitable attack.

Leaning back—though he didn't take so much as a single step away—he opened his mouth, only to snap it closed without uttering a sound. His frown intensified. A strange grimace flitted across his features, as if he were in acute pain. His emerald eyes widened and...dilated? Then he blinked and his expression went utterly blank, all emotion carefully tucked away, shuttered behind eyes that had gone strangely dark. She stared up at him, catching the edge of her lower lip between her teeth, baffled. What had just happened here?

Whatever it was, it felt...momentous.

Weird.

No, her mind must have been playing tricks on her. That's it. Nothing more.

Again, he took her by surprise. His brow crinkled with unexpected concern, and his odd stare turned serious. His voice was tight, thick, when he warned, "You be sure to get help moving that thing. Don't try doing it alone. You'll hurt yourself."

His eyes bore into hers for a moment more, intense and too discerning. He bent forward at the waist...just the slightest bit...and drew another deep, if cautious breath. He *was* smelling her. There was no doubt about it. And it made no sense.

Still, she couldn't move away.

The room seemed so full of him all of a sudden, too full. The scent of him went straight to her head. Soap and masculine heat. Woodsy and wild. All male. His hair was tousled, like he'd driven hell bent for redemption with the windows rolled down every mile of the way. Her fingers itched with the fierce need to tangle and grip.

Stunned, she forced another swallow, tore her gaze from his. Only now realizing Ginny hadn't followed them inside, JJ spun on her heel and hurried through the wide doorway as fast as possible without being too obvious. No sound of footsteps followed her down the hallway or back out onto the porch, but she dare not look, too afraid of losing herself in that unsettling emerald stare again.

Warm sunlight caressed her skin and fresh air enveloped her as she shot out of the house and skidded across the warped boards on the now empty porch. She drew in a greedy lungful of air, but she couldn't dispel the scent of him. It clung to her as if he'd rubbed himself all over her, intoxicating and alluring, lingering on the edge of her awareness, imprinting the memory of itself on her soul.

Bemused, she staggered down the stairs and over to the back of Ginny's truck. Stopping at the tailgate, she reached up blindly for another box. However, just as Ginny bent to hand the box down to her, two impossibly long, incredibly strong arms reached up on either side of her, and an all-too-familiar, rock-wall of a chest brushed at her back. Heat enveloped her, like the sudden blast of a torch, and her knees shook. Her head swam in the heady scent of him once more. Where had he come from? How did he manage to move so silently?

"Let me get that. It looks heavy," his deep voice rumbled close to her ear.

JJ froze, staring up into Ginny's amused brown eyes. A dimpled grin spread across Ginny's face as she completely ignored JJ's gurgle of protest and set the last box into Cam's steady hands. He couldn't have stood like that for more than a fraction of a second, with her body trapped between his and the tailgate, locked between his sinewy arms, but when he moved away, lifting the box over her head, the sense of loss nearly brought her to her knees. Dropping her hands to the tailgate, JJ's fingertips went white.

"Well, now," Ginny chirped, flipping an unnecessary glance at her watch. "I best head out. I have just enough time to swing by the school and pick Tanner up on my way back to the store." She leaped to the ground, agile as a feline, and dusted her palms on the faded thighs of her blue jeans. She shot an approving, meaningful glance from the sheriff to JJ and added, "You're in capable hands now. We'll talk later, JJ." Aiming a secretive grin over JJ's shoulder, she added, "I'll catch ya 'round, Cam."

"Ginny," he drawled. A hint of sarcasm waffled through each syllable.

The reverberation of the truck's creaking door slamming shut loosened JJ's death grip on the tailgate. Recalling herself, she stepped back, facing Cam as the truck began to roll down the lane. They were alone now.

All. Alone.

Irrational panic swelled. She remembered, all too well, the way his body had reacted the last time they'd been alone...and the way her own body had reacted. Of course, they weren't exactly horizontal this time, but it didn't take a very large stretch of her imagination to picture them that way. Nor did it stretch the boundaries of that same, overactive imagination to recall the tempered steel of his erection pressing against the juncture of her thighs. The mere memory brought back the flutter—and the ache—in the pit of her stomach.

Mortified heat rushed up her neck, exploding in her cheeks. Small wonder her hair didn't simply ignite, for steam was surely rolling from her ears. Her guilty gaze swerved to his, and her eyes widened. The grin tugging at his sensual lips was just a shade too smug for her comfort. The intense interest in his eyes was a tad too concentrated. Maybe his imagination was as boundless as her own. Then again, perhaps her face had been an open book with every sordid little image displayed with Technicolor clarity. The light in his eyes would have made the Devil's own blush like an inexperienced adolescent and look away in modest embarrassment.

"Um," she mumbled, drowning in a sea of confusion.

Never before had anyone...*anyone*...ever affected her as this man could with nothing more than a simple, innocent look. Damn him. Her gaze shot to his face, and she amended the innocent portion of that thought. There probably wasn't an innocent bone in his entire body.

"Miss Frost?" His voice was velvety warm, holding an odd note of curiosity that didn't seem to have anything to do with the box in his hands.

"Yes, this way." She whirled around and scurried back up the stairs before he could say anything more.

After a momentary pause, he followed her into the house and down the long hallway, into the kitchen.

"You can just put that box there on the table. Thank you." He did as she requested, and turned to face her once more, but she was already spinning away, edging toward the back door. Her head still felt muddled from the last time she'd gotten lost in his eyes. "I don't want to take up anymore of your time, since it's your day off. The shed's out this way."

Duh, JJ, she muffled a self-conscious groan. *Like he didn't already know that.*

She grappled with the doorknob. The door refused to cooperate, and she cursed beneath her breath. Before she could move away, a large, warm hand settled over hers on the knob. His other hand landed, slow and easy, on the doorjamb just past her left shoulder. He'd boxed her in again. His breath caressed the back of her neck. His scent and his heat surrounded her, filled her. Instantaneous and scorching.

"Let me," he murmured at her temple, sending a delicious shiver down her spine.

The door yielded to him with astonishing ease, and she cursed beneath her breath once more. A soft chuckle slipped around her earlobe, and she tugged her hand from beneath his. Jerking the door open, she fled the cage of his arms.

Again, his feet were silent as they followed her down the back steps and across the yard. Stopping beside the broken lock where it lay in the grass, she tried to marshal her wits. All she had to do was keep it together until he left.

"Were you storing anything valuable out here?"

His voice broke the silence, from just over her shoulder, and she jumped, inadvertently brushing back against him. How did he keep *doing* that? It's like he was always...*there*.

It took a long, shaky heartbeat for his words to click into place. Jerking a hasty step forward, away from him, she forced a swallow and angled sideways, though she was careful to keep her gaze on the shed when she responded. "No, just some old stuff I wasn't sure I wanted to keep."

"Has anyone tampered with the doors or the windows on the house?"

That gave her pause. "I...I don't think so."

"Well, all the same," he mumbled, his voice aimed toward the ground as he scanned the area. "You should replace those locks...they're old, not very reliable. You'll have to get yourself some sturdy deadbolts, too. Get someone to check the locks on the windows."

"I'll check them tonight," she assured him, her gaze following the fluid motion of his hands—strong calloused hands—as he examined the broken lock and the marks the intruder left behind on the wood planking of the shed.

Her answer must not have been what he'd been hoping to hear. The look he shot over his shoulder, unimpressed and rife with irritation, said as much. He let a long breath seep out, and the muscle along his jaw bunched. One corner of his mouth hitched up in a wry twist, and he shook his head as he turned back to his careful examination. A jumble of words rolled out of his mouth, low and muted, as though they weren't meant for her ears. All the same, she understood the gist of his one-sided conversation.

Her response was immediate and sharp, honed with the snapping edges of temper, "Excuse me? What did you say?"

"I heard you were hell bent on doing it all for yourself. Just didn't figure you for stupid." His head turned, and he pinned her with a hard stare while she sputtered indignantly. "Gambling with your safety is stupid. Much as I hate to say it, Sutter Hollow isn't exactly crime free...not lately at least. Do I need to remind you of the dead woman we found out in those woods?" He shot a thumb over his shoulder toward the tree line behind him. She was beginning to think that thumb thing was a local's specialized way of communication. Just sling a thumb in a general direction, and people will know exactly what you're talking about...or where. "You should have a professional come out and take a look at—"

"Why?"

"What?"

"Why? Why do I need a professional to take a look at anything?" She glared at him, building a fine head of steam. That was the second time he'd called her stupid. She didn't care for it one little bit. Crossing her arms over her chest, she lifted her chin, narrowing her eyes. "Because I'm a woman, I can't protect myself? Because I don't have the right set of chromosomes, I can't defend myself? Because I don't have a pair of—"

"I didn't say that," he growled as he straightened, facing her fully. Little grooves dug in between his brows. "I just meant a professional will know what points of weaknesses to focus on. It's just a matter of common sense."

She was sure her arched eyebrow spoke volumes, but he completely missed the warning sign and jumped head first into his topic, paddling on in blissful male ignorance. "It's not just the locks on the doors and windows, it's little things like parking your car in well lit areas, carrying your keys in your hands just so, always having your cell phone charged, and learning some basic self-defense moves."

His condescending attitude slapped at her pride. Any woman with half an ounce of common sense in her head already knew everything he was telling her. The fact that he figured she needed to hear it was just...insulting.

"Tell me, Sheriff, do you offer these helpful tidbits to all the women...or just the ones you've personally assaulted?" JJ's other eyebrow joined the first, and her gaze dropped to points south of his belt for the briefest flicker of a moment. "In case you've already forgotten, I can handle myself."

Courtesy of Jerry Dewitt, JJ knew better than anyone that the only person she could trust to take care of her...was her. She was the last person he needed to provide with self-defense pointers. When she wasn't at a severe disadvantage, namely with a two hundred pound male pinning her to the ground, she wouldn't hesitate to bring a man to his knees anyway she needed to.

The cringe of remembrance wrinkling his brow brought an unexpected surge of laughter gurgling into the back of her throat. That brought her up short. Biting the edge of her lip, she took a step back. She only wished the extra space could lend her the perspective she was missing. The good sheriff also took a step back, angling his head to the side. That same, oddly pained expression he'd worn in the house earlier settled on his face again.

"Right..." He drew the word out, letting it trail away into an awkward silence. Turning back to the shed door, he took a chip of the peeling paint into his fingers, shaking his head as it crumbled to tiny fragments in his palm. Clearing his throat, he adopted a cool, professional tone. "It's doubtful I'll be able to lift any prints from this." He pulled a pen from his back pocket and hooked it through the loop on the lock. "I'll take the lock in though, might be able to get something from this." He set the lock on the rough ledge of a windowsill. "Let's go in, see if anything is damaged or missing."

JJ drew a deep breath and followed him inside. It took a moment for her eyes to adjust to the shadows. Mellow sunlight gleamed in sparse streaks here and there, wherever wood had aged and separated, gilding dust motes, turning them to fairy dust. The small doorway provided enough illumination to keep them from stumbling over the haphazard array of clutter filling the small space, but shadows lingered around the edges, making the storage area seem smaller than it was. The large, double doors along the far wall were still braced from the inside.

Preoccupied with taking mental inventory, JJ was half a second late in realizing he'd stopped walking. She crashed into his back, and, once again, it was like hitting a brick wall. She bounced back a step and collided with a table lamp, knocking it to the hard packed dirt. The clatter echoed inside the shed, and the bulb shattered. She gasped, her arms flailing at her sides as she tried to regain her balance. The room tipped to a dizzying angle and darkness swam before her eyes as another flash jerked her off kilter.

Jerry would know right where to look, and he'd find her faster than she was prepared to die. Not that she wanted to die. She'd never be ready to die. Oh, God, Sarah... She fumbled the vase for a moment in palms damp with sweat and blood, her mind screaming desperate prayers. The white crockery stayed in her hands, its blue, hand-painted flowers and vines remained intact, and a ragged whisper of relieved breath slipped past her bloodied lips...

A large body whirled on her. Strong hands clamped down on her shoulders, steadying her, jerking her against a solid chest, back to the here and now. Desperation clawed through her and she pushed him away with shaking hands. It took a moment to focus on the present.

"Are you all right? What happened?" The sheriff peered hard into her face, concern shadowed his brow. She shoved at him again, and he dropped his hands to his sides. "You're as white as a sheet."

"I...I'm f-fine, I'm *fine*," she stuttered, pushing the words through trembling lips. Maybe if she said it enough it would start to *feel* like it was true.

She must not have been convincing enough, because his hands were back, stroking up and down her chilled arms in an extraordinarily familiar, comforting way. His rich voice murmured gentle sounds—the words weren't quite discernable—but the overall effect soothed the rough edges. Then his face was close, so very close, and she could taste his breath as it feathered over her lips. Unsettled, JJ braced her hands against his chest, and the heat of his flesh burned her palms through the thin, soft barrier of his cotton shirt. The dark shape of a tattoo, covering a large portion of his chest, appeared through the worn material. She could barely make out the outline. What mark would he have branded on his perfect body? The mere thought was intriguing.

Her focus swerved back to his mouth. A sensual mouth if ever she'd seen one. She wanted his lips on hers, with an intensity that terrified her.

But it was all happening so fast, the swift kick of desire so close on the heels of another terrifying flash. And there was just so much of him, in such a small space. Again. She was overwhelmed. So much so, that even as she prepared herself for his kiss, she abruptly pushed at his chest and insisted, "No."

He didn't move an inch. All she accomplished was shoving herself back against the rough-hewn wall. But that was safe. Distance. Space. She pressed herself there for a moment and watched him, wide-eyed, a mouse waiting for the cat to spring. Rough splinters of wood and the sharp tip of a nail bit through her worn T-shirt, abrading her skin.

He wore that pained, vaguely horrified expression again, and she couldn't quite figure that out. Drawing a ragged breath, he stepped away, taking his own precious bit of space.

"I'm sorry—"

"Nothing's missing—"

Clearing her throat, JJ began again. Her words tumbled out in a wobbly rush. "Nothing's missing as far as I can tell. I'm sure whoever broke in realized this was a waste of time. I'm sorry Ginny called you out here for nothing."

Why was he wearing that strange expression? Why did he look like someone was flaying him alive? He reached a hand out to her, but before he could speak, she spun away, desperate to flee the shed, frantic to escape into wide-open space and fresh, mind-clearing air. A soft ripping sound accompanied her first step, but it took two more steps and the bright, warm caress of sunlight before she realized she'd left half her threadbare T-shirt hanging from the nail back inside the shed. It didn't matter. She had to get inside the house...away from the turbulent chaos in his disconcerting eyes.

A dark, vicious roar stopped her dead in her tracks. A band of steel locked around the crook of her elbow, spinning her around until her palms braced against his granite chest once more. His muscles quivered beneath her palms. His hands clutched convulsively at her shoulders, bruising and unyielding. His wild eyes were black with the faintest hint of a green ring. His nostrils flared, and his chest heaved. His face was livid, and a vein throbbed in his neck. A low, dangerous snarl rippled through his chest, vibrating against her palms.

Her mouth went bone dry. She froze.

She'd never seen anything so fierce in all her life.

Chapter 8

The rending of her shirt echoed in the shed, pricking at Cam's sensitive ears. For a split second, he didn't move as she fled. He couldn't. Confusion, then vile, outraged shock held him rooted to the spot as sunlight filtered across the satiny flesh of her exposed back. The thin, pale pink straps of her bra held no hope of concealing the long, jagged scar slashing its way across her back, over one shoulder blade, and down around the curve of her ribs where it disappeared beneath the ragged edges of frayed cotton. The faint pucker left behind from dozens upon dozens of stitches only served to highlight the pearly scar tissue.

Rage roiled through his system, and black, acidic bile rose in his throat. In a sudden spurt of motion, he was behind her, the sight of her scars ravaged his control. The wounds had healed well, but they were still relatively new, and the urge to protect her from some unseen threat clawed through him. How dare anyone harm her? How dare anyone cause her one second of fear or pain? Fury seethed inside him, snarling for release. He'd kill the son of a bitch that had done this to his female.

He'd maim and dismember before he ever let something like this happen to her again. Ever.

She jerked at her arms, eyes wide and frightened as they stared up at him. With superhuman will, he uncurled his fingers from her elbow, swearing beneath his breath at his own thoughtlessness. Shit...he'd probably bruised her. If he were lucky, that was all he'd done. He'd lost his head, and with his strength, he could have snapped her bones like a damned pencil. He shuddered, cringing inside because now *he* was the source of that raw emotion swimming in her glassy, fearful eyes. It was a feeling he never wanted to experience again.

His words tumbled out, a dark, and mighty growl, "Damn it, JJ! What the hell happened to you?"

The alarmed groove between her brows slowly faded, as did all the color in her face, and her eyes widened with understanding. She shook her head slowly, gaining momentum as she backed away from him. Her lips moved, but she didn't seem able to find her voice.

Her hiking boot pivoted as she prepared to flee, but he was faster, latching on to her wrist with viselike strength. Though she fought him, he tugged her back with inexorable purpose. That's when he noticed the pair of scars, one long and jagged and the other short and straight, each with stitch puckers of their own, running along the underside of her forearm. Defensive wounds if ever he'd seen them. His gut churned anew with rage, and his teeth threatened to shatter.

"Please, let me go. Please," she whispered, trembling like a leaf in his hand. Her anguish tore through him. "Please."

She was frightened. Terrified. She had that same deer-in-the-headlights look he'd seen in her eyes that first morning in the diner. Those beautiful, blue eyes held both demand and plea as she struggled to break his hold. He forced his voice to level out, but the driving need to protect her, to hold her and comfort her was firmly entrenched now.

"JJ, what happened? Who did this to you? Tell me," he demanded.

"It's over, it's over now," she chanted, her eyes

darting around them. Was she expecting someone to jump from a hiding place and cut her down? She sure as hell was acting like it. "He's dead. He's dead, and it's over."

Cam's brows drew together, and his jaw tightened. The horror in her eyes didn't diminish despite of her chant. Gone was the defiant spitfire who'd wrestled with him in the mud and kneed him in the balls to gain her freedom. The woman before him was fragile, delicate.

Breakable.

No, perhaps a more accurate assessment would be that she'd already been shattered, and still hadn't put all the pieces back together yet. The jagged edges of his own, inexplicable fear began slicing at his control. The wolf within snarled and snapped and began pacing, restless and alert. Dangerous.

The analytical part of his brain engaged, the cop in him wanting to press the questions, demand answers. He wanted a name. He wanted a reason. He wanted retribution. He wanted *vengeance*. The emotional side of him—the wolf within—needed to protect what was his with a ferocious urgency that bordered on fanatical. He wanted to comfort her, to kiss her and offer her a safe haven. He wanted to *be* her safe haven, with every cell in his body. He wanted to take her into his arms and make it better for her. He wanted to claim her for his own so that he had the right to protect her with his life, if need be. Compulsive. Obsessive.

Unsettled, he faltered, blinking at her in bewilderment. What was wrong with him? Only a...a *mate*...should engender this dangerous level of emotion. Burned to his soul, he dropped his hands from her and stumbled back. A bolt of lightning come down from the heavens to strike him where he stood wouldn't have stunned him more.

No way.

It wasn't possible.

Then he remembered his initial reaction to the sight of her scars. *How dare anyone hurt his female...*

His female.

He stared at her, his mouth hanging open, unable to string two words together to save his life. Every nerve in his body ached...*raged* for her...even as his mind rebelled. His heart lurched inside his chest. His soul staggered.

She backed away from him once more. Slowly now. Cautious. As one would from a wild, predatory animal. Staring at him with wide, bruised eyes, her voice trembled. "It's none of your business, just...just go away!"

She bolted for the house. Her long, blonde ponytail bobbed and swayed as she ran from him, ran from memories he couldn't see. Instinct demanded he follow, but he let her go as he tried to wrap his mind around what had just transpired. His hands shook. Hell, his entire body shook. His mouth went dry. His head spun. And he couldn't move. He didn't dare so much as blink.

His female?

He couldn't go after her, and he couldn't walk away.

Her anguished sobs tore at him. Through wood and glass, he could hear them plain as the pulse of the forest around him, and each sob raked through his body like icy claws, shredding his heart. A flicker of motion in one of the windows caught his attention, and he stared in morose grief as she wrapped her arms around her middle and collapsed onto a sofa. She was so pale, so tormented as she folded in half, dropping her forehead onto her knees, her delicate frame shaking with the force of her suffering.

The need to hold her, to comfort her finally pushed him beyond the borders of shock. Yet he stifled the urge to go to her, to break down the door and force her to accept his comfort. It took more willpower to stop himself than he realized he was capable of. He had to think this through. Dissect and examine what had happened here. There had to be a rational explanation. Something beyond the obvious. Something less threatening to his peace of mind than a...than a...

Son of a bitch...

She couldn't be.

But ancient, feral instincts argued with sanity. *His mate?*

He needed to get the hell out of here. Far enough away to look beyond the wolf's instinctive response to its mate's pain. She wasn't his mate. She was *not* his mate, damn it. She was a virtual stranger.

Yet she called to him on a primal level. And she was hurting. Damn it all to hell! What was he supposed to do?

Cam bore down on the emotions wrenching his system in too many different directions. Grinding his teeth together, he stomped through the yard and jerked the truck's door open with enough force to leave the imprint of his fingers on the handle. The impression on the metal gave him pause and he froze again. His mind raced, swamped with jagged pieces of memories and old lore. Impression. Imprint...

Imprinting?

Was it possible the old legends could be true?

He'd humored the others in the pack...the ones who'd claimed the legends held true and claimed their own mates. Reed, Charlie, Todd... He'd humored them, but he hadn't truly believed. He'd kept his love life free of any threat of permanency, free of the tangled web of emotional ties for a reason. A mutual sharing of physical pleasure that went no deeper than the here and now was his mantra. Essentially, love 'em well and leave 'em happy.

Leave being the operative word.

His own mother hadn't been capable of fidelity to his father. How, then, could he expect any different of any other woman? His mother's betrayal had been deeper than the usual, though. With far reaching consequences no one could have anticipated. Well, no one, perhaps, but the Werewolf she'd willingly taken to her bed. The Werewolf who'd supposedly imprinted on Cam's mother. The Werewolf who'd sired Cam...while Cam's mother had still been married to Seth Walker.

Bowing his head, he thrust that upsetting train of thought forcefully away.

Imprinting...

Pulling himself up inside the cab of his truck, he slammed the door shut behind him, shaken to the core, praying the sound of her gut wrenching sobs would cease with the barrier. They did, at last, but he knew she wept on, knew it in his soul, and the impact of her tears rocked him. It still wasn't easy to bear, wasn't easy fighting instinct, but he cranked the radio to an eardrum-shattering decibel, and let Daughtry's *"What I Want"* pound the shakes from his system.

Cam stomped on the accelerator with unnecessary force as he aimed the truck toward the road, leaving a wide spray of gravel and a billowing cloud of dust in his wake. Unfortunately, he couldn't steer his mind as easily as he could his truck.

Imprinting...shit.

Remembered lore swamped him. The old ones claimed that once the time was right, and a Werewolf imprinted on his female, there was no turning back. No denying fate. The Werewolf would be unable—on every level imaginable—to connect with another female. Unable to form an emotional, intimate attachment with another. Unable to *mate* with another, regardless of his chosen female's loyalty or emotions. The urge to protect would be irrefutable. The need to claim and possess inescapable, irrational. His very existence would center around his female. Her safety. Her happiness. If the Werewolf in question were extremely lucky, the emotions wouldn't be one sided.

If those emotions weren't reciprocated, however, the results could be disastrous.

Destructive.

Case in point...his own biological father. He shuddered at the thought, at the very term. When his mother had been unable to deal with the...the wilder side of her lover's true nature, she'd gone back to her human husband. Right up until the day he'd died, Seth Walker had never known the truth of Cam's paternity. His mother's life had gone on as if her infidelity had never happened, and the resulting child passed off as a Walker.

Her lover, on the other hand, had never recovered.

In one of the rare, real conversations Cam had had with her lover—Cam refused to acknowledge him as his father—the bastard had claimed moving away from her, severing all contact, would have been harder than carving the heart out of his own chest.

He'd been too much of a coward. Instead, he'd wasted his life loving a woman who could never return his love, desperate for a glimpse or a smile, finding what solace he could in the bottom of countless bottles of alcohol. Cam couldn't find any respect for him, couldn't summon anything but the meanest pity for a man who refused to lick his wounds and walk away.

No, he wouldn't be that man. That pitiful excuse, a burden to his pack, emotionally shackled to a female who couldn't or wouldn't accept him for what he was. Besides, what female in her right mind would willingly bind herself to a monster...the big, bad wolf?

Nickleback's *"Come for You"* finally broke through the haze of angry confusion clogging his brain. He gritted his teeth as the gravelly voice sang of searching forever to bring his love home. The song hit just a little too close to the way he was feeling right now. With an angry jerk, he twisted the knob, effectively killing the sound.

Shaking his head, he guided the truck into his designated parking space in the lot adjacent to the sheriff's department. Turning the key, he yanked it from the ignition, and drew several deep breaths, calming his mind. He felt better...almost. He was being stupid. Paranoid. Yes, he felt a connection to JJ Frost. Yes, he was attracted to her. She was sexy and intriguing, and her eyes hinted at a fiery passionate side. And the smell of her...

His entire body shuddered, head to toe.

It was simple enough. He'd see her again...later, when things settled down, when *he'd* settled down. He'd pursue, he'd have his fun—make sure she had hers too, of course—and then he'd walk. Imprinting was bullshit. It was lore. Nothing more.

He'd never be pitiful.

Feeling slightly more comfortable now that he'd reasoned it all through, he hopped out of the truck and strolled across the asphalt, nodding respectfully to the elderly Mr. and Mrs. Cross as they passed, hand in hand. The familiar clack of computer keys, the ring of the phone, and the chatter of the scanner greeted him as he pushed the door open and stepped inside the office building. Emma glanced up. Her smile took some of the exasperation out of the roll of her eyes.

Holding up a slim finger, she spent a long moment in silence before responding to the headset with intermittent pauses, "Yes, Ms. Potter. I'll send a deputy right over... That's right... That's no problem. I'm sure everything will be fine... No, you don't need to stay on the line... Yes, Ms. Potter. You have a nice day too." She flicked a button with practiced ease, transitioning from the headset to the radio. "Austin, Ms. Potter called in again. She says that sound is back."

The aggravation in Austin's voice was unmistakable, even beneath the layers of scratchy static. "You gotta be kidding me."

"Nope, I assured her you'd be right over."

The pause was long, the sigh audible, the drawn out response sarcastic. "Thanks..."

Turning back to Cam, Emma grinned like an evil pixie as she leaned back in her expensive office chair. The pencil in her hand joined the two already lodged in the wild spikes of her hair. Her clothing was black, as usual. Goth, right to the tips of her thick-soled boots.

Her hair was another story all together. This week her spikes were a stark, white-blonde. That didn't necessarily mean she'd be blonde next week, of course. Or tomorrow for that matter. Last week her hair had been flamboyant red, the previous week jet-black, and electric blue the week before that, if he remembered right. He half expected her to get confused someday and come in with rainbow stripes.

Her hair color seemed to change with her whims, although, thank heaven, her disposition always held steady. She was invariably bubbly, unfailingly cheerful, with a mischievous streak a mile wide, and a peculiar coolness under fire that belied her youth.

Cam could find no fault with the way she ran his office, and so she could dress any damned way she pleased. The sheriff's department was a well-oiled machine beneath the watchful eye of a master mechanic...despite the fact that the mechanic looked a bit like a wild-haired Wednesday Addams. Everyone loved her, from Ms. Potter, the senile old lady down on Maple who lived with fifteen cats and swore up and down that someone was walking around in her attic on a regular basis, to all the teenage boys who thought she was the coolest thing since somebody got the notion to screw wheels onto a short piece of wood.

"Hey there, Cam," she called in her trilling voice. A voice completely different from the one answering 911 calls. Then her expression turned foreboding, her tone scolding and suspicious. "What are you doing here?"

"Came to file a report," he told her, leaning an elbow on the high counter between them. "How'd the other calls turn out?"

"Same as before," she grumbled, passing him a stack of papers and a thick manila file. "Looks like the same vandals...those little bastards." Her tone changed, edging into reluctant admiration. "They painted up one of the screens at the movie theater." Her lips twisted in a wry smirk. "Did an interesting...mural. Judy took some good photos, they're in the file."

Huffing out a long, aggravated breath, Cam tapped the edge of the stack against his palm and headed for his office. He couldn't wait to get his hands on those little shits. Halfway through the door, he spun on his heel and paused, hand on the doorknob. "Did Jarvis—"

"On your desk," she cut in before dismissing him so she could answer the ringing phone.

Nodding to himself, he closed the door behind him, flipped the switch on his coffee maker, and settled himself behind his desk as the first chugs and hisses escaped the aging machine. Before long, the inviting scent of fresh coffee perfumed the air, making the autopsy report for Lori Watson only slightly more tolerable.

Tossing the photo's aside, he stood and crossed his office. As he poured a cup of the steaming brew, he glanced out the window and surveyed the street before him. Despite the grisly photos on the desk behind him, the cozy familiarity of his town offered comfort. Maggie'd changed the daily special's sign in her front window. Meatloaf and mashed potatoes. He'd have to stop in for supper.

Doc Templeton's receptionist/assistant had set out a fake fire hydrant in front of his place. An amazingly lifelike plastic terrier grinned at passersby as he lifted his leg in tribute. Ginny had her front door propped open with a garbage can full of discount scoop shovels. He couldn't blame her. It was too damned nice outside today not to savor every last ounce of fresh air, work or no work.

Turning his gaze in the other direction, he scanned the tidy faces of the library and the town hall. No changes there. Heaving a sigh, he took a quick sip and scalded the roof of his mouth as he turned back to his desk. Cursing, he forced the swallow, and sucked in a sharp breath to cool his mouth. It didn't help much. Unable to face the photo's, he flipped them upside down on the edge of his desk and reached for the report as he returned to his seat.

The technical jargon floated on the surface. Words and phrases popped at him from the page. Obstruction of venous drainage. Occlusion of the internal jugular vein. Cerebral edema and cerebral ischemia. Cyanotic. And the classic sign of strangulation—petechiae—little blood marks on the face and in the eyes from burst blood capillaries.

Ligature marks, as well as fibers taken from the victim's skin, indicate the stockings found around the victim's throat were indeed the murder weapon.

The hyoid bone was broken, pointing to manual choking rather than execution via hanging. Jarvis tagged time of death somewhere between midnight and one a.m. given the corpse's temperature at time of discovery, and the woods as the place of death given lividity. Lori's death would have been immediately following her shift at Maggie's.

The ME hadn't been able to recover any prints or viable DNA from the body, or from the crime scene evidence. The only prints on the rosary were those of the victim. The killer had used paint to form the gruesome letters on her back, not blood as they'd initially assumed. That made sense, given the rain. Blood would have washed away. He must have been more off balance than he'd realized to have missed that.

The condoms scattered about the crime scene were your garden-variety condoms, available in dozens of pharmacies or retail stores across the state, as were the magazines. None bore any trace of bodily fluids. Red was following up, even now, on the videos. With any luck, they might get a hit when they ran serial numbers. All in all, the sum of the report left Cam with more questions than answers. Who would kill Lori? Why? And why leave her like that? Why strip her of her dignity in such a base, cruel fashion?

Tucking the photos and the reports back into the manila file, he dropped the packet into a tray on the corner of his desk and leaned back in his chair, considered the stack of work that had accumulated since the last time he'd been in his office less than two full days ago. Hell, anymore a day off was more work than if he spent a double shift in uniform.

It took him just over two hours to review the rest of the papers in the stack Emma had handed him. He signed off on requests for concealed weapons permits, approved purchases for a new K9 unit, and then read reports for the latest rash of vandalism. Still no lead there either. It only took a few minutes to fill out a report for the call he'd taken at JJ's. He'd long since given up the absurd notion that formality equaled distance.

His mind circled back to the incident outside her shed. Rocking back in his chair, he closed his eyes and pinched the bridge of his nose between his thumb and forefinger. Hell, who was he trying to fool? His mind had never left her place, never left her.

Those scars had been vicious. It didn't take a genius to figure out where the fear in her eyes came from. Someone had done some serious damage. And not just to her body. From the look in her eyes earlier, she had much deeper wounds that were still bleeding.

"It's over now. He's dead," she'd said. That was little comfort to him. Then again, it was probably just as well. It was a very real possibility the man's life would have been forfeit should Cam have ever met him face to face. He'd have taken great satisfaction in ripping the man's throat out with his bare teeth, badge be damned.

Cam's narrow-eyed gaze swerved to the computer screen on the left side of his desk, and he chewed the inside of his cheek as he fought curiosity. It would be an invasion of her privacy. Under any other circumstances this wouldn't be something he'd ever even consider. Even now, it didn't sit well. Digging into someone else's secrets was taboo for him.

And yet...

He rubbed at his chin, dug at the knot at the base of his neck. He drained the cooling coffee in his cup and drummed his fingers on his desk blotter. Pushing to his feet, Cam paced to the window and back again. And all the while his eyes never strayed too far from the blank computer screen. Cam all but gnawed a hunk of his lip off while his conscience lost the battle with the merciless need to know all there was to know about JJ Frost.

With a snarl of self-disgust, he plopped down behind his desk and reached for the mouse. His conscience made one last stab at him, and his fingers hesitated. But that long, jagged scar across her back flashed through his mind again, and conscience was hamstrung without another whimper.

He began with a basic search and came up with more than he'd expected. She'd graduated at the top of her class, with honors, from a highly distinguished academy of the arts. Miss Jillian Josephine Frost, AKA JJ Frost, age 26, born and raised in Minneapolis, was a critically acclaimed artist the art world watched with baited breath. She'd had several very successful showings, both here in the United States, as well as abroad.

Then, with no warning or explanation it seemed, she'd fallen from the face of the earth...at least from the face of the art world.

Cam called up some old clippings, as well as pictures of her and a few other select artists at a fashionable gala event a couple years back featuring celebrated works. The woman smiling back at him took his breath away. She was different...and still the same. The proud tilt of her head, the glint of steel in her eyes was the same. The self-assured, unguarded happiness glimmering in her eyes in these pictures was missing in the woman he knew. What had happened?

Without giving it a second thought, he dug deeper. A phone call to the proper authorities in Minneapolis lasted less time than it took to pour another cup of coffee. Having secured the sergeant's assurance she would fax their files on JJ to him at the earliest convenience, he returned to his computer. He typed in more keywords and waited.

A brisk rap on the door—followed by the click and hum of the outer offices as the door opened—interrupted his concentration just as the next article popped onto his screen in startling, bold print. *'Brutal homicide leaves promising young artist fighting for life.'*

Biting off a particularly nasty expletive, he glanced toward the door, fully prepared to rip into the intruder. The angry growl died on his lips. Emma's pale face was chalky, her eyes round as saucers.

"Sheriff…"

Oh, hell…

Coffee curdled in his stomach, and he held his breath. Emma only called him sheriff when there was serious trouble. Trouble in all caps. Trouble beginning with a *Holy shit* and ending with an *Oh, fuck.*

"Just got a 911. A couple kids over at Angel's beach," she paused to draw a shaky breath, forced a swallow. "They found another body."

Chapter 9

Cam parked his truck alongside Austin's Tahoe and took a moment to brace himself. He couldn't shake that sick sense of foreboding swimming in the pit of his stomach. In a jurisdiction this size, odds were pretty damned good Cam was gonna know the victim, whomever it was. He'd been so startled, so appalled at the news of another dead body he hadn't stopped to ask Emma if Austin had a positive ID on the vic. He should have. At least he would've had the drive over—short as it was—to prepare.

Prepared or not, he still felt as though this was his fault...somehow. Common sense argued no one would have expected this—a second murder—so fast on the heels of the first. Which begged the question...what was going on here?

Well, hell, at least this time he wasn't dead on his feet, wearing a coat of sheetrock dust and sweat. He secured his sidearm and leaned across the seat, digging in his glove box for a pair of latex gloves. He should have put his uniform on this morning, not that it really mattered. His was the kind of job that didn't recognize the meaning of the terms day off or vacation time.

He followed the narrow trail through the woods toward a secluded little lakeside cove, Sutter Hollow's version of lover's lane. If he hadn't been aware of what awaited him at the end of the trail, this could have been nothing more than an ill-timed trip down memory lane. Moving with the natural grace of a lithe predator, he made not a sound as he drew closer to the beach. His heavy boots left no trace of his passing. His movements bent not a single leaf.

Ducking beneath the fluttering yellow ribbon of crime scene tape tied between two saplings across the trail, Cam broke into the clearing and paused. He dragged in a deep gulp of air through flared nostrils, careful not to let his gaze fall to the body just yet. He needed to assess the scene objectively...before the victim's identity could impinge on his clarity of purpose.

Distinctive earthy scents, lush and verdant, mingled and swirled through the air. Lake water. Damp sand. Then the wind shifted, and a wave of stale liquor washed over him. His gut clenched. No. No, he told himself adamantly, it couldn't be *him*. He was mistaken. Shaking off that impossible thought, he dragged in more scent. Sifting. Isolating.

And that familiar scent hit him again.

Denial gripped him by the throat.

Although he hadn't had the advantage of a night of rain to aid in washing away his trail, the killer had left no trace of himself behind. Again. Nothing, but for the scents of liquor and old blood...and the dead body, of course.

He took the scene in with a wide sweep of his keen eyes, deliberately avoiding the corpse. Desperately ignoring the unexpected lump in his throat. A plethora of glittering glass—broken shards and intact bottles with a wide assortment of liquor labels—littered the sand in a fifteen-foot radius of the body. Each and every one appeared empty beneath his quick glance.

It looked like the beach had been the sight of a wild, booze-soaked party.

Not a likely scenario. Local partygoers would never leave the beach in this user-*un*friendly condition. Everyone in the county old enough to have a hormone in their body knew this beach—and this sand in particular—was far better put to use in more *recreational* ways. No, whoever the killer was, he couldn't have had any sentimental attachment to this location, defiling it the way he had. Wide arcs of rusty splatters tinted the pale sand. Blood-stained, shattered glass peppered the ground. A massive, uneven hunk of stone near the center of the clearing—also drenched with dried blood—half concealed the discarded corpse, like a pagan sacrificial altar, used and abandoned.

Cam's gaze slid to the kneeling deputy, trepidation slithering through his veins. Austin's silver-streaked head bent to examine the area surrounding the body. With cautious, latex-covered hands—apparently oblivious that he'd gained an audience—Austin used the tip of a slim golden pen to lift the victim's wrist a few inches from the ground. His brow puckered as he angled his head this way and that, scrutinizing the victim's frozen, bloody fist.

Cam's gaze edged from the suspended wrist upward, over the thickly muscled, tattooed forearm to the bulky shoulder. His eyes widened as he identified the familiar tat, and the ratty plaid shirt. Stunned, he sucked in a sharp, horrified breath and staggered forward a few steps. The exposed and mangled, gaping chest cavity left Cam clutching at the nearest tree for support. The victims other broad, long-fingered hand lay open on the ground, palm up, gently cradling a silent heart.

The bastard had left him sprawled on the beach like a half-carved Thanksgiving turkey.

It took every ounce of Cam's self-control not to howl in bewildered disbelief.

A violent gash yawned beneath the victim's chin, ear to ear, in a macabre smile. The victim's features locked in eternal pain and shock. Garish red paint scrawled the word GLUTTONY across the man's forehead.

He knew that face as well as he knew his own. He saw similar features in the mirror every morning as he shaved. He'd never forget the first time he'd seen this man's face. Cam's mother had set up their first contact, urging Cam to listen carefully...and to believe in the impossible. Yes, Cam knew this face.

And he hated it.

It was the face of Ed Whitlock, town drunkard...

The face of Cam's own biological father.

A crackle and a snap from somewhere behind him swung his head about, but he couldn't make his feet move, couldn't release the tree, though his fingers were fast going numb, the bite of bark against his palm all but unnoticeable. Only by sheer determination did he manage to keep the instinctive snarl of warning locked deep in his chest.

"Oh, Cam," Jarvis muttered, stumbling over a gnarled hunk of tree root that didn't seem to understand it belonged beneath the ground rather than above it. For being so athletic, the good doctor could be unnaturally clumsy sometimes. "I didn't realize they'd called you already. Judy will be along shortly. She's gathering some things from her car."

Tugging his medical coat free of a clinging branch, the doctor drew closer, hesitated. His alarmed gaze swept over Cam's face. His brow creased. "Cam...are you all right? You look like...well, you...you don't look so good."

That was the understatement of the century. Blood pounded in his ears, though his head felt vastly bereft of the warm oxygenated fluid. His stomach was oddly hollow, though nausea rolled. His knees had gone to jelly.

Once he'd pushed beyond the shock, past the raw grief he couldn't fathom, his mind locked onto and whirled around one inescapable fact. Ed was a Werewolf...*had been* a Werewolf. Although they were not immortal, they were notoriously fast healers. There were few ways to kill one of his kind beyond the natural aging process. A severe trauma, say a slit throat for example—since the example was glaring him right in the eye—would temporarily incapacitate a Werewolf...provided he didn't bleed out, a risky gamble that. If the trauma, however, were followed quickly enough by another lethal strike—say something like having his heart removed from his chest—death was a given.

Jarvis wondered closer to Cam, mumbling beneath his breath, "Why slit the throat, and then cut out the heart—isn't that overkill?"

Cam bit his tongue, though the thought circled in his head like a swarm of angry bees, *Not if the victim is a Werewolf. It wasn't overkill...it was necessary.*

A sudden dawning crashed through him like a runaway freight train. The killer stalking Sutter Hollow knew the legacy...but was not one of his kind. Cam couldn't scent him. If a human did this...knew *how* to kill one of his kind...then the killer had the potential to expose his pack. Cam's own secrets weren't safe anymore, in more ways than one. But why had the killer targeted these specific people? Ed and Lori were nothing to each other.

What was the common thread here?

"Cam?" The concern—both professional and personal—in Jarvis's voice drew Cam back from the brink of panic.

"Yeah, yeah," Cam hedged. "I'm okay." He could panic later. Right now he had a job to do. "C'mon."

Jarvis shot him a look rife with disbelief, but followed him into the clearing anyway. At the sound of their approach, Austin glanced up, and pushed to his feet. "Hey, Cam...not much of a day off, huh?"

Ignoring Austin's off the cuff remark, Cam

visually searched the rest of the empty beach. "Who found...the body?"

"Noah Simpson and Tess Palmer. I took their statements and sent them on home with stern orders not to discuss the scene with anyone. Tess was in rough shape. I figured the best place for her to be was with her mama."

Cam stepped aside as Judy shuffled by with a large duffle bag slung over her shoulder. He would've liked the chance to speak to Noah and Tess himself, but what was done was done. He'd just have to track them down later.

Jarvis snapped on a pair of gloves and stepped up to Ed's body to begin the preliminary exam. Unable to watch, Cam turned away under the pretense of helping Judy remove crime scene equipment from the bag. Once Jarvis began with the body, Austin was in the way so he stepped aside as well. He crossed to the edge of the clearing to stand beside Cam.

Dangling a broken, brown bottle between his thumb and forefinger, its ragged edges liberally coated with dried blood and little pieces of torn flesh, Austin announced, "Near as I can tell, this seems to be the murder weapon."

"Oh, my Lord," Judy gasped. Her pale face leeched of all color, then filled with a ghastly shade of green. "The killer carved his heart out with a broken beer bottle?"

"I always figured the booze would get him sooner or later, I just never imagined it'd be like this," Austin interjected in what Cam assumed was a poor shot at wry humor.

A harsh growl ripped from Cam's chest about the same time Jarvis cleared his throat in heavy disapproval. The remorseful deputy shot Cam a guilty glance, muttered a hasty apology, and quickly focused his attention on bagging up the suspected murder weapon. Turning his back, gritting his teeth, Cam walked away, making a show of searching the sand for evidence. His temper was boiling, seething just beneath the surface. He was hard-pressed to keep it contained. The last thing he needed to do right now was shift in the middle of a damned crime scene.

Being a Werewolf himself, Austin wouldn't be surprised...except maybe for the fact that his Alpha couldn't control himself any better. It might give Jarvis a moment of pause, but then, Cam was sure, he'd start in with the fascinated scientific questions and observations. He was one of the extreme few humans who knew the truth. Werewolves were a breed unto themselves, complete with their own set of chromosomes and their own hybrid blood type. Being the only doctor in a small town—a town with a healthy-sized Werewolf population—it had just been a matter of time before something out of the ordinary sparked more questions than Cam could find excuses for.

Judy...

Well, trooper that she was, Judy would probably just pass out straight away. That or put a slug between his eyes. With Judy, you just never knew.

"The killer would have needed something stronger than a broken bottle to open his chest up that way." Jarvis crossed his arms over his own chest, tipping his head to the side.

He studied the position of the body, bending to peer closer at the snapped ribs. "Garden sheers perhaps. Mm-hmm... Long handled garden sheers. That would allow the proper leverage and pressure." He spoke to himself, but his words carried through the now silent crime scene as if he'd used a bullhorn.

Beer bottles... Garden sheers...

Shit.

"Interesting," Jarvis murmured, pricking Cam's

ears.

"What?" Cam moved to the doctor's side, his footsteps reluctant. Careful to keep his eyes averted from the corpse without *looking* like he was keeping his eyes averted, he stared at the doctor.

"Cadaveric spasm," Jarvis explained, eyes on the prize, as he pried Ed's resistant fist open.

Cam held his breath as Ed's fist finally yielded a string of small beads and a flash of silver. The delicate rosary, identical to the one found with Lori Watson, poured out onto the blood-soaked sand. A rosary in one hand, his heart in the other. What message was the killer trying to send?

Like Lori, Ed was not Catholic. The only altar he'd ever worshipped at was the long, scarred bar down at Pappy's, his communion taken not with blessed wine and wafers, but with whatever liquor he could lay paws on—the stronger the proof the better—and a handful of stale pretzels. Cam rocked back on his heels as he finally stared into the face of the father he could neither denounce, nor claim.

He'd find no closure here.

And his heart held no forgiveness.

Chapter 10

As the sliver of a crescent moon edged over the ridge behind Suttor Hollow, bathing the landscape in deep shadows, Cam slipped through his backyard on silent feet. Pausing just inside the curtain of the forest long enough to shed his clothing and stash them in the hollow of a well-marked tree, he drew a long breath and centered himself. Not an easy task given recent events, but shifting this way was easier, much less painful through centering and focusing rather than giving rage or grief free reign.

His head swam for a moment as searing heat built in his core. Muscle, tendons, and tissue stretched and bunched. Bones snapped and cracked, reshaping and reorganizing themselves. Skin shivered and twitched as fur sprang forth.

Planting all four paws on the ground, Cam flexed his claws, digging them into the loamy soil, shaking himself from the tip of his snout to the last hair on his bushy tail. A thin ribbon of moonlight trickled through the dense canopy overhead, glinting off his honey-toned pelt.

The forest fell unnaturally silent, as if sensing a new threat had entered its domain, a dangerous predator of unequaled abilities far beyond the natural world. In tentative stops and starts, the woods reanimated, swamping Cam's sharpened senses with distinctive scents and a symphony of sounds. Everything became sharper now, each leaf and every branch, separate and vivid despite the darkness, just as it did whenever he shifted.

Something was wrong though, not *everything*

was the same. He waited a moment, and then disappointment rushed through him. Cam dropped back on his haunches, pointed his nose skyward, and let a low, plaintive howl ripple up through his chest and throat, pouring forth into the night. A lone, eerie howl.

In the far distance, a reciprocal acknowledgement pierced the night, once. Then silence. His pack. They would keep their distance tonight, sensing he wished to be alone with his loss. One of the many benefits of the pack...the unspoken understanding. Sort of a special, emotional telepathy. No verbal explanations were necessary. Cam had the added bonus of being Alpha...his word was law. None would challenge him.

The anticipated, heady sense of freedom didn't fill him tonight, not as it usually did. The carefree desire to run wild—to roam at will—did not sink into his bones. Tonight his heart was heavy, confused. Any other night, he'd have immediately taken off at a steady trot, letting his paws carry him wherever they would. He'd have chased the scents. He'd have raced the moonlight, dancing in the shadows as he reveled in his sometime gift sometime curse.

He'd have hunted. The hunger in him was always a gnawing ache—a driving force— particularly after shifting, when his metabolism had kicked up and his body demanded nourishment. Even after shifting back to human form, he'd have to hunt again, though his prey would be far different. In human form, his prey often consisted of not one but two of Maggie's blue-plate specials, or a large pizza supreme from Tucker's. With Cam and the rest of his pack running around, it was little wonder the town's food service businesses were booming.

Tonight the ache inside was different. Hollow. He hadn't anticipated that. He still craved something, of that he was certain. He just didn't understand what that craving was exactly. Pushing himself to his feet, he forced his paws to move, but they were heavy and uncooperative. Restless, he wandered through the undergrowth. His heart just wasn't in his ramblings tonight, his head filled with too many troubling thoughts.

Dappled moonlight flickered across a small stream, turning the water to a ribbon of molten silver, and the small, silver crosses at the end of the identical rosaries came to mind. The rosaries left little doubt the two murders were connected, as did the grisly letters painted on the victim's bodies. He had a serial killer on his hands, and he didn't dare call in the pros for help. The last thing his pack needed was a bunch of FBI poking their noses in Sutter Hollow secrets.

He'd tried all afternoon, but he hadn't been able to come up with any common threads between Lori and Ed, at least none beyond the obvious familiarity bred of small town acquaintances. Lori...effervescent and efficient at her job. With a husband who worshipped the ground she walked on, and not a faithful bone in her body. Then there was Ed...a drunken loner who'd turned his back on his pack and couldn't hold a job to save his life. Faithful to his dying breath to a woman who would have nothing to do with him.

Different as night and day.

No common denominators.

Cam slid to a stop, his breathing arrested. That wasn't true. There was a common thread. Him. He was the tie that bound them together. He'd slept with Lori, once upon a dark and lonely night, though no one should have known about that. Ed was his father, though few knew of the connection either, only those of his pack and the elders. But they would never tell, never break loyalty with one of their kind.

No, there had to be something else. Something

he was missing. Whatever it was, he'd find it. He just couldn't believe this had something to do with him. These murders had to have more behind them, more than the fact both of the victims were key players in scenes from a past he wished to high heaven he could forget. There was a bigger picture, he just needed to step back a little, and maybe he'd get a better view. He'd thought shifting might help to clear away some of the sludge. Being in wolf form usually had that effect on him.

Not this time. This time he was just as confused, just as weary as before.

His paws slowed as he entered a small clearing deep in the heart of the woods. In the very center of that clearing, the forest floor lay blackened and empty, charred from centuries of ceremonial bonfires. The Circle of Beginnings. The sacred site the elders visited for their visions, and the honored location where the pack banded together on special occasions such as welcoming a new member to the pack, or for Lifemate ceremonies.

Incense and smoke clung to the ancient trees, kindling old memories.

He, like every other youngster, had heard the old legends as the naïve citizens of Sutter Hollow knew them. Old wives tales and campfire stories. Unbelievable tales of shapeshifters and demons of the night. Fiends who prowled the woods, enslaved to the phases of the moon. Animals that killed randomly, without hesitation or remorse. Evil beasts that preyed on careless hikers and unsuspecting innocents. Monsters that bathed in the blood of children and forced themselves on beautiful young women.

All untrue.

Cam had learned the truth of his existence in The Circle.

At the edge of the clearing, he crouched on his

haunches once more, silent and alert, yet his mind drifted far, far away. In his mind's eye, he watched the billowing gray smoke, thick with incense, swirling into the midnight sky the first time Ed had brought him here. A rite of passage. The stars twinkled overhead, ancient and timeless. Naked but for loincloths as a show of respect for their Winneoten forbearers, the old men gathered around the crackling fire, their chanting low and constant. Around them, another circle formed. Another generation...the future of the pack.

That night, myth had been dispelled and true understanding gifted through the traditional stories the elders passed down. He and others of his kind weren't brainless killing machines or rapist controlled by the moon's cycles. No, they were the average Joe next door, with a few extra...*perks*, courtesy of a common ancestor who'd made a pact with the Great Spirit in order to thwart his enemies and keep his tribe safe.

The moon held no sway for a Werewolf. His emotions were the only key to his unique shifting abilities. So once he learned to control those, he could shift...or not shift...at will. A silver bullet—hell, any bullet for that matter—directly in the heart, or head, would end his life. All other wounds no matter how severe, aside from outright amputation of course, would heal with preternatural speed.

But the Werewolf's heart was the key. The only thing a Werewolf feared more than a mortal wound to the heart was the loss of a mate. A bullet meant instant death, escape from the pain. The loss of a mate meant protracted suffering, a long and painful death of the soul until the body succumbed to the effects of time...or the subject in question could stand the pain no longer and took his own life. Like their wolf brethren, Werewolves mated for life.

Cam had resisted the truth at first, refused to accept what he'd heard, and what he'd seen with his own eyes...what he could do with his own body. It had taken him several years to come to grips with the reality of his life, to realize that it *was* reality and not some absurd break with sanity. He'd come to relish the freedom—the wild, unadulterated liberty—as well as the support of the pack. He'd even come to terms with his place in the pack, his position of authority and responsibility. He was Alpha now. Grandson of an Alpha. Great-grandson of an Alpha. Ed had refused the Alpha position, preferring to drown himself in the bottom of a whiskey bottle...that damned mate thing, again.

Why did it always circle back to that?

Bounding to his paws, he prowled The Circle, pacing with angry energy. Lifemate. He snorted at the word. Impossible. The very idea sent a shiver of fear undulating through his coat. On a burst of adrenaline, he shot from the clearing, legs pumping for all he was worth. His massive chest heaved as his breath sawed in and out. His teeth clenched tight as he pushed the word from his mind with determined force. Mile after mile passed in a blur. Sights and sounds, smells were here and gone before they could register.

He'd just rounded a curve in the river at a dead out sprint, intent on filling the hole in his stomach with the rabbit he'd just caught a whiff of, when something else drew his attention. Something much stronger, much more alluring than the juicy bit of fluff darting for its burrow. A distinctive scent, unimaginably powerful and uniquely enthralling, wafted to him on the gentle breeze, summoning him like a siren's call. All thought of the hunt slipped from his mind, his head whipped around. His agile paws tangled up in themselves, and he tumbled headlong into the thick trunk of an ancient spruce.

Fazed, he picked himself up, shaking his great, shaggy head. Lifting his snout to the wind, he dragged in a series of sharp sniffs, and took a cautious, reluctant step forward. Another round of sniffing snared him, like a fish set to well-baited hook. Her scent, drifting through the medley of raw foliage, seized him by the soul and reeled him in. His paws moved now of their own volition, with a fervor he'd never before known.

JJ...

He drew near, slowed. Following his instincts, he crept forward, head low to the ground, prowling the blurred line between her yard and the woods. He lurked in the shadows, his keen eyes searching for her. She was outside. Her scent was powerful, unmuted by the confines of a house, drawing him ever closer.

His ears pricked, twitching forward as he picked up the soft, velvety sound of her low humming. The bars were sporadic, the melody vaguely familiar. All his senses locked on her, he edged closer, savoring the sound of her song as she secured the new lock on the shed door.

The palest hint of silver moonlight limned her delicate profile. Her hair was unbound now, streaming down her back in rippling waves of gilded perfection. Her jeans were frayed around the edges, snug around that luscious bottom of hers. Her boots bore deep scuffmarks, her T-shirt was well worn and a size too big. Her slim, bare arms almost glowed against the encroaching darkness. She was gorgeous, her scars inconsequential.

Raw desire ruthlessly shoved any frustrated thoughts of thwarted revenge against the man who'd harmed her from his mind.

A rustling in the trees caught his attention, and he froze. His heightened senses kicked up a notch. Downwind as he was, he sifted the scent without even trying. Across the yard, she gathered her tools, oblivious of the threat.

His heart thundered.

His female was in danger.

He crept forward, low to the ground, his steady gaze trained on the tree line just beyond JJ. Her back was to him now, and she'd gone still. Had she finally noticed she wasn't alone? He slunk closer, his hackles lifting. He was a little over three yards away, when the bear broke free of the trees. Cam was closer to JJ, but not by much. The bear lifted his dripping snout to the air and snorted, rising up to stand on its hind legs. It let out a long, warning wail, its great lips flapping as it sprayed drool.

Cam closed the distance in two leaping bounds. He landed directly in front of JJ and backed up until his tail brushed her stiff legs. He crouched there, protective and threatening. Her breathing was shallow and fast, whipping over his senses. He could smell her fear.

Baring his fangs, he snarled warning at the bear. He would protect his female with his life, if need be. He was considerably larger than your average wolf—as was typical of his kind—but the bear towered over him, outweighing him by a solid two hundred pounds.

At least.

If he fought this bear, it might well cost him his life. He only prayed JJ got away before the bear finished with him. He could call to his pack, but it would be a waste of energy and focus. Fast as they were, they'd never make it here in time.

The bear's massive paws slashed at the air, wicked black claws glinting in the sparse moonlight. It growled, deep and loud. Its size indicated it was male...a full-grown male, easily topping four hundred pounds...but it shouldn't be this close to town. Sutter Hollow had never had a problem with bears before.

And this one seemed particularly irritable.

Though he couldn't communicate with the bear the way he could with his pack, Cam's preternatural sensitivity keyed him in to the animal's hunger. It had probably come to investigate the delicious aroma drifting from JJ's kitchen windows. Well, it would just have to find its midnight snack elsewhere. The black bear couldn't have whatever it was she'd baked...and it sure as hell couldn't have *her*. Cam snarled again, edging back half a pace until his rump pushed against her thigh. Shit, why wasn't she running for the house? He wanted to yell at her to go, but the best he could do in this form was growl and push at her again.

Damn it, JJ, run.

The bear dropped to the ground, and, finally, she bolted.

The shaggy beast advanced, his stench preceding him, his beady eyes swinging from Cam to JJ, and back again. Cam edged to the side, keeping his large body firmly positioned between the bear and JJ, preparing himself to fight. He had to hold out, at least long enough for her to get to safety. The door slammed behind him. The bear took two feinting steps forward, snorting and pawing at the shrinking space between them.

Cam crouched, tensing to spring. Now that she was safely out of the away, he could focus. He needed to keep his head, think smart. If he could manage that, he just might survive. The bear's hide quivered. It lifted its front paws from the ground, slammed them back down, emitting a thunderous roar. Cam's claws dug into firm soil, seeking traction.

The crack of a handgun pierced the night, spraying dirt in the bear's face. Startled, the bear snorted and backed up a pace. Instinct flattened

Cam to the ground. Bellowing, the bear advanced, only to be driven back by a second shot and another shower of dirt and grass. Cam didn't dare peek his head up and around for fear of having it blown off. Damn it...did she actually know how to use that thing? Or was she just getting lucky? Was she missing the bear by accident...or hitting the ground on purpose?

The bear hesitated, eyeing its quarry. Both of them. A dark growl ripped from deep in Cam's chest as he took up his defensive position again, praying now that she wouldn't shoot him too. The bear must have decided the meal wasn't worth the effort. It wheeled around and lumbered back into the undergrowth, wailing his disappointment, disappearing from sight and smell.

Cam waited, just to be sure. His sides heaved as adrenaline coursed through him. His nostrils flared, but the bear's scent grew weaker by the moment. The bear's bulky crashing grew fainter. Slowly, Cam turned to face her. His great head first, then his massive body.

JJ was a sight to behold. She stood at the bottom of the stairs with a Springfield Armory XD Subcompact in her hand, her hair a wild tangle around her shoulders. Her eyes were wide, glittering blue. Her chest rose and fell in quick spurts.

When he didn't immediately move to attack, she tentatively lowered the muzzle to point at the ground. A good sign. Her finger remained on the trigger. Maybe not so good after all. Should he run away now? Should he go to her...or let her come to him?

Would she come to him?

The very idea excited him. Tilting his head to the side, he relaxed his stance and tried to make himself look as nonthreatening as possible. She didn't move, just stared at him, tense and expectant.

Desperation grew. The need to gain her acceptance—in this form—was overwhelming. Maybe, if she could see he wouldn't hurt her, then...

Then what?

He didn't want to consider the 'then what,' but he couldn't resist the urge to gain her trust either. But how? He could try approaching her, slowly...but the way she held that gun made him doubt the wisdom of that idea. Like as not, she'd put a bullet in his stupid ass for his efforts.

A thought occurred to him then, and he almost snorted aloud. He couldn't believe he'd even think about stooping this low, but she wasn't *moving*. He focused on the woods for a moment, and breathed a sigh of relief. Sending up a silent thanks no one else was around to see this, he plopped his ass on the ground, offering her as close to a harmless grin as he could muster, given the circumstances. He even let his tongue loll out the side of his mouth, heaven help him. She'd better come around soon. He didn't think his pride would suffer him to lift a paw. He wasn't some domesticated retriever, damn it.

No, he definitely drew the line at shaking on command.

An eternity seemed to pass before she finally expelled a long whoosh of breath and tucked the gun in the waistband of her jeans at the small of her back. Sexy. If he'd been capable at that moment, he'd have whistled like a pack of New York construction workers.

JJ took a hesitant step forward, then another, one hand outstretched. Her voice was quiet, the tremor barely detectable. "Come here, pretty boy," she crooned, clucking her tongue, crouching a little at the waist. "Come here, beautiful. I won't hurt you."

He did roll his eyes this time. Pretty boy? *Puh-leeze...*

139

Shifting to his feet, he loped forward, and she froze. Her eyes widened the closer he got.

"Okay, *big* pretty boy," she murmured, edging a cautious foot back half a step. She left her hand out for him, but her words betrayed her fear. "What say you don't hurt me either, huh?"

He really shouldn't do this. It was setting a bad example. But he couldn't seem to help himself. He nuzzled his cheek along her palm, nudging her hand until she scratched behind his ears. A shiver of pleasure rippled down his spine. Cautiously, she sank the fingers of first one hand, then the other into his coat. A long, slow smile broke over her face, one that was mirrored on his heart. Why couldn't she smile at him like that when he was in human form?

"Oh, you're a sweetheart," she breathed, going down on one knee before him. He smirked as this actually put his head above hers. Then her words robbed him of his dignity. "Are you tame? Huh, sweet thing? Do you have an owner? Where's your collar, baby?"

Despite her demeaning words, her gentle hands felt like sumptuous sin, smoothing over his neck and shoulders, down his sides. Her silky voice did funny things to his insides. *Temptation, thy name is JJ Frost.* If he were in human form, he'd have her naked and writhing beneath him faster than she could fire that sexy little gun of hers again.

The pull was too strong. Cam edged closer, careful not to frighten her. He pushed his face against her collarbone, snuggling his wet nose up the side of her neck, startling a giggle from her. She smelled so incredibly good, better than anything he'd ever scented in his life.

"Playful, aren't you?" She giggled again, pushing his head back when he slathered his tongue along her jaw. "You saved me from that bear, didn't you?

Didn't you, big boy? Are you hungry?"

If she only knew how much...

"The least I can do is offer you something to eat," she coaxed, rubbing his head.

Oh, yeah, that sounded good. He'd start with a thigh, and work his way to a breast...or two. Then he'd—

"I don't have any kibble...how about some hamburger?"

Kibble? Hamburger?

Oh, hell, no...

Shaking the fog of lust from his head, he backed up a step. Her hands fell to her sides, her expression so disappointed his heart ached. "Are you leaving me now? Will I see you again?"

He surged forward, knocking her off balance. She landed on her butt, gasping as she clutched at his fur for balance. He licked every inch of her face and neck, savoring her flavor, as she fell back, laughing. Then he froze. She was right where he'd wanted her...under him, and he couldn't do a damned thing about it. This was too much. He'd gone too far, and he was just torturing himself now.

With a low growl, he spun around, racing into the woods. Mile after mile flew by as he struggled to contain his baser instincts. Without warning, her scent caught him again. He'd circled back and hadn't realized it. Dropping to his haunches, he peered through the dense foliage at her as she climbed the back stairs and disappeared inside the house.

His gaze flickered to the kitchen window, and he watched as she moved around the room, storing food, wiping counters, filling the teakettle. She'd begun humming again, the gentle melody drifted to him from the small opening in the window. Once the teakettle whistled, she poured the steaming liquid into a large mug, dropped a tea bag in, and shut the light off.

A few moments later, a muted light in the next room blinked on. Curious, he crept around the side of the house, and plopped down in the shadows to observe her through the window. She snuggled into a rocker, tucking her feet beneath her. Pulling a blanket around her shoulders, JJ settled back in the chair, clicking the TV remote on. She wrapped both hands around her mug as the soft wash of color from the TV bathed her face.

He should go now. He didn't have any reason to linger, and yet he couldn't force himself leave. She'd shocked him earlier. He'd never expected her to go for a gun. Then again, he hadn't expected her to approach him once the bear left either. She was a walking contradiction...fearful of man, yet brave enough to lavish affection on a wild animal of disproportionate size.

A mate?

His mate?

Could it be true? If it was, just because he'd found his mate didn't mean he had to be weak, like Ed...but he still wasn't convinced. Not entirely.

He lay down on the cool grass, resting his head on his paws, and stared up at her through the window. Heaven help him, what he wouldn't give to be able to walk inside that house and lay his head on her lap, feel her fingers run through is hair again.

Chapter 11

The Apostle leaned an elbow on the counter, benignly watching the elderly lady hobble through the door, past the storefront and out of sight. Bells jingled against the glass, announcing her departure.

Ginny's cheerful voice called out to him from behind—and beneath—the counter. "What time does the school board meeting start?"

"Seven."

"Where do you find the time? I don't know how you can stand to sit in on all those meetings...the school board, city council, church council..." Ginny grunted as she hefted a large box to the checkout counter and brushed the back of her forearm across her brow. "Doesn't it get to you after a while?"

"Sometimes, I guess." He slid the box over as she plopped two rolls of blue paper shop towels beside the cash register. "But I just keep telling myself it's for the greater good."

"The greater good would be to put up some new damned equipment on the playground," she grumbled. "I dug a splinter the size of Noah's Ark out of Tanner's palm last week."

"I'm really sorry about that, Ginny." He shifted his weight from one elbow to the other, peering into her eyes. "We tried, but we just couldn't get enough votes."

"I know," she assured him, reaching out to pat his hand. Then she moved on to pull a plastic bag from beneath the counter. "You do what you can."

He nodded, holding one edge of the bag as she dropped his purchases inside. Ginny was a good

143

woman, a good mother. Her son was well behaved, and she conducted herself with dignity, as befitting a widow with a small child. It was sad she had no one to rely on now that her husband was gone. Todd had been a good man. His accident had been a real shame. Just as well not too many knew the truth of the situation though. The poor hunter who'd shot Todd swore up and down he'd thought he'd shot a huge wolf.

Closer to the mark than he'd realized.

He handed her his money and gathered the bag in one hand as he reached for the box.

"Oh, I almost forgot," he murmured, easing the corner of the box back onto the laminate countertop. "I need batteries, the eight-pack up there, please."

She snagged the package he indicated from a hook high on the wall behind her, and dropped them into the bag with a smile.

"How much do I owe you for them?" He made to juggle the box, but she waved him away.

"Don't worry about it, that box is heavy. You can take care of it the next time you come in."

"Thanks. Tell Tanner to keep practicing his curveball," he called over his shoulder. "That boy of yours is a natural, Ginny."

"He is, isn't he?" Her pride in her son was a joy to see. Too often, parents didn't appreciate what a blessing their children were. "Thanks for giving him the pointers, by the way. I haven't been able to pry that baseball you gave him from his hand till he falls asleep at night."

Grinning, he nodded and pushed the door open, maneuvering the box through the doorway. He wasn't exaggerating when he'd told Ginny that Tanner was a natural. That boy had an arm on him that would make someone important sit up some day and take notice. Children were such a wonder to him. So innocent. So pure. Unblemished by the sins of adulthood. They deserved to be protected, given every chance to grow and bloom.

Free of the sins of the father.

He glanced across the street to the Sheriff's Department as he crossed the sidewalk. Speaking of sins of the father... He'd done Cam a real favor with his last mission. Maybe now that Ed Whitlock was out of the picture, Cam would be able to focus on clearing the rest of the trash out of town. It was a real shame Ed hadn't lived up to anyone's expectations. Poor Cam had suffered so many years in silence. Well, he didn't have to suffer his shame any longer. God had seen fit to ease his burden.

A muffled cry, a muted slap, and an angry hiss jerked his gaze a short distance down the street. Angie Berg cuffed her teenage son on the side of his head, shoved him inside their family minivan. The boy's shamed gaze darted around, and he ducked his head, buckling his seatbelt.

The Apostle's brow creased as he pushed the box onto his passenger seat and closed the car door. He felt that slap himself. Remembered, all too well, what it was like to be humiliated, degraded in front of others. The memory of the belt, administered in private, tensed his back even now.

Squaring his shoulders, he stepped forward, calling out to Angie. He would stand up for the boy, as no one had cared enough to stand up for him.

It was his duty now.

"Angie, I think, perhaps, he might be better dealt with if you..."

"You don't have children, do you?"

"Ah," he paused, taken aback by her tone. "No, but—"

"Until you have children of your own, don't you dare stand there and take that holier-than-thou attitude with me. He's my goddamned kid and I'll discipline him how I see fit."

She spun away and climbed into the van, slamming the door behind her. The engine revved, the tires squealed as she backed out of the parking stall. He watched her taillights with narrowed eyes until she rounded the corner a few blocks away.

And so says the Book of Psalms, 'They repay my kindness with evil, and my friendship with hatred'.

Children were to be protected, cherished.

The Apostle turned away, but he would not forget. God had spoken.

****

Cam stepped through the gym's doublewide doorway, reaching for the mike clipped to his shoulder of his uniform. "Emma, the board meeting ended late. I'm stopping off for supper at Maggie's."

The scratchy reply chirped, "Sure thing, boss."

Before long, Cam found himself seated at the horseshoe counter at Maggie's, a pile of roast beef, mashed potatoes, and homemade bread in front of him, Jim on his right, and the quiet, aging veterinarian, Doc Templeton, on his left.

"You ought to stop down Saturday for the little league game, Cam. The kids would get a kick out of having the sheriff showin' an interest in them." Jim shoveled in a gravy-laden spoonful of potatoes, and nudged him with an elbow. "Better still, I have an assistant position open. Best way to pick up votes come the next election. Schmooze some parents."

Ignoring the barb, Cam scraped up a healthy bite of roast. "I have enough on my plate right now. Maybe next season..."

Unfazed, Jim swung his focus to Brandi. She topped his coffee off with a tolerant, if immune smile, and turned her attention to Cam's cup as Jim lined her up in his sights. "That's all right, Cam. You ain't pretty enough to be my assistant. Now, young Brandi here...she'd be just perfect." His smile was a mile wide, and as lecherous as the day was long.

"I don't know the first thing about baseball, Jim," she hedged, slipping the coffee pot back onto the burner. "You'd be better off talking to Dr. English, or Red, for that matter. Good heavens, you'd have better luck with Noah Simpson or Mike Becker...that is if you could catch 'em when Noah wasn't chasin' a girl, and Mike wasn't chasin' a dollar."

"Oh, now, sweetheart," Jim coaxed, wiggling an eyebrow. "I could teach you everything you need to know...and then some."

"Ease off, Jim. I'd hate to have to haul you in for harassing Brandi."

"Aw, Cam," Jim grumbled. "You wouldn't be such a tight ass if you had a pretty little thing to snuggle up with at night."

Cam lifted another bite of Maggie's mouthwatering roast to his mouth, chewing it with unnecessary precision. He grimaced as it began to take on the unappealing flavor of sawdust.

Maggie chose that moment to make an appearance, catching the tail end of Jim's ill-advised comment. "He's got a point, ya know."

Oh, hell. Here we go...again. He should've picked up a pizza and headed back to his office. Then maybe he could have enjoyed his meal. Behind locked doors. With Emma as his watchdog.

Maggie wasn't happy unless she was motherin' somebody. Unfortunately, her idea of motherin' entailed marrying off every eligible bachelor stupid enough to stumble into the wrong end of her hunting scope to any unsuspecting female she could toss in his path.

"Speaking of pretty young things," Brandi chimed in a moment later, joining Maggie's Matchmakers-R-Us club, "That new artist that just moved to town wouldn't exactly be taking home second place at any beauty contest, if you catch my drift."

"Brandi—"

"Now, Cam, don't go gettin' your boxers all in a twist," Maggie cut in. "A man your age ought to be thinkin' about settlin' down. You ain't getting' any younger, ya know, and I'd say you about got to be scrapin' the bottom of that pail of wild oats, boy."

Eyes tearing, Cam sputtered into his coffee. Jim obligingly pounded on his back as Brandi and several others around the diner chortled with glee.

"A man my age..." he wheezed. "I'm only thirty-one, Maggie. For the love of—"

"My point exactly." She took a rag from Brandi and slapped it on the counter, scrubbing the shine off the laminate with work-reddened hands. "Wait much longer, and you might as well head on out to pasture. You get set in your rut much more, ain't no woman in her right mind gonna wanna hook up with the likes of you."

Once again, he sputtered. If she kept this up, he'd be squirtin' coffee from his nose like some damned circus performer.

Oblivious...or, more likely, uncaring...she pressed on. "Now that little JJ, she's a fine piece. Just missed her as a matter of fact. She was in here not too long ago with Ginny and her boy. Only been in here a few times, but I can tell," Maggie shot him a wink, flicking the end of the towel in his direction, "that girl's got spunk...and she's beautiful as those paintings of hers, too. Heard June's gonna ask her to donate a piece or two for the charity auction next month. Big name like hers ought to draw some money." She eyed him for a shrewd moment, then murmured slyly, "Won't be long before certain other males I know start beatin' a path to her door."

Males...not just *men*.

Point taken. A wild rush of jealous possessiveness surged through him at the very thought. Then he snapped a perceptive gaze over his shoulder, toward the hardware store. As far as anyone else knew, he'd only been to see JJ on official business. He'd hardly even batted an eyelash in her direction. Now here Maggie was, next thing to dragging them off to the altar. Purposefully provoking his relentless instincts...tossing an unsuspecting JJ out there like a virgin sacrifice.

What would JJ say if she knew half the town was trying to feed her to the wolves...literally?

He chewed his next bite in silence, well aware of the speculative looks the other patrons were shooting him. It irritated him to admit it, but Maggie had made a good point...several actually. It *was* high time he settled down. He could be content going on the way things were, but content didn't mean happy. And, if he were being honest, JJ called to him on an elemental, pagan level. Everything about her drew him in. By the acceleration in her heartbeat whenever he got close and the increase in her pheromones, he knew she wasn't adverse to him either.

As long as he was being honest, he might as well admit he suspected she might very well be his mate. He couldn't seem to stay away from her. The way he'd been behaving...the jealous possessiveness, the nearly uncontrollable animalistic attraction ...certainly pointed in that direction.

Like a flashing, neon sign in Vegas.

Why was he fighting this so hard? He'd been resisting the very cornerstone of his nature. Squaring his shoulders, he pushed to his feet, tossed a fold of cash on the counter beside his plate, and stalked to the door without another word to any of them. He was a man on a mission.

It was high time he tracked his female down and set matters straight.

Chapter 12

JJ tugged her jacket off, juggling her keys as she flipped lights on, chasing darkness away from the hallway first, then the parlor. Humming, she dropped the jacket on the back of the rocker and bent to remove her boots.

The air had taken on a distinctive chill tonight. She hadn't worried about it when she'd left this afternoon, but the bite of it nipped at her now. She didn't waste any time before plugging in the small space heater she'd purchased from Ginny yesterday. As many times as she'd been to Ginny's store this last few days alone, she may as well have gotten a job there. Maybe she'd be able to get an employee discount.

Her quick trip into the store today had lengthened into several hours. She'd only intended to stop for mulch, but she'd ended up going to Maggie's for an early supper with Ginny and Tanner. Tanner was a pure delight. As they'd strolled the short distance to the diner and settled into a booth, he'd regaled JJ with a play-by-play accounting of his little league game earlier in the week. With a seven-year-old's vivid attention to detail, his freckled face glowing, he'd told her of the umpire with hair sprouting from his nose, who'd popped not one but two buttons from his uniform as he bent to declare Andy Gifford safe.

At the diner, they'd drawn quite the crowd, and, for the most part, she hadn't minded a bit...again, another oddity for her. Brandi had been as friendly and as efficient as ever. Maggie had even come out of the kitchen for a warm hello. Jim from the Post Office had been there. He was nice enough...maybe a little *too* nice. Did the man have a clue how thick he was laying it on? Really, that much testosterone in one man ought to be illegal. At the very least, it should come with a warning label. Caution...testosterone known to cause brain damage, retreat with all due haste.

Then one of the local preachers, one Reverend Mathias, had come round to introduce himself and offer her a personal invitation to join his congregation. At first, she'd given it serious consideration, but then he'd creeped her out a bit when he'd climbed up on his proverbial soap box and started spouting an impromptu sermon on temptations of the flesh and sins of the father...whatever *that* had been about.

She'd also met a few other, less-offensive fellow diners. Jarvis English, the town's only doctor and Fulwick County's Medical Examiner, made her acquaintance. He was very gracious, possessed a wicked sense of humor, and was very handsome. The other had been Doug Weston, a shy and unassuming insurance agent and member of the city council. He'd turned ten shades of red when she'd smiled at him and held her hand out for him to shake. It had been kind of...well, kind of cute.

JJ made her way down the hallway, back toward the kitchen, humming a new, upbeat melody she'd caught over the radio on the way home. A nice, steaming mug of tea, or maybe hot chocolate would be the perfect way to end the night. She snagged the teakettle, thrust it beneath the tap, and hissed a ripe curse as water sprayed from a loose fitting on the faucet handle.

Holy crap. Couldn't she have one day...just one...without these nasty little surprises. Well, she'd probably asked for it buying the house like she had.

Things like this were an annoyance, but she didn't regret them.

She might curse them...but, a tiny part of her, also reveled in them.

Right now, that reveling part of her was tiny indeed.

One hand thrust forward in a defensive maneuver, cupping the spray to minimize saturation. The other fumbled, jerking a drawer open, yanking out a stack of hand towels. Piling them on top of the faucet, thereby containing the shower of water, she stepped back, using a spare towel to mop at her drenched face and dripping hair, blotting at her shirt.

Brilliant.

She had to shut the water off. Oh, Lord, let there be a shut-off valve up here. She hadn't been into the basement more than once, and she sure as certain didn't want to have to go down there right now. In the dark. Alone. The very thought sent a chill rippling through her.

Getting down on her knees, she tugged the cabinet doors beneath the sink open. Cursing softly beneath her breath, she leaned to the side and dug in another drawer. There it was. The flashlight she'd found when she'd went to search for her gun...in the bright light of day, of course. Thank heavens she'd found both. Clicking the flashlight on, she aimed the bright beam into the dark corners beneath the sink and then thrust her head into the opening. Thank you, Lord...shut-off valves.

She propped the flashlight on a can of Comet, stretching her arm into the opening until her fingers grasped the valve. It wouldn't budge. Gritting her teeth, she used two hands and twisted with all her might.

Her hands slipped off the valve at the exact same moment the doorbell emitted its sickly wail.

Already off balance, JJ jumped, slamming her forehead against the edge of the cabinet. A sharp stab of pain lanced its way across her scalp. Sucking in a sharp breath between clenched teeth, she rocked back on her knees, her palm pressed to her forehead, and the goose egg forming there. The leaking faucet no longer held her attention. The doorbell faded into nothing.

She fumbled the vase in palms damp with sweat and blood, her mind screaming desperate prayers. The white crockery stayed in her hands, its blue, hand-painted flowers and vines remained intact, while a ragged whisper of relieved breath slipped past her bloodied lips. Vision was becoming more difficult as the swelling around her right eye increased. The fear coursing through her veins kept the pain in her face and body manageable...for now. Water sloshed onto the shiny floor, and the lush spray of yellow tulips—Sarah's favorites—spilled from the delicate vase. JJ's fearful gaze swerved to the stairs behind her. Her heart lodged in the back of her throat.

The sounds of movement on the landing below arrested. The harsh echo of his breath in the darkness ceased.

She caught her own breath, biting down hard on her swollen, split lip. Dead silence fell over the house. Only the incessant ticking of the grandfather clock in the foyer echoed through the unnatural stillness. Then the bottom step creaked. Slow and easy. Assured.

Oh, no. No, no, no. Not yet. Please not yet...

"JJ?" A familiar deep voice broke into her awareness. A large, warm hand cupped the back of her shoulder with immeasurable gentleness. "JJ, are you all right?"

A terrified shriek tore from her throat, and she jerked away, scuttling back toward the stove on heels and wobbly arms.

"Whoa!" He backed up a step, holding both hands up, palms out. "It's all right. I'm sorry. I didn't mean to frighten you. Your door was open, and the light was on, but you didn't answer the doorbell. I was worried..."

Dropping her butt to the floor, she pressed the heel of her palm to her heaving chest, struggling to subdue her racing heart and slow her bursting lungs. Gasping, she clapped the other hand over her mouth.

Pull it together, JJ. You're making a fool of yourself.

Using the stove for leverage, she dragged herself to her feet. The sheriff moved to help her, but she thrust a warning palm at him, cautioning him to keep his distance. "I'm sorry. I didn't...I, I'm sorry. You startled me...I didn't hear you come in."

Of course. It had to be *him*. The sexier-than-should-be-legal sheriff of Bossyville. His bright-eyed, emerald gaze swept over her, making her uncomfortably aware that she looked like a bedraggled participant in a wet T-shirt contest. Glancing down at herself, she grimaced. The waves of heat from the space heater hadn't yet reached the kitchen...and it showed. Crossing her arms over her chest, heat climbing her neck to fill her cheeks, she stared him down, brazening it out.

She wouldn't even let herself think about the fact that he'd seen her scars...at least, some of them.

The muscle in his jaw leaped to life beneath the dark shadow of whisker stubble as he dragged his smoldering gaze up to her face. Burning every inch of her on the way. Then she got the full impact of him. She caught her breath, scars and embarrassment completely forgotten. She'd thought he'd looked good enough to eat that first morning in the diner in stained jeans and dusty T-shirt. When he'd come to see about the broken lock on her shed, in clean jeans and T-shirt, he'd been a girl's dream.

Tonight—in uniform—he was walking carnal sin.

And the look in his eyes...

Despite her recent fright, she couldn't suppress the shiver of awareness. His smoldering stare was intoxicating.

"Are you all right?" He lowered his hands, taking a cautious step forward. "You're still as white as a sheet. What happened?"

Dragging in a deep breath, she recalled the reason she'd been under the sink in the first place. Refused to think about the flashback at all. She could almost hear Dr. Greene's voice droning in the back of her head. *"This is a classic symptom of denial, Jillian."*

Only Dr. Greene and Gloria ever called her Jillian. It drove her crazy. Then again, now that she thought about it, perhaps it was more their tone than the actual name itself that bothered her.

"I'm fine. The faucet's not. It's spraying water everywhere. There's a shut-off valve under the sink," she muttered, forcing her legs to move. "But I can't quite get it to—"

He'd taken another step closer, bending at the same time to look beneath the sink as well. Her forehead thumped his. He straightened, strong arms shooting out to steady her. JJ rocked back, cupping her throbbing head, groaning. The man had a head like a chunk of granite.

"Are you all right?"

"I will be...as soon as Tweety finishes his song and dance around my head."

"Here, sit down," he insisted guiding her to a chair. "Let me see." His hands captured hers, pushing them away from her injury. His brow wrinkled as he examined her head. "That's a nasty

155

bump."

He didn't wait for confirmation, didn't bother to ask her preference. He moved away, a blur of motion, and she closed her eyes to keep the room from tilting. A moment later, after much painful clatter, he was back, pressing something very cold and very hard to her head. She leaned away, hissing her displeasure, but the compress followed.

"Here, now," he murmured, cupping the back of her neck in his free hand, holding her steady. Her eyes popped open as he dropped to his knees before her. A worried frown creased his brow. Instinctively, she parted her knees so he could lean closer as he held the compress in place.

He was so close now she couldn't miss the baby-fine scar at the edge of his left eyebrow, or the way his jewel-green eyes glittered with concern. His skin was sun-kissed. What would the stubble on his jaw feel like if it rasped against her collarbone? His shoulders and chest were so broad they filled her vision completely. His hands on her were gentle, yet unrelenting, his fingers soothing tiny circles on the nape of her neck. His scent...woodsy, crisp, and oh-so-masculine...surrounded her. The warmth radiating from him tempted her to press closer, to ease the ache in her breasts.

His lips were smooth and sensual, parted slightly with the lingering freshness of double-mint gum. They pulled her like a magnet. She moistened her suddenly dry lips, squirming uncomfortably on her seat, and his hips slipped farther into the cradle of her thighs.

He went utterly still. Chest frozen, fingers motionless, no breath escaping his lips. She tore her gaze reluctantly from his mouth, locking onto his eyes. He looked stunned, sucker-punched. His eyes dilated right before her startled gaze, black all but engulfing emerald.

That same, mesmerizing stare he'd leveled her with zeroed in on her mouth now, completely devastating in its intensity. A long shuddering breath escaped him. The fingers cupping her neck tightened. Not enough to hurt her, but strong enough that she knew there would be no escape unless he wished it.

Letting her go looked to be the last thing on his mind.

He was going to kiss her. He was going to kiss her...and she *wanted* him to, wanted it more than her next breath. Oh no, oh no, oh no...

She panicked, rearing away from him until her back slammed against the chair. Spell broken, he recoiled, thrusting the compress into her hands. Muttering to himself, he moved back to the open cabinet, squatted down, and reached beneath the sink. In less time than it took her to recover her equilibrium and regain her feet, he had the valves twisted off and the faucet in pieces on the counter. Wiping his hands on a discarded towel, he swiveled to face her.

"You won't be able to use the sink till the faucet is replaced, the insides are rusted clean through, and the fittings are cracked." She wobbled on her feet, still floored by her unexpected longing, but before she could thank him for the assistance with the valve, he steamrolled ahead. "I'm pullin' the night shift tonight, but I'll stop off at the hardware store and pick up a new faucet in the morning. I'll be over first thing."

She was still sputtering when he tossed the towel aside and caught her head between his large palms. Tilting her head toward the light, he examined her injury. "You didn't break the skin, but that's a pretty good sized goose egg. You need to be more careful. Don't take on projects you don't know how to handle, you could seriously hurt yourself."

"Look, Sheriff—"

"*Cam.*"

Irritated now, she batted his hands away, backing up a step. Of all the nerve. How dare he come barreling in here, as if *he* owned the place, tear apart *her* faucet, and then chastise her as if she were some child in need of guidance. So what if he'd been helpful with the valve, solicitous with the compress. He was overbearing and conceited and...

"*Cam*, what are you doing here?"

"Ah..." He stepped away from her, clearing his throat. "I, ah... I figured I should check back...see if you found anything else missing, or if you'd had any more trouble."

Her mind circled back to the bear...and the wolf. "No...no trouble, except..."

Frowning, he stepped closer. "Except what?"

She hesitated a moment, chewing the inside of her cheek. She didn't want to put the wolf in danger—now she realized that's what it was—after all, it had saved her. At first, given its tameness, she'd assumed it was just a dog, a very, *very* large dog. Like a hybrid mix roughly the size of a mastiff...or a Shetland pony. But the face and size had finally clued her in. She'd researched it on the internet, and had been shocked to realize she'd not only come face-to-face with a black bear, but she'd also wrestled on the ground—and been licked on the face and neck—by a full grown, wild wolf...a natural born predator.

What a glorious creature he'd been, with a luxuriant, golden coat and eyes like... She stared into Cam's eyes, blinked, and peered closer. It had to have been a trick of the light that night, because she could have sworn the wolf's eyes had been this exact shade of green. But that was impossible, wasn't it? Wolves' eyes were usually brown...or in a few exceptions blue. Never had she heard of a green-eyed wolf. But, then again, anything was possible.

"Except what?" he pressed.

"Nothing."

For a moment, he looked as if he might argue. Instead, he caught her by surprise, reaching out to feather his fingers through the hair at her temple. "I don't like the looks of that bump. You might have a concussion. I better take you in to see Jarvis."

"Don't be ridiculous...I'm fine." She batted his hand away again, then spun on her heel and marched down the hallway to the parlor.

He dogged her footsteps. "I'd still feel better if he took a look at that."

"The clinic wouldn't be open at this time of night, and I'm *not* going to a hospital." Glaring over her shoulder at him, she stalked to the space heater, shivering a little as the welcome waves of heat caressed her chilled skin.

Undaunted, he extracted a cell phone from his pocket and flipped it open. "You won't have to go anywhere. He'll come here."

"No," she gasped, leaping toward him, grabbing his wrist. His skin was a furnace beneath her icy fingers. Again, she battled the urge to shiver and curl herself around him. "Oh, no you don't. You just put that away. I'm not hurt...it's just a little bump. Thank you very much for your help, Cam, but you don't need to come back tomorrow. I am fully capable of fixing the faucet on my own. Now, I don't want to detain you any longer. You must have all sorts of official police business to attend to."

She all but shoved him toward the door. A loud pop overhead jerked her to a halt, and the parlor went dark. Pale golden light filtered in through the hall doorway, but her eyes took a moment to adjust to the alteration in lighting.

"Oh, for heaven's sake, what next?"

Sighing loudly, he pushed past her and stepped

back inside the parlor. "I'll fix this before I go. Where are your spare light bulbs?"

Cursing beneath her breath, she stomped back down the hall to retrieve a light bulb from the pantry off the kitchen. Light bulb in hand, she hurried back, a small, three-step ladder tucked beneath her arm. He held his hand out to her, but she elbowed past him. Scowling, she stood directly beneath the fixture.

"I can change a damned light bulb myself," she snapped, slamming the ladder open and thumping it onto the hardwood floor.

JJ clambered up to the second step and stretched, but her fingers were several inches shy of her target. Mumbling beneath her breath, she climbed up on the final step, went up on tiptoes.

"I bet you used to cheer for Yosemite Sam when you were a kid, right?" His wry remark rubbed her the wrong way.

"Better him than Elmer Fudd..." She whipped her head around to glare him into silence, but the precariousness of her balance didn't allow room for the movement. Her eyes widened, and she had time for one sharp gasp before she tumbled from the ladder.

Straight into his waiting arms.

Cam grinned at her, cradling her against his chest. His eyes twinkled with mischief. He was smug, and so damned sexy she couldn't catch her breath. In the blink of an eye, his gaze turned sultry, and his heady stare locked on her lips. Suddenly she didn't care that she couldn't breathe anymore. The arm cradling her back was unforgiving, turning her, pressing her closer to his heat while the arm beneath her knees slipped free, sliding around her waist. Trapping her.

She already had one arm hooked around his neck. She lifted the other to lay her hand flat against his chest in warning. His heart hammered an aroused cadence against her palm. She couldn't tear her gaze from his. She couldn't *see* anything but him.

She didn't *want* to see anything but him. Not anymore.

Not ever again.

His stare branded her for a moment that seemed an eternity before he dipped his head, his lips swooping down to seize hers. His tongue swept past her lips, plunging and ravaging until her head swam. His large hands splayed against her body, searing her with their heat, filling her with the need to feel them running over her naked skin. He pressed her close, and closer still, until she couldn't tell where she ended and he began. The thick bulge pushing insistently against her hip was unmistakable. Deep in the core of her, desire pooled, thick and molten.

As if sensing her acceptance, he tilted his head, changing the angle of the kiss, deepening it, slanting his mouth over hers. In reply to her unspoken need, his hands began to roam, one to cup and massage the side of her breast, the other to slide lower, until he grasped and squeezed her bottom. She moaned, deep in the back of her throat, opening for him like a greedy flower soaking up rays of sunshine.

She'd been kissed before. She'd been with a man, *before*. But never had anyone *ever* held her, or kissed her with such systematic ferocity. His kiss was like a drug, went straight to her head and incinerated her inhibitions.

Until something vibrated against her belly. Jerking back, startled, she broke the kiss and struggled to put space between them. He swore softly, anchoring her against him with one arm as he reached between them to tilt the pager attached to his belt.

Closing his eyes, he dragged in a deep breath

through flared nostrils. When his eyes snapped open, they seemed...sharper, the green more brilliant, if that were possible. The lines of his face were harsh with his desire, his frown unambiguous. He wasn't happy the pager had interrupted.

His stormy gaze lowered to her lips, locked. His voice was harsh. "I have to go."

Was he trying to convince her...or himself? But still he stood. Holding her. Staring at her lips.

The pager vibrated again, just as his head began to lower toward hers once more. "I have to go," he repeated, softly this time.

Definitely to himself.

Nevertheless, his supple lips skimmed along hers as his hand slipped around her nape, fingers lacing into her hair, cupping her skull with an unexpected gentleness. He tilted her head back, and she was powerless to resist the inescapable heat, the unexpected tenderness in his gaze. Then his eyes closed as he claimed her mouth once more. Her own eyelids sagged closed, until touch and taste and smell became the ruling senses. Until her world revolved around Cam. This kiss was as lavish and thorough, as sweet, as the last had been consuming and greedy.

The cell phone in his pocket rang now, and he broke the kiss with a reluctant groan. He waited until she dragged her eyelids open once more, and offered her a lopsided smile, dropping a soft kiss to the tip of her nose before releasing her.

Staring at him, wide-eyed and open-mouthed, she wobbled backwards on legs that would no longer function properly. The back of her knees bumped into something solid, and she dropped like dead weight to the loveseat. Grinning ear to ear, he filched the light bulb from her numb fingers, bound up the steps, and swapped the old bulb for the new. Hopping from the ladder, he dropped the old light bulb onto the table at her side. Grinning, he bent down and stole one last fleeting kiss.

"I'll see you in the morning, honey." No words had ever sounded so portentous...or more ominous to her.

In a flash he was gone, and yet she continued to sit, exactly where he'd left her, fingering her lips. Bemused.

****

Duty called. *Damn it all to hell.*

Cam stopped on the porch, resting his palm against the splintered paint on her front door. His body was on fire for her. His heart raged inside his chest. Another few minutes, and he'd have claimed her...just as he had in his dreams every night since the morning he'd seen her in the diner.

The pager vibrated on his hip again, as did his cell. Before he changed his mind and said the hell with duty, Cam leaped down the front steps and sprinted across the lawn toward his truck. There was no doubt in his mind now. No doubt whatsoever. She *was* his female. She just didn't know it yet.

But now *he* did.

And it changed everything.

He'd learned something else tonight. Imprinting was real. And, now that he'd experienced it firsthand, he'd determined imprinting wasn't a strong enough word.

Branding might be a more appropriate term.

JJ Frost had seared herself upon his soul.

Chapter 13

The next morning, as the sun spilled its gentle rays over Sutter Hollow, burning away the mountain mists, Cam angled his truck down 123 Shady Lane, thumping his thumbs against the steering wheel in time to Matt Nathanson's *"Come On, Get Higher."* After his shift, he'd stopped off at home long enough to grab a quick shower, then he'd beat feet to get her faucet and get back here before she got a wild hair to take off and go somewhere for the day. Now that he'd made up his mind she belonged to him, he wasn't going to give her the chance to run or hide.

Every time he got close to her, she turned skittish as a colt. He'd seen the surprise, the stunned disbelief in her eyes after they'd kissed. The memory of her response sent euphoria coursing through his veins. She'd felt it too.

Cam hadn't been able to stop thinking about her all night. He'd finally faced the facts, and not even the latest in a long string of vandalisms had dampened his mood. He'd found his mate. And, just as important, she was not indifferent to him. He'd hang around until she got used to him. He'd make himself indispensable to her. He'd woo her. He'd seduce her if need be, and she'd fall in love with him.

She had to.

Cam couldn't live as Ed had...imprinted on a woman who didn't return his feelings. He refused to even consider that horrifying possibility.

Once she'd fallen in love with him, once he was sure she could handle his secret, then he'd tell her about the pack. He'd tell her everything.

Once he was sure she wouldn't leave him because of that secret.

At least that was the plan.

One corner of his mouth hitched up in a self-satisfied grin. JJ's new faucet lay in a white plastic bag on the seat beside him. Cam eased the truck up her drive, drew the key from the ignition, and gathered up the bag before hopping out of his truck. Reaching into the back of his truck bed, he snagged the handle of a small red toolbox and lifted the dented metal case out. He whistled the closing bars of the song he'd been listening to on the radio as he took the steps two at a time, swinging the toolbox at his side. The aged boards creaked beneath his feet, giving a little with every application of weight.

Stepping to the side of the doorway, he bounced a little on a particularly splintered board and grimaced. He'd have to replace that board before his female hurt herself on it. He considered the rest of the porch and sighed, shrugging. Screw the board. He'd replace the whole damned thing. No sense taking chances.

Stepping back to the door, he jabbed a finger at the antiquated doorbell, hissed as a jolt of faulty electricity shot from his fingertip to his shoulder. He added replacing the doorbell to his list and rapped his knuckles on the door before stepping back to wait.

And wait.

Flicking a glance to his wristwatch, he frowned at the door. It wasn't quite eight yet, but he'd assumed by now she'd be out of bed. Her vehicle was still here. Had she gone for a walk? No, she was probably working on something. The nasty bump on her head flashed through his mind.

What if she'd hurt herself again?

What if she'd cut herself and was laying there, bleeding? What if she'd electrocuted herself, this place had to be a nightmare of outdated wiring. What if...

Without stopping to think, he rattled the doorknob, pounding his fist on the aged wood, shouting, "JJ! JJ, are you in there? JJ, can you hear me? JJ!"

The snick of a rusty lock disengaging finally caught his attention. He withdrew his fist seconds before smacking it against her forehead. Good Lord, what had gotten into him? He'd never overreacted like that before.

Cam got a good look at her, and his breath deserted him in a startled, lust-filled whoosh.

JJ braced herself against the doorframe, glaring up at him through sleepy eyes. A hearty yawn ruined her glower. Her long golden tresses were a tousled mess, all but standing straight on end. Her skin was a soft, fresh-from-bed pink. His hungry gaze skimmed down over her spaghetti-strapped, faded tank and her threadbare boxers. Her nipples puckered against the thin material in the chilly morning air, teasing him, reminding him of how they'd looked last night beneath her wet t-shirt.

His hand itched to touch.

Her legs were long and slim, toned. Her dainty feet were bare but for the pink polish on her toenails. It was more than apparent she'd literally just rolled from bed...and he wanted nothing more than to roll her right back in.

"What?" She frowned, irritably grinding a palm against her eye. Her voice was husky, rippling through his system like aged whiskey, smoky and sensual...with enough bite to knock a man on his ass if he wasn't careful. "What do you want?"

Another yawn broke free.

Oh, he could answer that last question in so many ways...most of which would probably get him slapped, given how testy she looked just then. "Do you always wake up grumpy?"

"Usually," she snapped.

He grinned down at her, lifting a suggestive brow. "Maybe you just don't wake up to the right...incentive."

"Doubtful," she growled, shoving petulantly at her tangled hair.

She was more tempting than one of Maggie's steaming caramel rolls, fresh from the oven, paired up with a supersized mug of black coffee strong enough to chew the end off a spoon. Waking up to her every morning would be more than enough incentive to put a smile on *his* face.

His grin stretched wide. "Wanna bet?"

Before she could respond, he stepped closer and brushed his lips over hers. Leaping back, blinking in groggy surprise, she banged against the door, providing him with the opening he'd been waiting for. Slipping past her, he sauntered down the hall.

"You should close the door," he advised over his shoulder. "You're going to catch a chill standing there like that...then I *will* call Jarvis."

The door slammed behind him hard enough to rattle the pictures on the walls. He chuckled.

"What do you think you're doing?" She staggered down the hallway after him, rebounding off the kitchen doorframe. Thrusting out a hand, she steadied herself against the peeling wallpaper, demanding, "I didn't invite you in."

"So call the cops." Smirking at her over his shoulder, he set his toolbox on the floor, the bag on the counter.

She sputtered at that for a moment, muttered beneath her breath, and ground her palm against her eye. Then she tossed her hands in the air with a disgusted growl, and stumbled toward the coffeepot. It took her two, blurry-eyed jabs before her finger connected with the right button, and then she yawned again—lustily—as she leaned a hip against the counter, crossed her arms over her chest, and glowered at the coffeemaker. He wanted to laugh. He wanted to sweep her off her feet and swirl her around the room. He wanted to kiss her senseless, and carry her back to her bed. She was adorable when she was disgruntled.

"You really aren't a morning person, are you?" Warm humor drenched his observation.

"What was your first clue, lawman?"

Touchy, touchy.

"Here's an idea," he offered peaceably. "You take a mug of coffee on upstairs, take a nice hot shower and wake up a bit, then come on back down and we'll start over. I'll have this faucet changed out by then." He gave her hair a long, considering stare, imagining it wet and lathered and clinging to her delectable curves. His palms began to burn, and he cleared his throat, forcing his thoughts to safer routes. "I'll probably have your doorbell torn apart by then, too, and I'll have a better idea what to pick up at Ginny's later to fix it."

She glared at him for a long moment, as if trying to assemble the right words to tell him exactly what he could do with his suggestion. In the end, she grunted, poured herself an enormous cup of coffee, and proceeded to dump enough sugar and creamer into it to send a diabetic straight into a coma. Just as she had that first morning in the dinner.

Without another word to him, she picked up the mug and took a long sip, eyes closed in bliss. The look on her face in that moment did funny things to his insides. *He'd* like to put that look on her face.

A moment later, after heaving a resigned sigh, she staggered from the room, holding the steaming cup well away from her body in cautious hands without so much as a backward glance.

It was probably a good thing she didn't turn

around. He was doing enough *glancing* at her *backward* to get himself a black eye if she caught him at it. The song he'd been listening to on his way over surfaced as he watched her walk away, and he caught himself humming the melody. He scrubbed his fingers down the sandpaper edge of his jaw. The swing of her hips had him thinking about a hell of a lot more than faith and desire.

Well...mostly.

Grinning to himself, he poured a cup of coffee— straight up black like he preferred, snickering to himself over her addiction to sugar—and took a long draw of the bitter brew before setting it aside as he reached for the new faucet. Before long, the ancient pipes nestled in the walls began to rattle and hum. He gritted his teeth as torturous images began to swamp his mind to the point he could barely focus on the project at hand. He'd just had to suggest a shower, hadn't he? She was up there right now, naked, with water and soap bubbles sliding over her luscious little body.

Lord, have mercy. He'd be lucky if he wasn't on his knees, begging, by the time she came back downstairs.

Or worse...

****

Refreshed, feeling human again, she stepped back inside the kitchen as Cam lifted the lever and stared at the flawless stream of water. Her alert gaze drifted over him, catching details her sleep-numbed brain had missed earlier. Details...such as how his muscles rippled and bunched with natural ease, sinuous and defined, every time he moved. Details like how his faded jeans hugged him in all the right places, setting wild flutters loose in the pit of her stomach. Apparently satisfied with his handy work, Cam nodded, pushed the lever back down before reaching for a hand towel. Glancing up, he

aimed a sexy, come-and-get-me grin in her direction.
Whaa...

Working hard not to stutter, she stepped into
the room and quipped, "So, Mister Plumber, what do
I owe you for the faucet?"

He appeared to roll the matter of payment
around in his head for a moment, his oh-so-
expressive eyes twinkling diabolically, as if debating
how far he could push her before she slapped him
down. After a long moment, the tiny grooves in his
cheeks deepened, and he conceded, "I'd settle for
breakfast."

For a split second, a little devil rode her
shoulder. She considered asking him what his first
choice was, but she changed her mind. The
expression on his face was far from innocent.
Besides, she wasn't sure she really needed to know
all that badly anyway.

"I can do breakfast. Do you have a preference?"

He blinked and froze, all but for his glittering
eyes. They roved down the length of her body, slow
and methodical, incinerating her where she stood.

Eyes widening, she cleared her throat and
scurried toward the refrigerator. "I, I ah...I have,"
she cleared her throat again, "bacon and eggs...and
pancake mix." *God, could she sound more breathless,
more desperate?* JJ opened the door, ducking her
head inside, praying the chilled wash of air would
cool the burning in her cheeks. "Or would you rather
have—"

An irresistible wave of heat pressed against her
backside. Her throat closed, tight. Cam's warm
breath feathered over her cheek as he curled himself
over her, the rough skin on his jaw caressed her ear
as his hands settled on her hips, tucking her tighter
against him. "Fix whatever you like, honey. I'm sure
I'll like it just fine." He nuzzled her neck then, his
lips grazed her skin, and then he moved away,

leaving her staring blindly at nothing in particular.

With a little shiver, she pulled herself together and thrust a shaking hand into the fridge, latching onto the carton of eggs. Never before had cooking been such a chore for her. It took all her concentration to crack the eggs without breaking the yolks, to flip the pancakes without sticking them to the ceiling, or to fry the bacon without setting off the smoke detector.

JJ scooped four eggs from the skillet, sliding them onto the plate in front of him, before she plopped two onto her own plate. They spent several moments passing syrup and butter, salt and pepper, the process both awkward and yet oddly domestic as they settled in to share the meal and a quiet bit of conversation. Surprised at how natural being with him like this felt, JJ leaned back against her chair and watched him chase syrup around his plate with a forkful of eggs and pancakes. There was something to be said for a man with an appetite like that...and a body like his.

Oh, mama...

Later, as Cam handed JJ the last dried dish to put away, his thoughtful eyes scanned the room around them. "You know, for being such an acclaimed member of the flighty, artistic society, the house looks pretty good."

Flighty? Slanting him an irritated frown, she slammed the cabinet door with slightly more force than necessary. Now why did he have to go and ruin a perfectly nice morning? "Was that supposed to be a compliment?" One fist found its way to her hip. "'Cuz if it was, you'd better practice some more."

The last word had no more than cleared her lips, when the door she'd slammed snapped free of its hinges. Cam's arm shot out, lightning quick, and caught the panel of wood before it cracked her on the top of the head. He'd moved forward in the process, until her nose brushed the bare skin at the v of his white cotton T-shirt. Startled, she gasped. Her wide-eyed gaze shot up to his. Slowly, he tilted his head down, angling it slightly to the side. His eyes were heavy-lidded, captivating. His lips slightly parted.

The weight of his large hand settling on her hip, just above her fist, sent heat rocketing through her system, all but melting her bones. Without lifting his gaze from hers, he tugged the cabinet door free of its remaining hinge and placed it gently on the counter at her side. Then he feathered the backs of his knuckles over her cheek, along her jaw, down the line of her neck.

She was frozen, unable to draw away, unable to speak, lost in the verdant clarity of his entrancing gaze. She tried, desperately, to remind herself of all the reasons she shouldn't be allowing this to happen. He was rude and overbearing.

Bossy.

He was controlling. Everything she hated in a man.

And right now, if he didn't kiss her, she'd surely die.

"Everything about you calls to me." His voice was deep, husky, brimming with need. "The fire and the vulnerability in your beautiful eyes, the layer of steel running down your spine."

A delicious shiver coursed through her. He thought her eyes were beautiful?

"Damn it, woman, your scent drives me crazy. No matter how far away from you I get, it's always there...pulling me back." His lips twisted in a grimace, the next admission tore from his lips on a groan, as though he couldn't believe he was admitting it aloud. "I can't stay away from you."

His hand slipped around to cup the back of her neck, drawing her forward. She didn't resist. The notion never even crossed her mind. His lips were so warm, so smooth. So demanding. His tongue traced the rim of her lips, and she parted them, inviting him in.

He invaded.

The flavor of him decimated any lingering doubt, any residual protest. His knee pushed between her thighs at the same moment his hips twisted, pressing her back, pinning her against the counter. Fingers splayed, the hand at her waist slid beneath her shirt, skimming her skin. He held her, touched her with a level of passion she'd never encountered, kissed her...seduced her...with every part of his body.

JJ clung to him, floating on the sensations. His hands were gentle but calloused, rough against her sensitive skin, shooting fireworks through her bloodstream. His scent, fresh and clean, muted out the lingering aroma of their breakfast, dragging her under, until everything else faded away. His hands grew bolder, his kiss voracious. In that moment, nothing else mattered. Cam simply *was* her world.

Lightheaded with need, she floated on a cloud of desire. Her ears were ringing.

No. His cell phone was ringing.

She crashed.

He muttered a dark curse against her lips and pulled away, leaving her empty, bereft. How could she be so stupid? Her hands shook as she braced them on the counter at her sides to steady herself. Her traitorous knees wobbled.

Pull yourself together, JJ, you moron. It was just a stupid kiss.

She couldn't tear her gaze from his face. His frustrated expression took on a serious, analytical edge. Anger and anxiety edged his tone as he bit out, "Get Judy over there, and call Red in. It'll take me a little bit to get there, I'm at JJ's."

Great, she could already hear the buzz down at

Maggie's.

Didn't you hear? Cam was at JJ's at the crack of dawn this morning.

Wonder what he was doing there?

I heard he was fixing her faucet.

I'll just bet he was. Wish he'd come on over and take a look at my faucet...

He listened to the phone for a short moment, the muscle in his jaw began to tick. "Don't start with me, Emma." On that terse note, he snapped his phone closed and shoved it back into his pocket. Tossing a thumb in the direction of her cell phone where it lay charging, he addressed her, "I programmed in my personal cell number, speed dial one..."

JJ wrinkled her brow at his nerve, but before she could make comment, he shrugged, adding, "You weren't using it anyway. Call me if you need anything or have any more problems. I have to get going. There might be a break in the vandalism case. I'll be back as soon as I can."

Where did he get off?

He didn't live here, and yet he was acting as if he owned the place, going about...fixing things. It wasn't his place, and she resented his attitude. Her problems were not his responsibility, and yet he acted as if she belonged to him, like a girlfriend, or a wife, only his behavior was more possessive...more *proprietary*.

A tiny edge of fear tickled down her spine. Proprietary...hadn't Jerry been that way with Sarah? Proprietary and controlling.

No. Cam wasn't Jerry. Deep in her heart, in her mind, she knew the truth of that—somehow—and it went a long way toward squelching most of that tickle of fear.

Temper took care of the rest.

"I'll take care of the doorbell, and anything else that needs fixing. Don't worry about coming back…I'm sure you have plenty of other things to take care of."

"You are so damned cute when you get mad." He tilted his head down, angling it slightly to the side, and peered at her through the thick rim of his golden lashes. His voice dropped an octave, his tone intense. "I'll be back, JJ," he murmured, stepping closer. Her knees knocked together. His warm palm cupped her cheek, his thumb tracing the petulant curve of her lower lip. "After all, I've only just gotten a taste of you." His smoldering gaze dipped to her lips. "And I'm hungry for more."

For half a heartbeat, his unmistakable implication hung heavy in the sparse air between them. Then his lips claimed hers for one brief, searing kiss. All too soon, he eased away, nipped her bottom lip lightly, and angled his head, winking at her before swaggering from the kitchen.

JJ sagged against the counter, staring after him, mentally sputtering. The man was impossible. The growl of the diesel engine as it roared down her lane snapped her resolve back into place.

As she straightened from the counter, a red glint caught her eye. He'd left his toolbox on the floor beside the table. The big jerk. So now he thought he could just leave his stuff lying all around? Just because he'd fixed her damned faucet?

Just because he could knock her silly with one freakin' kiss?

Huffy, she stomped to the toolbox, and, before she gave it better thought, she kicked it. The toolbox scrapped across the old linoleum less than half an inch. The metal didn't give, but her toe did. Wincing, cursing, she hobbled to a chair and dropped onto the seat. Cradling her damaged foot in her hands, she scowled at the doorway. If he thought, for one lousy second she was some meek little woman—content to let him boss her around—he had another thing coming.

JJ Frost would never let any man rule her the way her sister had.

The shrill cry of her cell phone broke into her dark musings. She crossed the room, savoring the pain lancing through her foot at every step, a sharp reminder to keep her head screwed on straight. No man was to be trusted.

Picking the phone up, she flipped it open and snapped, "Hello?"

"JJ? This is June over at Paper Cutouts," a cautious voice replied with sticky-sweet cheer. "The rest of your order just came in. Would you like me to bring it out to you?"

"No, that's okay." She dropped a narrow-eyed glare to Cam's toolbox. "I have a delivery of my own to make."

****

As the Apostle bent down to ruffle Mrs. Tisdale's puppy's cheeks, a dark Grand Cherokee eased into a parking space across the street, catching his attention. A pair of long, slim legs swung out from the open car door, then the rest of her hopped out. From the corner of his eye, he admired JJ as she crossed the sidewalk and disappeared inside Paper Cutouts.

She was a beautiful woman, elegant and timeless. Even dressed in tattered jean shorts, running shoes, and a faded T-shirt, with her gorgeous hair pulled back into her ever-present ponytail, she was a traffic stopper. The good Lord knew she was enough to stop his heart, dead in his chest.

Straightening, he made small talk with the elderly woman as she struggled to restrain the vivacious retriever. All the while, his mind fixated on JJ. The poor thing had suffered her share of heartache. Such a shame, the things her brother-in-law had done...killing JJ's sister like that, attacking JJ. From the articles he'd read, she'd barely survived the encounter.

He'd carefully studied everything he could get his hands on about that night, and about JJ herself. The internet had its uses, Devil's tool that it was. It was all too easy nowadays to find every sordid detail on any unsuspecting soul.

When JJ struggled through the doorway of Paper Cutouts, arms laden with shopping bags, he bade Mrs. Tisdale a hasty goodbye. Bounding across the street, he hailed JJ.

"Here, let me help you with those."

Glancing up, she blew a stray wisp of hair from her eye and lit up his morning with a bright smile. "Oh, thanks so much. There was more here than I realized."

Relieving her of her burden, he followed her to the rear driver's side door of her Jeep, waited for her to unlock the door and open it. He leaned inside the vehicle as he settled the bags on the seat and drew a deep breath, sweeping his gaze over the interior. The vehicle was spotless and smelled just like her. Clean and fresh.

Edging clear of the doorframe, he smiled down at her and closed the car door. "All settled."

"Thank you again. I should have made two trips."

She was so very courteous. He beamed down at her. "It's all right. Just be careful next time. We wouldn't want you to hurt yourself."

"I will." She reached up and slid a pair of large, round sunglass up the bridge of her nose. There was no subtle flirtation in the motion, no coy, come-hither glance. No Devil's guile.

He couldn't have been more pleased.

"I heard June was going to ask you to donate a few pieces for the charity auction. Has she spoken to you about that yet, or did I let the cat out of the bag?"

Smiling, she thrust her hands into her front pockets and nodded. "She caught me just now."

"Are you? Donating pieces for the auction, I mean?"

"Yes, I told her I don't really have any completed works with me, but I should be able to have something for her by the end of next month without any problems."

"That's very kind of you, JJ."

He thought then of the things he'd read about her. *A promising young artist,* they'd called her. *A natural talent.* It was right that she not ignore the talents God had given her. Too often talent was taken for granted, or, worse still, exploited. And she was such a pretty thing, so friendly. A woman like her deserved to be cherished.

He smiled, stepping to the side for a young mother pushing a stroller. A bright-eyed child gurgled, drooling through his cherubic grin as he pounded on the tray in front of him. A small, fuzzy bear tumbled free from the child's pudgy fingers, bouncing across the sidewalk, rolling to a stop at their feet. Without a moments hesitation, JJ scooped the bear up and returned it to the child with a warm smile before the toddler could so much as whimper. Thanking her, the mother moved on.

JJ had such a beautiful, innocent smile.

She obviously liked children, was good with them. She'd give her children the kind of childhood he'd always envied of others. She'd make a wonderful mother, sweet and loving, nurturing. Not like the cold, selfish bitch that'd whelped him. He knew God forgave him for not honoring thy mother in this instance.

God hadn't forgiven her either.

She'd been such a hypocrite, hatefully preaching

God's word as she'd beaten the verses into him. No one else had seen. No one else had cared to look. But God had watched every vicious blow.

God had judged her, and she'd died unrepentant.

Someday soon, once he'd finished purging the town of sinners—making it safe and fit once more for God's faithful—he'd like to settle down, have a few tykes of his own. Of course, he'd need just the perfect woman at his side...someone just like JJ.

He swallowed the bitterness and let his smile grow.

Surely, she was God's reward for his unwavering faith.

He considered asking her out for dinner. That would be the next logical step in courting her. Before he could form the words, however, the door to Paper Cutouts opened, and June came bustling out into the sunlight.

Resentment bubbled in his chest.

"Oh, JJ... I'm so glad I caught you before you drove off."

June was a tall woman, pencil thin with hawkish eyes. The woman could glean the most innocent bits of information from a conversation and twist them into reputation shattering gossip faster than the ladies-aide could organize a bake sale.

"Oh, well, hello," she crooned, smiling at him. Already vicious lies were brewing behind those beady eyes as they passed between him and JJ. "I didn't see you there. I'm so sorry to hear about you mother, such a kind lady."

"Thank you." Nodding gravely, he shuffled his feet to keep from snarling at her insincerity. Everyone who knew his mother knew she was one of Satan's minions. Pivoting on his heel, he caught JJ's concerned frown and added, "She was ill for some time. It broke my heart to have to put her in the nursing home. She passed in her sleep a few weeks back."

Her illness left her too weak to fight the pillow.

God's will be done.

"I'm so sorry," JJ murmured. A shiver of pleasure coursed through him at her sympathetic stroke on his arm.

"Yes, well," June changed the unpleasant subject. She held a colorful pamphlet out for JJ. "I forgot to give you this when you were in the store. The auction is very popular, draws quite the crowd. Not that you need the exposure, of course. I'm so excited we'll be able to showcase your work...and as a *local* artist at that."

"I've been...out of the public's eye for a while. I'm sure the publicity can't hurt. It will be good for me to be back in the spotlight, even if only for a short while, all the better if the auction is more profitable because of it."

A tiny furrow dug in between his brows. That wasn't very modest. Then he relaxed. Maybe all she needed was a little warning, nothing that would hurt her of course, just a gentle nudge. A little something to help her to stay on the right track.

She could rely on him to watch over her, help her make the right decisions. She could count on him to protect her from sin.

Excusing himself, he strolled down the street toward the Post Office. Inside, he emptied his box, sorting envelopes as he headed for the door.

"Hey there," Jim called from behind the counter.

Heaving a sigh, the Apostle stopped at the door and spun back, pasting a smile on his face. "How are you, Jim?"

"Great, just great." The postman leaned an elbow on the counter. "'Specially now that pretty little JJ moved to town. Bet she's a real wildcat in bed...the quiet ones always are."

The Apostle saw red. Jim was a pervert, an abomination. His palms dampened the stack of envelopes he crunched in his hands. Murderous rage boiled through his veins. It would be so easy to snuff out such a worthless life. He could almost feel the degenerate's final heartbeat pulse beneath his fingertips.

It would feel good.

Appalled at his own thoughts, the Apostle stammered a quick, absent reply and ducked outside. Black, acidic hatred clutched his stomach tight. His breath sawed through his nostrils. It took every last ounce of his composure to smile at passersby as he made his way back to his office. The Devil was insidious, ever watchful for weakness, tempting the faithful to stray. Murder was against God's will. He would not stray from his path of righteousness.

Murder was a sin.

Chapter 14

JJ laughed as Ginny vaulted into the air, doing her patented boogie-woogie, chicken dance as bowling pins crashed and ricocheted at the end of the long lane. Overhead, the electronic scoreboard blinked, flashing a new score.

"That's worth another round," Ginny shouted over the busy din of the crowded Bowl-a-Rama. She staggered to the padded booth and plopped beside JJ, jostling her with a loose shoulder, knocking her into Brandi. "See, ain't this fun?"

How Ginny could bowl, much less manage a strike in her current condition was beyond JJ. Yet she'd had four strikes tonight...or was it five? She'd lost count. Never had she seen anyone down so much alcohol and remain upright, either. Then again, there weren't many at her table tonight who'd been slacking as far as the booze went.

Giggling, JJ lifted her beer in tribute, tipping it to her lips. She'd gone well past her own limit, and the room had taken on a pleasant, golden glow, as if all were right with the world. Her only surprise was the alcohol had given her this enjoyable, fuzzy feeling rather than sending her straight to the ladies room in disgrace, as it usually did.

Across the table, her new friend, Carol Ann Metcalf waved a twenty in the air, batting her artificially enhanced eyelashes at the tall blond behind the counter. Grinning, he nodded acknowledgement and began loading up a tray.

Brandi snaked an arm around JJ's shoulder. "So...what's the JJ stand for?"

JJ had just enough alcohol in her to own up to the awful truth. "Jillian Josephine."

"That's not so bad." Brandi giggled when JJ made a face. "What's your poison, Jillian Josephine?"

"JJ, please...just JJ. And I'll have another beer, I know better than mixing."

"Sspoil-ssport," Ginny slurred. "C'mon, JJ, just one li'l ol' shotsy. Ya gotta have one... 'S a rule. 'S girl's night out. We all got ssittzers tonight." She waved her arm flamboyantly toward Carol Ann, Brandi, and Lacy—though Lacy had no children— then thumped her own chest. "No kids to worry 'bout...no men folk to slow us down. 'S high time to get all lacquered," hiccup, "licked," she shook her head, giggling, "liquored up." Ginny nodded soberly, grabbing twice before she snatched the slippery tip of her tongue between her sluggish fingertips. Her tongue wiggled loose, and she shrugged, beaming at the room at large. "Damned tongue quit working after that lasss Capt'n."

Across the table, Lacy Becker dropped her head to Carol Ann's shoulder, humming blissfully. The blond arrived with his weighted tray, slid the edge onto the table, and began passing drinks around.

"How about a pizza, ladies?" He aimed the question at the group in general, but his eyes—and his smile—were for Carol Ann alone.

"That's a great idea, Adam." Brandi elbowed JJ as she gave a stage nod in Carol Ann's direction. The calf-eyes were mutual.

Carol Ann tried to pass her money to Adam, but he waved it away with a shy grin. "Now you know better, Carol Ann. Your money's no good here." The heat in his smile sent a wave of female twitters around the table. Clearing his throat, he promised he'd return with a large double pepperoni, and sauntered away.

Five female necks craned to follow his exit.

"What a man," Carol Ann sighed, patting a hand over her heart dramatically.

"I'll say," Brandi chimed in. "You get tired of playing with him, be sure to toss him my way."

"Ssspeaking of what-a-man, take a gander at that hunk-a-raw-sssex that just ssswaggered in. That one looks right," hiccup, "right up your alley, JJ."

Whipping her head around, JJ's gaze zeroed in like a heat-seeking missile on the tall drink of water leaning against the service counter...and oh, was he sexy. His ankles were crossed, his thumb hooked in his utility belt. He was in uniform again, with a gun strapped to his hip and a star pinned to his chest. He was insolent, cocky. He oozed sensual bliss. He was...

Dear Lord help her, he was edible.

And Cam was staring right at her, as if there wasn't another soul in the entire building.

Forcing herself to turn away, her face on fire, JJ couldn't help grinning like a loon at the blurry label on the half-empty beer bottle in front of her. Ginny jostled her again, sloshing her caramel-colored drink over the side of her glass. Brandi leaned close, whispering—loudly—that JJ ought to go on over and be *friendly* with the good sheriff. After all, you never knew when being on *first-rate terms* with the long arm of the law might come in handy.

Embarrassed, JJ shushed Brandi and took an unsteady gulp of her beer. She shouldn't be reacting like this, like a giddy schoolgirl the high school jock just winked at. She hadn't seen him since he'd left her house yesterday morning. He'd told her he'd come back...and then he hadn't—not that it mattered.

Because it didn't...not at all.

She'd delivered his toolbox to the sheriff's department after her stop at Paper Cutouts. The odd-looking young woman with glow-in-the-dark green hair and a familiar voice staffing the front desk had smiled as if JJ were the answer to some sacred prayer, and politely asked if she'd like to leave a message for the sheriff. JJ had been so flustered by that knowing look and bizarre smile she'd sputtered, backing from the office without passing on the scathing set-down she'd rehearsed.

Now there he stood, gorgeous as a Chippendale dancer. She stole a sidelong glance, and silently cursed when she realized he no longer leaned against the counter. Had he left? Disappointment settled in the pit of her stomach.

Facing her companions, she reached for her beer again, only to gasp and freeze. How did he *move* so fast?

Cam stood beside the table, feet spread, both thumbs hooked on the corners of his belt buckle. She ogled that belt buckle...or round about that area...and licked her lips. Snagging her bottom lip between her teeth, she stifled a whimper. What would he do if she stuffed a wad of cash in his belt? With that sexy grin and that taunting uniform, he certainly fit the part. Did male strippers give lap dances?

Holy crap, what was wrong with her? Appalled, she leaned back in her seat and slowly, carefully lifted the beer bottle to her lips with trembling fingers. Her brain must be pickled. There was surely no other excuse for her wayward thoughts.

Dragging her gaze up to his face, her cheeks went up in flames. He smiled at her as if he'd read her mind—every naughty little thought—and she wondered if spontaneous human combustion were possible.

"Ladies...JJ," he drawled, angling his head. His voice dipped an intimate octave on her name, sending a tremor of delight trilling through her

Brenda Huber

body. "How are we this evening?"

"We'd be a lot better if *you* joined us, sssheriff." Ginny wriggled a limber eyebrow, leering at JJ. "Wouldn't we, JJ?"

"Well, now. I can't think of many things I'd enjoy more," he said, his gaze sweeping over the group, lingering on JJ, "but, to my regret, I have to pass. I'm on duty tonight."

"Aw...p-party-p-pooper." This from Lacy, her head lolling from Carol Ann's shoulder back against the seat.

Cam's lips twitched, but he adopted a stern expression. "Lacy Becker, I think you've had about enough to drink. You'd better have a ride home. Want me to call your brother for you?"

"Red's p-pickin' me up when I call him," she informed him, wobbling her head with a sober expression. She was half a Jell-O shot away from sliding under the table.

"That goes for the rest of you, too." His eyes came back to rest on JJ, and she fought the urge to squirm in her seat. "I'd hate to have to haul any of you in tonight."

Grinning, Brandi tossed her arm around JJ's shoulders again. "Will you cuff us, Sheriff?"

"Yeah..." Ginny threw an elbow at Cam, clipping his hip. "You better ssstrip-sssearch JJ, Cam. Ssshe's been awfully *naughty*."

Gasping, JJ all but knocked Ginny from the booth. Her heart thudded against her ribs. Cam simply tilted his head again, stripping her with his eyes, and murmured, "I'll be sure to keep that in mind." Then, louder, he added, "Have a nice night ladies...JJ." Again, the sensual octave dip on her name.

Grinning, he swaggered away.

Once again, five female necks craned for a better view.

"I'd take a p-piece of that with a scoop of ice cream on the side," Lacy purred, adding, "Even if he is Red's boss."

"You and me both." Brandi bobbled her head. Recalling herself, she shot a guilty glance at JJ. "Course I wouldn't dream of poaching, but, oh the stories I've heard... You are definitely one lucky woman, JJ Frost."

Frowning, JJ glanced from one confirmatory nod to the next. What were they talking about? Maybe she'd had more to drink than she'd thought. She did a quick mental tabulation of her drinks, and shook her head in amazement. She'd definitely had more than her limit. As carefully as if it were a coiled snake poised to strike, JJ pushed the beer bottle away with the tip of one finger.

Then their words finally began to register. She didn't know quite what to think. Her head was spinning. Surely that was the reason they were talking like this...as if trying to make inroads with her on Cam's behalf. It was ridiculous. They were bragging him up like proud mother hens with a prodigal son.

Though they claimed none in the small group had ever actually been with him in *that* sense of the word, they admitted rumors of his conquest were the stuff of local legends. From all accounts, he was a living god in the bedroom. It was a lamented fact, at least by said conquests, that he never returned to the same bed twice. It was also purported he was cool under fire, never once losing control in the heat of passion. He left every last one of his lovers with a smile and fond, *fond* memories. In short, he was a Casanova. A generous, considerate lover without an ounce of possessive tendency. He was never jealous, never controlling of his women, more often than not remaining on friendly, though emotionally shallow terms with his ladyloves.

On some hops-soaked level, she agreed with their claims. Wholeheartedly. If his kisses were any indication, his god-in-the-bedroom status would remain unchallenged. She must have had too much to drink. He was sounding better and better by the second. "He sounds like a hound dog without a loyal bone in his body," JJ snorted, anxious to put the evening...and the man...back into proper perspective.

"Naw...he just hasn't found the right woman." Ginny thrust JJ's beer back into her hands, suddenly looking far too serious for JJ's comfort. "When a woman finally tags him—the *right* woman, mind you, you better believe it will be for keeps."

"I doubt he'd hold still long enough for the shot." Unmindful of her resolve to cut herself off for the night, JJ tipped the bottle to her lips. "Besides, given his history, I'd say he lacks the ability to make a commitment to just one woman."

"For the right woman, he'll hold still all right," Ginny insisted stubbornly. "Once he commits, he'll never look twice at another female...and that you can bet your lacy Saturday-night panties on."

"What makes you say that?" JJ didn't believe a word of Ginny's claim, and yet a tiny part of her was strangely hopeful.

Ginny shot her a lopsided smile as she rubbed at the wide leather strap of her watch. Her sage tone was all too sober...and oh-so-sad. "It's the nature of the beast."

JJ cast a wary, thoughtful glance at the door Cam had disappeared through.

The nature of the beast...

What an odd expression.

****

It took four jabs at the lock before JJ finally managed to get the key where it belonged. Staggering around, unsteady on her feet, she waved

188

at Red as he shifted into reverse and backed the police cruiser down the lane. Lacy slumped against his shoulder, passed out cold. Brandi and Ginny wailed a rousing rendition of *"I will survive"* from the back seat.

Imagine. JJ Frost...delivered home in a cop car. She giggled. *Another first.*

Once inside, she staggered down the hallway, dropping boots and shedding clothing as she went. In the kitchen, she tugged the refrigerator door open, shivering as the chilly blast of air poured over her bare skin. Snagging a bottle of water from the fridge, she worked the cap loose with severe concentration before stumbling into the small washroom where she dragged an oversized T-shirt from the dryer. Carefully propping the water bottle on top of the washing machine, she battled the hooks on her bra, gave up, and wrestled the cursed thing off over her head. Dropping it onto the dryer beside the water bottle, she tugged the shirt on, grabbed her water and the bra, and wandered back down the hallway.

Pausing at the foot of the stairs, JJ frowned at the bra in her hand, glanced at the scatter of clothes on the floor, and giggled again, draping the bra over the banister with a careless shrug. She'd just placed her foot on the bottom step, when a loud thump came from somewhere overhead.

Ice shot through her veins. Just enough for panic to set in.

A flash of her sister, drenched in crimson, lying motionless in a pool of blood, eyes lifeless and open, hand outstretched, begging for mercy that would never come, flickered through her mind. She hadn't been able to save her sister, though she'd tried with every ounce of strength she possessed. Now he was coming for her. She wouldn't be able to save herself either. This time she'd failed them both. That gruesome realization left the bitter taste of desperation clinging to the back of her raw throat, a throat that already bore the bluish marks of Jerry's angry hands.

The silhouette of a man separated from the shadows, and then he was there, looming over her, his left arm raised high. In Jerry's fist, the enormous butcher knife gleamed, dripping the gore of her sister's death. The smile on his once handsome face was serene, twisted with justified vengeance. His muddy brown eyes glittered with vindicated, diabolical glee. She would pay for turning Sarah against him. She'd never interfere with his marriage again. His hand descended with brutal purpose, again and again. Pain seared across her ribs, her forearm, penetrated her thigh.

Clutching her side, she stumbled back, gasping. No. No...that wasn't real. It was just a memory. Though the shadow of remembered pain sliced at her, she did not bleed. She was safe. She was alive. She wasn't in Minneapolis anymore. Jerry was dead.

The ceiling above her creaked.

Silently sobbing, she dropped to her knees and frantically rooted through the scattered clothing until she found her phone. Crawling on hands and knees into a small closet beneath the stairs, she flipped the phone open. The screen swam before her eyes. Her thumb hovered over the number nine, but she didn't press it.

The house was just settling. It was just her imagination, intensified by another flashback. Please, let it be just another damned raccoon. The stairs groaned, and she bit down hard on her lip. The salty taste of blood coated her tongue. Her wide-eyed gaze darted around the small closet, but it was so dark...too dark. Like someone had poured ink over her vision. A tiny crack of light below the door offered little to no definition. She scrabbled back into a corner, huddled there.

Oh, please, oh, please...

She *so* didn't want to dial 911. Eventually, they were just going to look at her like the boy who cried wolf...or the lady with the cats Cam had told her about over breakfast the other morning. But neither could she drag herself from the closet. What if someone was out there? There was a killer lurking in Sutter Hollow, after all. Earlier tonight, Ginny had told her they'd found another body...a man this time...with his chest carved open by a broken bottle.

One half-drunk, neurotic woman wouldn't offer much resistance.

No. No, it wouldn't end like this. Not for her. She was a survivor. She'd face whoever it was out there, face them...and face her fears. She wouldn't die hiding in some dark corner like a rodent. Her body vibrated with the need to do...something. And for once that something was *not* to reach for her car keys. Praying it was a true dose of courage and not the booze talking, she struggled to her feet, and eased closer to the door, straining to hear sounds of movement.

Nothing.

Closing her eyes for a split second, she plucked up her courage, and placed her hand on the doorknob, turning it slowly. Cracking the door open, she peered out into the hallway. Her gun was in the nightstand upstairs. With that goal in mind, she crept from the closet and tiptoed up the steps.

Feeling slightly better now she had a gun in her hand, she skulked through the house like a burglar, checking beneath every bed, behind every door, inside every closet. By the time she'd reached the kitchen pantry, she was feeling very foolish.

Relieved, she headed back to her bedroom. She just needed a good night sleep. All the windows and doors were locked...she'd checked and double-checked. She was alone in the house. And she had a gun. She was safe.

All the same, when she climbed into bed in the wee hours of the morning, the lock on her bedroom door was firmly in place, her gun tucked safely beneath her pillow.

****

JJ woke up cold, chilled to the marrow of her bones. Her first instinct was to burrow farther under the pile of blankets. Why was it so cold in here? Shuddering, she peeped from beneath the soft edge of her comforter. A flutter of movement in the darkened room sent chills of a new kind racing down her spine.

Her heart leaped to her throat. She bolted upright in bed. Her hand shot beneath the pillow, searching for her gun. JJ's frightened gaze locked on the whisper of movement, and she stilled, gun clutched in her white-knuckled fist. Near the bed, just on the other side of the nightstand, the sheer curtains swayed softly in the chilly breeze. Pale moonlight illuminated a patch of hardwood floor beside the bed. Her brow puckered. She hadn't left the window open before she'd gone to sleep.

Had she?

No. Impossible. Even on the second floor, an open window would have posed a security issue. Slipping from the bed, shivering when her bare toes connected with freezing hardwood flooring, she darted to the window. It was wide open...had been opened from *inside* the room. Slamming the window shut, she whirled to face the open door, gun aimed and ready.

She'd closed that door tight before she'd gone to sleep.

Closed it...and locked it.

JJ's heart threatened to hammer a hole clean through her chest. The hall light was on. Edging forward, she ducked her head into the hallway, scanning for intruders. Padding silently on feet as cold as her icy heart, she checked every room on the second floor. Every light was on. Every window, every door was wide open. A hasty glance down the stairwell confirmed the lights appeared to be on down there as well. The front door banged gently against the wall with every caress of the night breeze.

Tears streamed down her face. Dashing back to her room, she slammed the door, forced the lock to engage, and raced to the nightstand, snatching up her phone. Without hesitation, JJ speed-dialed the number Cam had programmed into her phone. Her fearful gaze darted around the room as she waited for the call to connect, flickering over and then locking on the large mirror above the dresser in astonishment.

Garish red lipstick scrawled the word *Beware* across the antique mirror.

"JJ?" Cam's curious deep voice cut through the haze of fear clouding her thoughts. "JJ, is that you? Honey, are you all right?"

She couldn't make her voice work. Her lips were moving, why wouldn't any sound come out?

"Damn it, JJ, talk to me," he barked, anger and fear lanced through the phone line. "Honey, are you there? Hello?"

"Cam," she finally croaked.

"JJ! You sound scared out of your mind. What's wrong? Are you hurt?"

"No, Cam. Someone's here...or they were here. Inside...the windows," she broke off on a stifled sob. "Oh, God, they opened all the windows."

"Shit! I'm on my way. Stay on the line, okay." The roar of an engine growled through the phone. "Stay with me, honey."

"Yes," she breathed, forcing herself to stay calm.

Give him the facts. Don't let him rush in here blind. "The front door's wide open. I locked it before I went to bed. I think all the lights are on, too. He was in my bedroom...while I was sleeping...he was in here." The breeze stirred, more forcefully now, coursing a fresh wave of goose bumps over her flesh. She shivered, whether from the frigid night air, or from the fear, she wasn't altogether certain. "It's so cold...all the windows are open. I closed them. I know I did. I always close them, and I locked the door. The bedroom door, not just the front door. Oh, but I locked the front door too, and the back. Who would have done this?"

She was rambling. She couldn't stop herself.

"Honey, I'm almost there. Where are you? Right now, where are you? Do you have your gun?"

"Upstairs," she mumbled into the phone, only now realizing what she'd done. She was hiding again, cowering behind the bed in fear.

So close to reaching for her car keys.

Something inside her snapped. Maybe it was her fear. Maybe it was common sense. She didn't know...and right now she didn't care. This was *not* happening again. No more. She was taking control, once and for all.

She would *not* run.

"I'm going downstairs. He's not going to get away with this."

"What?" Cam bellowed. "No...baby, don't do—"

She snapped the phone closed, possessed, brimming with the fire of indignation. Firming her grip on the gun, she dropped the phone onto the mattress and stalked to the door. Whoever the hell thought he was going to get his jollies by frightening her had another thing coming. She liked it here. She was making friends...at last. By all that was holy she wouldn't run, not again.

Storming from the room, she pounded down the

stairs, with a cold, single-minded sense of purpose. She wasn't a victim, not anymore. Suddenly, inexplicably empowered, she tossed her wild hair over her shoulder and began combing the house for intruders. Heaven help the fool if he'd decided to hang around. She'd shoot him just on principal now.

Before she could complete her search of the main floor, the snarl of an approaching vehicle warned her Cam had arrived. A car door slammed in the night. Boots pounded across the porch, followed by a loud crack and a louder curse.

"JJ," Cam yelled.

Another crack echoed in the darkness outside the house a bare moment before Cam bound inside the hallway, gun palmed, eyes alert, chest heaving, scowling with frightening menace. The moment his gaze connected with her, a shaky breath escaped him. He lowered his gun and loped forward.

She offered him a thin, apologetic smile. "I didn't find—"

He thrust his gun into his holster, clutched her by the shoulders, and gave her a rough shake, looking far more dangerous than he had the moment he'd burst through the door. "Don't you *ever* do that to me again, do you hear me?"

Speechless, JJ stared up at him, her own gun hung in a limp hand at her side. The lines of his face were harsh, the muscle in his jaw twitched. His eyes shot green fire. He was beyond furious, and he wasn't making the least little effort to hide it.

"Look, I'm sorry I called—"

"You little *idiot*—"

"Idiot! Where do you get off—"

"Idiot! Never again will you do something so dangerous," he snarled, shaking a tiny, bewildered nod from her. "What if he'd still been here? What if he'd attacked you before I got here? My God, JJ, he could have—"

The look in his eyes went wild as his gaze swept over her from tousled hair to bare toes. His words broke off on a furious growl, and he jerked her into his arms, crushing her to him with a vicious curse. His erratic heartbeat pounded against her cheek like a jackhammer. Cam's breathing was ragged, harsh against the top of her head. His wide, uniform-covered chest smothered her. His long arms were bands of unforgiving steel. If it weren't for the fact she couldn't breathe, she'd have happily stayed in the circle of his warm, protective embrace for the rest of eternity.

Her head began to swim. Struggling, she wrested a slip of air between them. Tipping her head back until she could peer up into his face, she opened her mouth to demand her release. His lips sealed over hers. His tongue filled her mouth. She drowned in the rage of his passions.

His mouth was fierce. Demanding and possessive. Inescapable. His body was rock hard...and growing harder against her by the second. One large, unyielding hand settled on her backside, hoisting her against him until her toes barely grazed the floor. His other hand fisted in her hair, tugging her head back as he deepened the kiss. A low, dark sound rumbled deep in his chest as he thrust his thigh between hers.

Raw need swam through her veins. Her gun clattered to the floor at their feet, and JJ wrapped her arms around his neck, surrendering with a whimper. Without warning, he growled again and pushed her from him. Gaping at him, bewildered, she braced herself against the back of the sofa. Her knees wobbled beneath her.

Scooping her gun from the floor, he tucked it back in her palm, and, steering her by the shoulders, he guided her around the sofa until she plopped down onto the rocking chair. "Stay here." His voice was a hoarse, pained rasp. "I'm going to check the house over. Don't shoot me when I come back."

Then he was gone.

And, doing exactly as he'd warned her not to do—shooting him—began to hold a great deal of appeal. How dare he kiss her senseless, and then just walk away...unaffected?

Cam prowled the main floor, flickering in and out of her line of sight, securing each room he passed through, turning lights off as he went. The ceiling creaked above her as he moved through the second floor. Windows banged closed, then his boots thumped up the second flight of stairs to the attic. In short order, he thumped back down both flights of stairs and crouched in front of her. With gentle hands, he extricated the XD Subcompact from her trembling fingers, gingerly depositing it on the small, piecrust end table. Drawing her icy hands onto her lap, he chafed warmth back into them before enveloping them in his large palms.

His touch was so tender, so comforting. "Whoever it was is long gone. I could try dusting for prints, but I doubt I'll find anything. JJ, promise me you will never risk your safety like that again. When we were on the phone...and you said you...damn it, woman, you scared ten years off my life."

"I'm sorry."

She hadn't thought about it from his perspective. She'd been so consumed with taking back control she'd lost sight of the fact there was a fine line between bravery and stupidity. Clearly, tonight she'd danced on the edge. She was lucky she hadn't tumbled over on the wrong side.

"I didn't mean to frighten you, I just...I had to..." She trailed away, unable to express what had motivated her to descend those stairs and hunt danger down. Gritting her teeth, she started over. "He was in my house, Cam. He forced his way into my *home*. He came into my bedroom while I slept. He wrote on my mirror."

Now Cam was the one gritting his teeth. "I saw," he bit out.

"You don't understand..."

She made to stand up, but he held her firm, his eyes imploring. "Then tell me."

She stared down into eyes the color of a warm spring day. He was so serious, so intent on her, she felt like she was the center of his universe in that moment. "I've run for too long, Cam. I've tried to hide." She shook her head, forcing a swallow. "Running doesn't help. Hiding doesn't work."

His eyes flashed. His grip tightened. Did he know then? Did he have any inkling of her past? He remained silent, and she could only speculate.

"It's not safe for you out here, isolated like this, honey."

His endearment thawed a layer of fear, melting it away like welcome spring sunshine on a winter lake. Squaring her shoulders, she lifted her chin. "He's not scaring me off. I'm not going anywhere." Her voice dropped, whisper thin but laced with steel. "Not this time."

Some of the tension eased from the lines on his face, and a long, slow sigh eased from his lips. She frowned at him, but before she could question his abrupt shift in mood, he stood, tugging her to her feet. His eyes swept down the length of her, before locking onto her face. "Much as I hate to say this, you'd better go put some clothes on. I'll take you down to the station. You'll be safe there until I can figure out what to do."

"Until *you* figure..." She couldn't believe she'd heard him correctly. Shaking her head, she untangled her hands from his. One winsome smile, one staggering kiss and how quickly she forgot his tendency to control things. "I told you, this is my home, and I'm not going anywhere."

"Honey, I need to know you're safe. You can't—"

"The hell I can't. I'm staying, Cam."

His jaw clenched, the muscles in his cheek leaped and bunched. She could see the battle in his eyes. His hands fisted at his sides before he shoved those fists deep in his pockets.

"I can't believe I'd even consider asking this," he muttered, clearly to himself. Then, louder, he addressed her, "Is there somewhere you can go, somewhere away from Sutter Hollow that you could stay...just until I catch this guy?"

He was tense again, his body rigid. It was a small wonder he had any teeth left in his head for as tightly as he seemed to be gritting them right now. His request had been reasonable enough, given the circumstances, and she wouldn't take offense over his preference that she run away but, having asked it of her, he looked as if he was, even now, kicking himself for making the suggestion.

"There's nowhere else for me to go. I won't be run off."

"It's not safe for you here right now, JJ. I'm trying to be rational here. Isn't there a relative or a friend you could stay with?"

Even when he'd come roaring out of the shed after her shirt ripped, demanding to know who'd hurt her, he'd never looked so...so...good heavens she didn't even have a word in her vocabulary for how he looked at the moment. It was almost as if the mere thought of her leaving town disturbed him beyond words. But that was just ridiculous. Wasn't it?

"What about your parents?"

"No." The word came out much harsher than she'd intended. Relenting, she explained, "Last I heard, dad was somewhere in the Bahamas...or maybe it was Spain." She tossed a shoulder. "It doesn't matter, we haven't spoken in years."

"What about your mother?"

How did one explain Gloria?

She rolled that one around in her mind for a few minutes. He moved aside, grudgingly, and she paced her way across the room and back. "I think I'd rather take my chances here than go stay with her in LA."

"JJ, come on. It couldn't be that bad. At least you'd be safe."

"I'd end up behind bars, Cam. One of us would kill the other for sure." JJ snagged a straggling lock of hair and ruthlessly jammed it behind her ear. "Cam...you'd have to meet Gloria to understand. Right now, she's estranged with husband number five, probably already hunting for victim number six. But that's Gloria for you, eyes on the prize...always looking for the next bigger thing." She rubbed her hands briskly up and down her arms. "You see, I was a mistake of the unsuccessful union with number three, Sarah was the product of union number two. We're both little more than distasteful reminders of unpleasant periods in Gloria's life. Reminders, I might add, she'd like nothing more than to forget."

Agitated, she paced away again, well aware his discerning eyes were following every step she took. Chilled to the bone, she chafed her hands harder against her bare arms as another flash of memory sucked her where she hadn't gone in years. Though not as debilitating as her flashes of Jerry's attack, this one was just as powerful. Gloria may have never raised her hand to her children, but JJ had learned the hard way that words left bruises just as easily as a fist.

Two little girls, their dresses damp and pretty hair bows askew, cowering beside a piano and a broken vase, water and lilies pooled on the floor. Gloria's stern face, filled with disgust and contempt, glaring at them.

"Why can't you two behave yourselves for a little while? Why must you always ruin everything? I swear, you two live to torment me. You are my own version of perdition. What did I ever do that was so terrible to deserve such little monsters?"

"It was my fault, Gloria," Sarah whispered, stepping forward, placing herself squarely between the livid woman and the whimpering child. *"Jillian didn't do anything."*

"Jillian doesn't ever do anything, does she? She's just a worthless, whiny brat. Well, she hides behind you well enough. You both are a sorry disappointment to me. Just...just go away. I don't want to see either of you for the rest of the day."

Gloria stormed away, and Sarah's comforting arm slipped around her slim shoulders.

"She didn't mean it, Jilly. She was just mad about the vase. Come on, let's clean this up and then we'll go talk Flora out of some ice cream."

Sarah had always been her buffer, and she'd failed Sarah so badly.

JJ didn't realize she was wringing her hands together, until Cam's warm palm slid between hers. He pulled her to a halt, tugging her around to face him.

"Take a breath. Take a deep breath." Cameron smoothed his hand down her arm, shoulder to elbow. His breath was soft against her temple. "Don't fall apart on me now, honey. You're safe."

She'd already fallen apart...it hadn't helped then, it wouldn't help now. But she still felt fragile, like one good tap, and she might shatter. No, she was hanging on tooth and nail. It would take more than a few open windows and some pathetic letters scrawled on a mirror to send her over the edge again. Even so, it didn't take a genius to realize she had, once again, stumbled into the sights of a demented psycho. Was she just genetically predisposed to attract these brutal monsters?

"Excuse me, someone just broke into my home. The bastard's trying to play nasty little mind games with me. Don't think for one minute I don't know about the murders. For God's sake, Cam, I've already lived through this once." She slapped at his chest and bit down hard on the sob swelling up inside her throat. "I think that entitles me to fall apart. It's my God damned right to fall apart, not that I'm going to fall apart, damn it. So don't you tell me not to..."

Her words fell away as the sob finally got its way. Her hands fisted in his shirt. Her breath caught, hitched in and out. She pinched her eyes closed, willed the burn of tears to stay firmly locked away. Her lips moved, but only the tiniest shadow of a whisper emerged.

"Oh God, not now...not now."

Cam laced his fingers into her hair, cupping the back of her head in his large, warm palm, pressing her face against his solid chest. His arm slid around her, and he drew her stiff form tight against him, firmly holding her there as she trembled like a leaf in the face of a twister. He caged her until the tension in her body eased and her own arms slowly crept around his waist. Only then did he loosen his hold, albeit marginally.

Seconds passed into minutes, and those minutes ticked by in silence as he simply held her, offering her a safe, protective harbor in the wild storm of her emotions. Finally, she drew back to look up into his face. Her cheeks were damp, as was his shirt.

He refused to release her. Emotion swirled in his heady gaze. Without a word, he lowered his head, capturing her lips with his own. His tongue swept inside without invitation, without apology. Lips meshed, teeth scraped, tongues danced until her head began to swim.

When he pulled away, they were both breathless. "I'm on duty tonight. I can't stay—"

"I didn't ask you to." Slipping from his arms, skirting him, she paced the length of the room once more, raking irritably at the loose tangle of her hair.

Those emotions swimming in his eyes shook her, far more than anything else she'd encountered since she'd moved into this house. Instinct demanded she rely on herself, lean on no one. He may have slipped beneath her radar, and she wasn't quite sure how to deal with him just yet, but she'd never allow him to dictate to her. This was her home now, and she was staying. End of discussion.

"I'm not leaving you alone, JJ." Glaring at her now, he clutched his fists at his sides, radiating frustration.

"I'm not your responsibility, Cam."

He caught her around the waist midstride and swung her about until their noses brushed. His eyes burned into her with enough force to drive the air from the room. "You are *mine* to protect," he snapped.

Okay, so he took his job seriously. Still, that didn't give him the right to dictate to her in her own home. Unsettled, she lifted her palms, warning him to back off. He released her, but didn't back up an inch. "Okay, look. I appreciate you're trying to do your job, but I can take care of myself."

"I'm not talking about my damned—"

"Look, if you want me to call you again the next time I have trouble, back off now," she interrupted. She had him over a barrel on that point, and, judging by the mutinous scowl on his face, he knew it.

A long, tense moment passed between them, and he visibly stiffened.

"Fine." He spat the word out, grimacing as if it had left an unpalatable taste behind. Whoever taught him the finer points of conceding with good grace had failed. Miserably. "You can stay."

She scowled. How dare he? Grant permission, would he? Of all the stinking, obnoxious, conceited...

"I'll be back as soon as my shift is over. I'll replace all the locks on the windows and the doors...and I won't hear a word about it. When I finish with that, I'll work on your new porch."

"My new porch..." she sputtered, completely lost now. What was wrong with her porch?

"You will barricade yourself in your bedroom. You'll sleep with your phone in one hand and your gun in the other tonight."

She dragged in a deep breath, intent on letting loose a tirade at his overbearing demands. But he beat her to the punch. "I'll increase patrols around this place. You'll call me if you think you hear the wind rattle a window. You will call me if the house so much as settles too loudly."

Crossing her arms over her chest, she narrowed her eyes, pursing her lips. He was beyond controlling. He was unbelievable. He was... He was just...

Ooooh...

She stifled the urge to stomp her foot. Just barely.

"You'd better get used to having me around, honey." He leaned close, his eyes glittering with newfound purpose. "Because *I'm* not going anywhere either. You are *mine* to protect...and that has absolutely *nothing* to do with the job." His lips seized hers, though he didn't touch her anywhere else. That simple contact was enough to hold her immobile.

Awestruck.

The first few moments of the kiss were fierce, violent and consuming. Then, by slow degrees, his lips softened. The urgency was still there, but it was tempered now, soothed. He nibbled her lips. Lapped at her tongue. Moaning into her mouth as if he'd never tasted anything more exquisite. Abruptly, with a low growl, he withdrew.

"I'll be back in," Cam flicked a glance at his watch, "three hours and forty-six minutes. How 'bout waffles this morning? I'm partial to blueberry."

Stalking to the doorway, Cam paused, turning back long enough to singe her with a long, heated glance designed to curl her toes.

And then he was gone.

She didn't sleep a wink. She wasn't stubborn enough to blame it on her nighttime prowler. No, she knew exactly who to blame.

The taste of him lingered on her lips long after the indignant anger cooled.

Chapter 15

JJ drained her third cup of coffee and wiped the toast crumbs from the counter. *Waffles, my ass.* He wouldn't be getting a single bite in this house, not a nibble.

Curious, she'd poked her head out the front door after he'd departed last night—or rather earlier this morning—and gawked at the damage. He'd stomped a hole the size of a crater smack in the center of her precious porch. The big jerk.

Not a crumb.

Her hand hesitated in its circular wiping motion. In all fairness, the boards had been rotting, and she'd intended to replace them sooner or later anyway. She couldn't help the tiny smile tugging at her lips over the memory of how he'd come bursting through the door, a brave knight charging in to slay her dragons. She really should cut him some slack, after all, he'd...*volunteered*...to fix the damage.

Heaving a sigh, her lips twisted in a wry grimace as she considered the black kitty-cat clock high up on the kitchen wall. Twenty-five minutes left until his promised return. Not that she'd been keeping track. Shaking her head, she rinsed the dishrag in the sink, wrung it out and draped it over the center divider. Why was she so impatient, so excited about the prospect of seeing him again?

He probably won't show up anyway.

She dug out a mixing bowl. He'd have to settle for Belgian waffles. She didn't have any blueberries.

She'd pick some up the next time she stopped at the store.

Not that she'd be making him waffles again, of course. These waffles were just payment for changing her locks and for coming so quickly when she'd called about the intruder. That was all.

Okay, so he could have a nibble. Where was the harm in a nibble?

Would he stop at the waffles, or would he nibble on *her* again? Never had she encountered a man who could use his mouth like *that*. One little kiss, and she'd been ready to beg.

God help her if he truly decided to press his suit.

She wouldn't stand a chance.

On automatic pilot now, she drifted around the kitchen preparing the breakfast she swore she wouldn't make, for a man she wasn't sure she wanted to see. Sausage sizzled in a covered skillet on the stove. The coffeemaker hissed and chugged, brewing a fresh pot as JJ retrieved a carton of eggs from the fridge.

The man's lips were a wonder. Where had he learned to kiss like that anyway?

JJ whipped the batter with excessive force, all but gnashing her teeth. He'd probably honed his skills on the local cheerleading squad. He'd probably played tonsil-hockey with half the women at college, the womanizer.

The memory of his glittering eyes stilled her hand. When he'd looked at her like that—like she were the only woman in the world...in *his* world— she hadn't been able to think straight.

When he'd claimed she was *his* to protect, with such fierce conviction...

A delicious shudder rippled through her.

She still couldn't fathom the emotions that had surged through her at his forceful declaration. What would it be like if only it were true? What would it feel like to be the object of such devotion, such intense emotion?

JJ set the bowl on the counter in front of her with a tiny, wistful sigh.

She reached for a bottle of vanilla, and a large, warm pair of hands slid around her waist, a bristled cheek nuzzled the side of her neck. JJ jerked, biting back a scream. The hands held her fast, firm and unyielding, waiting her out, gentling her. His heat, his very scent—all too familiar for such a short acquaintance—comforted, even as it excited.

"Mornin', honey," he murmured, smooth and soft. "Smells scrumptious." He nipped her earlobe, chuckling when she shivered. "Breakfast smells good, too."

Her lips parted in surprise. She didn't have the slightest clue how to respond to his comments. Then again, she often found herself in this state when he was around, speechless and floundering. Swiveling round, spatula in hand, she began piecing together a stern rebuke, but her reprimand died a quick and painless death as her gaze slid over his face.

He was tired. Dark shadows lingered beneath his eyes. His skin was pale. His hair was damp, the honeyed edges curling at the nape of his neck. He must have stopped at home for a shower and change of clothes. His jeans and T-shirt were fresh, and oh-so-sexy.

He was dead on his feet, and still he'd come.

Her heart melted...just a little.

"When was the last time you had a decent night's sleep?"

He'd released her when she'd twisted round to face him, but he hadn't stepped back. Settling his hands on her hips, he shot her a rueful smile...one that lacked his usual vibrant devilment. "Not since the day you came to town, honey."

A disgruntled compliment if ever she'd heard one.

Yep, speechless and floundering.

Unable to help herself, she reached for his face, her palm cradling his cheek. What a strange sensation, the gritty texture of his whiskers where they pressed against her sensitive skin. His brow winkled for a moment, then eased. His eyes glowed from within, lowering to her lips.

With excruciating slowness, he lowered his head. His lips claimed hers. Not with heat, though it was there, sparkling just beneath the surface. No, this was a warm homecoming. A tender meeting of desire and comfort. His hands crept around her waist, easing her closer. No force, no coercion was needed. She melted into him, boneless, pliant. She started to sink without a fight, but he ended the kiss on small, nibbling pecks. Instead of drawing back, as she'd expected, he pressed her head to his chest, resting his cheek on the crown of her head, holding her as if she were a precious package, a priceless treasure he'd guard with his life. Her arms slipped around his waist, tentative, testing.

Wonderful.

She snuggled closer, content to just be.

The sausage crackled, popped, and she eased back, reluctantly. Pressing her palms to his chest, she urged him to sit at the table. "I'll get you a plate. I made coffee, but you look like you need a pillow instead."

"Coffee please, black as tar. I'm gonna need broomsticks to prop my eyelids open at this rate."

"You should go home, get some sleep."

"Too much to do." He smiled gratefully as she slid the loaded plate before him, then he frowned at the tall glass of orange juice she set down next to it.

"Coffee will keep you up, and you need to rest." He wasn't the only one that could be stubborn. "When you're finished eating—since you won't go home to sleep—you can take a nap here."

"But the locks—"

"Will wait..." Unsettled by the utter domesticity of their interaction, she spun away to tend the dirty dishes as he dug into a small mountain of waffles. A casual observer might mistake them for a couple.

No. It wasn't like that. They hardly knew each other.

And yet...

She bit down on her lower lip and set to scrubbing the little blue flowers off the mixing bowl.

A short while later Cam's chair scraped across the linoleum as he pushed back from the table. He carried his dishes to the sink, sank them into the soapy water, and dropped a kiss on her temple. "Thanks for breakfast, JJ. You're a damned good cook, in case I forgot to mention that. You must have taken the old saying seriously."

"What saying would that be?"

"About the way to a man's heart."

She whipped her head around to challenge his assertion, but his lips swooped down to cover hers, stealing her head of steam, robbing her of her breath. Robbing her of every thought in her head.

"Are you sure you don't mind if I crash here for a while?"

"Ah..." He tasted of like maple syrup and orange juice. It took a moment to regain cognitive ability. "Positive. Go, lay down."

"Don't let me sleep too long."

"Do you have to work today?"

"No, I've got a couple days scheduled off. Though given the situation down at the office, I probably shouldn't be taking them right now."

"You're no use to anyone if you collapse...go...sleep." She shooed him from the kitchen.

Once she'd finished with the dishes, JJ tiptoed into the living room. Cam lay stretched out on the long couch. He'd tucked his boots beneath the edge of the couch. With one arm flung above his head, the other draped across his chest, he slept like the dead. His face softened in repose. His lips were slightly parted—his breathing deep and even. She snagged her lip between her teeth as tender emotion swelled.

JJ retrieved a warm throw and draped it over him, tucking him in. She couldn't resist slipping her fingers through the stray shaggy lock of hair feathering over his brow. With infinite care, she eased the hair from his face, relishing the texture of each silky strand against her skin. Bending, she brushed a fairy-light kiss over his cheek. Then she crept from the room.

Collecting her gardening tools, she wandered into the side yard. Despite the dull throb in her temples and her poor night of sleep, the day looked promising. The air was fresh and crisp, the sunshine bright and warm. Yes, it looked to be a fine day indeed.

****

Cam yawned and stretched. The scent of JJ surrounded him, and he smiled, sitting up. As he did, a warm, soft blanket fell from his shoulders. She'd covered him up. Warm fuzzies blossomed in his chest. He leaned back against the cushions, uttering a soft, shocked oath. His splayed hand rubbed at his chest, just over his heart. Warm fuzzies? Him?

When the hell had *that* happened?

Shaking his head, he reached for his boots. A quick glance at his watch told him it was pushing noon. He'd slept a solid six hours. Again, something new for him. He was a light sleeper, one who had trouble drifting off and who woke frequently. On the average, he was lucky if he could string together more than three hours at a time. And here he'd been, passed out—dead to the world—for just over six hours. Unbelievable.

He pushed to his feet, rested and mellow, and made his way to the kitchen. The sink was empty, the counters spotless but for JJ's half-empty mug of coffee. He ambled forward and reached for the mug. The flowery painted ceramic was cold. A congealed, creamy skin coated the top of the liquid. He stood motionless, closed his eyes and listened. He could detect no sound from within the house. His brow wrinkled, and he strode for the door.

A quick search of the yard brought him up short. Freshly turned dirt in two flowerbeds, and a pile of limp weeds near the shed indicated how she'd spent her morning while he'd been playing at Sleeping Beauty. A small hand spade and trowel glinted on the bottom step of the back porch beside a dainty pair of dirt speckled gardening gloves.

"JJ?"

His bellow echoed through the yard, unanswered.

Damn it. He rounded the house, cursing aloud when he spied her Jeep parked beside his truck. Where the hell was she? Lifting his nose to the wind, he drew the morning in. A myriad of smells assailed him, the flora and fauna of the woods, the freshly worked earth, the recently clipped grass. And there, just at the surface hovered a trace of her. Just a trace. Faded with the day, and impossible for him to track in his current form.

Stifling a vicious curse, he tore around the house and ducked into the woods behind the shed. There he stripped down, stashed his clothes, and began the transformation. His focus was fuzzy, shadowed by fear for her, and shifting was more painful than normal. Where was she? Had she wandered away on her own?

Or had she been forced away against her will? His blood turned to ice.

The change in his face was near to excruciating.

Bones shattered and reformed, muscle and sinew ripped and bunched across his body. The griffin on his chest rippled as if alive. He nearly writhed on the ground from the pain. *Damn it, Cam, focus.* A thick pelt replaced smooth skin, and only by sheer dint of will did he prevent himself from tearing it back out as the searing burn of its rapid growth lanced across his flesh.

Dropping to all fours, he shook himself from snout to tail, panting, forcing himself to focus through the throbbing in his joints. He sniffed and snuffled the ground near him but could pick up no trace. Trotting back to the porch, he picked up her trail once more. Nose all but pressed to the ground, he loped across the yard and into the woods to the north of the house. Her scent grew stronger the farther he ran. He breathed an inward sigh of relief.

She was alone.

Then anger flared. *She was alone.* He could detect the familiar scents of man-made weaponry. At least she was carrying her gun. All the same, he was still upset. Was she insane? Had she forgotten so quickly the black bear who'd nearly dined on her not so very many nights ago? That puny little gun she had wouldn't have stopped it from taking her down if Cam had given it half a chance. Had she forgotten there was another predator out here, one far more dangerous than that bear? One who walked upright on two legs and stalked the community's citizens without remorse?

Had she forgotten the wolf?

Growling low in his chest, he charged onward. Maybe he ought to scare her. Remind her that these woods weren't safe.

Then he located her, and he couldn't find it in himself to frighten her. On the contrary, once he found her, the pull of her was too strong to resist. He couldn't stand the thought of causing her fear. The instinct to protect was too strong. Dropping to his haunches, he angled his head and observed her with all his heightened senses. His acute vision drank in every greedy drop of her appearance, from the top of her golden head to the scuffed tips of her hiking boots, and every luscious inch in between. Her breathing was gentle and even, caressing his sensitive hearing like the caress of her hands on his body.

She stood in the middle of The Circle, gazing about her in unmistakable wonder. Her stance was completely relaxed, totally at ease. Even so, she examined her surroundings with infinite care, as if cataloging every microscopic detail. Was she planning her next painting even now? He could almost see the wheels in her head turning.

A quick slash of wind gusted through the clearing, tearing her hair from the clip at the nape of her neck. Her golden tresses lifted in the breeze and swirled around her face until she captured it and ruthlessly restrained it once more. Her essence slammed through his system like a shot from a twenty gauge fired at close range.

His female.

The subconscious assertion exploded through him, savage and primal. If he'd had any lingering doubts before, seeing her here like this laid them to rest. On those few occasions when his cynicism had lapsed and his imagination had run away with him, she was all he'd ever dreamed of and so much more.

After the incident with the bear, he hadn't been able to stay away, unable to resist the urge to watch over and protect his female. Every waking hour he wasn't either on duty or tied up with the murder investigations, he'd been skulking in the woods near her house, like some hungry, love-sick pup starving for a glimpse of her.

Hell, even when he was on duty he had trouble

staying away, enter exhibit A...last night at the bowling alley. He'd been on duty, only a few hours into his shift, and he hadn't been able to resist tracking her down. He had a vandal harassing his town, one he couldn't wait to get his hands on. He had a killer on the loose, should have been focusing solely on hunting the bastard down and putting an end to his spree of terror, but he hadn't been able to look beyond his own personal need. Another first for him. Always the pack...and the town...had come first.

Now JJ did.

Unequivocally.

With the newfound senses of a Werewolf who'd found his mate, he'd singled out the sound of her voice, the sound of her laughter through the din of the crowd as she'd discovered new friends. The tenor of her laughter had left him achy and wanting. He'd tried to tell himself that he'd gone there simply to see for himself that she was all right. Hell, he hadn't been able to fool anyone, least of all himself. He'd needed to be near her with a driving instinct that would not be denied. He'd needed to see her, to breathe the same air as she breathed.

For the first time in his life, he began to understand. Perhaps Ed hadn't stayed for Cam's mother because he was pathetic. Maybe leaving truly hadn't been an option. Granted, there was still no excuse for the way Ed squandered his life, shunned his pack. But maybe...just maybe...there'd been more to the story than Cam had previously been prepared to consider.

He hadn't been joking when he'd told her she'd scared ten years off his life last night. Never before had he experienced the blood-curdling terror he had when she'd announced she was going downstairs, implied she'd meant to confront her intruder. Even now, the mere thought sent chills through him.

Being with her in her kitchen as she'd made breakfast for him had been surreal, given him a taste of a future he could cherish with every ounce of his soul. He hadn't even claimed her yet, and already he looked forward to waking to her every morning. She made him want things, things he'd never before even considered. A real home. A wife.

Children.

She stiffened suddenly, and he went on full alert. Sifting scents on the wind, he couldn't distinguish anything amiss. His inner instinct didn't sense any danger, any threat. What had spooked her?

Then, as she twisted around to gape in his direction, he realized the truth.

She'd sensed *him*. How...odd. He hadn't made a sound, hadn't twitched an eyelid. Yet she'd unerringly found him, as if he'd tossed his snout in the air and howled for her attention. Just as she'd found him in the bowling alley last night. Was she as aware of him as he was of her?

He rose to his paws and padded forward, slow and easy. The last thing he wanted now was to frighten her. Please don't let her run from him. Given his current state of emotion, he wasn't all together certain how he would react. Would he be able to let her go?

Or would he give in to his innate predator's instinct to give chase, to track her down? And once he caught her...then what? Would he shift and claim her as he longed to do? Would she accept him? What would happen if she fought him?

God help him, he'd rather cut out his own heart than cause her a moment of pain, and yet, with the fierce emotions roiling through his system, he wasn't at all certain he could contain himself.

His mind raced as he drew closer. She stood her ground. He stopped at last, only a few feet away, and tipped his head to the side, trying to reassure her with his eyes. Did she understand he would willingly die for her?

JJ bent slightly at the waist and reached a hand out to him, clucking softly. Narrowing his eyes, he snorted. He knew he'd set a bad example before, but he'd just had to reassure her. And now look at her. She was treating him as if he were some tame lap dog. He was a freakin' Werewolf, not some pathetic poodle.

Her eyes widened, and she sucked in a sharp breath. Slowly, she lowered her hand and edged back a step.

Damn it all to hell.

Loathing himself for his weakness where she was concerned, cringing at what he was about to do, he let his tongue loll out the side of his mouth.

Humiliating.

Thank God, the other guys weren't watching this. He'd never live it down.

She relaxed again and offered him a blinding smile, making his degradation worth every second. He crept closer, all but purring like some lowly, disgusting cat when she stroked his head. In this form, he was eye-level with her breasts. Ever since he'd seen her bra hanging from the banister last night, caught a glimpse of those pert nipples puckered against the thin fabric of the tank she slept in, he'd been dying to bury his face against her. Right now, those soft, womanly curves were more than he could resist. A devil rode him, and he gave her a wolfish grin before nuzzling his face against her breasts.

Heaven had nothing on her.

The only thing that would have been better would be if he were in human form, and if she were naked, writhing beneath him as she screamed his name.

She giggled, pushing him away. He butted up against her, unwilling to yield her softness just yet. She laughed aloud, wrapping her arms around his neck, holding him close. It took every last ounce of his willpower not to shift then and there. He nuzzled her a moment longer, gave her a long, indolent lick up the side of her neck then edged away. He wouldn't be able to stand much more of that torture before he caved to instinct and shifted to claim her.

She might not be afraid of him right now, but he could damned near guarantee if he shifted right here in her arms, he'd be lucky to catch her before she sprinted across county lines. Oblivious to his discomfort, she laced her fingers through his fur, over and over, stroking his back, humming her pleasure. She was killing him.

To take his mind off the pleasure of her hands, he pushed his head under her arm and nudged the small of her back where she'd stuffed her gun. It smelled as if it had been recently cleaned. Good. At least she was taking that much responsibility for her safety.

"What are you... Oh, the gun," she answered herself. Turning to face him fully, she smoothed both hands down the sides of his neck. "Can you smell it? I bet so, huh? Bet you don't like guns. Can't say as I blame you there. I don't really like them either." Her tone grew wistful, her gaze pensive. "Someday I'll be strong enough, I hope. Then I won't need it anymore."

The pain in her eyes sliced at his heart. Is that what she thought? That she was weak? That her courage came from the gun she carried? The things she'd overcome would have destroyed a weak person. No, JJ was a survivor. Couldn't she see the remarkable things he saw when he looked at her?

He nuzzled his face against hers. A low whimper rumbled around in his chest. She buried her face in his fur for a long moment, then seemed to shake off her melancholy.

"It's so beautiful out here." She smiled as she straightened. Her appreciative gaze swept the clearing. "I had no idea this place even existed."

She spoke to him as if he were human, as if he were a long lost friend. She was a wonder that never ceased to amaze him. "What is this place?" She toed the charred debris from the last ceremonial bonfire. "This doesn't look that old, I wonder who comes here? What do they celebrate?"

She sighed wistfully, and faced him. "Would you listen to me? Standing here asking you all these questions, like you can talk to me?" She snorted softly, scuffing the toe of her boot against a huge, fallen log.

Oh, but he *could* tell her. He wanted to. Everything. He could tell her of the ceremonies and the legends.

He could tell her the *truth*.

She scratched that wonderful spot behind his ear, and he closed his eyes, nudging his cheek into her hand. Her gentle laughter soothed him. "You're awfully friendly. You know...that first time...I'd begun to think I'd only imagined you."

He growled softly, nudging his shoulder against her hip, tilting her off balance. "I know, I know. You *are* real." Then she cast a thoughtful gaze at him. "Would you like to come home with me? You're used to running free, though. I bet they don't even make doggie doors in your size." She heaved a deep sigh. "What am I even talking about...I don't know where you'd even sleep."

With you...only with you.

She scratched that spot again, and his fur twitched appreciatively. "You like that, huh? I've been thinking about getting a pet...a puppy, or a cat or something."

A cat? Eww...that was just *wrong*.

"But you'd be so much better." He wasn't sure if he should be offended, or flattered. He was seriously leaning toward the former, until she admitted, "I feel...safe with you. I don't feel safe with anyone, you see, so you should feel special...well, I didn't feel safe with anyone until I came here..." Her voice grew wistful, quiet. "He makes me feel safe too."

Who made her feel safe? No doubt about it, she was killing him. Dare he hope?

Smiling to herself, she eyed him with a devilish twinkle in her eye. "I wonder...what would Cam have to say about you? I bet you two would get along pretty well. You remind me a lot of him in some ways." She crouched down, holding his big head in her hands, peering deep into his eyes. Then she smiled playfully, teasing, "He's awfully handsome, too. Maybe it wouldn't be such a good idea to take you home. I don't think you look like the type to share your turf."

She had *no* idea.

JJ's stomach rumbled and she ruffled his hair. "I better head back. Cam's probably still sleeping, but I'm getting hungry. Don't be such a stranger, huh? I enjoy these little talks of ours." Laughing, she patted him on the head, and made to move passed him.

He followed, sticking to her side like Velcro. Her own personal bodyguard. She beamed down at him, sinking her fingers into his fur once more. "Are you going to walk me home? Aren't you just so cute."

She made small talk the rest of the way through the woods, and he padded along at her side, content to bask in the sound of her voice. It turned out, in fact, that she had been considering doing several paintings of The Circle, as well as the surrounding woods. She'd even decided to do some of the lake.

Once he'd shifted, he'd have to have a talk with her about wandering around alone. At least until he caught Lori and Ed's killer. Painting might make her happy, but he refused to allow her to put herself at risk like this again. She was too precious to him.

As they neared the edge of the woods, Cam drew to a halt.

"C'mon, boy," she coaxed. "It's okay."

He turned his big head and nuzzled the curve of her breast, taking one last deep breath of her warmth before he backed away from her.

Her disappointment was palpable, and he almost changed his mind. But how would he explain where he'd gone when she returned to find his truck still parked in her driveway and him nowhere in sight. Besides, he'd rather be pressing his advantage while he had *hands*. Now he had leverage. She said she felt safe with him...in *both* forms.

And she thought he was *awfully handsome.*

Grinning, he trotted off, looping around until he reached the tree where he'd stashed his clothes. He had locks to change, a porch to work on, and a woman to seduce. The locks he would change with all due haste. Her safety was something he wouldn't mess around with, but he wondered how long he might be able to drag out fixing that porch. At the very least, that ought to earn him a few more meals...and maybe dessert.

He all but licked his wolfy lips in anticipation.

****

The Apostle leaned back, resting his arm along the back of the park bench. A little girl giggled and squealed as a handful of ducks quacked and waddled closer, squabbling over the bits of bread she tossed in their direction. He smiled, nodding a pleased hello to the girl's watchful mother. Turning his focus to the apricot-streaked western sky, his thoughts wandered.

Had JJ understood his message? He worried about that. Had he been clear enough?

Normally he didn't second-guess himself like this. He didn't worry so much if those he tried to help had difficulty understanding. But there was just something special about JJ. What if she rejected his help?

What if she rejected *him*?

No, he wouldn't see it like that. She was kind, compassionate. She wouldn't reject him. She wouldn't laugh at him behind his back. Not like those others. JJ was worthy. If she didn't understand his warning, well, then he'd just have to give her another. Something more tangible, something less ambiguous. If she didn't understand his first warning, then it was his fault. He would be more thorough next time...if there *was* a next time.

Maybe she had understood and was, even now, repenting her sins.

Why was he doubting himself?

It had to be Satan at work again, filling him with self-doubt, tempting him to stray from his path of righteousness.

His eyes narrowed on the setting sun, and he chewed the inside of his cheek, drumming his fingers on the painted wood. It was the Devil. That's what it was. The Devil was just trying to confuse him.

Well, it wouldn't work. He wouldn't be distracted from God's mission. He would save JJ from herself. She wasn't like the others. There was a core of goodness within her. An inner light. A radiance. God had meant for her to be his reward. He just had to *earn* her.

That was it. It suddenly became crystal clear. He had to save her to earn her. God did work in mysterious ways, didn't he?

Movement at front of the bank drew his unswerving regard. A few moments later, a flashy red sports car pulled from the bank's parking lot. Drawing a deep breath, he rose and smoothed his palms down his slacks to shake the wrinkles free.

God's will be done.

He climbed into his car and eased from his parking space. He didn't need to follow the sports car. He knew exactly where it was going. The sinner was taking the same route he took every Friday night. He'd stop home long enough to change clothes. Then he'd head out of town, drive along the interstate for half an hour. He'd stop off at a fast food drive-thru, then he'd slip from his car three blocks farther on where he'd proceed to lose most, if not all of his paycheck in a few sweaty hands of Texas Hold'em. The loss of his weekly wages wouldn't matter though. Come Monday he'd recoup his losses from the bank's funds.

Not this week.

This sinner had more than enough opportunity to see the error of his ways. God had given him another chance, in the form of a winning scratch ticket. Instead of repenting, instead of confessing his sins and turning the funds over to those he'd stolen from as God had surely intended, the sinner had merely anteed up in a higher stakes game.

He'd lost, of course.

Well, what could one expect when one relied on the Devil to hedge his bets?

He circled the block, and pulled into the parking space beside the empty sports car in the back of the dark, nearly vacant parking lot. He killed the engine. Pulling a paperback from the glove box, the Apostle settled himself in to wait.

Almost two hours later, the back door of the illegal card room opened. Mayor Chuck Hughes stepped into the night. His tie was loose, the ring of graying hair around his head stood in cockeyed tufts, his wrinkled suit coat draped over his arm. Apparently, he hadn't had time to stop at home this evening before he'd come to gamble away his soul.

His shoulders bowed as if the weight of the world rested upon them.

Rough night at the tables, old man?

As Mayor Hughes tugged his keys from his pocket, the Apostle rolled his passenger window down and leaned across the seat.

"Evening, Chuck."

A dropped pin would have echoed like a crashing cymbal in the ensuing silence. Hughes became a granite statue of shame. Motionless. Breathless. Then he stirred, lies filling his shifty eyes. "Oh, ah... I didn't see you there. What are you—"

"I'm waiting for you, Mayor." Oh, the effort it took not to let anger and revulsion color his tone.

"Me?" Hughes affected an innocent pose, edging toward his vehicle. "Well, now, I—"

"We need to talk...about a certain bank account, Chuck."

All the color drained from Hughes face. He visibly forced a swallow. Perspiration began beading across the barren expanse of his wide forehead. "I'm sure I don't know what you mean."

"Now, you and I both know that's not true, Mayor. Why don't you get in the car? We'll go for a little drive, talk a bit." Then he tightened the noose. "I'd hate to have to go to the council...and Cam...with my information."

Deadpan, cornered, the mayor nodded and climbed into the passenger seat.

"Put your seatbelt on, please, we wouldn't want anything unfortunate to happen."

"Look, you can't say anything about this." Hughes twisted in the seat, bracing a hand on the dash, ignoring the seatbelt request. His eyes pleaded for understanding. A thin trail of sweat trickled passed his receding hairline and down his temple. "This will ruin me. What will it take to make this all go away? I'll cut you in."

The Apostle eased his vehicle out onto the interstate. "So, you think to bribe me now?" He cast a quick glance at his passenger, then monitored the road ahead. "With what? Stolen money? Embezzled funds?"

"No one would be able to trace the money. I've been very careful."

"Obviously not careful enough...or I wouldn't have found out."

Hughes ran a nervous finger around the collar of his shirt as his Adam's apple bobbed. "You gotta understand. Being mayor in that backwater town...it's an honorary title. There's no money in—"

"What about your day job, Mayor? Doesn't that count for anything? Last I checked, loan officers earn a decent income."

"Jeanie...Jeanie bleeds me dry." Everyone in town knew about the mayor's ex-wife. She saw it as her personal calling to stimulate the economy, every chance she got. But that was beside the point.

"*You* stole the money, not her. Thou shalt not steal, Chuck. You siphoned it off dozens of accounts. Then, what you didn't give to her, you gambled away." He flashed a condemnatory smile at the accused. "Then there was that scratch ticket last month. Where'd all that money go, Chuck? Thirty thousand, wasn't it?"

"Now see here," Hughes objected, banging the heel of his hand hard against the dash. His face took on a livid hue. "That's none of your damned—"

"Isn't it, Mayor?" He kept his voice calm as he eased the car off the interstate, pleased that Hughes was more concerned with defending his actions than paying attention to their destination. "What do you think your citizens would have to say about the true state of the city's finances? How many others are aware the account for the new Rec Center is all but empty? How many thousands did you go through there?"

Hughes blanched.

The Apostle slowed the vehicle, navigating through the twists and turns of a forest-shadowed road as he angled toward his favorite little spot in the woods. It was as if God had reached his own hand down from heaven and blessed this precious corner of the world. Parking a short distance away, he reached in front of the mayor and opened the glove box. "I have something for you."

A flash of silver glinted against his palm in the moonlight. He let the rosary drop until it dangled by two fingers, and he held it up for Hughes. The small silver cross sparkled with the promise of redemption.

"Go on," he encouraged. "Take it."

Hughes eyes locked on the bit of silver. The moment the cross landed in the mayor's greedy palm, the Apostle swung the gun around, driving the grip hard against the mayor's temple. Hughes slumped forward on a strangled whoosh of breath.

Easing his passenger back against the seat, the Apostle retrieved the rosary from the floor of his vehicle, then placed it reverently in Hughes' palm once more. Reaching down, he popped the trunk latch, and climbed out of the car to retrieve his tools. Slinging two long coils of rope over his shoulder, he stuffed a clean handkerchief into his pocket, snapped on a pair of latex gloves, and shuffled around the car to the passenger door.

He reverently polished any dirt from the floor, and any lingering prints, from the rosary, before securing it in his pocket. He looped a quick knot around the mayor's wrist, and dragged the mayor's inert body from the car, slinging him over his shoulder with a slight grunt. Whistling the opening bars of "*Amazing Grace*," he trudged down the hill toward a tall oak.

By the second verse of "*Old Rugged Cross*," he'd

secured the kneeling Hughes to the oak with the first length of rope. The Apostle looped the second length of rope around Hughes' wrists, and wrapped the loose end of the rope around the stout trunk of an elm a few feet from the oak. He tugged the slack from the rope until the mayor's arms stretched taut before him, as if in supplication, and he tied the rope off.

The Apostle gently placed the rosary in Hughes' cupped, ruddy hands before gently patting the man awake.

The moment lucidity settled in the mayor's mind, he began fighting his restraints with every ounce of his strength, cursing and ranting until he grew hoarse, his eyes round with helpless fear.

Squatting on the forest floor, the Apostle opened the small duffel bag he'd retrieved while Hughes had still been unconscious. With methodical resolve, he drew forth his blessed tools of redemption. A bible. A small bottle of holy water. A sterile, razor-sharp hacksaw. Then he drew forth a thick plastic bag filled with the Devil's tools. Cold, crisp cash and a couple handfuls of poker chips.

After carefully arranging the chips and the cash, he settled back to wait for Hughes to repent and accept his judgment. At last, when Hughes' struggles grew week, the Apostle stepped forward, bible in one hand as he made the sign of the cross with the other. "In the name of the Father, and of the Son, and of the Holy Ghost..."

Reaching out, he adjusted the rosary until Hughes held the first single bead in his limp fingers. "I believe in God, the Father Almighty, Creator of heaven and earth..."

Chapter 16

The reading lamp in the parlor flickered off. Frowning, JJ set her book aside, and flipped the switch a couple times. Nothing happened. She retrieved a light bulb from the pantry and switched it out. Still nothing. Gnawing on her lip, she glowered at the lamp.

Lifting an uneasy scowl to the darkened windowpane, JJ crossed her arms over her chest. The twin to this lamp was in the shed. Outside. In the dark. All the way across the back yard. It was ridiculous she should be afraid to set foot outside her locked door in the darkness—she was a grown woman after all. But the thought of crossing that dark yard was near paralyzing. Fear gripped her by the throat and shook her like a rag doll.

Chiding herself for her cowardice, she paced the length of the room and chewed on her thumbnail.

It wasn't so much the need for that particular lamp. Any other lamp in the house would work just as well. It was the principle of the matter. Why shouldn't she be comfortable going outside after dark? Why shouldn't she be able to go to her shed and get a damned lamp?

Recognizing the pep talk for what it was, she groaned aloud and forced herself to walk toward the back door. Cam had replaced all the locks on the main floor before his dispatcher, Emma-of-the-green-hair, had called him in on a domestic disturbance while the deputy on duty had been off on another call.

He hadn't gotten around to replacing the porch

yet, a job he assured her would take at least a solid two weeks if not longer, and he had extracted JJ's solemn oath she would avoid stepping anywhere on the front porch...for any reason...until he'd replaced the entire structure. It wasn't safe, he'd insisted. Even while part of her chafed over his domineering, caretaker mind-set, another part of her secretly delighted in his solicitous attentions.

He hadn't tried the whole *'me, big strong man, you little helpless woman, go get my beer'* thing.

Yet.

So she figured, all in all, she could let him off the hook...for now. After all, he was seeing to her safety.

JJ's hand hesitated on the shiny new lock on the back door. Cam had told her—in no uncertain terms—that she was to remain inside tonight while he was gone. *While he was gone*...as if he lived here or something. Danger lurked in the woods. He'd tried to make it sound creepy. Done a pretty damned good job of it too. Except she now knew not everything out there was malevolent.

Her wolf was out there—somewhere.

She trusted her wolf to keep her safe. Was he out there even now?

What would Cam think of her not-so-little friend?

She should get her gun. Cam would have a fit if he knew she'd even considered stepping out the door without it. But her one-sided conversation with her wolf had opened her eyes, so to speak. She was becoming dependant on that gun. It was a crutch. The whole reason she'd bought this house was because she'd wanted to start over. Yet, she continued to carry around the fear, carry around the reminder that she couldn't trust anyone. No, she wouldn't run for her gun every time something went bump in the night.

She did *not* need her gun to get some damn lamp.

To hell with it. She'd go out, get the damned lamp, and be back inside before you could scream Jamie Lee Curtis. After securing a flashlight, JJ scurried across the pitch-black yard, holding her breath every frightening step of the way.

She wasn't afraid, she told herself. But the reassurance was flimsy at best.

She'd dug through the darkened shed with minimal help from the thin beam of her flashlight and secured the lamp in question. No creepy monster had crawled from the shadows. She started to feel pretty cocky. It hadn't been so bad. She'd just psyched herself out, that was all there was too it. Stepping back out into the night, she propped the lamp against the side of the shed and reattached the lock.

A blood-curdling shriek shattered the stillness, sending a river of razor-sharp icicles arrowing straight to her heart. The piercing wail went on and on, like a wounded animal being viciously tortured. Only it was a *human* voice screaming for help, screaming for mercy. Then the scream died...or rather, it gurgled away, strangled off.

She stood immobile, paralyzed with horror. Someone was out there. Someone needed help. She knew that feeling all too well. The terror. The pain. The need for help that did not come. Common sense urged her to race to the house, barricade herself inside, and call for help.

Human compassion refused to let her hide.

Neither would she be a fool. Sprinting back to the house, the lamp completely forgotten, JJ ran up the stairs and grabbed the gun from her nightstand. She raced back down the steps and from the house in time to hear one last sickening wail.

An eerie silence fell.

The shadows weren't nearly as intimidating as that first night she'd made a similar, foolhardy foray into the unknown. Strong, silvery moonlight sliced its way through the canopy of foliage overhead. She hesitated, just inside the tree line, and thumbed her flashlight off. Her grip on the gun tightened as she slipped the flashlight into her back pocket. There was more than enough light for her to see by, and, as on that first night, she didn't want to draw attention to herself. Not that it had mattered *then*.

Hopefully it would make a difference *now*.

She slipped around the trees, wending her way through the woods on nearly silent feet, careful to keep her bearings as best she could. She should have brought breadcrumbs to guide her way back home. Stifling a nervous giggle, she crept forward. The security of her yard light slipped farther and farther away. The trees began to close in on her, surrounding her until she had difficulty distinguishing which way was back, and which was forward.

Staggering to a halt, she dragged in a long, deep breath and centered herself. She could do this. She could. Someone was out here, hurt and needing help. She couldn't turn her back and walk away. Patting her back pocket, she breathed a silent sigh of relief. At least she had her cell phone should she find anything she couldn't handle alone. She wouldn't call 911 until she had a better handle on the situation. People in town probably thought she was crazy enough as it was.

Leaves rustled somewhere to her right. Far to her right. Praying she'd meet her wolf and not another bear...or worse...she changed directions and slunk toward the sound. What was that anyway? That strange shuffling and thumping?

The shuffling grew silent, and the night grew still. Unnaturally still. A sick ball of dread settled in the pit of her stomach. She had to be close. The rustling sound had seemed to come from just beyond those big pines. She veered closer.

Was she too late to help? Should she turn back?

With trembling hands, she reached out and clutched a fragrant branch of the nearest evergreen. Its bristles poked her skin, fracturing beneath her touch, releasing a fresh wave of pungent aroma. Sap stuck her fingers together.

Forcing a swallow, she drew the branch down and away. Her eyes widened, and her startled cry choked off on a smothered gasp. For a moment, the world tilted on its axis. She couldn't catch her breath, couldn't rationalize beyond the gruesome sight before her eyes. Oh, yeah...she was in *way* over her head.

She'd been too late to help, though by the steady stream of blood coursing from the stumps of his wrists, she hadn't been too late by more than a minute or two.

An icy wave of shock washed over her, numbing her to the unbelievable violence in the secluded, blood-spattered clearing. Even in the silvery shadows, the colors were vibrant, the details inescapable to her artist's eyes. All around the body, trees and small clumps of bushes—pulsing vivid green with life—were slashed with dark, unmistakable crimson arcs. Glistening, scarlet pools had formed at the base of the old oak, one on either side of the kneeling man in the gray suit. The pools grew wider by the moment as his life's blood drained from arms that hung limp at his sides. The grisly drizzle tapered to a slow drip before her stunned gaze.

The man was bound to the ancient oak with the length of a thick, sturdy rope secured around his chest. His head lolled forward, chin to chest. She could see little of his face but for his receding hairline. His banker's tie looped around his throat and up over his shoulder like a noose.

But the most shocking, most disturbing aspect of the carnage was not the body, nor was it the frenzied splashes of blood. It was the small pile of cash—sprinkled with party-bright poker chips—strewn on the ground a few feet from the dead man. Upon the small, haphazard pile of crisp bills rested a pair of severed, blood-soaked hands. The cash beneath the hands greedily absorbed the spilled blood, just as a sponge would filthy water.

And those hands...

Those lifeless hands—cupped as if in prayer—clasped a beautiful rosary with a gleaming, silver cross.

Lurching back, letting the pine's branch swoosh back into place to conceal the horrific sight from her unblinking gaze, JJ slid to her knees and gasped for air. The gun fell to the ground at her side with a soft thump. *Help...*

The useless word echoed inside her head. *Oh, please... Somebody, help me...*

But no one came.

Then she remembered her phone.

Cam... Cam would come. Cam would know what to do.

A lone tear slid down her cheek as she tugged the phone from her pocket. This time, the shaking hands that held the phone, the trembling fingers that speed-dialed Cam's number did not belong to a petrified woman cowering behind a bed in a locked room. They did not yearn to reach for car keys. She was stronger than that. She was a survivor. And she was reaching out, putting her trust in someone else.

Putting her trust in Cam.

Pressing the phone to her ear, she struggled to her feet and wobbled to the pine. She would not leave this man—dead or not—to lie alone...abandoned...while she ran for safety. She didn't know him, didn't even know his name. But she wouldn't leave him.

Not the way she left her sister every night in her nightmares.

****

The roar of the truck's engine was near deafening. The steering wheel vibrated beneath his sweating palms as he battled the loose gravel. The rear end of the truck whipped around until it vied for the lead with the headlights. Swearing, he yanked the steering wheel, snapping the tires back in line. His truck skidded to an abrupt halt, pelting JJ's Jeep and her front porch with a shower of sand and tiny pebbles.

Exploding from the truck in a blur of motion, his heart lodged in his throat, Cam tore across the yard. It was a struggle—pure living hell—not to simply tear his uniform off and shift. He had to get to JJ...fast.

But he didn't know *exactly* where she was.

He wouldn't let that slight complication matter. Human or wolf, he'd find her. His female was in serious distress, he'd heard her terror, loud and clear, in every quivering note in her voice. She'd given him an extremely abbreviated explanation, next to nothing really. Three short, terse sentences. She was in the woods somewhere behind her house. She'd found a dead body. And then she'd sobbed the one sentence that trumped all else.

"I need you, Cam."

I need you, Cam. Then she'd hung up. Those four words had been the beginning and the end for him. Though she hadn't exactly spoken them in the context in which he'd been hoping for, she had said them. She was in trouble, she needed help, and she'd called *him*.

His female *needed* him.

He jerked to a halt a few steps inside the woods and threw his head back, closing his eyes. Dragging in the innumerable scents of the woods, he sifted through them until he found her, the task not nearly as difficult as it usually was when in human form. Was this another aspect of imprinting? Strange, his sense of self and of his abilities had never been this powerful, this...overwhelming...before. He could scent her, as easily as if she were standing right next to him. Her fear was palpable, and it was driving him insane.

Trees whizzed by right and left as his boots kicked up clumps of mud and debris. Branches and leaves slapped at him, biting the naked human skin of his face and arms, making him truly appreciate how well his thick pelt protected him when in wolf form. Still, he didn't slow. He was getting closer. Her scent was growing stronger...as was the distinctive, metallic scent of blood. Lots of blood.

Oh, God, please *don't let any of it be hers...*

The scent of pine was pungent. His vision sharpened the closer he got to her, as did his hearing. His muscles and joints began to ache. He was losing control of his emotions. Instinct roared through him. He must protect his mate. Shift.

Not good.

He shoved his way through the tacky pines, resisting the changes already taking place inside his body. The physical wash of pain was enormous, damned near crippling. Never before had it been so hard to stop, to keep himself from shifting. Then again, he'd never tried to stop once the process had gone this far.

Shift.

His. Female. Needed. Him.

Shift.

Bursting into the clearing, he absorbed everything at once. But the only thing that fully registered was the woman huddled at the far edge of a clump of brush. In three leaping bounds, he was at her side, scooping her up into his arms.

"I'm here, JJ. Everything's going to be all right, I'm here now. I'll keep you safe." His canines were lengthening, effecting his speech.

What in the hell was happening to him? *That* had never happened before. Animal instinct had a firm grip on him now, making human logic all but inconsequential.

Guard. Protect. *SHIFT!*

He had to stop this. He had to pull back from the edge. If he didn't get a handle on his emotions, a leash on this pounding need to defend his mate, he'd scare her far worse than anything she'd seen thus far.

Seeing her safe and unharmed, touching her went a long way toward easing the primitive creature inside. Unable to help himself, Cam wrapped his arms around her, pressing her hard against him. Burying his nose in her hair, he utilized her scent to force the changes back. One by one, beginning—thankfully—with his canines, the changes receded. By the time she leaned back in his arms, by the time he sealed his lips over hers, he was in control once more.

For the most part.

His lips lingered for a brief moment, but all too soon he had to draw away. His emotions were still bubbling too close to the surface to risk that kind of temptation. In his current state, he'd be lucky if he didn't end up marking her. He couldn't do that, not until she understood what bearing his mark would mean for them both. And he sure as hell wouldn't be marking her *here*. When he claimed JJ as his mate, he didn't want anything to mar the memory for either of them.

His perceptive gaze swept the clearing. Nudging

her face against his neck, cradling her in careful arms, he catalogued details of the murder. The blood, the money, and the severed hands.

The rosary.

Why had she had to see this?

Never before had he needed to protect anyone with such fanatical intensity. Then again, he'd never allowed himself to *feel* for any of the women he'd been intimate with either. Hell, he'd gone out of his way to make sure he'd never spent more than one night with any of them, specifically to guard against feeling what he was feeling now. The sheer magnitude of his emotions where JJ was concerned was...frightening...to say the least. And he hadn't physically claimed her yet. Good Lord, how would he survive *after* he claimed her?

What would it do to him once he saw his mark upon her skin?

Shaking himself free of that tangled web of speculation, he dragged his attention back to matters at hand. The physical changes in his body had receded, but his sensory capabilities were still intact, still acute. That hadn't happened before either. Was he closer to the edge than he'd thought?

At long intervals, a lethargic droplet of blood slipped from the stumps of the victim's wrists. This was a fresh kill. If she'd been minutes—hell, even seconds for all he knew—earlier she might have stumbled upon the killer in the act. His arms tightened about her until she squeaked in protest.

Forcing his arms to relax, he sucked in a sharp breath. But he couldn't bring himself to let her go, couldn't stand the thought of not touching her right now. Each tiny breath she puffed against the base of his throat, every flutter of movement was confirmation she was alive.

Cam didn't need to lift the victim's face into the moonlight to identify the corpse. *Son of a bitch.* His job just got a whole hell of a lot more difficult. Mayor Hughes.

What next?

Who next?

Damn the FBI. Damn their pernicious, bureaucratic red tape and their frustrating, useless waiting lists. His citizens were dropping like flies, and he couldn't justify keeping them out of the loop any longer. So, against his instinct to protect his pack at all cost, he'd called them. And he'd been put off. He didn't have time to wait for profiles and official documentation. He didn't give a damn that other serial killers were stalking other towns. He didn't give a rat's ass about statistics and behavioral analysis. His town, his citizens were under fire...*now*.

He needed help *now*.

Dipping his head to the side, he squinted at Hughes' forehead. That garish red scrawl was becoming sickeningly familiar. This time the letters were meticulous. Inimitable. GREED. What did *this* mean? The last two messages hadn't exactly taken a degree in criminology to figure out. What nasty little secrets had the mayor been hiding?

"JJ, did you touch anything, disturb the scene in any way?" Cool professionalism fell by the wayside. Helpless fury roiled through his system. "Don't you have more sense than to go walking in the woods alone at night? Where's your damned gun? You swore to me you'd stay inside tonight. I swear to God, woman, I need to lock you up just to keep you safe."

She tensed in his arms, and shook her head, pushing away from him, but he was having none of it. He palmed her head like a basketball, burying her face against his shirt, tugging her closer. She didn't need to see anymore of this gore than she already had. She struggled for a moment, then simply collapsed against him, all semblance of resistance completely gone.

Her muffled voice murmured, "I had my gun...I did. I dropped it, over by that big pine I think."

She'd dropped it. Just great. Lot of good it did if she couldn't hold on to the damn thing. But he stifled the urge to tell her so. She didn't need that now. Now she needed comfort.

For the first time in his life, he truly cursed his responsibilities, and he felt the depth of his failure. He'd always been proud of his position, deeply satisfied with the knowledge that day in and day out he protected this community and led his pack, keeping them successfully—if covertly—integrated. Now his citizens were no longer safe. His pack was at risk.

If that wasn't bad enough, the whispers had begun. Twisted, of course. Some so far off the mark it was almost laughable...almost. Twitters at the grocery store. Murmurs at the library. Rumors at the Post Office. Gossip raced through the town like wildfire. Pappy's, the bowling alley. No place of business was immune from the gossip...no place but for Ginny's hardware store, the Sheriff's department...and Maggie's of course. No one dared slander the word Werewolf around Maggie.

But the whispers were still there. A monster haunted the woods of Sutter Hollow, some claimed. A demonic beast from the days of yore, brutally slaying at random. A mutated, lupine fiend with human characteristics that existed on its victim's blood...or their immortal soul...depending on who was doing the whispering.

Bloodthirsty Werewolves.

Ludicrous.

Werewolves were protectors by nature. They'd watched over this community for over two hundred years, and for countless decades before that they'd guarded the small Winneoten village that once stood near where Cam's own house was now, rising up as a bulwark between loved ones and their utter destruction at the hands of evil, ruthless enemies.

Now, his responsibilities chafed. Now, he wanted—needed—to devote his attention to his female. She'd surely been traumatized seeing this. Her dilated pupils confirmed she was, most likely, in shock. Instead, he had a crime scene...*another* crime scene...that needed securing. Another family to notify. Evidence to gather. A killer to find...

Who the hell was this demented, sadistic executioner?

Whoever he was, Cam would be damned if he'd let the bastard pin these atrocious murders on his pack. The sooner they caught this killer, the sooner his pack, his community, and his female would be safe.

"I have to call this in, honey," he murmured against her hair. She trembled in his arms, but made not a sound. His hand smoothed up and down her spine, steady and comforting.

Slipping her arms around his waist, she nodded. The warmth of her embrace leveled him out, calmed his erratic heartbeat. Hooking one arm across her back, Cam pulled the phone from his back pocket and began dialing one number after another, barking terse orders. Then he snapped the phone closed and jammed it in his pocket, tucking her gently back inside the shelter of his arms.

"Tell me what happened, how you ended up out here, how you found...this. Tell me everything, every detail. No...don't look at...at him. Just start at the beginning."

Haltingly, JJ recounted her rash decision to hunt up the lamp from the shed, and how she'd heard the horrific cries from somewhere in the woods. He stiffened, clamping down on the rabid temper bubbling just beneath his tranquil surface. Even so, he couldn't contain his reaction for long.

"Let me get this straight...you heard someone screaming out here in the dark, and you thought...hey, maybe I should go out and have a look around," he exploded. She pushed back, but he captured her shoulders in an unyielding grip, giving her a sharp, helpless shake. "Did you stop, for one damned second, and consider it might be *dangerous?*"

She glared up at him, shoving at his chest with her small fists. "Do you want to hear this or not, *Sheriff?*"

Closing his eyes, he struggled to compose himself. Raw emotion seethed, volatile and foreign. Twin points of pressure—her small fists—pushed and thumped his chest, but a greater pressure built within him. He couldn't stop touching her. Cutting off his arm would have been less traumatic.

Damn it all to hell...maybe he was beginning to understand Ed far better than he'd ever imagined. It was no small wonder Ed had sought oblivion. He had the sinking sensation he would too if JJ refused to let him touch her ever again. Gritting his teeth, Cam jerked her back into his arms, caging her there. She was stiff as a two by four, but she didn't bother trying to escape him, apparently realizing the effort would be futile.

At length, she finished recounting her tale. He was more convinced than ever that she'd been moments from stumbling upon the killer. She finished speaking, the last of her explanation snagged in the tension between them, and, with a stifled sob, she sagged against him once more. Chills kissed his spine. She'd heard the actual murder, of that he was certain. His heart stuttered in his chest.

She'd been so close...

What was taking everybody so damned long to

get here? He needed to get her away from here, needed to get her somewhere safe. And that bothered him too. The mere thought that these woods were unsafe was sacrilegious. The woods of Sutter Hollow had always been secure. They'd always been a safe haven for those of his kind, and their mates.

Evil should fear walking here.

Somewhere in the distance, the blare of a siren shattered the pale façade of tranquility. The piercing wail died on the murmured rev of a V8 engine. Cam's heightened senses picked up movement and scents that hadn't been there a moment before, his nose twitched and his ears trained on the swish and crackle of approaching human. Jarvis.

Jarvis didn't have a siren...he must have arrived about the same time as Austin.

"Over here," he hailed, dropping a fleeting kiss to her hair. Then he used the curve of his knuckle to lift her face to his. "I can take you home in a few minutes...just hold on a little longer, honey."

He couldn't stand having her out of his sight, not even for a minute, but neither did he want to expose her to this gruesome spectacle any longer than necessary. She was a magnet for trouble, and his heart couldn't take another shot of fear like this. One more phone call like tonight, and Jarvis might as well haul out another body bag for him. Thankfully, she was holding herself together. He didn't know what he'd do if she fell apart on him. As it was, her face was pale and drawn, and dark shadows lined her eyes. Feeling as though he were tearing out half his heart, he dropped his arms to his sides, releasing her.

"Cam, I'll have to make another trip back to the van, I didn't grab my..." Jarvis pushed passed the shroud of trees and drew to a sudden halt, blinking at them in owlish surprise. "Oh...ah, JJ...I...I didn't realize—"

"She found the body," Cam interrupted.

"Oh," Jarvis murmured, tugging at his collar. Sympathy furrowed his brow. "I'm so sorry, JJ. I hate for you to have to see this..."

"Thank you, Dr. English...Jarvis," she amended at his pointed look. Then she fell silent, her gaze drifting to the toes of her hiking boots.

Clearing his throat, Jarvis shifted the bulky black bag from one hand to the other and moved into the small clearing with professional efficiency. At this time of night, Cam had half expected him to show up sporting pajamas and yawning, at the very least. Instead, Jarvis was bright-eyed and bushy-tailed. In fact, by the crisp scent of Irish Spring and the lingering moisture in his hair, Cam felt it safe to assume he'd just hopped straight from the shower.

Hell, maybe he'd just had a late night session at the gym, for all Cam knew. He'd done that himself often enough when he couldn't sleep. A few hours on the machines and a nice long shower worked wonders for a mind that refused to rest.

"Red should be along shortly. I believe he said he needed to gather some things from his trunk."

"Red...I told Sandy to call Austin in."

"Ah, you'll have to speak to Red, but I seem to have overheard something about a possible arson over at the abandoned warehouse on the other side of town. Seems they flipped a coin...I'm not sure which won—or lost—whatever the case is in this particular situation."

Flipped a coin? What the hell? Heads were gonna roll. The whole damned town was going to hell in a clown car, and Cam couldn't decide if he was behind the wheel, or if he'd been stuffed somewhere in the trunk.

The way his luck was holding out, he figured for the trunk.

Cam glanced from JJ to Jarvis and back again. His duty hung like an anchor about his neck. He reached for her, running his hand from her shoulder to her elbow, and downward until he clasped her hand in his. "I have to go back to my truck and get my gear. I'll walk you back to your house." He swung his gaze back to Jarvis. "You all right here till I get back?"

"Huh? Yeah, yeah, sure..." The doctor's head was all but stuck in his bag as he methodically extracted the tools of an ME's trade, arranging them on the ground near the victim with meticulous precision. Plastic bags, sterile swabs, rubber gloves...

As Cam guided JJ through the woods, he couldn't help but reflect on the last time he'd walked by her side along a similar path. Her fingers, sunk deep in his fur, had felt every bit as good to him then as her hand in his—palm to palm, fingers laced—did now. Would that this could have been just another casual stroll...

They broke through the trees and rounded the shed just as Red slammed the trunk on his cruiser, one hand fiddling with a button on his uniform shirt. He didn't appear aware of them as he ruffled a hand through his bright locks and then stuffed the tail of his shirt into his trousers. He retrieved a large black duffel bag from the ground near his feet and pivoted in their direction. He faltered midstride, but then he ambled on.

"Ms. Frost...Sheriff," he greeted them, readjusting his grip in the bag. "Where do you want me to get started?"

Once again, Cam felt like an elastic band, pulled in too many directions. Sooner or later, he was just going to snap beneath the pressure.

"I'll take the kit," Cam growled, releasing JJ so he could pluck the heavy bag from Red's hands. "I was first on the scene, I'll head back now."

"But I—"

He cast a murderous glance at Red, cutting him off mid sentence. "You will stay with JJ. You will *not* leave her side until I personally get back, am I understood?" Red nodded, frowning at Cam as if he'd lost his mind. Cam ignored the petulant look and snapped, "Keep her inside...and out of trouble." Cam stepped close, until his nose was inches from Reds. "And for your sake, I better never hear another word about you flippin' freakin' quarters for dibs on a crime scene."

Red's eyes were the size of aforementioned quarters by the time Cam finished. Bobbing his head, he stepped back, his face matching his hair.

Cam veered back to JJ, consciously softening his tone. "You'll be fine now. Go on inside, stay with Red. I'll be back as soon as I can."

She was still too pale for his liking, but there wasn't a damned thing he could do about it. He had to get back to the crime scene. He shouldn't have left it to begin with, but he hadn't been able to stand the thought of her walking through those woods alone...or with someone else. Thank heaven Jarvis knew what the hell he was doing. The last thing he needed right now was to worry about some damned novice screwing up any possible evidence.

Before he realized what he was doing, he feathered an anxious caress over her cheek. Biting off a vicious oath, he stomped passed her and then broke into a steady jog, the black duffel bag tossed over his shoulder.

Chapter 17

Oddly bereft, JJ gawked as he disappeared around the side of the shed. A gentle wind brushed at her bare arms, and she shivered. When had it gotten so cold out here? She hadn't noticed the chilly night air since...well, since Cam had come charging to her rescue...again...scooping her up into his arms. Nearly every minute since then, he'd been touching her in one way or another. The loss of contact left a cold physical ache, bone deep.

Rubbing her arms, she staggered around to face Red. Her knees were fast turning to jelly, and she wasn't altogether certain how much longer they would last before they gave way completely. Red scowled at the shed, or rather the edge around which Cam had disappeared, lost in thought.

"Deputy?"

Seeming to stir himself, Red offered her a somewhat bashful smile. "Sorry...I better get you inside or he'll have my hide."

He reached for her elbow and led her toward the house with the same solicitous care a boy scout might offer a senior citizen to cross the street. His touch was confident, but a bit stilted. Then again, maybe she'd just grown used to Cam. He didn't so much *touch* as he *possessed*. Shaking her head at her own fanciful thoughts, she assumed the lead up the steps and into the house.

The kitchen light was still on, and JJ went straight to the sink to wash her hands. Sap stuck to her fingers, compounding the *soiled* feeling. She half wished she were alone. Then she wouldn't have thought twice about going upstairs and sinking into a deep, boiling-hot tub of bubbles.

"Come in and have a seat. Make yourself comfortable, Deputy," she offered over her shoulder. The way he stood awkwardly by the door, thumbs hooked in his utility belt, shifting from foot to foot, made her strangely uneasy.

"Now, JJ," he chided. "Just 'cause you don't have a few beers under your belt don't mean you have to go all formal on me. Red worked just fine the other night when I give you girls all a ride home, it'll work fine tonight, too."

Drying her hands on a dishcloth, she pivoted and leaned a hip against the cabinets. "You're right. I'm sorry. I guess I'm just a little...shaken up."

"Given the circumstances, I'd say you're allowed." Red settled himself on a chair, crossing his ankles. "Is there anything I can do for you? Anyone I can call?"

"No, thank you," she murmured, sliding onto the chair at the opposite end of the table. "Where are my manners? Can I get you something, Red? Coffee or water...I believe I have a couple sodas..."

"A soda would be just fine...though, if you don't mind my saying so, you look like you could stand something a bit stronger." One corner of his mouth quirked up. "Course, Cam probably don't want you drinking right now, I'm guessing he's probably gonna want to talk to you again, take an official statement and all."

JJ plodded to Red, soda in hand. As she held the icy-cold can out to him, her gaze finally registered his appearance. "You're a mess."

His alarmed stare shot to hers. His eyebrows lifted to his hairline, and then he glanced down at himself as he patted his chest with one hand, as if searching for something. "Excuse me?"

Realizing her mouth had run away without her

brain, she lifted a hand to cover the offensive body part, and let out an exhausted giggle. "Oh...I'm sorry. That was rude."

Red wasn't paying her apology much attention. He was too busy examining his shirt and his arms and hands.

"Your shirt buttons are misaligned," she offered helpfully.

"Oh...ah, thanks," he muttered as he set to work righting his buttons.

She paused then, tilting her head. "You've a bit of dried blood on your neck...right there..."

His fingers paused, the button halfway through the hole, and his gaze shot to hers once more. Following her indication, button forgotten, he slapped a hand to his neck. "Do you have a mirror? I, I must have...cut myself shaving."

"There's a small powder room down the hall and to your right."

She cast a bemused glance at Red as he sprang to his feet and disappeared down the hallway. A few moments later, he returned. The blood was gone.

"Just a nick," he assured her. His appearance was impeccable now.

Spotless.

She had to stop this. She was overanalyzing everything. Shrugging it off, she took a long swig from her can, savoring the bite of the soda behind gritted teeth. "How long do you think it will be before Cam gets back?"

"Depends on the crime scene, how difficult it is to process...could be a while."

"Do you think it would be all right...I just feel so..." She trailed away on a shiver of revulsion. "I'd like to go up and take a long, hot shower. Would that be all right?"

"I'm sure that'd be just fine."

"Thank you." Maybe after she lost the disgusting

layer of fear coating her skin, she'd feel normal again.

Checking the impulse to search for car keys, she left Red to his own devices and hurried up the stairs. In a matter of minutes, lavender-scented steam filled the bathroom, blunting the jagged edges of her evening in the woods.

****

Cam rapped sharply on the back door, and stepped inside as Red opened the door for him. The house was silent, but for the groan and clank of the pipes in the kitchen walls. The kitchen was empty, the rest of the downstairs dark.

"I thought I told you not to let her out of your sight," he snapped.

"I checked the windows and the front door, the house is secure. She wanted to take a shower...looked like she needed something to calm her nerves," Red interjected, eyeing Cam warily. "Given the circumstances, I didn't figure you meant for me to stick to her side...literally."

At the mere suggestion, a low threatening growl rumbled in Cam's chest, filling his throat, but he caught it before it snarled through his lips. Cam was on edge, raw...and knew it. Besides, there was no excuse to take it out on his deputy. He honestly couldn't even be upset over the whole quarter thing. After all, it wasn't as if Cam had never done anything similar when he was a deputy himself...and with Austin, no less.

Threading his fingers through his hair, he sagged onto a kitchen chair. It had been a hell of a night. He'd been across town investigating his first solid lead on the vandalism cases. Of course, now the vandals had stepped up their game. The warehouse fire had definitely been arson, the place saturated with accelerant—gasoline, by the smell of it.

What was that old phrase...when it rains, it

pours?

That was his life right about now. It was pouring...and not timid little kittens and puppies. No, in his world, it rained full-grown bobcats and Great Danes. He wouldn't dream of prodding fate by asking what next.

"You can take off now." He leaned back in the chair, propped his ankle on his knee, and crossed his arms over his chest, pinching at the bridge of his nose between his thumb and forefinger. His heightened senses had yet to dull, and the sensory overload was beginning to take its toll. "I'll bring your kit to the office in the morning."

Nodding, silent, Red ducked out, leaving Cam alone with his desolate thoughts, thoughts too troublesome to bear for long in the face of inactivity, and so he puttered about JJ's kitchen, checking the faucet to make sure it still worked all right, brewing a fresh pot of coffee. Responsibility weighed heavy upon him. He should shift, go back and search the crime scene. But, knowing the futility of that, he opted to stay here.

Opted to guard his female.

A short while later...as Cam sat at the table with a cooling, untouched cup of coffee before him, his elbows propped on his knees...he caught the faint creak on the stairs. He detected her scent moments before she entered the kitchen. Alluring.

Home.

Bright-eyed and pale, JJ shuffled into the kitchen smelling of lavender soap and innocence. Fresh. Vibrant. Her damp hair hung down the length of her back, nearly to her waist, in fragrant strands. The soft curls beckoned him, tempting him to lose himself in her, forget everything else. Her skin glowed pink from scrubbing. His mouth watered for a taste. Cloud-soft, baby blue cotton pajama pants caught low on her hips by a thin drawstring. Her tiny feet were bare. Her white T-shirt was worn soft with time, a V-neck like he preferred for himself. It wasn't hard to imagine her wearing *his* shirt.

Or nothing at all, for that matter.

She blinked, as if surprised to see him there. Then her eyes softened, warmed. Something twisted, deep in his chest.

"I sent Red home," he offered by way of explaining his presence, "Or back to Brandi's...whatever the case being..."

"Do you need to take an official statement now?" She floated to the counter, taking down another coffee mug and filling it.

"No, I think I have everything I need. I wrote it up before I came back."

Turning to him, she held the steaming mug in both hands. Her brow wrinkled. "If you don't need a statement...why are you here?"

"I was worried about you. I didn't want you to be alone tonight."

He didn't want to be alone.

"I'll be fine."

What about me? Will I be fine?

"You scared the hell out of me," he barked. *Where'd that come from?*

"I'm sorry, Cam...I just...I didn't know what else to do, so I called you." Without taking her eyes from him, she set the coffee cup down with an unsteady hand, and rubbed at her arms as if she were cold. "I kept seeing..." Her gaze drifted beyond him. Her voice dropped, broken and strained. "I keep seeing Sarah...I couldn't leave...couldn't leave him like that...alone..."

Sarah...of course.

Sarah DeWitt. JJ's sister. The article he'd read on the internet, the faxed police reports he'd received from Minneapolis came flooding back. Those vicious

251

scars. What he wouldn't give to make it all better for her, to take away the horror and the fear. His skin crawled at the thought of what she must have gone through out there in the woods tonight. Alone.

But she'd called him.

In the minutes she'd needed someone, she'd called *him*.

That had to count for something.

Her focus came back to the here and now, to him. "Who was that man?"

"Chuck Hughes...the mayor."

Another pang of guilt clawed him. Three murders and not one scrap of evidence pointing to a suspect. He'd gone over every square inch of each crime scene. He'd reviewed every file front to back and back to front. He'd stared at crime scene photos until the images had burned themselves into his nightmares. And he was no closer to catching the killer than he had been the night Lori had been murdered.

Damn it.

"I was so scared, Cam." Her words were soft, carrying with them the bite of shame.

Everything else faded to nothing. He was on his feet and across the room before he realized he'd moved. Gathering her into his arms, he pressed her close, murmuring soothing sounds against her hair. "I was scared, too."

"You?" She snuffled against his shirt, and gave a tiny snort of disbelief. "I doubt anything could scare you."

"Not much scares me," he admitted. He took hold of her shoulders, edging her back just a little, just enough so that he could look down into her face. The next words that poured forth shocked him to his core, even as he realized the gleaming ring of truth in them. "But you do...you terrify the living bejesus out of me."

Her beautiful blue eyes widened, and she went utterly still beneath his hands. The lush curve of her lips parted on a soundless breath. He couldn't resist. Cam brushed his lips, ever so softly, across hers. Once. Twice. Three times.

Those tiny nibbles only fueled his hunger.

He'd intended his kisses to be those of comfort and reassurance, but they swiftly turned to voracious, blatant, carnal need. Blazing out of control. Consuming his restraint.

With a low growl, he slipped an arm around her waist and hauled her flush against him. Cam seized her lips, thrusting his tongue inside her mouth as he claimed the sweet curve of her bottom with his free hand. Squeezing possessively, he held her immobile as he thrust his hips against her, leaving no room for doubt as to how much he wanted. Her tongue parried with his, tangled, danced. Her lips were so soft. The taste of her pulled him under, straight into a riptide of emotion. He knew she was vulnerable, knew in his heart that if he were a better man, he'd walk away now.

Evidently, he wasn't a better man. He was a Werewolf. There would be no turning back now, no time for second-guessing, and no room for self-doubts.

At last.

He would claim his mate.

He'd waited a lifetime for this it seemed...without *knowing* he'd been waiting. Her hands slipped up his chest, over his shoulders, and her fingers laced through his hair as she yielded to his demanding kiss. She was paradise, pliant in his arms. He had to remind himself how tiny she was, remind himself of his strength. He had to be careful with her.

She wasn't making it easy. She was so responsive, so damned *willing*. It was hard to slow down, and getting harder by the moment, difficult to rein in the instinctual need to mate. He should know better than to try. The others had often warned him—with smirks and sly winks—that when a Werewolf found his mate, sex was anything but civilized.

Understanding now dawned...with a vengeance. In his current state of arousal, civility was nothing more than a thin veneer masking the slavering, lusting beast within. Something deep inside, something primordial and fundamental was changing inside him. It snapped at his control, shredding his will. Nothing short of divine intervention could stop him from claiming her as his own now.

In one seamless motion, he swept an arm beneath her knees, lifting her high against his chest. His mouth still locked on hers, Cam strode from the room and down the hallway. The stairs disappeared beneath his boots, two at a time, and he carried her inside the first open bedroom doorway. The scent of her was stronger here.

The moment her feet touched the bare floor beside her bed, she tore her lips from his. Her arms remained locked around his neck. Luminous blue eyes stared up at him through a haze of passion as she swayed against him. "Cam," she whispered breathlessly, "what are you doing?"

His wry laugh was harsh, ragged in his throat. His entire body vibrated with the depth of his need. His hands shook from the fierceness of his desire as he fumbled his phone from his pocket, thumbed it off before tossing it on her bedside table. His dead pager followed a second later. The muscle in his jaw snapped and pulsed as he strained for some semblance of control.

"I sort of thought you'd have figured that out by now."

The pink tip of her tongue slicked over her bottom lip, leaving a trail of inviting moisture in its wake. The mask of civility shattered. Cam wound his hand in her hair, fisting it at the base of her skull, dragging her head back. His other hand jerked at the string tied at her waist. His ravenous focus locked on her lips for a moment before he jerked his hungry gaze to her eyes. He was dead serious now.

"I'm claiming you, Jillian." He stole one swift, soul-deep kiss as the tie at her waist gave. Yanking his lips from hers, he nipped and suckled his way to her earlobe. Panting in her ear, he snarled, "From this night forward...I claim you as mine."

She whimpered soft acquiescence, trembling against him. The soft cotton pants slid down her trim legs, pooling around her bare feet. With a hungry growl, he released her long enough to whip the T-shirt over her head, leaving her in nothing more than a shell-pink, lacy bra and matching panties. If he hadn't been so overcome with the need to mate, he would have fallen to his knees to worship at her feet. Thankfully, the sight of her, so stunning and delicate, harnessed some of the power surging through him. So many emotions seethed inside him, difficult to isolate or identify, and they all—each and every last one—centered around his stunning female.

Remembering his vow to make their first time together special, he made a conscious effort to slow down. Slow was pure living hell, a nightmare of tormented desire. He whisked his own shirt over his head, not bothering with the buttons. A faint ping echoed in his ears as one of the buttons bounced off the far wall. It was a small wonder his zipper continued to hold against the heavy, excruciatingly painful weight of his erection.

She gasped, staring goggle-eyed at the wide expanse of his naked chest, and he froze. Oh, hell...

He'd gone too fast, lost his head and scared her. He hadn't prepared her, hadn't explained *anything* to her at all. He was a bastard. A selfish, horny bastard. How could he have let things get out of hand so quickly?

He struggled to find his voice, working to form the words of apology, but then she lifted her hands, splaying them on his chest, just over his heart. Her fingers, light as the stroke of a feather, traced his griffin. A murmur of unmistakable female approval bubbled in her throat. His words of remorse emerged as a greedy rumble of pleasure. With butterfly strokes, she touched him, smoothing her cool palms over his burning, aching flesh, exploring him, his chest, his ribs, his shoulders. Her eyes followed her hands. Then her lips did, and he thought he'd surely die from the pleasure alone.

She glanced up at him. Her blue eyes glittered in the moonlight. She moistened her lips again.

He was a goner.

In seconds, he stripped the rest of his gear and clothing away. Cam snaked his arms around her, hauling her to him, crushing her against him. His throbbing shaft pulsed against her stomach, the contact of skin on naked skin ripped a tormented hiss from him. The lace and silk of her bra and panties—previously enticing—thwarted him now, providing far more barrier than his body could stand.

Her bra came loose with a deft flick of nimble fingers. Impatiently sweeping the scrap of lace out of his way, Cam filled his hand with her silky smooth breast. Her pebbled nipple thrust against his palm, driving him out of his mind. He sank to his knees before her, caged her hips in his hands, and sealed his lips over her nipple, flicking his tongue over her, suckling her hard until her knees buckled.

Bracing her meager weight against him, he

continued his thorough ministrations on the other breast. JJ tossed her head back, moaning low and deep. She laced her fingers through his hair, cradling his head to her. The scent of her arousal wreaked havoc on his control. Cam buried his face against her flat stomach for a moment and inhaled, soul deep, savoring the flavor of her, absorbing it, letting it sink through him...become a part of him.

Turning his lips to her flesh, he tasted her skin, trailing hot, open-mouthed kisses from sternum to the scallop of lace below her navel. His hands slid from her hips down over her thighs. Her skin was the finest of silk beneath his fingertips. On the return trip back up her thighs, his thumbs hooked in the thin straps banded over her hips. With inescapable deliberation, he drew the lacy barrier lower and lower until her panties joined the pile of light blue cotton at her feet.

Cam rocked back on his heels as he stared up at her. Never in his life had he seen anything...anyone...so beautiful, so precious. She made to shield her body with self-conscious hands, but he wouldn't allow it. He captured her wrists, pulling them down to her sides. His eyes, worshipful and greedy, devoured every inch of her. When at last he found his voice, his whisper couldn't have been more reverent, more sincere had he been standing at God's altar, surrounded by a choir of heavenly angels.

"So beautiful..."

She blushed beneath his steady regard, but her attention focused now on his straining erection. He flexed his proud, masculine strength for her, stifling a devilish grin. Her eyes widened and she caught her breath. His grin broke free.

Dropping a swift kiss to the perfect, golden skin of her taut stomach, he rose, gathering her against him. Twisting, he levered onto the bed with one knee, laying her on the mattress before him like a feast...like a virgin sacrifice to an insatiable god. He claimed her mouth again, weaving a heady spell with his lips and tongue. Her hands grew restless upon him, tracing over his back, squeezing his shoulders, caressing his chest, trailing a blaze of passion across his skin.

When they slid lower, their goal unmistakable, he captured her wrists once more, pinning them to the mattress above her head, strung too tight to risk her hands on him there. He was too close to that precarious edge of wild, unrestrained abandon. The reins of his control were slippery at best now. One tiny tug of those beautiful hands of hers, and he wouldn't stand a hope in hell of keeping the starving animal inside him tethered.

Keeping her wrists manacled with one hand, he trailed his fingers down the length of her arm, over the outer slope of her breast, across the shallow valley of her stomach. He traced tender kisses down the length of the scars along her forearm. She was perfection. He couldn't get enough of her. Angling his head, he slanted his mouth across hers, taking the kiss to a new level. Cam nudged her thighs apart with his knee, feathering his fingers over the delicate skin on her stomach, down to the mound of soft curls at the apex of her thighs. She started—just a tiny jolt of awareness—and puffed a tiny sigh against his lips. She was already damp against his palm. He'd done that to her, effected her so strongly. The knowledge cranked his blood from a bubbling simmer to a hard, rolling boil.

She was so hot, so wet, his shaft jerked against her hip, ready and eager. Groaning into her mouth, he slicked his fingers against her, burrowing them into her heat, teasing and satisfying as she squirmed and strained for more, bucking her hips against his hand—whimpering against his mouth.

Determined to make this last as long as possible, he shifted above her, nudging her thighs farther apart. He meant to slide lower, to take her with his mouth first and taste her passions, savor them. But the moment he knelt between her thighs, she thrust her hips up, brushing the length of his straining erection with her damp womanhood.

Her blatant invitation was his undoing. If he didn't bury himself deep inside her, right *now*, he'd go out of his mind.

****

JJ strained against the iron band of his hand around her wrists. He'd drugged her with his intoxicating kisses, and now he was tormenting her with his body. The sight of him, kneeling on the floor before her in all his aroused splendor had brought her a whole new meaning to the word terror. His size alone was daunting—daunting, hell, the man was freakin' enormous—but the very thought of not going through with this—not making love with Cam—was more than she could bear.

He'd caught her by surprise when he'd carried her up the stairs, but she wouldn't have—couldn't have—told him to stop if her life had depended on it. Honestly, what woman wouldn't melt...just a little...at literally being swept off her feet and whisked away like Scarlett? He hadn't declared himself, hadn't spoken the sentimental words of promise most women needed before they would even consider allowing things to progress to this point. But words weren't important to her. Words could be a lie just as easy as they could be the truth.

Actions held sway with her, and Cam's actions—though at times arrogant and bossy—were noble. With Cam, she felt safe...she *was* safe. With Cam. He'd set her skin on fire with his bold, possessive strokes. Her head swam with his kisses. And if he didn't ease this burning ache deep inside her, she'd scream, go utterly mad. Insane. A drooling, blathering idiot.

His lips branded the side of her throat, sending shivers of molten desire racing through her veins. She rocked her hips, lifting them, rubbing the sensitive nub of her need along the rigid, steely length of his shaft, and he growled against her skin.

Her wrists were free at last, and she sank her fingers deep in his hair. His fingers bit into her flesh as he slammed her hips back onto the bed, holding them immobile. His chest rubbed against her breasts with every ragged pant...both hers and his. He moved, settling himself between her thighs, nudging them farther apart. She obligingly wrapped her legs around his waist, tilting her hips despite his efforts to restrain her.

Did she have to beg?

She would...in a heartbeat.

His fingers tightened on her hips. She'd have bruises tomorrow, but she couldn't have cared less. He muttered a harsh expletive against the ridge of her jaw, and the broad head of his penis parted her. At the intimate contact, his body shuddered atop her, his muscles quivered, straining and rock-solid. He pushed inside her, inch by excruciatingly slow inch, stretching her, filling her. The burning need increased exponentially. But he held her fast, refusing to let her move.

Holy Crap. He was going so...damned...*slow.*

She clutched at his shoulders, digging her fingernails into muscle. "Cam," she pleaded.

"No...hold...still," he ground out, teeth gritted, panting. "So...tight...don't want...to hurt...you..."

She nipped at his chin with her teeth, seeking his lips. He gave them to her, and she immediately sank her tongue inside his mouth, assuming control of the kiss. She *would* get her way. Her hands cupped his buttocks, pressing him closer, gaining only one more precious inch of him. Frustrated, she clenched and relaxed her inner muscles, clenched and relaxed, drawing him deeper, tugging at him.

"Damn it, JJ," he growled against her mouth. His grip on her hips tightened painfully, and he shifted for better leverage.

JJ clamped her legs tight around him, fearful he intended to retreat. Without warning, the world suddenly shuddered beneath her as he gave one short, angry hiss, and slammed himself to the hilt inside her. Startled, overcome by the blissful friction, she cried out, but he didn't stop. He was like a madman possessed now, wrapping his arms around her, pounding urgently inside her, over and over, grinding himself deep, groaning.

Even as he drove into her, he whispered apologies in her ear, his voice hoarse, guttural. But she wasn't in pain, couldn't understand why he kept telling her he was sorry. She'd never felt better. She could die right now, a happy, satisfied woman.

JJ fisted her hands in his hair, jerking his head back until he finally focused glittering, contrite emerald eyes on hers. The lines of his face were strained, his gaze troubled, even as his hips continued to pump frantically between her thighs.

"Stop apologizing," she ordered. "I happen to be enjoying myself here."

Then she seized his lips, pouring every ounce of feeling she possessed into her kiss. Abruptly, buried deep, he froze. Cam tore his lips from hers and stared down at her with an odd mixture of awe and desire etched upon his face. It was as if a strange peacefulness had come over him, soothing the jagged edges of his need.

Cam lowered his head to hers once more, his lips sliding over hers with newfound control, though this kiss was every bit as powerful, every bit as soul-consuming as his carnal possession of seconds before. Just as she began to sink under the tide of his desire, he pulled away. Not just from the kiss, but from her body as well.

Confused, JJ gurgled a protest. Without warning, Cam flipped her over onto her stomach and spread her legs. Faster than she could blink, he gripped her hips, pulling her back and up. In one long thrust, his shaft sank deep inside her, deeper than ever before.

But he wasn't done.

Cam splayed his hand under her chest, pulling her up until his chest pressed against her back. His calloused palm covered her breast, kneading, caressing. His free hand slid around her waist and down, nimble fingers furrowing through her curls. With his lightly bristled cheek, he nudged her head until she looked up. Straight at the large mirror above the antique dresser across the room.

Her startled gaze locked on the entwined couple writhing erotically on the bed. Then Cam parted her golden curls, and she couldn't tear her gaze from what he'd revealed. He kneed her thighs farther apart, pulling her back against him, tilting her as he began thrusting up and into her. His fingers massaged the tiny nub between her legs. The thick girth of him stretched her as he sank deep. The sight was almost as erotic as the sensation.

His hand released her breast, only to capture the other. He rolled her taut nipple between his thumb and forefinger, and stroked his way over her ribs and her stomach. His mouth seared her throat. His teeth nipped. He was pure seduction now. Every move, every caress, every kiss, every thrust was raw sensuality, inescapable and intense.

Her head lolled back against his shoulder, but she continued to observe the couple in the mirror through hooded, passion-glazed eyes, surrendering her body—surrendering everything inside her—to him.

"You belong to me now, JJ, as I belong to you." Cam's deep voice was hoarse in her ear. The reflection of his bright emerald gaze bore into hers for one defining moment. Then he caught her earlobe between his teeth, nipping lightly. She gripped the sides of his thighs as he continued to glide in and out of her. He caged her to him in strong arms. "I swear...I will cherish you."

Tension built and crested until she teetered on the brink of shattering. With every word he spoke, his thrust held more power, more purpose. His lips slid to a point, just behind her earlobe, a sensitive spot that sent delicious shivers coursing through her, pushing her closer to the fall.

"I give you my loyalty...and all that I am," he panted raggedly against her skin. "I will keep you safe...always..."

With his final words, something happened...something strange. A tiny flare of pain scored that sensitive place behind her earlobe where his mouth rested, pulsing and throbbing at first, then dulling to a faint twinge. At nearly that exact moment, he rocked hard into her, touching her just so, setting off a chain reaction deep inside her body she had no way of controlling, no way of resisting. With a sharp cry, she shattered in his arms, her body's inner muscles clenching hard on his shaft as she dug her nails into his thighs.

A dark growl rippled up from Cam's chest, vibrating against her back. He tossed his head back, letting the roar pour forth as he crushed her to him, spilling pulsing warmth deep inside her.

Exhausted, limp, JJ let Cam maneuver her until she lay on the bed, cradled in his arms. He kept her back pressed tightly to his chest, surrounding her with his warmth. A contented smile curling her lips, she drifted to sleep with his bicep as her pillow, his arm her blanket. His large, hot hand splayed over her stomach.

His shaft—still surprisingly hard—buried deep within her.

Chapter 18

JJ woke to the muted warble of cheerful birdsong. Yawning, she rolled over, stretching the stiffness from her abused muscles. Cam had been a demanding lover—more demanding than she'd ever imagined possible—waking her up several times last night for vigorous bouts of lovemaking.

In the middle of one such session, he'd growled in her ear—almost a complaint—that he couldn't get enough of her. More importantly, he'd shown her...every time he took her. Even when they weren't making love, he hadn't stopped holding her, hadn't stopped touching her. In the quiet times between loving, he'd kissed her, nuzzled her, laced his fingers through hers, whispering warm affections against her skin. He'd been like a man possessed, driven by the need for constant physical contact. By turns dominant and possessive, and then playfully yielding and affectionate.

Satisfying warmth crept into her cheeks as she recalled the last time he'd taken her, in the early shadows before dawn. Before she'd fully gained consciousness, Cam was already kissing her senseless, cradling himself between her thighs, thrusting slow and deep. He'd teased her with gentle kisses, nuzzling her until she giggled, then he'd gazed deep into her eyes with an impassioned intensity, made her heart flutter beneath her breastbone. His lips returned—time and time again—to the responsive place behind her earlobe, the place that had briefly stung last night.

At last, when he'd carried her to the peak and

swept her over, he'd sealed his lips over hers, drinking her cries in like the elixir of life. He'd thrust harder, faster for a moment, then stiffened in her arms, pulsing and exploding deep inside her. Before she'd drifted back to sleep, he'd whispered in her ear that he needed to go in to the office, but he promised her he'd be back later in the day. He'd dropped a kiss on the tip of her nose, and one behind her ear, given her a strange, fierce look, and slipped from her bed.

JJ fingered the skin behind her ear. There was no welt now, as she'd have expected from a bug bite. It felt normal. It didn't hurt anymore either. Shrugging, she rolled back to her stomach and wrapped her arms around her pillow, grinning like a loon.

Her friends hadn't been just a-kiddin', she mused with a smile. He *was* a sex-god in bed. Surely, it was a sin for a man to have a body like that. And that tattoo. She'd never seen anything so...so sinfully sexy. In the wee hours of the morning, she'd asked him about it, why he'd chosen that particular tattoo, and what it meant. He'd told her that in medieval legend, griffins were said to be guardians of kings and treasures. They were ferocious protectors, unquestionably loyal, lethally strong, and fiercely intelligent.

The griffin was a perfect symbol for Cam. She giggled at the whimsical thought.

She was exhausted, and she'd never been more relaxed, more satisfied. It should probably have bothered her, the fact that she'd fallen so readily into bed with him, especially given the fact she'd known him for such a short time. That wasn't like her, not at all. JJ just wasn't a girl to play fast and loose, in fact, she could count on one hand how many men she'd been intimate with...and still have several fingers left.

More disturbing, however, was the confounding feeling it wouldn't have mattered whether she'd been with one man or a hundred before Cam. Nothing would have compared with what she'd found in his arms. There was, quite simply, a before Cam. And then there *was* Cam.

The question now remained, would there be an *after*?

Pushing those unsettling thoughts away, she shoved the comforter aside and crawled from the bed, limping to the bathroom. She ached in places she hadn't known it was possible to ache. A long, steaming shower helped to ease her muscles, but the tenderness between her thighs remained. A pleasant reminder of how she'd spent the long hours laced in shadows and moonlight.

In Cam's warm, strong arms.

A brief pang of guilt flickered over her as she recalled how her evening had begun...and that poor man in the woods. Being with Cam had driven those horrid memories completely from her mind.

Now, in the bright light of day, they'd returned.

Subdued, she dressed, ate a quick breakfast of cinnamon sprinkled toast, and stepped out onto the back porch with her brimming coffee mug in hand. Sunlight bathed the day in cheery rays. The early morning air was warm and crisp, filling her with the promise of a pleasant, warm spring day. She surveyed her flower gardens. Vibrant spring buds were thriving now that she'd banished the choking weeds. She could work there a bit more, but she was too restless for that.

Stepping back inside the kitchen, she refilled her mug, and made her way to her studio in the attic. She had obligations now—work to do. Golden sunlight flooded the room, just as she knew it would that first morning she'd set foot here. Crossing to the window, she pushed it wide open and breathed deep of the fresh air. A promising hint of rain hung on to the day. Perhaps her flowers would get a shower later. Smiling, she positioned her easel and paints. It was a beautiful day, and, thanks in large part to Cam, she was filled with inspiration.

Death would not trespass here.

She wouldn't allow it to color her work, not anymore.

Several hours later, JJ stepped back to survey her canvas. Bright splashes of color, bold and true, commanded the eye. The smaller, equally important details were perfect. It was finished.

Lovers...

The fundamental word drifted through her mind from out of nowhere. So simple, yet so intrinsic.

Intimate.

She'd call this one *Lovers*. Satisfied, she removed the canvas from the easel and propped it on the table at the far end of the room. After equipping the easel with a fresh canvas, blank and eager for life, she cleaned her brushes, reorganized her paints, and tossed the rag she'd used to wipe her hands into a small bucket on the floor at the end of the table. The warm breeze wafting through the open windows called to her, caressing her with tantalizing, eager fingers. She couldn't resist any longer.

In short order, JJ donned her hiking boots, crammed her keys and a small fold of cash into one pocket and her cell phone into the other. A nice long stretch of the legs sounded wonderful. With any luck, the rain would hold off until she got back, and if it didn't, so what. She wouldn't melt.

Despite the agreeable possibility of seeing her wolf again, she couldn't face the woods, nor did she want to remember what she'd discovered there last night. She wandered down her lane, turning her boots toward town instead.

JJ glanced at her watch. Maybe she could talk

Ginny into a late lunch. Wouldn't it be icing on her cake if Maggie's special of the day were that delicious meatloaf again? That thought put a spring in her step. Nodding and smiling, JJ greeted pedestrians on the street with an ease she'd never felt in Minneapolis. Pushing the door to the hardware store open, she smiled at the cheerful jingle of bells.

"Well, good afternoon there, sunshine," Ginny greeted her. She finished lining up a row of extra stock on the top shelf, and climbed down from the stepladder. Dusting her hands on the hips of her faded jeans, Ginny joined JJ at the counter.

"Afternoon," JJ beamed. "You have lunch yet?"

"Nope. Got busy after this morning's delivery and lost track of time." She shot a glance over her right shoulder, whispered conspiratorially, "Soon as Ms. Potter here decides which garden hose she wants, we can make a break for it. You'd swear she was pickin' out fine china for the White House for all the time she's taking."

JJ propped a hip against the counter and settled in to make small talk while the hunch-backed, elderly woman in a ratty, old-fashioned shawl waffled between green coils and colorful labels.

"How's Tanner?"

"The little stinker finally managed to wear me down," Ginny complained with a good-natured smile. "We're going over to Doc Templeton's when Tanner gets out of school. Sadie's pups are weaned."

"I bet he's over the moon."

"Yeah...till he gets pooper-scooper detail," Ginny joked, then she canted her head and considered JJ for a long moment, adding, "You know...a puppy sure would make that big old house of yours a bit less lonely."

"Maybe I'll go with you." JJ chewed on the tip of her thumbnail. A puppy might be fun. Then she thought of her wolf. How would he react? Hesitantly, she inquired, "Say...have you heard anything about...wild wolves in the area?"

"Wolves?" Ginny's tone was sharp, but she ducked her head, suddenly fascinated with eradicating a strip of dust from beneath the edge of the cash register. "Heavens, why would you be wondering about wolves?"

"Well, I...I have one," JJ admitted. Ginny's fingers stilled, then she scrubbed at the dust line with renewed, fierce determination. "I mean, that is to say, I don't necessarily *have* one. It's just...there's one in the woods near my place."

Ginny glanced up swiftly, her eyes piercing. "You've seen it?"

"Actually..." Drawing a deep breath, JJ toyed with a tin can full of generic pens beside the register. "It sort of...comes to visit me on occasion." She told Ginny of the incident with the bear, and of finding the wolf in the strange gathering place in the woods. By the time she'd finished her tale, she had Ginny's undivided attention.

And Ms. Potters as well.

"What does this wolf look like?" Ginny frowned, rubbing absently at the wide leather watchband on her wrist.

"Oh, he's beautiful," JJ blurted. "And big! I never realized they were so large up close. His coat is...well, it's like honey, rich and golden, and so thick...amazingly soft," JJ trailed off with a slight shake of her head. "He has the most unusual eyes...like emeralds." Like Cam's. She paused for a moment on that disconcerting thought before pushing on. "I didn't know wolves could even have green eyes."

Ginny's eyes had gone wide at JJ's description. The corners of her mouth had begun to hitch upward. "His coat was golden, huh? With green eyes—"

"Oh, my dear, that's not just any wolf you're talking about. You've met one of *them*." The nosy little old woman hobbled down the aisle in her tan, orthopedic shoes and her faded blue housedress. Short steel-wool hair clung to small pink curlers, haphazardly secured in place by a large, faded red handkerchief. Her cloudy, gray eyes were round with eager delight. "Green eyes, you say?"

"Excuse me?" JJ cast a frowning glance at a curiously motionless Ginny. "One of *them*?"

"One of the protectors, my dear," Ms. Potter insisted adamantly.

An image of Cam's griffin tattoo flashed through JJ's mind, his words filtered into her subconscious. Ferocious protectors, he'd said. JJ shook her head mystified. Ms. Potter nudged her horn-rimmed, rhinestone-studded glasses back up the bridge of her beak-like nose, and slung a coil of garden hose onto the counter with a pop of an arthritic hip. "Oh, that's right...you're new...probably haven't heard..."

Tight-lipped, Ginny hustled behind the counter, where she began ringing the sale up with astonishing speed. "Will that be all for you today, Ms. Potter?" She rushed on, not waiting for a response, "That comes to eight—"

"Protectors, I say," Ms. Potter insisted dramatically, ignoring Ginny as she warmed to her subject, "a whole pack of them."

Despite herself, JJ tilted her head and regarded the wizened woman with bemused curiosity. The poor old dear was clearly off her rocker. "A whole pack of what, ma'am?"

Ms. Potter shot a suspicious glance over her shoulder, then she whispered conspiratorially, "Werewolves, my dear. Werewolves..."

Ginny swore softly beneath her breath. JJ blinked, utterly speechless. The woman truly believed a pack of Werewolves ran loose in the woods of Sutter Hollow. Not only did she believe, fanatically, but she seemed bent on making JJ believe as well.

Werewolves! Imagine. Next she'd be insisting Vampires haunted the night, and Faeries and Leprechauns were real. Would she be offended if JJ offered her the name and number of a good shrink? Maybe she'd get a special discount or something for drumming up business for Dr. Greene.

On a sudden spurt of motion and another muttered curse, Ginny ripped a plastic sack loose from below the counter. She crammed the hose inside the noisy bag and thrust the tangled mess at her persistent customer. "Here you go, Ms. Potter," Ginny all but shouted, her teeth bared in nothing remotely close to a smile. "I'll just run a tab for you, and you can take care of the bill later. JJ, I'm positively starving! Why don't I close shop, and we can—"

"Oh, you mustn't listen to that craziness some people spout. They're just superstitious old fools. They don't know the truth." Ms. Potter glowered, shaking her knobby finger at JJ. She slung an accusatory grimace in Ginny's direction, adding, "The girl has a right to know, young lady...especially now." Her shrewd eyes locked on JJ, and her whole demeanor changed, became almost reverent. "Fearless warriors protected the old Indian village that once occupied the woods near Sutter Hollow against an encroaching evil so vile it threatened to drain the village of its very life force.

"Those warriors' descendants roam our woods now, slipping into wolf form at will, ever watchful for evil's return. They are ferocious protectors, possessive and loyal to their bones." Ms. Potter bobbed her head knowledgeably, taking the bag from Ginny only to lay it down on the counter at her side.

Her gray eyes were piercing as she reached out a gnarled hand to clasp JJ's wrist. "But you mustn't be afraid, my dear. They are fiercely protective of their mates. Your protector will never harm you."

Her protector? Mates? What nonsense was this old woman spouting? Was she trying to tell JJ that her wolf was some kind of...of mutant beast? Some shape-shifting creature? Absurd. Her wolf was just that...a wolf. There wasn't anything supernatural about him. He was a normal wolf.

Just a very *large*...tame...wolf.

No way was she going to mention she'd actually talked to the wolf, petted the wolf, wrestled with the wolf...or that it had licked her. What this batty old woman would make of that, JJ didn't even want to know.

"You've been blessed, it seems." Ms. Potter's voice was strangely worshipful, her eyes wandered to the side of JJ's neck, lingering just at the bottom edge of JJ's ear. JJ instinctively lifted her hand, smoothing her hair self-consciously along her neck. Why was the woman staring at her, at her neck like that?

"Blessed?" The word whooshed from a wide-eyed Ginny, and her gaze swerved to JJ, widened further still. Then she compressed her lips, as if trying to prevent any other slippery words from sliding past her guard.

"Blessed indeed," Ms. Potter gushed. "Our young artist here has captured his heart, little Ginny." She patted JJ's forearm, smiling kindly. "Oh, this is wonderful news. He was such a lonely boy, lonely on the inside...where the others couldn't see. You are just what he needs, dear." She patted JJ's forearm affectionately.

Frowning, JJ narrowed her eyes and backed a half step away. "What who needs? What are you talking about?" The old woman wasn't making any sense, and JJ was baffled. "Captured whose heart?"

Ginny couldn't have flown from behind the counter faster than if someone had set the place on fire, catching Ms. Potter and her purchase up and propelling them toward the door with a pained grimace. JJ couldn't quite catch the muttered words Ginny rasped into Ms. Potter's ear. The whole situation, the entire conversation had been so bizarre, JJ could only stare.

A half hour later—as Ginny all but shoved her from the diner—JJ was still just as lost. Perhaps more so. Things had seemed normal when they'd first arrived, but then suddenly—about the time JJ had swept her hair up into a ponytail, come to think of it—half the conversations in the diner hitched mid-stride. The other half ceased outright. She'd had more people stare at her in that last twenty minutes than she had the entire time she'd been in town...including her first morning there.

What was with everyone anyway? You'd think they'd never seen anyone put in a hair-tie before. Strange as everyone else was behaving today, Maggie's reaction had been the most bizarre of all. She'd come out from the kitchen to say hello as she always did. Halfway to their table, the ever-unshakable Maggie had gasped, skidded to a stop, and over-balanced a platter heaped with food. Her eyes had been as round as the saucers clattering on the floor, her mouth gaping open. She'd sputtered for a moment, then scurried over to JJ, hugging her like there was no tomorrow, gushing about how she was so pleased.

Just that fast, Ginny had begun making a strange, strangling sound in the back of her throat. JJ strained to glance around Maggie to make sure she wasn't choking on something, but by the time Maggie moved away, Ginny was dabbing at her lips with a napkin, eyes carefully averted. Maggie'd backed up, a look of severe consternation creasing her smoke-weathered face, and planted fists to bony hips.

"He's a bloody, damned idiot." Her declaration exploded through the silent diner like a volley of cannon fire before Maggie tromped away to see to the spilled food.

When JJ'd questioned Ginny, her evasive friend had begun twisting anxiously at the wide leather strap on her wrist, unable to make eye contact. Soon thereafter, Ginny had rushed JJ from the diner and sent her on her way home. Puzzled, muddling through the strange reaction in her mind, JJ glanced over her shoulder, unexpectedly catching Ginny as she snuck furtively across the street and ducked inside the sheriff's department.

JJ paused, eyes narrowed. Her teeth gnawed of the edge of her bottom lip. What in blue blazes was going on here?

Chapter 19

JJ shuffled her feet as she paced up her drive. Her troubled gaze tracked the small pebble bouncing a few feet ahead of her as her stomach twisted uneasily. It didn't take a rocket scientist to figure out Ginny was doing her damnedest to keep JJ in the dark about something, and Maggie—if not half the damned town—was in on the secret. Chewing the inside of her cheek, she tore the elastic band from her hair and thrust her hands deep in her pockets, jiggled her change.

She'd never felt like an outsider in Sutter Hollow. Even that first morning, she'd felt—in some strange way—connected. She was definitely out of the loop on this one. The question remained...what did everyone else know that she didn't?

Why was Ginny being so cagey? Disappointment chewed at her. She'd really thought she'd found a good friend in Ginny. Obviously, she was going to need to re-evaluate. Digging the keys from her pocket, JJ rounded the side of the house. A dark shadow moved across the porch, down the steps, slamming her heart into the back of her throat. She leaped back, a raw scream clawed its way free.

"I'm so sorry. I didn't mean to startle you," a gentle voice called out. Pale, thin hands thrust up in the space between them, empty palms out.

As her heart hammered its way back down her throat, JJ stared hard at the man on the top step. His face was vaguely familiar, and, as it turned bright red with embarrassment, she finally remembered. Don...no, Doug. Doug something-or-other, from the diner. The painfully shy insurance salesman. Right now, he looked like a salesman, put together and properly pressed to present a confident, competent appearance in pale slacks and an equally washed-out blazer.

One might consider him mildly attractive, once you looked beyond the computer-geek façade. Too bad he flushed like a schoolgirl at her first dance every time he got within ten feet of a woman. She'd seen firsthand proof of that in the diner. How did the man function in a business that demanded he deal directly with the public?

Slapping her palm over her thudding heart, she took pity on the horrified man on her steps, offering him a reassuring smile. "It wasn't you. My mind was…elsewhere. Doug, isn't it?"

"Yes, Doug Weston." He beamed down at her, his Adam's apple bobbing with his pulse. If he turned any redder, she feared she'd need to dial 911 for an ambulance. "You remembered."

"Of course." She brushed a stray lock of hair out of her eyes, tucking it behind her ear.

Her initial gut reaction was to back up a few paces, slip her keys between her fingers just so, even as she kept a steady smile plastered to her lips. Then she chided herself for being ridiculous. The man was harmless as a gangly pup, tall and reed thin. She could, in all likelihood, snap him in half without breaking a sweat. He was probably more afraid of her than she was of him. In fact, she cautioned herself not to smile too big. He just might keel over on her.

"Umm, can I help you with something?" Why did he keep staring at her like that? Was he waiting for her to sprout another head or something?

"Oh," he stuttered, jerking back a step. "I, ah, I b-brought you, ah, a welcome b-basket." Every word out of his mouth deepened the color burning his neck and face. He turned away, bending at the waist, and plucked up a whicker basket with long, narrow fingers. A large bow shimmered, pale pink, in the late afternoon sunshine.

"Oh, goodness, you didn't have to do that." Flustered now, she moved forward accepting the heavy parcel.

"I didn't...I mean, it's not from me. Well, not all of it. That is I..." He paused, visibly battling the bullfrog in his throat. "It's a welcome b-basket from the city council. Everyone who moves to town gets one. It's really just a b-basket of promotional stuff from local businesses."

She could see that now upon closer inspection. Dozens of multicolored pens, three rolled-up t-shirts, and a wide assortment of magnets, all meticulously printed with business logos, filled the basket to overflowing. Two tiny bottles of liquor advertised Pappy's Bar and Pool Hall. A tiny bowling pin keychain nestled among a small, colorful spray of scratchpads. A silver coffee mug bore Maggie's name in bold, artistic script. A red-handled claw hammer announced Connor Hardware in plain, no-nonsense lettering.

"Thank you." Then she glanced around, only just now realizing there was no car in her drive aside from her Jeep. "Did you walk all the way out here just to bring this to me?"

The flush had begun to recede from his cheeks. It surged once more, and he slipped a finger into the collar of his shirt, tugging uncomfortably. "Oh, ah, it was nothing. Should've brought it out before now. Just a good stretch of the legs..."

Stepping up onto the porch beside him, JJ glanced over her shoulder as she inserted the key into the lock. "Would you like to come in for a glass of iced tea or something? I baked chocolate chip cookies last night."

His face brightened with a cheerful smile, his eyes lit up. "That would b-be—"

Gravel crunched and sprayed beneath large tires, cutting his reply short. The muscled purr of a diesel engine cut away, and a vehicle door slammed.

"JJ?" Cam's voice curled a giddy fist of anticipation deep in the pit of her stomach.

Like the flip of a switch, Doug's face closed down, his eye went oddly vacant. "I have to go."

"Oh, but..." JJ set the basket by the back door and trailed him down the steps. "You don't have to leave yet."

"I have to get b-back to work," Doug called over his shoulder, all but trotting away. He offered Cam a curt nod as he passed, then scrambled off without another word to either of them.

"Well. That was strange," JJ mumbled as she reached Cam's side.

"*He's* strange...but about as dangerous as a day old doughnut with a few missing sprinkles," Cam remarked, catching her around the waist, spinning her into his arms. "Hey there, gorgeous."

He didn't give her a chance to respond. His lips sealed over hers, thorough and possessive. By the time he drew back, JJ's head spun and pleasant warmth crackled like heat lightning through her limbs.

"I missed you." He nipped and nibbled at her lips as though he had the next century or two to sample her flavor.

Doug Weston might be harmless, but Cameron Walker had lethal stamped all over him. A girl's willpower could happily go down in flames with just a slow, sinful curl of those skillful lips. JJ leaned back in his embrace, more than a little pleased despite herself when his arms remained locked around her waist. He was in uniform again. She could almost smell the beginning whiffs of smoke rolling off her self-control.

Then she got a good look at his face and stilled in his arms, her hands resting on his shoulders. Her gaze cruised his features, picking up on the finer details one might miss if they weren't paying close enough attention. The fine shadow of stubble on his jaw made the faint shadows beneath his eyes just a little more pronounced. The smile curving his lips deepened the lines of strain at the corners of his mouth. His eyes might glitter with sensual promise, but they were also tired, care-worn.

"Are you still on duty?"

"For a few more hours yet."

"Have you eaten today?"

The crease in his cheek deepened as the corner of his lips hitched up. He traced the curve of her lips with the heat of his stare. "Not for a while. I could use a bite or two...if you're offering."

Tilting her head, unable to fight the smile, she scolded, "You just said you're on duty."

"I'll take my lunch break."

JJ shot a glance at her watch. "At three in the afternoon?"

"C'mon, honey," he murmured, nuzzling the side of her neck. "I haven't been able to get you out of my head all day. Invite me in."

"I should be working on those paintings I promised June."

"You can work on them later." His hot mouth suckled the sensitive flesh beneath her ear. Her stomach quivered in response. "Please?" His plea was one hot breath feathered over her skin as his hands grew bold.

"Yes," she conceded breathlessly, but as soon as he released her, she planted a finger in the middle of his chest and pinned him with a stern frown despite the stars she was certain were still circling in her eyes. "I'll fix you a sandwich, make you some coffee.

But that's it mister. You are on duty."

Ducking his head, he still couldn't hide the amused grin. "Yes, ma'am."

Stifling a snort, JJ led the way to the back door. Cam snagged the welcome basket before she could give it a second thought, carrying it inside and setting it on the table for her. She went straight to the fridge and dug out the makings for Cam's late lunch, turning quickly as soon as she sensed his presence behind her.

Her arms were laden with foodstuff, a poor defensive shield when pitted against the hunger in his eyes, but use them she did. He glanced down once at her burden, then slowly lifted his smoldering gaze to hers, leaving no doubt in her mind what his preference for a meal was.

Undeterred, she lifted a brow, frowning him back. Heaving a dramatic sigh, he took a seat at the table to wait while she spread her supplies out on the counter and began assembling his lunch.

"How's your day going so far?" Her gaze lingered on his face as she slid a full glass of milk and a loaded plate on the table in front of him.

The grimace flickered across his face at her question, gone so fast she might have missed it if she'd blinked.

"Milk?"

"It's good for you." Frowning, she drew the chair beside him out and sat down. "Talk to me, Cam. What's going on?"

He scrubbed his palm down the side of his jaw, leaning back in his chair, tossing his shoulders in a weary shrug. "Same old, same old."

She lifted her brow again, eased an elbow onto the table, and waited.

Taking his time, Cam lifted the sandwich and took a healthy bite, chewed slowly. "Have I told you lately what a good cook you are?"

"Cam." His name was an admonishment this time, drawn out and firm, warning him she wouldn't be put off or patted on the head and ignored.

His gaze cut to hers. She could see the battle raging in his eyes, but, in the end, he yielded. "The break in the vandalism—now arson—case fell through. The kids had an alibi."

She didn't want to bring it up, didn't want to remember the gruesome scene in the woods, but she refused to cower from reality. "And the killer?"

He paused, staring at the sandwich. He took so long to answer, she wasn't sure he would. "No leads. The guy's good, hasn't made a single mistake."

Gnawing on the tip of her thumbnail, JJ watched in silence as Cam finished his lunch. When he drained his glass and set it aside, she coaxed, "I know there's probably all sorts of rules and regulations about what you're allowed to discuss with a civilian, but if you ever need to talk—"

"I don't want this to touch you," he interrupted. His eyes were hard now, his lips compressed. "You've been through enough."

"It already has, Cam. Whether or not you like it, I am involved. I was from my first night in town when some cowboy cop tackled me in the mud for being in the wrong place at the wrong time." She shot him a smile to soften the remark, show there were no hard feelings.

She leaned forward in her seat, reached a hand across the table, smiled when his palm landed in hers. She considered him with a shrewd gaze, and she bit the bullet. "I figure you already know about what happened to me...and to Sarah. Even without the badge, it's not that difficult to get information about that night."

"JJ, I don't want you to think that I—"

"No, Cam," she cut in, giving his hand a gentle squeeze. "I don't know if now is the time to have this conversation...but I guess now's as good a time as any."

"Honey, you don't need—"

"Yes, Cam," she insisted. "I do." She needed to do this, for herself as much as for him. "I still have...flashbacks of that night sometimes. I never know when it's going to happen, or why. But something always happens, triggers a flashback, and..." Dropping her chin, she studied their linked hands. "And I run. Sometimes I don't even realize what I've done until I'm a hundred miles away from wherever I was."

She dragged her gaze to his, the confession sour on her tongue. What would he think of that? Of her? He remained silent, but his fingers tightened on hers, lending her the support to go on. "I've run a lot, Cam. I'm trying...really trying to stay put this time."

"Have you had any of these flashes since you came to Sutter Hollow?"

She blinked, moistened her lips, and skimmed a scrape along the back of his hand with the pad of her thumb. Slowly, she nodded, admitting, "A few."

"But you didn't run."

"No, I haven't run." *Yet.*

"You won't run. Not anymore." There was such conviction, such fierce assertion in his voice, in his eyes that she almost believed him.

Almost.

But she knew herself, better than anyone. She knew better than to lay odds on a long shot, and she was a long shot, straight out of the gates.

"The point, Cam, is that I've stuck it out...so far. I've stayed longer here than I have anywhere else since that night Jerry... I am a survivor. At least, I'm trying awful hard to be. I won't break. I won't shatter if things get too scary." She hoped. "After Jerry...I never thought I'd be able to trust a man again. But I trust you." Her heart stuttered at the admission, then it froze solid in her chest as she offered the one thing she feared more than making herself vulnerable to someone else. She offered the chance for someone else to count on her. "I want you to trust me too."

He stared at her from across the table, stared hard. The glass, coated with milky residue, and the crumb-speckled plate could have been a barbed wire fence, his expression was so solemn. The muscle in his jaw leaped to life as he drew his hand slowly from hers. Her icy heart suffered a tiny crack, and she couldn't breathe. The scrape of chair legs on old linoleum echoed in the kitchen as he pushed back from the table, but he didn't rise. He sat there for a moment, tense, eyes closed. Then, with a muttered curse, he leaned forward, resting his elbows on his knees. Splayed fingers tunneled into his hair as he dropped his head onto his palms.

She didn't know what to say, completely at a loss as to how to go on from there. How could she have been such a blind fool? Obviously, she'd seen something that wasn't there. She was a grown adult, should have known not to assume just because they'd stolen a wild night between the sheets that it automatically meant any level of intimacy. After all, hadn't Ginny and the others told her he'd never returned to the same bed twice? Somehow, she'd convinced herself that it would be different between them, more fool she.

She wanted to hide, but her pride held her to the chair, held her chin up, pushed her to ignore the bruise forming on her heart.

His voice startled her.

"The son of a bitch wrote on them."

It took a moment to process his words. Once she did, once she realized he was letting the barriers down, she could breathe again. Then his words clicked into place, and she stuttered in shock,

"He...he writes on them?"

"Yeah," Cam growled at the floor. His voice cracked, laced with angry confusion, riddled with weary guilt. She didn't need Dr. Greene to analyze that one. JJ would have recognized that tone anywhere. She'd used it herself often enough. "He leaves a silver rosary with each victim, and he writes on them."

"A rosary," JJ murmured to herself, eyes narrowed with concern as she watched Cam struggle with his emotions. "What does he write?"

"He wrote...lust, he wrote lust on Lori. On Ed...gluttony."

"And Mayor Hughes?"

"Greed."

"Lust. Gluttony." She recited the words quietly. Something nagged at her. "Greed?" She tapped her finger on the table for a moment, gnawing on the edge of her lip. "And a rosary? Were the victims Catholic?"

"None of them were. It just doesn't make any sense."

"Hmm," she murmured, frowning. Reluctant to step on his toes—or his pride—she hesitantly inquired, "Have you requested help from another agency...the state police or the FBI?"

"The Feds are too busy with other cases...too much red tape, too many hoops to jump through. Oh, they had some behavioral analysis unit come up with a profile, lot of help that was. Hell, it pointed the finger at half the males in town between the ages of 17 and 35. I could be a suspect for all the damned good that thing did."

"What about these words...lust, gluttony, greed?"

"Damned if I know."

JJ nibbled on her thumbnail as something tugged at her memory, something from long, long ago. With a small gasp, her gaze flew to Cam. "Cam...the victims might not have been Catholic...but maybe *he* is? A rosary? Lust, greed, gluttony...those are three of the Seven Deadly Sins, aren't they?"

His head whipped up and around. His eyes pierced hers with the first glimmers of hope. That hope quickly died beneath a landslide of self-recrimination. "Shit, that never even occurred to me. How could I have missed it?" Then his expression fell, and his face went white as a sheet. "Ah, sweet Christ...he's not done."

"What do you mean?"

"There are seven sins, JJ...he's only taken care of three. He's not done yet."

A long moment of silence, pregnant with deadly implications, hung heavy in the air between them. Cam dropped his forehead into his palms again. She'd never seen him this way, and it was killing her. Cam—always so self-aware, confident to the point of arrogance—hunched forward in his chair like a man condemned.

Outside, the wind began to pick up, rattling the windowpanes, as if stirred by the roiling emotions bottled inside the man before her. The room grew dim as dark thunderheads rolled across the azure skies. The first whiffs of rain wafted through the open window above the sink, stirring the pale lace curtains JJ'd found in a packing box in one of the bedrooms upstairs.

Following instinct, she slipped from the chair to kneel at Cam's feet. Slowly, gently, she clasped his wrists in her hands, drew them down and held his hands between them as she gazed up into his face. The strain of the burdens he carried etched deep lines on either side of his mouth, dug a deep groove between his eyebrows. His eyes burned her, glittering with emotion at which she could only guess. At present, he was a man carrying the weight of the world on his broad shoulders...undoubtedly capable shoulders that could rival Atlas...and yet, just now, he looked so vulnerable. Utterly exposed.

"I'm sorry," he rumbled. Dejection had never sounded more hollow. "I shouldn't have come here, shouldn't have..." He trailed off, shaking his head, as if he couldn't find the words he sought. "I just couldn't... There was nowhere else I could think of... I needed—"

JJ laid a palm softly against his cheek, shushing him. Pushing up on her knees, her waist cradled between Cam's thighs, JJ sealed her lips over his in unspoken understanding. There had been a time when she too hadn't known where to turn, had needed someone to just be there. That he would turn to her...that he needed her...spoke directly to her heart, bypassing all those roadblocks she'd so cleverly set up, decimating all those walls she'd so meticulously erected.

Cam needed her.

She fell. Heart first.

For the barest fraction of a moment, Cam sat motionless as her lips moved softly over his. Then, with a strangled groan, his large hands lifted to cup her cheeks. Wresting control of the kiss from her, he leaned back, slipped one hand around her waist, and hauled her up from the floor.

Cam's hand cruised down her thigh, bold. Possessive. He hooked his fingers around her knee, drawing it up, up and over his thigh. In one fluid motion, he hooked her other leg, and tugged it up and over as well, until she sat on his lap, straddling him. She gripped his shoulders, yielding all to him. His hand cupped her bottom jerking her forward until she pressed tight against him. His rigid erection pushed, hot and hard, against her core.

Cam lifted his hand, tangling it in her hair. He

wrapped the golden mass around his fist, tugging her head back. His greedy mouth ravaged her senses. He dragged his unrelenting lips from hers, and she whimpered protest. But his lips never left her skin. They seared their way down the side of her neck, suckling and laving at her sensitive flesh. They paused, there at the base of her throat, to pull at the hummingbird flutter of her pulse, and then they skated back up the opposite side of her neck

He paused then, going still as a block of granite in her arms. JJ forced her eyelids open, gazed down at him through the blurry haze of desire. His hungry gaze was locked on her ear...no, just below her ear. Holy crap. What the hell was it with everyone and her friggin' neck lately?

A gurgle of sound formed in the back of her throat, one of confusion...one of frustrated desire. Then Cam's burning gaze skated to hers, shocking her speechless. Never had she seen such raw need, such unfettered greedy hunger. His stare was feral, frightening in its intensity. A spurt of teeth-rattling panic darted through her bloodstream like a ninety-proof shot of adrenaline. Stiffening in his arms, her breath hissed out as the passion-induced haze cleared from her vision. Before she could take flight, however, his arms tightened around her, the steel bands of a trap sprung.

She thought he would claim her lips again, looked forward to it with greedy excitement even as fear made her tremble. He wanted her. She could see it in his eyes, in the harsh need that sent healthy flush into his neck and cheeks. His hand cupped the back of her head, determined and powerful, and she braced herself.

She could never have prepared herself for his masterful, albeit gentle assault. Where she'd expected fierce and unyielding, she received soft and languid. Where she'd bargained for force and driving need, he gave her coaxing and savoring. He lavished her lips with tender passion so at odds with the boiling emotion in his eyes, and JJ drowned in his kisses, and in her own need, squirming closer to the fire, eager to be consumed.

At length, Cam tore his lips from hers, a harsh growl rumbled deep in his chest. His large hand pushed her head to the crook of his shoulder, held it there when she resisted. His chest heaved with his ragged breathing. The hoarse demand torn from his lips betrayed the jagged edges of his desire. "Just....damn it, just let me hold you."

She shifted restlessly against him. With a muttered oath, he pinned her to his chest.

"For God's sake, JJ, hold still," he growled in her ear. "You have no idea how much I want you right now, want to finish what we just started." Oh, she had a pretty good idea. The hard bulge of him still pulsed against her, unsated and demanding. "I'm on duty. I shouldn't... No, I can't...I can't do this. Not right now..."

Who was he trying to convince here?

"Just a couple more hours," he muttered beneath his breath. "Just a couple more hours and I'll be back."

She giggled as he chanted the phrase to himself. His hands soothed up and down her back, soothing the burn of need coursing in her veins. Yet she could feel the tremor in his hands, the hint of shaking restraint in his arms, and the knowledge fixed a smug smile to her lips. He wasn't nearly as composed, as in control as he would like her to believe...maybe even as he would like himself to believe.

He buried his nose against her hair, and his chest expanded beneath her cheek with the depth of his indrawn breath. His heartbeat continued to hammer. The hard thud of it against her ear pushed her smile wider. The scent of him—all masculine heat and the fresh scent of pine and the outdoors—wrapped itself around her, as securely as his arms, and she wanted nothing more than to sink in and never come up for air.

"You should go home, get some rest when you get off work," she reluctantly chided.

"Don't you get it yet, honey?" His voice held a new edge, one that cut straight to her heart, made it sit up and take notice. "When I'm with you...wherever we are...I *am* home. Sweet Christ, woman, you...you rub at my soul."

His words touched something deep inside her, something no one had ever gone near. Her heart purred and melted. Nothing had ever affected her more strongly, more completely. Nothing had ever meant more.

Echoes of the approaching storm crashed in the distance, a resounding exclamation point to a statement that left her thunderstruck. Against her thigh, Cam's phone began to hum. Heaving a bone-deep sigh, Cam shifted her in his arms and glanced at the display, swore softly beneath his breath.

"I have to take this." He stole a fleeting kiss, promising, "I *will* finish this when I come back later. You should go on up, get some work done...I don't plan on giving you much time for it later." His grin told her exactly why she wouldn't have time.

Still flustered from his declaration, she climbed from his lap as he flipped the phone open, pressing it to his ear with a terse, "Yeah?"

Cam followed JJ down the hallway, listening silently to his caller. At the bottom of the stairs, he stole one more fleeting kiss, his mind obviously on his call, and then he sent her on her way up the stairs while he stepped out onto the porch.

Dazed—still more than a bit dazzled—JJ climbed the stairs, reminding herself to put one foot in front of the other lest she fall flat on her nose. *'You rub at my soul.'* Those words circled in her head…in her heart. She knew, without the slightest doubt, she would carry those words with her to her dying day. And finally, JJ was forced to face the truth. She'd fallen in love with Cam. Hopelessly, senselessly, no-holds-barred in love.

With Cam.

He'd slipped past all her defenses. No, she corrected. He'd smashed right through them, demolished them, leaving her with nothing to hold on to but his need for her. Was it enough? Halfway up the stairs she paused, icy terror suddenly ripping through her.

She could hear his voice, muffled by the door. He sounded tense, agitated.

Holy crap. What if he didn't feel the same? What if his words were just carefully constructed, premeditated tools to ensure her vulnerability? What if…

No. Cam was not Jerry.

She closed her hand on the banister, squaring her shoulders. She wouldn't do that, wouldn't diminish Cam or his words—words that meant so much to her—by comparing him to that monster. Cam was honorable. He was protective and caring. He'd never lie to her, never hurt her. He was nothing like Jerry.

Smiling, reassured, she ascended the second flight of stairs. The storm rumbled all around the quiet house now, slashing angry torrents of rain against the roof. Her steps were so light, her heart so buoyant she could have been floating on puffy white clouds, accompanied by a symphony of harps, serenaded by a choir of celestial beings.

Opening the door to her attic studio, JJ stepped inside and crashed headfirst, straight into hell.

Wide arcs of brilliant crimson slashed the walls,

splattered the floor, stained the ceiling. Her worktables were overturned. Mangled paint tubes were scattered about the floor amid the smashed debris of oak and maple frames. Snapped brushes had been tossed around the room. Her palette—or what was left of it—lay in splintered pieces beneath the paint-soaked window.

But the thing that horrified her the most, the thing that raked pain across her heart were her works...paintings that had come from the depths of her heart, expressions of emotion straight from her soul. He'd flung her paintings upon the floor, slashed them to ribbons, defiled them with the same slashes of crimson that marred the walls.

All except *Lovers.*

He'd used five huge, gleaming spikes—forming the rough pattern of a cross—nailing *Lovers* to the wall directly across from the door. Gaudy, deep scarlet letters sprawled across the painting, excess paint dripped from the lettering, running down over her vision.

PRIDE.

JJ clamped her hands over her ears to block the horrid screams filling the room. She could deal with this...if someone would just stop that screaming. Oh, God, why wouldn't they stop screaming?

The paint turned to blood before her eyes, pulsing with the grief of life lost.

The hot ball of fear in her stomach turned cold, detached. He would kill her now, just as he'd killed Sarah. And there was nothing she could do to stop him. How had she ever been taken in by this man? How could she have mistaken him as a gentle, loving soul mate for her sister? How could she not have seen the monster hiding behind his beguiling smile?

He lifted his arm again. How many times had Sarah seen that sight? The sight of his lifted arm, his fist clutching that bloody blade. This time, the blood dripping from his blade was hers.

JJ sucked in one sharp breath after another. Her hand flew to her ribs, clutching the dry cotton material in a sweaty death grip. The phantom burn lingered even as she scooted sideways across the threshold, scrabbling for the light switch. Soft yellow light flooded the room, and she yanked the hem of her shirt up and out of the way. Her finger traced the jagged, pink scar across her side. A scar that had taken no less than twenty-eight stitches to close. She couldn't even remember how many stitches it had taken to close the countless other wounds her brother-in-law had inflicted.

Sarah hadn't been so lucky.

Some wounds even the best medical attention just couldn't heal.

And the screaming continued, curdling her blood in her veins. She could handle this...she wouldn't run. If only the screaming would stop.

Her gaze dropped to the floor, snagging on the bright gleam of silver. There, in the middle of the floor was a large butcher knife, the blade splattered with red.

"Interfering bitch," Jerry ranted, slashing at her again, catching her across the forearm this time, only a shallow nick when compared with some of the other wounds he'd inflicted so far. "Why couldn't you keep your nose out of our business? This is your fault, JJ. All your fault..." He slashed again, kept the blade shallow, and she finally understood he intended to toy with her—punish her—for her crimes. "You should never have convinced her to leave me. A wife shall cleave only unto her husband."

Slash.

Blood splattered across her face, but she felt no sting. The knife had missed her. Her gaze focused on his face, on the whites of his eyes as his eyeballs rolled back in his head. His left temple and cheek bore streaks of crimson, and shards of white crockery with tiny blue flowers fluttered from his hair. Her stunned gaze slid to the shattered vase in her hand, and the remaining pieces tumbled to the floor.

Like a scene from a horror movie, Jerry dropped to his knees in slow motion. She scrambled back on bleeding heels and battered palms. Her lungs burned, but she locked the scream deep, unwilling to cry out lest she wake him. The front stairs beckoned her, but she was too weak now to pull herself to her feet. Nothing more than sheer determination dragged her across the hallway. Then the whole world tilted, spinning madly as she rolled, pell-mell, down the stairs, the sharp edge on every one of the steps rising up to meet her with vicious stabs of hope. Each step was raw pain. Yet each step took her closer to the door...and farther away from him.

Large hands descended on her shoulders. Her throat, already raw, burned with another scream. She struggled, fighting for her life. Jerry wouldn't catch her. She'd get away. She had to get away, had to get help for Sarah.

The room spun as those hard hands gripped her and whirled her around. Heat enveloped her...heat and a familiar scent. Strong arms subdued her, warm breath panted against her temple as a deep voice called her name.

Where was she? Oh Lord, she had to get out of here...wherever she was. She had to get away.

Run, JJ. Run.

"JJ, baby, I'm here. I'm here—it's going to be okay. I'm here now, honey. Shh..." Cam's voice called to her, from so far away. His hands, so gentle and warm, comforted her. His arms held her tight. Cam. Why was he here?

Oh, no, Jerry would hurt him. Jerry would kill Cam, and she wouldn't be able to stop him. Not Cam. She couldn't lose Cam too.

She crashed in an undignified heap at the bottom of the steps, only a few precious, precarious feet from the door. Her brain rolled inside her skull. Somewhere above her, footsteps thundered closer. She was too dizzy to form words of her own, and yet Jerry's words were all too clear...all too chilling.

"What God hath joined together," he snarled, staggering down the steps after her, bracing a shoulder against the wall, clutching the knife in one fist and his head with the other. Rage flashed in his eyes, ugly and murderous.

His face, twisted with pain and fury, flashed blue and red before her eyes. No, not just his face. The whole room flashed blue and red. The swirling lights glanced off the walls and stairs, glinting off the blood-spattered glass covering photos of smiling faces. Had the fall, the loss of blood scrambled something in her brain?

His eyes were demented, gleaming desperation. His pace quickened as he staggered closer. The knife lifted. "Let no little bitch tear asunder..."

JJ struggled against the arms that held her, sobbing. No, no, no. She didn't want to die. She'd finally found happiness again. She had a reason to live. She'd found love. She had Cam. She could hear him, calling to her, his voice muffled and insistent.

But Jerry's face leered closer.

The door burst open behind her, and frantic male voices shouted words she could no longer decipher. Biting wind raced over her and a spray of white floated inside the room, a snow globe shaken and set down, left to swirl in a flurry of bitter white all around that glistening red blade...that blade that continued to descend, promising an end to her pain.

Promising an end to her...

From somewhere far away, the explosion of gunfire echoed in the room, and above her Jerry's body jerked once, twice, three times. Fury darkened his face as he tumbled sideways, thwarted in his quest for righteous vengeance. New blossoms of crimson spread across his chest.

A stranger's face swam in the murky soup of her vision. A kindly face crinkled with lines of worry, framed with wiry gray hair. His blue uniform blurred and wavered. A silver badge, old-fashioned and yet timeless in its honor, flashed on the man's shoulder, catching her eye, and then darkness began to descend.

The uniform before her eyes was no longer blue, but sandy beige. The badge wasn't quite the same, but it still gleamed. Bright with golden hope, bright with the promise of safety.

JJ lifted her confused gaze to the face above the badge, then she tumbled into the dark void where blood and pain and loss held no significance.

Chapter 20

Cam's hands fisted on the steering wheel, his knuckles bleached white beneath the pressure. The image of JJ—eyes rolling back in her head as she collapsed in his arms—kept flashing through his mind like an endless loop from a nightmare he couldn't wake up from. His heart had stopped dead in his chest.

Hell, even the seconds that had passed while he raced up the stairs to her, as her screams had rent the air around him, had been jolt enough for his heart. She'd been trapped in one of her flashbacks when he'd burst into the room. He'd figured that out the second he'd looked into her eyes. Her studio had been destroyed, her work ruined. But her eyes had been dilated, trapped by things he could not see. Her screams—and the broken recollections he didn't think she was aware she cried out—had shredded him, leaving him helpless and filled with black rage.

Then she'd passed out in his arms.

A hard wave of nausea rolled through him just thinking about it.

Slowing for a corner, Cam pushed the residual anger down deep. Lightning slashed across the sky. Wind ripped through the streets, bowing saplings, making older established trees shudder and twist. Small branches danced and skittered across wet roads in front of his headlights. Torrents of fat droplets of rain splashed against the windshield, waging war with the windshield wipers. It was fast becoming a draw as to which was winning.

He'd had a busy day, and, by the looks of this

storm, it didn't look as though it were going to get any easier. He'd be lucky if he wasn't dealing with downed power lines before the night was through.

At least the rain had taken hold before the fire had spread. God help the little bastard that kept messing up his town and tearing him away from his woman when she needed him. He'd be hard pressed not to strangle the son of a bitch with his bare hands when Cam finally caught him. The only thanks Cam could offer was that the arsonist had continued to target abandoned buildings. How long would it be before he grew bolder, upped the stakes?

Slowing again for another corner, Cam let a long, slow breath hiss from between his teeth. The streets were abandoned. Apparently his citizens had enough sense to stay in out of the rain. Thank heaven for small favors.

Primal instinct demanded he stay with his female, protect JJ at all cost, but, thanks to the arsonist's latest bit of handy work, Cam's sense of duty as an officer of the law demanded he leave her, even if only for a short time. He'd also had to process the scene in her attic. He hadn't wanted her there for that, hadn't wanted her to see that room again until he'd had a chance to clean up the mess. But he couldn't leave her alone. A small, begrudging smile nudged its way to his lips. She'd argued, claimed she didn't want to bother anyone. She could clean the mess up on her own, she'd insisted. She'd be just fine.

Oh, she'd stood her ground, and he couldn't help admire her courage...even if she had been ten shades of white and shaking with the last tremors of her flashback. But he'd won.

In the end, when it counted, he'd won.

He'd left her with Ginny to cluck and fuss like a mother hen over her. He hadn't missed Ginny's glare. What the hell had that been about? He hadn't missed JJ's parting scowl either. Ginny, he couldn't do anything about, but he'd taken great pleasure in kissing JJ's scowl from her lips, then he'd slipped out the door before she'd had a chance to regain her senses.

As she'd turned away, he'd caught a flash of the mark he'd left upon her skin, just below her ear. It had been all he could do not to simply toss her over his shoulder and carry her up the stairs to the nearest bit of privacy. Sheer dint of will had pushed him out the door and toward his duty.

That reminder lead him down another path, one he wasn't sure how to handle. He had to tell her. About himself, and about what he was. He had to tell her what he'd done, that he'd marked her as his. She wouldn't be happy, he'd wager. Not at first. He'd talk her around though.

Losing her wasn't an option he could live with.

Cam eased his pick-up into the driveway beside Ginny's battered relic of a truck and killed the engine. Drawing a deep breath, Cam scrubbed both hands over his face. Exhaustion nipped at his heels, but he couldn't afford to let it catch up with him. He had too much to do yet, and a conversation that couldn't wait any longer.

Cold rain pelted him as he slid from the truck and sprinted across the yard. He didn't bother knocking on the door, just let himself in with a quick shout. "Ginny? It's Cam."

"Back here," she called. By the tone of her voice, he felt it safe to guess she hadn't let him off the hook...for whatever he'd done. A rustle of movement wafted to him from the back of the house. He wiped his feet on the mat by the door and followed the homey sounds of dishes clacking together as a little boy's homework was checked down the hallway.

Stepping into the kitchen, Cam's gaze went straight to JJ. She sat at the table beside a sleepy-eyed, freshly scrubbed Tanner, a blanket tucked around her shoulders. Her face was chalky white around a smile that didn't quite reach her eyes. Her hands clutched a steaming mug on the laminate surface before her, but she didn't seem interested in drinking...indeed, she didn't seem to be paying much attention to anything going on around her. Cam shot Tanner a fond, if somewhat distracted smile, ruffling the boy's damp hair, on his way to JJ's side.

"How are you, honey?" He drew the chair beside her away from the table, perching on the edge as he reached for her.

Expression blank, she blinked up at him, allowing him to draw her limp hands into his.

Cam frowned. His questioning gaze darted to Ginny where she stood beside the sink, wiping her hands on a small towel. Ginny gave a helpless shrug, shaking her head, and mouthed the words, "She hasn't spoken much."

Closing his eyes, Cam took a moment to steady his nerves. When he opened them, Ginny had set aside the towel and was crossing the kitchen. She leaned close to his shoulder and whispered into his ear. "She keeps asking where her car is."

Cold fear crawled into Cam's belly. Was this what she'd meant before, when she'd spoken about not realizing she'd run until she was already on the road, driving away? Well, she wouldn't be going anywhere. Not this time.

Not ever again, if he had anything to say about it.

Nodding to Ginny, Cam turned his attention back to the woman at his side. He was relieved to hear Ginny speaking quietly to Tanner as she drew him from his chair, gathered up the papers and pencils before him, and led him from the room.

"JJ, honey..."

"Cam?" She blinked at him, frowning. "When did

you get here? I can't find my car, Cam."

Forcing a swallow, Cam pushed what he hoped was a reassuring smile to his lips. "I came in just a minute ago, honey. Do you know where you are?"

She blinked at him and, frowning, glanced around the room. It took a long moment for recognition to sink in. Cam's insides iced over as he watched understanding slowly fill her eyes. Understanding and horror. Her breath came faster now. Tears trembled on her lashes. "Did I run? Oh God, did I run again?"

"No...shh. It's okay, you're all right. You didn't run. I brought you here, honey. Do you remember?" She shook her head, a sob escaped her, and he drew her on to his lap, cradling her there like a lost child. "You're not going anywhere."

She leaned against him with a muffled sob, melted into him, and he rocked her, murmuring against her hair until she quieted.

"I'm sorry," she mumbled against his damp shoulder, snuffled.

Leaning back in his arms, she accepted the napkins he'd filched from the small, plastic holder shaped like a little boys hands in the center of the table. He regarded her silently as she mopped at her face, and, when she was done, he drew her to her feet.

"Let's go home, honey."

"I can't...Cam, he was there again. He was inside my house again. I can't go there—"

"My place, JJ," he cut her off, cursing himself for the quick spear of panic flashing in her eyes. He took her chin between his thumb and forefinger, forcing her gaze to his. "We'll go to my place tonight. Tomorrow we'll get some of your things, figure out where to go from there, but for now...from tonight on...you're staying with me."

He'd expected an argument, braced for one. He'd

already practiced logical arguments, perfected his reasoning. Relief washed through him when she simply offered a grateful smile and nodded.

The drive home was treacherous. He breathed a silent sigh of relief when he pulled into his own driveway without incident. The wind was kicking up, swirling through the streets. Cam sent JJ back to the bathroom for a long hot shower while he set to work in the kitchen. He was starving, and, chances were, she probably hadn't had anything to eat since this afternoon when she'd gone to Maggie's.

Aw, hell...

Now Ginny's glare made sense. They'd seen the mark, and they'd realized that he hadn't explained anything to JJ. Maggie had chewed a couple layers off his hide over that one when he'd bumped into her earlier. By Ginny's glare, he was due to lose a few more layers before it was all said and done.

Cam carried a loaded tray of food into the living room and set it on the coffee table in front of the fireplace. The lights flickered as he straightened. Blinked on, and then cut out completely.

"Damn it," he muttered, searching for the box of matches on the mantle. He made short work of starting a fire, and made his way back to the bathroom. The rush of water ceased as he knocked on the door. "Honey, are you all right in there?"

"Yes, what happened?"

"I'm betting we lost a power line somewhere. I'll call in and check. Do you need a flashlight?"

"No...I'm fine. I'll be out in a minute."

Cam drew his cell phone out and made a series of short calls. The big tree in Emerson's yard a few blocks away split beneath a lightning strike, tangling itself up in the power lines at the intersection. Emma assured him she was on top of things, urging him to stay home. There was no need for him to come in, she'd insisted. He'd been there all day, after all, and it wasn't as if he didn't have capable help. Duly chastised, he hung up and returned to the living room as JJ stepped in front of the fireplace to warm her hands. Her wet hair dampened the soft material down the length of her back.

That T-shirt had never looked so good on him. Miles and miles of bare, shapely legs peeped from beneath the hem. Her bare toes curled against the thick rug beside the hearth. Warmth glowed to life inside his chest, building with every moment he stood in the doorway mesmerized by her. At last, when the pressure in his chest threatened to choke him, he cleared his throat and stepped inside the room.

She beamed a smile over her shoulder. He was more than a little relieved to see her color had returned.

Then a shadow fell over her brow as she eyed the phone in his hand. "Do you have to go back in?"

"No, Emma threatened she'd shoot me with my own gun if she saw my face before nine a.m. tomorrow."

"I'm glad. I was hoping you'd stay with me." She caught the edge of her bottom lip between her teeth as she turned back to the fire. Her hands twisted together, and he didn't think the motion had anything to do with seeking warmth now. "I...I didn't want to be alone."

It had been a difficult admission. He could see that from the troubled lines forming between her brows, the ridged set of her shoulders. Vulnerability would be tough for JJ to face. Instinctively, he sensed an admission of that vulnerability was monumental. He closed the distance between them, rested his hands on her shoulders. The pressure in his chest increased when she leaned back of her own accord, leaning into him.

He slipped his arms around her waist, rubbing his cheek against her hair. Even beneath the scent of his soap, his shampoo, the essence of her was still there, tugging at his insides. At length, he drew her down onto the sofa beside him, tucking her against his side. She snuggled in with a grateful murmur, curling her legs up under her. Cam swiped a throw off the back of the sofa and tossed it over her, wrapped her in his arms, pulling her against his chest.

Having her here like this felt right. He'd always had a certain restlessness inside him. Could barely sit through a whole game on the TV without having to get up and just move, work on some project or other. Maybe that was why he'd spent so much time at the office, spent so much time on remodeling projects. But now—cuddling with her by the fire—he couldn't imagine being anywhere else.

The small heirloom clock on the mantle, a precious inheritance from his paternal grandmother, quietly ticked away endless minutes as they snuggled and shared the mountain of food Cam had brought in earlier, conversing in muted tones. Her nerves had settled. Her voice was stronger with every word she spoke. It pleased him that—though she seemed to have gotten over the shock, and was well onto getting over the fear—she continued to recline in his arms, continued to draw warmth and comfort from him.

"Cam…"

"Yeah?" He pressed his lips to her temple, toyed with the damp ends of her hair.

"I…" she fidgeted with a button on his shirt, "never mind."

"What?"

"Well, I… Ginny said I should talk to you about it, but I don't see as how you would have any answers."

"Talk to me about what, honey?" Frowning, he held very still.

"I..." Her voice trailed away, as if she waged some inner argument. Heaving a sigh, she tipped her head back so she could look into his eyes and admitted, "There's a wolf in the woods. He comes to see me sometimes."

Cam's entire body went rigid. His mind raced. This was the opening he'd been looking for.

But the very thought of telling her scared the living hell out of him.

'She keeps asking where her car is,' Ginny had said.

What if she wasn't ready to hear this? She'd dealt with so much already. What if this were the last straw? What if she couldn't accept—

"He's tame, Cam. I swear he won't hurt me." Her frantic words tumbled out, fast and furious, as she pushed up, peering into his eyes with a worried frown. "I don't want you to go after him, or hurt him. Please, Cam, promise me you won't let him be hurt."

Shit. Screwing up his courage like a man about to walk the plank, Cam leaned forward, took both her hands into his. Would the waters be warm and inviting, or filled with blood-thirsty sharks? "Baby, that wolf would never, ever hurt you."

The delicate arches of her eyebrows crunched together. Her eyes narrowed on him, and he could read the confusion in their beautiful depths. "But I... How do you..."

Drawing a deep breath, Cam leaned forward, brushing his lips across hers in a whispered plea for understanding. "Honey, I have something I need to tell you...something you're probably going to need to see to believe. I don't want you to be frightened. Can you please do something for me? Can you try to remember what happened with you and the wolf...how protective he is of you...how he kept you safe from the bear? How he walked with you in the woods? He'd never hurt you. *I'd* never hurt you."

Her eyes clouded; her skin went cold beneath his fingers. "The bear...how did you know about the bear? I never said anything about—"

"Honey, have you heard the tales...the stories about the protectors?"

Frowning, she nodded slowly. "Yes. That Ms. Potter started to talk about it at the hardware store...then Ginny got all weird and shoved her out the door."

"What did she say?"

"Cam, I don't understand. What does that have to do with my wolf?" She tried to pull back, pull away from him. He held her fast. Fear dug icy finger holds along his spine even as her proprietary attitude over his other form fed his ego. Her face had gone pale again, but he couldn't stop now. She needed to hear this.

She needed to hear it from him.

"There are a lot of legends about the woods of Sutter Hollow," he began. *Dear God, where to start?* "A lot of them are wrong. A lot of them talk about monsters, beasts that prey on the innocent. I guess part of that was true...a long, long time ago, but not the way some mean now." He squeezed her hands gently, stared hard at her. "Back then, according to Winneoten legend, a brave warrior stepped forward, dedicating his life to battling the evil that had invaded the woods of his ancestors. He was brave, crafty but honorable. Strong and loyal. His tribe had been attacked, over and over. Many innocents were defiled and killed, their bodies ravaged and drained of every last drop of blood. Soon after a particularly gruesome attack, in the light of the full moon, he prayed to the Great Spirit. He prayed for the power to stop the demons."

She remained silent, her head tilted slightly to

the side, absorbing his words with a curious frown.

"The Great Spirit came to him in a vision, granting him...special skills. He was to become the protector of his tribe. His descendents would bear the responsibility of his prayers, of this...this special gift from the Great Spirit."

"A protector..." She fidgeted, lifting one hand to brush it across his shirt, resting her palm just over the mark he bore beneath the cotton, beneath the badge. "Your tattoo...you said that was a symbol of a protector, right?"

A slow smile spread across his lips as he caught her hand, pressed a kiss to her palm. "Yes, that's right."

"Ms. Potter claimed..." She trailed off, frowning again.

"What did she say, JJ?"

"It's silly, really." She leaned back against the cushion, tucking her legs back up beneath her, absently tugging a stray lock of hair behind her ear. He captured her hand again, squeezing insistently.

"Okay. She claimed...she told me the same story you did, or one very similar...only she claims this warrior's descendants still roam the woods, protecting the town even now. Cam, I think that old woman needs help. She's...she's convinced there are Werewolves in the woods. That this warrior's descendants run around...slipping into wolf form at will. She said they were...um...fiercely protective and possessive...and loyal. She claimed that I met one of these protectors. She claimed that my wolf was one of them, one of these Werewolves. She even implied that he'd formed some kind of...of an attachment to me. That he was *my* protector."

"Shit," he muttered, barely suppressing the urge to close his eyes and snort in self-disgust.

Here he'd been going around all this time, smugly thinking he'd been so damned successful at keeping the truth under wraps, when apparently all you needed to do was go sit down and have a nice little chat with the cat-lady to find out all about Winneoten legend, and all about his pack. And the scariest part of all, she had all the facts terrifyingly straight. Someone had to have given her this information. There was just no way for her to know all this any other way.

"Honey," his cheeks puffed out as he blew out a long breath, then he took the leap he'd been dreading, "she's right."

"What?" The scowl on JJ's face expressed—eloquently—that she didn't appreciate what she perceived as a tasteless joke on his part.

"She was right. There are Werewolves in Sutter Hollow. But they would never harm the innocent, never ever hurt you. They are protectors. And, once they find their mate, they are loyal unto death. You have to believe you are safe...I guarantee you are safe. I wouldn't ever let anything harm you. You have to believe you are safe with me, safe with the wolf." He gripped her hands tight when she would have pulled them away. "And she was right about the wolf. He has formed...an attachment to you. Just as the man has."

She shook her head, jerking her hands more forcefully now. She wasn't going to believe, wasn't going to take on faith that which she couldn't see, couldn't witness with her own eyes. He'd been right about that. Damn it. He didn't want to have to do it like this, but he could see she wouldn't accept the story any other way.

"Why are you saying these things?" She fought to pull her hands from his, struggled to put space between them. "What are you trying to do here? Werewolves, Cam? I may be a little off my game tonight, but I'm not crazy. Why are you doing this?"

"JJ...just please, please let me explain. When

I'm done...just give me a chance to explain." And then, because he'd fought the truth for too long and realized he only had one chance to do this right—one chance to truly claim his mate—he gathered her resistant form into his arms and pressed her close. His breath skimmed her lips as his eyes bore into hers. "I love you, JJ. I need you to remember that, when you see... I need you to remember that I love you more than anything."

His kiss was explosive, fast and hard. His lips demanded a response, would accept nothing less than honest emotion from her. Her response was immediate. She wound her arms around his neck and surrendered with a small whimper. Satisfied, filled with dread, he pulled back and set her away from him before pushing to his feet.

He kept his eyes on her as he slowly worked the buttons of his uniform loose. His gear, boots, and pants followed. Once he'd stripped down to the skin, he offered her one last resigned smile. She was so beautiful—with her big, shining blue eyes, and her damp, golden hair falling all around her shoulders, curled up there in on his sofa, wearing his shirt— that his heart ached. "I love you, Jillian."

Then he closed his eyes, centered his focus, and gathered inside him all the power the Great Spirit had bestowed upon his ancestor so very long ago.

****

JJ leaned forward on the worn cushions, confusion tightening her brow. The taste of Cam lingered on her lips. *I love you, Jillian.* His words rang in her head. He loved her.

Cam loved her.

She couldn't catch her breath. Didn't understand why he'd told her those other things. So fantastical. None of the rest made any sense. But he loved her. She couldn't seem to be able to get past that.

Those long, deft fingers of his began working the row of buttons on his shirt free. Her eyes widened. That breath she'd tried so hard to catch got tangled up somewhere in her throat. Her hungry gaze followed his movements as he stripped away the last of his clothing until he stood before her in all his naked glory. Powerful muscle bunched and rippled beneath golden skin. Skin smooth as velvet beneath her fingers, she remembered.

There, upon his chest, soared his griffin tattoo. A symbol of vigilant strength, he'd once said. A protector of kings and treasures. Right now, it looked so very majestic, almost vibrant with life, a benediction.

A shield.

And a brand.

Desire pooled deep in her core. He was so handsome, but, more than that, he was everything she loved. Honorable, thoughtful, caring. He had become her safe haven.

He closed his eyes, a fiercely concentrated look settled on his features.

Unease clutched a cruel fist inside her chest, twisted. Something was wrong. She didn't know what was going on here, but she didn't like it, didn't like this sudden sense of...of power arcing through the room, swirling around Cam. Her feet hit the cold floor, and she scooted to the edge of the sofa. She'd feel better if he just held her.

She was halfway off the sofa when he threw his head back on his shoulders. His body tensed, and he bore down, clenched his fists. The muscle in his jaw leaped. And she froze. Her mouth sagged open on a soundless whisper as her breath left her. Her head spun, her vision blurred. No...she wasn't seeing this. She *wasn't*.

The muscles in Cam's body seemed to be bunching and rippling faster now, stretching…reshaping. And his face…

That just wasn't possible. Human faces weren't supposed to *do* the things Cam's face was doing…*couldn't* do those things. He folded onto the floor before her eyes, his body convulsing and shivering. No, no, no, her mind screamed. Yes, her eyes argued back. She was seeing this. She just couldn't believe her own eyes.

As fur began to…to sprout over Cam's body, JJ scrambled back up onto the couch, cowering there in shock.

Then he rose from the floor, braced himself on four paws, and gave one long shiver from snout to tail. Massively large. Golden fur. And the same brilliant, emerald eyes. *Her wolf.* He stood still, just stared at her with those eyes.

Cam's eyes.

Oh God, oh God, oh God.

She couldn't breath. Her chest heaved with the effort, but she just couldn't seem to draw a sufficient supply of oxygen. Surely, that was why she was having this hallucination. She clutched a fist to her chest. Air scraped down her throat, loud and ragged, as she crawled back across the sofa.

The wolf prowled forward.

Her wolf.

Her heart ricocheted inside her chest. How could this be happening?

She'd finally snapped. That was it. She'd finally taken the old header off the deep end of insanity. There was no other explanation.

No *logical* explanation.

She cringed in helpless horror as the wolf edged around the coffee table—slipping closer with every step—until he nudged her bare leg with his muzzle, a long, slow stroke from ankle to knee. Screaming, JJ vaulted over the back of the sofa like an Olympic hurdler. Her bare feet pounded across carpet, slapped against hardwood as she dashed for the front door.

He was already there, a honey-gold blur of motion, blocking her escape. She skidded to a halt a few feet shy of tumbling into the animal she'd once trusted. The animal she'd trusted as she'd trusted the man.

But they were the same, some dark corner of her mind argued.

No, no they weren't. That was impossible. Common sense argued against everything her eyes had witnessed.

Those haunting, expressive eyes peered hard at her, seemed to...to plead with her. He tilted his head, just so, the motion so familiar—familiar in the man, and familiar in the beast—that she pressed trembling fingers to her mouth to stifle the sob.

Spinning, she pelted down the dark hallway, searching, searching for a way out of the house. Why hadn't she paid better attention when she'd gotten here? Why hadn't she scouted out all the exits, noted all the possible dead ends the way she normally did?

Because she'd thought, for once, that she was safe...truly safe.

She'd been such a fool.

Stumbling blindly through a doorway on her right, JJ clattered into a straight-backed wooden chair. The scrabble of claws on hardwood followed her, close...closer. A streak of white light coursed through the skies beyond the windowpanes, flashing inside the room like a photographer's bulb, blinding her for a moment. Thunder crashed, rattling the windows. She jerked. A shrill cry ripped from her chest.

Choking off a sob, she skirted the table, desperately searching for another way out. The scrabble of claws stuttered into the thud and slap of human feet. Cam's breath was a hoarse, pained rasp in the darkness. "JJ, honey...please...please, don't run."

She whipped around, seeking the direction of his voice, sliding her feet slowly, silently backward. Her hands stretched out behind her as she edged toward the dark silhouette of a doorway. She bit her lip to keep the ragged pants of breath locked away, but her blood rushed, pounding in her ears like war drums. It was little wonder he hadn't found her by that relentless thumping alone.

"Honey, I won't hurt you...you know that. I would never hurt you."

Yeah, right. The big bad wolf had probably said something very similar to Little Red and her grandma...right before he chowed down. She might be a little slow on the uptake—ok, a lot slow—but she wasn't a complete moron. Then again, considering she'd gotten romantically involved with a...with a...

Holy crap.

Leading with fumbling hands, she navigated through the room. The night was pitch black around her as she groped her way down the cold length of a long counter. Trembling fingers fumbled over a cold metal rectangle, the long slots on top, the cold bare counter. The coffeemaker. A breadbox.

If only she could just get her hands on a weapon, something to defend herself with...a knife maybe. She shied away from that thought as quickly as it had formed. It was too easy to be overpowered, the knife taken from her...her weapon turned against her. But, dear God, she'd give her right arm for so much as a marble rolling pin right now.

A scrape from the doorway spun her around. She couldn't hear anything but the ragged gasp of her own breathing. Lightning streaked across the sky once more, and she caught the crisp outline of a window...the window on the back door.

She took three running steps.

An iron band snaked around her waist, capturing her, caging her against the solid wall of his chest. A wall of heat and muscle and smooth, bare skin. Another band of muscled flesh clamped around her, trapping her flailing arms.

The heat of his cheek pressed against her jaw. His body was unyielding, his breathing as jagged as hers. "Baby, shh...shh. Let me explain. I can make this all make sense...just let me explain. Shh..."

No way would this ever make sense. She had to get away.

Run, JJ. Run...

She struggled against him—struggled in vain—but he held her tight. He was gentle, pressing soft, desperate kisses to her temple, murmuring soothing sounds in the back of his throat. Flashes of Jerry sailed through her mind, but his face blurred, twisted, morphed into that of the man holding her now. And then that face—a face that had become so precious to her in such a short amount of time—shifted, morphing into the face of a wolf. No, this couldn't be happening.

"Honey, it's me...it's still me. You have to believe that I would never hurt you. This doesn't have to change anything between us..."

Yet, even as she resisted, even as she fought the surrender she felt deep in her bones, her body began to betray her, her determination to falter. The hands that gentled her *were* familiar to her. The voice whispering in her ear was the voice of the man she'd fallen in love with. His familiar body cocooned hers, cradled her, braced her as her knees buckled beneath her. His cheek absorbed the tears that tracked down her face.

At length, her sobs faded to muffled whimpers. Her head dropped forward, chin to chest in defeat. Her world—the one she'd worked so hard to piece back together—had shattered. The man she'd thought she'd loved had destroyed her fragile sense of security...no, she corrected herself, no, even now she knew in her heart of hearts she loved him still. She could feel that love burning through her, burning through the grief and the incredulity and the sense of betrayal. How could she feel this way, after seeing what she'd just seen?

It made no sense.

"That's it...that's it, baby. Just let me hold you." His muscles relaxed the tiniest bit, but he kept her trapped in the loose circle of his arms. His hands moved cautiously over her, her arm, her ribs. His lips cruised across her temple, her damp cheek.

"It's still me, JJ, the same man I've always been."

Her breath seeped out on a hiss.

And the anger came.

He'd lied to her, been lying all this time. Damn him.

"You...you son of a bitch...how could you...how could you keep something like this—"

"I know, I know, baby...I'm sorry. I'm so sorry...I just..." His teeth clacked together near her ear, and his breath skated over her skin as his arms tightened again. From the corner of her eye, she watched his eyelids sag closed. His chin fell to her collarbone. Guilt shadowed his face. "I should have told you, JJ...before, I should have told you. But I was so afraid you'd—"

"I'd what? I'd freak out? I'd run?" Acid laced her voice, but she just didn't give a damned. He'd played her for a fool, probably been sitting around with his...with his wolf buddies chuckling about her gullibility.

That thought sent a fresh wave of chilly fright rippling through her blood. Oh, dear God, how many more of them were there in this town? How many others walked the streets, passing themselves off as your average human, hiding the truth of what they really were?

"I was afraid you'd leave me." Those words, so hollow and yet so filled with anxious despair, cut through layers of anger, sliced through the panic. "I can't help what I am...can't help it any more than I can help the way I feel about you. I meant it when I said you rub at my soul. You do, in a way no one ever has...a way no one else ever will. You..." he shook his head, grimacing. "You've *become* my soul. I need you. If you leave me, JJ, I'm afraid I won't survive." His lips were hot on her neck, pressing one long, shuddering kiss against the sensitive skin beneath her ear. "Honey...I love you. I love you so damned much. Please, please give me a chance...give *us* a chance."

Despite the shimmer of fear quivering deep in her belly, she went utterly still at his words. For a long, long moment, the only sound in the murky room was the furious pounding of her heart...and, deep down, she swore she could hear his as well.

"Honey...feel the arms that hold you. They're the same arms that held you all through the night. Feel," he pressed his lips to her neck, to her check, "these lips. They're the same too." His long fingered, calloused hand flattened against her chest, directly over her hammering heart. "Feel these hands. They're the same. Your heart recognizes me. It thunders inside your chest for me even now, the same as it did last night when I made love to you...made love *with* you. Your body knows me, JJ. You know me. You know you're still safe."

Damn him, but her body did know.

And her heart knew him, just as he'd said.

He loved her. No matter how much she chastised herself, told herself they were just words—words from a man who'd lied to her—she couldn't

316

ignore the tingling thrill that darted through her system like an electrical charge, or the shot of warmth that followed the surge.

How was she supposed to fight this? Fight these feelings pushing through her?

As if sensing her inner battle, Cam laid his hands on her shoulders, pulled her around to face him. His palm slid up her neck until his hand cradled her cheek. His thumb smoothed across her bottom lip. His eyes glittered with a depth of emotion reaching out to singe her.

"Do you remember that day with the bear?"

Memory sparked, and her eyes flared. He'd been there. The wolf—*Cam*—had leaped between her and that huge bear. He'd been fierce as he'd defended her from the bear, but she'd never felt the slightest bit fearful of him, she'd felt only...only protected.

"If you hadn't come back with a gun," his lips twitched, then his eyes grew serious, "I was prepared to fight that bear...to keep you safe. And that was before I'd..." His voice trailed away as his eyes strayed to where the backs of his fingers skimmed along the line of her neck. "You are the only one for me now, JJ." His eyes probed hers. "You are my mate."

Her lips parted, and she sucked in a sharp breath. "Your mate? Cam, what are you...I don't—"

He captured her wrist, drew her hand up, pressed her palm against his chest...against the griffin's breast. "You. Are. My. Mate. This heart beating inside my chest, it beats for you, JJ."

He released her wrist, though he continued to trace the rim of her lip with the pad of his thumb, but she couldn't seem to pry her hand from his chest. His flesh was so warm beneath her palm. His heartbeat was steady, strong. His skin was velvet, warm rich velvet. Her gaze followed her fingertips as they traced along his tattoo, just the way she had last night.

All those times last night...

"You are a part of me now... just as the wolf is another part of me, part of who I am." His words drew her gaze back to his. His eyes were so clear, so green.

She reached up, her hand hesitated halfway to his cheek, and then she slipped her palm along his strong jaw. Her gaze devoured every inch of his face. So familiar, and yet it held new definition now, for all she'd seen it do. The rough, sandpaper scrape of his whiskers along the skin on her wrist tickled. She remembered how that same tickle had raced across her breasts last night, raced across her stomach and her thighs, the small of her back as he'd kissed and nipped every inch of her, scars and all. Her fingers feathered through the golden hair at his temple.

His fur had been so soft, so warm when she'd sunk her fingers in it as they'd walked through the woods.

She cradled his face in both of her hands, remembering the way he'd rolled and tussled with her on the new spring grass after the bear had gone. How he'd held her on his lap as he'd rocked her, kissing her face, calling her name after she'd fainted. How he'd cradled her on his lap at Ginny's, held her until she no longer wanted to run away...but wanted only to cling to him. He carried so many responsibilities, and yet, every second he was with her, he made her feel as if nothing were more important to him than she was. He was an amazing man.

More than a man, but still amazing.

This was Cameron Walker.

Her Cam.

Her wolf.

Sometimes what you wanted—what you needed—didn't always make sense. Sometimes you just had to take a leap of faith. Now, it seemed, it was time for her to make her leap. There was no fear in her now, only a happy confidence…a sense of certainty that nothing had been more right. Slowly, her gaze locked on his, she lifted up to her tiptoes and gently pressed her lips to his.

One trembling heartbeat shuddered past, and then he hauled her into his arms, crushed her to him. He slanted his mouth over hers, deepened the kiss, swamping her senses with hungry need.

Yes…the same firm, skillful lips.

****

The darker, primal side of his nature urged him to drag her to the floor, to ravish her then and there on the cold hardwood and claim her once more as his mate. The man in him—every bit as hungry and as possessive as the primal wolf—swept her up into his arms and carried her down the hallway to his bed.

Impatient hands stripped away the irritating barriers standing between him and her soft flesh. His lips drank in her impassioned murmurs, her cries of delight. His hands explored and pleasured every inch of her body, memorizing every curve and every dip, every sensitive place that wrung another moan from her lips.

The stimulating taste of her, the exhilarating scent and enticing texture, were a heady aphrodisiac to his already overheated system, one he imbibed with insatiable abandon. He could make love to this woman—*would* make love to her, would *love* her—for the rest of his life, and he'd never get enough of her.

She gasped and squirmed beneath his lips, beneath his hands, his body. By no means were her hands idle, stroking him, stoking the desire raging inside him. She left a trail of fire everywhere she touched, and he happily basked in the flames. Her flesh was damp with his kisses, damp with her need for him. A thin slice of lightning danced above the treetops, lancing through the room, and his mark upon her flesh flashed before his burning gaze. That sight was more than his flimsy grasp on control could handle.

With a harsh growl, he seized her lips, and he sank himself deep inside her molten flesh. She closed around him like a tight, silken fist. So hot. So very wet. Her legs clamped around his waist, her hands clutched at him, pulling him closer. The scent of her need cloaked him, until he tossed caution to the wind and eagerly dove beneath the waves of passion to seek the deepest wells of her desire.

This was coming home for him. Here—in her—was where he lived...not just the shallow existence he'd been passing off as life, but true heart-pounding, soul-binding life. He drove himself into her, over and over—unable to stop, unable to slow down—until she shuddered beneath him, sobbing his name. His release ripped through him as he poured himself out deep inside her body while his lips tasted the mark he'd placed below her ear. His soul reached out and touched hers, and together the two of them pulsed with life and glowed as one.

At length, once he'd recovered some slim grasp on his control, his lips savored hers, reverent and languid, before he moved to her side and pulled her into the curve of his body.

A long while later, as moonlight pushed through the angry storm clouds, turning the droplets of rain coursing down the windowpanes to liquid diamonds, Cam laced his fingers through JJ's, resting their joined fists over his heart.

"So...only the males of direct decent are able to...to change?"

"Shift," he corrected gently. "Yes...but not all of them. It seems to be a recessive gene."

Her questions had started soon after she'd

gotten her breath back. They'd been tentative at first, but they'd come faster and with more confidence as he'd opened himself up to her completely. And they hadn't stopped. She was, it seemed, a bottomless well of curiosity. He was just surprised and grateful she'd decided to keep an open mind.

"Are there many in town with this recessive gene?"

"Quite a few, actually." She tensed in his arms, and he smoothed his palm up and down her back in slow, reassuring strokes. "It's very important that we maintain anonymity, or, as I'm sure you can imagine, there'd be wide-spread panic." At length, she nodded against his shoulder, rubbing her thumb along the ridge of his knuckles. He explained to her about the elders, the significance of The Circle he'd found her in that day. Then he began paving the way to explain the mark he'd branded on her body...a mark she still seemed oblivious of.

"Including me, there are ten in the current pack." He rattled off a few names, some she was familiar with, and some he was sure she didn't know. Her head snapped up, and she'd peered at him with a comical, wide-eyed expression when he mentioned Maggie's awkward, gaunt husband Rich, and the handsome, laid-back, silver-tipped deputy, Austin Perry. "Until a few years back, Todd Connor was the pack's Beta. After Todd died, Austin's stepped into the role."

Her brow puckered. "Beta...so that's the hierarchy thing right? Second in command, so to speak?"

"Yes, that's right."

"So, if Austin is the...the Beta," she lifted her eyebrows on the word, and he nodded affirmation, "then that would mean there's an Alpha right? A leader?"

"Yes." His mouth kicked up at the edges. She was very quick-witted, had been following his explanations with intelligent, pointed questions.

"Who is the Alpha?"

He'd anticipated that question would come up sooner or later. He'd never felt as much pride in his position as he did in the moment when he answered, "I am."

"You are?" She stared at him for a long, silent moment. Admiration flickered through her eyes. Something else flickered there as well, what it was he could only speculate given the mysteries of a woman's mind. At length, she murmured a soft, "Hmm." Then she settled her head back on his shoulder, a soft smile curving her lips.

That small smile puffed his chest up, filling him with burgeoning pride. Then he remembered he had one point still to explain to her, and his confidence faltered. This conversation had gone so well, better, really, than he'd hoped. How would she react when she found out that he'd marked her as his, without her approval...without her knowledge? He drew a deep breath and prayed his luck would hold out.

"There's something else I need to explain." The tiny circles she traced on his chest with the tip of her finger were distracting, as was the lush press of her bare breasts against his chest when she squirmed around to looking up into his eyes again, but he firmly pushed his body's reaction to the back burner. It was crunch time now. All or nothing.

"According to legend...according to the elders, and some of the others in the pack, if a Werewolf is lucky, he'll find his one true mate...a Lifemate. When he finds her, when he imprints upon her, there's no turning back, no...no second choice. He'll be unable to take another as his mate, to love another. When he finds his female, the need to claim her as his own, to mark her as his will be undeniable...inescapable. He'll be faithful to her until his dying day. He'd lay down his life for her."

"Mark her?" She frowned, chewing on the edge of her lip.

"A mark...just like it sounds...he, well, he bites her." Cam shot her a sheepish look. The ball of anxiety rolled in his gut. He couldn't remember ever being this nervous in his life. "A Werewolf's bite leaves behind a mark...a permanent, um, brand if you will. Each Werewolf's bite is distinctive, the mark recognizable to all others in the pack."

"So just by this mark, all the others know she belongs to him—is that what you're saying?"

"Yes, but its more than that. This mark...it's like a beacon to the Werewolf, it draws him to her, links them together in a way nothing else can. The sight of a Werewolf's mark upon his female's skin will drive him out of his mind with desire, with the need to claim her again and again. He becomes fiercely protective of her, single-minded in his possessiveness."

"Maggie has one of these marks?"

Following her train of thought, Cam nodded. "She does...though I've never seen it, thank heavens." He chuckled at the thought of skinny, quiet Rich saddling himself with the bossy, irascible Maggie.

"And Ginny?"

"She bears Todd's mark on her wrist, under that wide watchband."

"Of course," she murmured softly. "Does the mark hurt? I didn't pay much attention before, but Ginny often rubs at that wrist, especially when she's distracted."

Cam peered hard at her, waited for her to connect the dots. "I'm told, at the moment the bite is given, there's a sharp flare of pain...it fades quickly, then the pain is gone completely, but the mark remains. It's permanent."

One moment ticked by, and then another passed in silence while JJ absorbed all he'd told her. Her brow wrinkled, as though she were trying to pin down some elusive memory. Suddenly she reared back, her eyes narrowed to twin points of burning accusation. Her hand flew to the spot below her ear, and she scrambled from his arms, scooted from the bed.

JJ leaned over his dresser, oblivious of the delicious view of her backside she'd unwittingly given him, and whipped her hair out of her way as she squinted into the mirror, tugged at her earlobe. Her fingers traced the small mark—a shape similar to that of a butterfly, only with sharp edges—there below her earlobe, and her breath hissed out.

Cam climbed from the bed and padded across the room until he stood behind her. Guilty green met furious blue in the mirror.

"You marked me?" She whirled around, thumped her fist against his chest.

Even now, with guilt weighing heavy on his shoulders and her eyes shooting daggers at him, the sight of that mark sent raw need shooting through his veins straight into his groin.

"You *marked* me? You never asked me, never checked to make sure I wouldn't mind?"

"I—"

Her fist pounded him again, cutting him off. "You *marked* me...and you never told me?" Then she went motionless, her lips parted and her gaze grew distant for a moment. Her mouth fell open on a gasp, and she drilled a finger painfully into the center of his chest. "No wonder they all kept staring at me...at Maggie's, when I pulled my hair up. They all saw it...and they all *knew*."

"You are my mate, JJ," he said simply. No apology. No regret. Had he been offered the chance to go back, do things differently, he'd have done everything exactly the same. Not having claimed her just wasn't an option he could live with, wasn't an option he would even consider. "I've given myself to you. All that I am, all that I have...it's yours."

He'd spoken the words softly, meant them with every ounce of his being. Those words drained the anger from her face. He didn't waste any time, didn't give her a spare moment for second thoughts. Instead, he swept her into his arms and carried her back to bed. He'd show her exactly what seeing his mark on her did to him, and when he was done, there wouldn't be any doubt in her mind.

Being his mate was a very, *very* good thing indeed.

Chapter 21

The Apostle slammed the car door and pounded his fists against the steering wheel, over and over. How could this have happened? How could she have let herself be corrupted like this? She hadn't heeded his first warning, had ignored his second. Now she was here, defiling herself with Cam...with his *friend*.

He'd been so sure she was pure of heart, free of sin. She'd been so damned sweet, so vulnerable. She'd said all the right words, done everything right. But she was just another one of *them*. Another sinner.

Satan was crafty, the true deceiver.

And God's Apostle had come so close to falling from Grace.

His weak human self suffered, tears of rage welled in his eyes, burning his lids, coursing hot, angry trails down his cheeks. He'd succumbed to weakness of the flesh and let himself fall for her. Pretty, helpless, sweet JJ Frost.

And she'd spurned him, giving herself to Cam like some common, lowly prostitute. Just like Lori.

JJ had been his test. And he'd nearly failed.

For a while, he'd actually contemplated setting aside his calling, thought he'd shown his devotion to God and already earned his reward. He'd even put off punishing that wrathful bitch Angie Berg. He'd assumed a woman—*JJ*—was his reward. He'd strayed from the word of the Lord. He'd been taken in by a harlot. A Jezebel. A Delilah. He should've known better. The only reward he should have wanted, the only reward he truly needed was God's love, God's forgiveness.

Angrily swiping tears from his cheeks with the backs of his hands, he leveled malignant eyes on the dark window at the rear of Cam's house. Cam's bedroom. Even now, the two of them were probably in there, rutting like disgusting, lowly animals.

That thought sent another cascade of tears— tears of humiliation—to soak his cheeks. He really had cared about her. Why had she been so weak? Why would she debase herself this way?

It was clear to him what he had to do. It broke his heart, but he would follow God's will. After all, God had called upon Abraham to sacrifice his beloved son Isaac. The Apostle could do no less than sacrifice this woman who'd proven unworthy.

Resolve firmly in place, he sat up straighter in the car seat, squeezed the steering wheel in an unforgiving grip. JJ's salvation lay between her and God now. He made a conscious effort to smooth his features and wipe the emotion from his heart. Even so, the cold rage of betrayal still chilled him.

Thou shall not suffer a witch to live.

Well, God would also not want him to suffer a freak...a Werewolf...to live either. Of that, he was now certain. As soon as he dealt with the prideful whore, he'd finish off the Devil's spawn. He'd kept silent about that little secret, convinced himself that Cam and his kind had harmed none, had earned the right to be left alone.

Well, no more. When he finished sending God's message about the sinners, he'd cleanse this town of those mutant freaks as well.

Calm now, he turned the key in the ignition and carefully eased the car from the road's soft shoulder. He had things to do, preparations to make.

The Apostle also had one more sinner in need of a guiding hand before he dealt with the Werewolf and the prideful whore.

****

In the early hours, before dawn streaked the sky with warm colors, JJ tugged her clothing and boots on and slipped from the bedroom, leaving behind a warm, empty bed. Where had Cam gone? Maybe he'd gotten a call while she'd been asleep. The storm last night had been a nasty one. She wouldn't be at all surprised if he had a grade A mess on his hands. At least the power had come back on in the wee hours of the morning.

She hadn't intended to get up quite so early. In truth, she was still a little groggy around the edges, but she'd been too restless to go back to sleep, her head swamped with Cam's mind-boggling revelations. She could barely wrap her head around it all.

She followed her nose, and the scent of coffee, to the kitchen. Bless his heart, he'd left her most of the pot. A speedy search of the cabinets yielded a mug and a sealed container of sugar. After stirring in the requisite mountain of sugar, she splashed a bit of milk into the mug. Smiling, JJ brought the mug to her lips, savoring the first long draw of caffeine like the addict she was.

Standing at the sink, JJ drained the rest of the mug. She had so much to do. Logically, she knew she couldn't go back to her place, at least not to stay. Cam was right. To stay there now, alone, was inviting trouble. Tomorrow? Well, she'd just have to take this one day at a time. JJ refilled her mug and took another sip as she enjoyed the view from Cam's kitchen. The woods were pristine, as if polished fresh by last night's downpour. Warm browns and vivid greens dazzled the eyes. Wild sprays of lilac clustered at one edge of the clearing, and she was reminded of the view from her attic studio. She had to return to her place at some point. She needed clothes, and, hard as she'd tried to push the thought from her mind, she needed to clean up the mess in the attic, see what she could salvage.

That thought no more than shuddered through her, when movement at the edge of the woods separating her and Cam's yards caught her eye. Going up on tiptoe, she used her palms on the edge of the sink to push herself closer to the window. What was he doing out there?

Cam rushed from the woods, obviously distracted. He dug in his back pocket with one hand, swiping the other palm over the side of his stomach, down across his hip, leaving behind a garish red smear across the pristine white cotton and faded denims.

JJ's heart slammed against her ribs.

Blood? Why did he have blood on his hands? She scanned his body as he loped to his truck. There wasn't blood anywhere else on him. He didn't move as if he'd been injured. Whose blood, then, was it?

Cam dragged a big, black duffel bag from the back seat of his truck, slung it over his shoulder, and trotted back toward the same place in the woods he'd just emerged from moments before.

Setting the mug aside with an unsteady hand, JJ hurried to the back door and slipped outside. Why was he rushing around like that? It wasn't like he was skulking around, and yet his very demeanor suggested he was in a rush, and, by the way he'd glanced at the house while he'd retrieved that bag, he didn't want company. If she didn't know better, she'd wonder what it was he was trying to hide.

But then, she didn't know better, did she? That sly little voice in the back of her head slipped the question in through a crack in her guard. And it wasn't done yet. Once it had managed to slice her with one niggling doubt, it seemed just a matter of time before others of its kind began scoring her self-confidence. Certainly, her confidence in the man she'd been sleeping with. He had lied to her after all, hadn't he? Lied about what he was. If he could keep something that big from her, what else, then, was he capable of?

Hadn't that been how things had started to deteriorate between Jerry and Sarah? The lies, the deceit. Small gambling debts here, a one night stand with a strange woman there. Then it had progressed. The accusations, the affair Jerry viewed as retribution against some imagined wrong on Sarah's part, and then the slaps started. The shoves. It has all spiraled out of control from there.

No, Cam wasn't Jerry. She'd already established that. There had to be some reasonable explanation for Cam's behavior.

JJ shouldered her way into the woods, pushing limbs out of her way as she scurried in the direction Cam had disappeared. Shadows danced around her, flirting with brilliant slices of dappled sunshine. Pine needles crackled beneath her boots, and the scent of the woods enveloped her. She stopped for a moment, peering hard in every direction, struggling to get her bearings. Which way had he gone?

A faint thud, a muffled curse seemed to rebound off the trees. JJ followed the sound deeper into the shadows, slowly now, hesitant. Just over the edge of a small hill, she caught sight of his gilded head. He was crouched, low to the ground, staring down at something. JJ slipped quietly up the side of the hill, her gaze sliding down Cam's back, down to the ground before him and the object he'd reached for. Blue, floral print fabric billowed in the wind, twinning itself around his legs. The wind changed course, and the fabric shifted, revealing the pale line of a bare, narrow foot and a trim, feminine calf smeared with blood.

Stumbling back, JJ gasped for air. Her vision blurred for a split second, then sharpened with brutal clarity. Cam twisted on his heel, one forearm braced on his knee as his brilliant emerald eyes sliced to her. He held the woman's limp hand in his. The glint of silver resting on her palm reflected a beam of sunlight, making JJ blink.

A rosary...

Shaking her head slowly from side to side, JJ began back-pedaling down the hill. She clamped a hand over her gaping mouth, but the sob wouldn't stay locked inside. It was Jerry...it was Jerry all over again. Oh, dear God, how could she have been so blind?

Cam jumped to his feet, dropping the dead woman's hand to the ground with a sickening thud. "JJ, wait..."

A small branch rolled beneath her heel, and she wobbled off balance. Righting herself, JJ scurried backward. Angie Berg's bloodless face, twisted in death, was all she could see. No, no this couldn't be happening.

Not again.

"JJ, honey, please..." Cam extended a hand, palm up to her. She refused to give in to the emotion on his face. All she could see was the blood on his hands. His gaze swerved to the body at his feet and back to her. "JJ..."

Sobbing, she pivoted on her heel and tore through the woods, running as she'd never run before. A slim branch slapped at her face, slashing pain across her cheek. The familiar burn of tears in an open cut seared through her, but still she ran. Loose vegetation rolled beneath her skidding boots as the woods flew past her in a confusing blur of leaves and sunlight. Only when her head began to swim did she realize she'd been holding her breath.

Gasping, she broke free of the woods. Staggering around the side of her shed, JJ raced toward the front yard, digging madly in her pocket for her car keys. Fumbling them free of her pocket, she dropped them on the gravel driveway. JJ skidded to a halt, twisted and scooped them up, her eyes glued to the woods, her chest heaving. He hadn't come through the tree line yet. But she'd seen him move. He was fast. She had seconds at best. Twisting as she straightened, she vaulted forward, colliding with a warm, hard body encased head to toe in black.

It took two long heartbeats for the black hood and ski mask to register. Before she could pull away, before she could let loose the scream clawing up her throat, a powerful, leather covered fist shot out and pain exploded in her jaw. JJ had the faint impression of strong arms breaking her fall as the world went dark around her.

Chapter 22

The blurry outline of a cartoon cat swam before her eyes, eyes that refused to focus. As she struggled to zero in on the cat's swishing tail, she realized it wasn't a cartoon, but the kitty cat clock on the wall in her own kitchen. Her jaw throbbed like an abscessed tooth, and her mouth was bone dry, felt stuffed with cotton. Her brain was fuzzy. Moaning, she let her head roll back on her shoulders. Worried it might just keep on rolling right onto the floor, she made to cradle her head in her hands.

Why wouldn't her hands move? Tugging, twisting at her wrists, reality began to swamp her. The black mask... She struggled in earnest now, but she was bound, gagged, and tied to a straight-backed chair. Blinking rapidly, filled with a sickening sense of vulnerability, JJ forced her defiant eyes to focus.

"There you are now," a soft voice called to her. Turning her head, she blinked owlishly at the dark figure leaning against her kitchen counter. Those eyes...those eyes were so familiar. Such kind, gray eyes behind that frightening mask of death. He crossed his arms over his chest. The wicked glint of silver flashed in his hand, and, for a moment, her pulse jumped. But no, it wasn't a knife. He held a cross...a rosary in his hand.

Questions, demands flooded her mind, but none would spew past the wad of material stuffed in her mouth. Suddenly her captor tensed, laying a leather-encased finger to his lips. His large frame glided soundlessly across the faded linoleum as he snatched a frying pan off the back burner of the stove and took up a covert position behind the kitchen door. A spare moment later, footsteps pounded across the back porch.

"JJ," Cam shouted. "JJ, are you in here? Come on, please, you have to listen to me. JJ..."

Cam bounded through the doorway. His steps faltered for a split second when his gaze connected with hers. The expression on his face was shocked, confused. His hand flew to his hip where his gun normally rested when he was in uniform as he charged forward. She cried out, her gaze shot to where her attacker crouched behind the door. Cam caught the movement of her stare, must have somehow discerned the intention of her cry, but by the time he spun on his heel, it was too late. The skillet was already descending, and Cam didn't have enough time to block the blow.

JJ watched helplessly as Cam toppled to the floor. Her muffled scream echoed inside her head. Her captor gave a small, satisfied grunt, tossing the skillet back onto the stovetop. He rolled Cam to the middle of the floor, near JJ's feet, before tying his hands behind his back and securing his feet together with a length of clothesline. He deposited a string of beads into Cam's palm, winding it around his thumb to keep the silver cross from falling onto the floor, then forced another, identical rosary into JJ's hands. The man in black patted Cam's back pocket and withdrew a small pocketknife. Then he stood and prodded Cam with the toe of his boot.

Cam seemed to come awake the same way JJ had, slow and groggy. He blinked up at her, then his eyes widened and he twisted around until he was facing their assailant.

"Who are you?" Cam fought his restraints. Under the guise of his struggles, he patted his back pocket, and swore loudly. "Damn it, who are you...what the hell do you want?"

The killer clucked his tongue and shook his head. "Now, now, Cam. Is that anyway to speak in a lady's presence?"

Cam went utterly still at the sound of the man's soft voice. Slowly, as if savoring the shock on Cam's face, he flipped the hood of the jacket back. Then, methodically, he peeled the ski mask off, revealing silver-streaked hair and gentle face.

Jarvis English smiled down at them.

"Jarvis..." Cam whispered. "Why?"

"Because this is what I was meant to do." Jarvis settled back against the counter again, crossing his arms over his chest. "This town was going to hell, Cam. Corruption, sin...it spreads like a disease."

"You killed them, Jarvis. You killed innocent—"

"No!" Jarvis stiffened, snarling the word. He sucked in a sharp breath through flared nostrils and relaxed his stance again. Calmer now, he preached, "No. They were all guilty. God gave them so many opportunities to repent their sins, to change their ways. *They* chose the Devil's path. Don't you see? They chose their own fates."

"What are you telling me? That *God* told you to murder them?"

"Murder is a sin, Cam." Jarvis shook his head, frowning his disappointment in Cam's lack of understanding. "I didn't murder anyone. I punished sinners, just as God wanted me to do. I even gave them rosaries, led them through their prayers. I did everything within my power to make sure their souls were as prepared as they could possibly be when they went to face their Creator."

JJ shuddered, imagining what those poor victims must have felt as they'd been forced to pray with the man who'd come to kill them. What a horrible torture they'd endured, far worse than anything Jerry had done to her. At least he hadn't toyed with her, hadn't taunted her with false hope.

He'd just gone straight for blood.

Cam lay at her feet, strangely silent as Jarvis went on, "You should have thanked me, Cam, instead of trying to hunt me down like some rabid dog. I was only trying to help you clean up your town, after all."

"Help me?" Cam sputtered. "Help me...by strangling Lori and leaving her...sprawled like that? By mangling Mayor Hughes, cutting his hands off? By leaving Angie Berg's children motherless? How could you possibly think you were helping me by cutting Ed's heart out of his chest?"

Jarvis didn't seem at all interested in addressing the first of his questions, but he latched onto the last. "You and I both know that last had to be done. Ed was a drain on you. He was a humiliation. How were you to focus on guiding your citizens with a father like that constantly distracting you? Sins of the father, Cam...sins of the father."

He jerked as if he'd been kicked in the stomach. "How did you... How did you know Ed was my father?"

"How do you think? I had access to all the files, Cam. Never could quite figure why you always seemed to cut Ed a little extra slack when anyone else would have locked him up for good. I did some digging. A DNA test was a little tricky, but I pulled it off. Did Seth Walker ever know the truth? Boy, it's a good thing that mother of yours moved away all those years ago, only enough room in a town this size for one whore like Lori. Too bad our little JJ wasn't smart enough to figure that out before she decided to pass out her favors."

"Bastard," Cam snarled, yanking at the rope on his wrists. "Let JJ go. She has nothing to do with this."

"Oh, but she does." Jarvis's cold gray eyes settled on JJ, and she cringed. How could she have ever mistaken those eyes as being kind? They were soulless. "You know, you almost had me fooled. I thought you were so sweet, so innocent. I was going to—" He broke off with an angry frown. Making a visible effort to smooth his features, he droned on, "That doesn't matter anymore. You were too conceited, to prideful over your work. You should have shown more humility over the talents God saw fit to give you. I tried to warn you. I gave you more chances to correct your sinful ways than any of the others. I saw such potential in you, Jillian." He shook his head, an odd glow began to kindle in his eyes, and JJ had the unsettling impression he viewed her like some science experiment gone sadly awry.

"You were the one that broke in, trashed her studio," Cam barked.

"Oh, yes. That was me." Jarvis turned his attention back to Cam. "You know, I really should apologize to you, Cam. But it's your own fault, if you weren't so good at sniffing out culprits, I wouldn't have had to distract you with all those vandalisms."

"You vandalized all those buildings?"

"Yes, to my shame. You were getting too close. I could only tamper with so much evidence before I ran the risk of getting caught. I had to distract you somehow, divide your attentions. Then again, I didn't realize our JJ here was doing such a bang-up job of keeping your attention focused elsewhere. Slipped that one right by me, didn't you?"

The unholy glow was back as Jarvis's malevolent stare centered on JJ once more. Her blood ran cold at what she saw in his eyes. It was the same righteous anger Jerry had skewered her with while he'd slashed his way over her body.

JJ pulled at her wrists again, twisting, desperate. Her skin stung, and the warm trickle of blood coursed down her fingertips. She wouldn't die, meek and helpless. She mumbled into the gag, fighting to be heard.

Jarvis stepped forward. A vicious warning snarl ripped from Cam as Jarvis reached for the band of material tied around her mouth. "Here now, where are my manners? Cam and I have been doing all the talking and we haven't given you any chance to speak."

The minute the gag slipped free, JJ lurched forward in her chair, until her tied arms jerked her back. "You sick, twisted, psychotic son of a—"

The back of Jarvis's hand cracked across her face. His chest heaved with sudden fury, his nostrils flared. Outraged moral anger dripped from every word. "If you can't speak like a proper lady, I'll gag you again. Filth like that is the Devil's work."

Even with her head reeling and stars spinning before her eyes, she could see Cam jerking violently on the floor. The growl that tore from his chest was feral, dangerous. "Touch her again, and I'll kill you, you bastard."

Jarvis ignored them as he strode from the room. In a moment he was back, toting a large red gasoline jug.

"You know, I had plans for you, Jillian. Very special plans. Then you went and turned yourself into a whore. The prideful whore of a freak. You're just like the others, unrepentant. Unworthy."

He slowly twisted the cap from the jug. The heavy, cloying scent of gas filled the room.

"I realized something when I set that warehouse on fire." He smiled down at Cam now. The demented smile of one who'd lost all grip on reality. "Fire is biblical, too. The warehouse was a symbol, just as He'd intended the burning bush to be a symbol. Fire will cleanse your souls." Jarvis hefted the jug, sending them a reassuring smile. "If you start reciting your prayers now...if you truly mean them, mind you...perhaps God might hear you yet and forgive you."

Jarvis splashed gas around the kitchen, over the counter, across the table behind JJ, along the floor in front of the doorway. Each wet slosh punctuated by a line from the Lord's Prayer. Then he disappeared down the hallway, leaving a trail of lethal liquid behind him. Despite her best efforts, a whimper slipped past her guard. How could it all end like this? Oh, God, she'd thought Cam had been the killer. She'd run from him.

"Cam...I'm so sorry," she sobbed. "I'm sorry. I shouldn't have—"

"Honey, don't cry. It's all right, baby. I know. It's all right. I'll get you out of this, I swear I will."

Cam rolled around, squirming on the floor until he lay on his back near the cabinets. Lifting his feet into the air, swinging them wildly, he tipped the strainer onto its side. Silverware tinkled across the counter. The creaking footsteps overhead paused. Cam snaked his feet up for one more swipe and knocked the wooden handle of a knife over the edge of the counter.

The silver blade streaked toward the floor, the tip embedding into the linoleum only inches from Cam's hip. Twisting, wiggling backward, his chest heaving, Cam began rotating his shoulders, faster and faster.

His breath expelled on a sharp whoosh and he flinched, but he kept sawing at the rope. The frayed restraint snapped free, and Cam wasted no time. He sat up and hacked his way through the bindings around his ankles. By now, smoke had begun to roll down the hallway. The deadly crackle of flames grew louder. Orange glowed through the hall and zipped into the kitchen, setting the room ablaze in a matter of seconds.

In a flash, Cam was on his knees before her,

cutting her free. Billowing black clouds began to fill the kitchen. Her lungs burned as she fought for each breath. The room swam before her, a blurred smudgy mess through the haze of involuntary tears. Cam scooped her up into his arms and sprinted through the flames guarding the rear door.

A wave of fresh, cool air washed over them as he bound down the steps. He didn't set her down until he was well clear of the house. She coughed, unable to catch her breath. "Here," he thrust something sharp, metallic into her hands. Her car keys. Where had he found them? Cam took her by the shoulders and propelled her toward the Jeep. "Get out of here. I have to go after him, have to stop him before he hurts anyone else."

"Cam—"

He cut her off with a kiss. Fast, hard. "Please, JJ, go...get down to the office, tell Emma what happened."

Cam whipped his shirt off over his head, tossed it to the ground. "Whatever happens, honey...remember that I love you."

He stripped the rest of his clothing away in record time, stole one last kiss, and shifted. He was gone in a streak of golden fur. JJ stared after him for a moment, too shocked to function. Then, with shaking hands, she scooped his clothes up and scurried to the Jeep.

She'd sit inside. She'd lock the doors, leave the motor idling.

But she would not run.

She'd never run away ever again.

JJ didn't have any idea how long she sat like that, hands gripping the steering wheel, eyes straining for any movement in the tree line around her. She'd only been able to bring herself to glance once at her house. The sight of greedy flames dancing in the windows, consuming the house she'd pinned her hopes on, had been too much to bear.

Not that watching the woods was much better. She kept seeing Cam streaking away from her, swallowed up by the forest. How could she have—for even one horrible minute—assumed the worst about him?

She hadn't even told him she loved him before he'd run off to chase down a killer.

What if he didn't come back?

Somewhere in the distance, the lone crack of gunfire startled a flock of birds. JJ jolted in her seat.

Unable to think, she leaped from the vehicle and raced forward, then froze at the edge of the woods. How would she find him? What if he were lying out there, wounded? How would she know where to look? Should she go for help? Oh God, what should she do?

The trees to her left rustled. Shadows shifted and green foliage parted.

Cam stepped into the clearing. His griffon tattoo was splattered with blood. Red smears stained his thigh and forearm. His right bicep poured a fresh wave of crimson. He staggered forward, his gaze locked on the Jeep, and he let out a low roar, "JJ?"

"Cam." She rushed forward, relief coursed so thick through her veins, it was almost impossible to speak.

He whirled toward her, raced forward, and scooped her up into his arms, bruising her as he crushed her against him. Without warning, Cam sat down, right there in the grass, in the blazing glow of her burning home, and pulled her down onto his lap. His hands swept over her, from the top of her head all the way to her feet. "Are you okay? Are you hurt anywhere? Jesus, JJ, you're bleeding!"

"No," she pushed his hands away, *"You're* bleeding. You've been shot, Cam. Your shoulder is bleeding."

Glancing down, he shrugged it off. "Just a nick. You're sure you're all right?"

"I'm not hurt." She trapped his face between her palms, forcing him to look her in the face rather than continue his fruitless search for wounds that didn't exist. "I love you, Cameron Walker."

Cam stared at her for a long moment, then cupped the sides of her neck and pulled her in for a long, searing kiss. "I love you too, honey. God, I love you so much."

Something clicked then. She'd only heard one shot. And Cam hadn't gone into the woods with a gun. JJ tensed in his arms. "Cam...did he get away? We need to—"

"No, he didn't get away. Jarvis won't ever hurt anyone else again."

"But, there was only the one shot. Where is he? How did you—"

"Sweetheart," Cam insisted, forcing her to face him this time. His eyes bore into hers. "Trust me. He's dead."

She thought to ask Cam how that was possible when he'd gone into those woods unarmed. Then she remembered he'd gone in as a wolf. It didn't take a map and GPS to connect the dots. She didn't need to ask any more questions, wasn't sure she was ready to deal with the answers just yet. He'd come back to her alive, and they were both safe. That was all that mattered. He squeezed her tight against him, and she followed his gaze toward the loud pop and crackle as flames finally breached one of the upper story windows.

"Well, I guess that's settled," he murmured.

She peered at him, confused. The orange glow of her burning home glistened over his sweat-slicked, soot and blood-smeared skin. She was sure she didn't look much better. "What's settled?"

"Where we're going to live." He nudged his chin

toward her house. "Looks like you'll be moving in with me. Good thing I finished that extra bathroom." Smiling, he smoothed her hair back from her face with his big hands and pressed a kiss to her lips. He trailed kisses from the corner of her mouth, nipped his way along her jaw, and dropped a long, slow kiss on the mark he'd placed behind her ear.

"I don't know, Cam. You keep some pretty crazy hours," JJ teased.

He eyed her speculatively, then his stare took on a serious bent. "I won't take anything less than forever. You understand that, don't you? Werewolves mate for life, JJ. There's no going back now."

"I like the sound of that." She sighed, savoring the feel of his hot mouth on her skin. "So...will we have a special ceremony in The Circle like the ones you told me about?"

His grin slowly grew to one of his heart-stopping, mega-watt smiles, and he nodded.

The blare of sirens broke the crackling stillness around them. Frowning, JJ glanced toward the woods. "How will you explain about...?" The image those words alone conjured sent a ripple of apprehension snaking down her spine.

His hand soothed down her back, offering warmth and reassurance. "I'll think of something."

She leaned back in his arms, a mischievous smile tugging at her lips. "While you're coming up with explanations..."

He lifted an eyebrow, continued to stroke her back. Despite the approaching sirens, his smoldering stare caressed her lips, and his hands grew bolder.

"Maybe you better work on an explanation for your deputies and the fire department as to why you're sitting in the middle of my yard while my house is burning...buck naked."

Cam's eyes rounded. A ripe string of curses tore from his lips. He dumped her on her butt in the grass and streaked into the woods.

JJ burst out laughing.

Life with her Werewolf was going to be anything but dull.

A word about the author...

Always a voracious reader, Brenda Huber closed the cover on a book by one of her favorite authors, and said to herself...I can do this! Ever fascinated by all things mythical and mystical, Brenda decided to try her hand at Paranormal Romance and dove into her second great passion...writing. She lives in Iowa with her husband and two children.